THE I
SE

* * * * * * *

BY

ANITA WARD

This is a work of fiction, Names, characters, businesses, organizations, places, events and incidents either are the product of the author's imagination or are used fictitiously. Any resemblance to actual persons, living or dead, events or locales is entirely coincidental

PROLOGUE

1951

It was late afternoon when Clara Renard alighted from the coach at Preston bus station. She was totally exhausted both physically and emotionally. She had been travelling for thirty-six hours, and the last thing she had eaten was a sandwich that morning.

As she took in her surroundings, she realized that the town had changed significantly. The bus station was exactly the same as when she had left fifteen years earlier, but otherwise, she found it difficult at first to get her bearings.

She recognized a few buildings, but she couldn't believe how much the main street had altered, even though Preston had been virtually untouched by the bombings of World War II—most of the bombings had hit East Lancashire.

She crossed the main road and slowly started to make her way home. Her legs felt like lead. She was so tired, having had no sleep the previous night.

She was concerned as to how her mother would react on her unannounced arrival. She could just hear her mother saying, '*you have made your bed, Clara. Now you must lie in it.*' What would she do then? She had no money, nowhere else to go, and she was definitely not going back.

As she got nearer, her heart started to beat faster. It felt as though it would jump out of her chest.

Clara arrived at the hairdressing salon owned by her parents; they not only managed the business but they also worked in their own areas on the ground floor. The living accommodation above the salon was her childhood home. She tentatively opened the door to her mother's side of the salon. The tinkling of the bell on the door announced her arrival.

Her mother looked up, taking a double take. "Oh my God! Clara, is that you?" Her mother ran over, taking Clara in her arms. Clara sobbed uncontrollably. "My dear girl, I can't quite grasp that you are here."

CHAPTER 1
1935

Clara Pape was so excited that today was her fifteenth birthday. She was not expecting much in terms of presents. Her parents had already given her some money to buy clothes, but her best present would come in two weeks' time when she would be able to leave school. It wasn't that she didn't like school; it was just that she thought it was a total waste of time learning history and geography. All of it, she felt, would be of no use to her in the future.

"Clara," her mother shouted, bringing Clara out of her daydreaming state and into reality, "if you want any breakfast, get into the kitchen now, and you will have to do your chores before going out this afternoon."

She was going to the cinema this afternoon with her best friend Mary, and she figured that there would be enough time to go shopping for clothes after the film before returning home for the birthday tea her mother had promised her.

Today was Saturday, and she was expected to help her mother in the hairdressing salon located on the ground floor of where they lived that was owned by her mother, Olive Pape, and her father, John Pape, who was mostly known as Jack. On one side of the building was the barbershop where her father looked after the men's needs, and on the other side, her mother looked after the ladies. There were two washbasins, three chairs with mirrors above, and two standing hairdryers. Olive hoped that in the future she would be able to employ a stylist to help her, but for now, there was only her. Clara had to sweep the floor and keep the salon generally tidy in exchange for a small amount of pocket money. Saturday was the busiest day of the week at the salon. The men from the local factories were paid on Friday nights which meant they could afford a haircut and their wives a shampoo and set in preparation for their weekly outing to the working men's club.

There were a number of working men's clubs in the town, and it was the highlight of the week for most workers. Here they could relax, enjoy a drink and the entertainment. Every Saturday night, there was sure to be live entertainment—be it a singer, or a comedian or bingo—the best being talent night when anyone brave enough would get up on the stage and entertain the audience.

Preston, Lancashire in the 1920/30s was fast becoming a booming industrial town, although the cotton industry, which had once been the main source of employment, was now in decline. However, a number of new industries were arriving in town. There was a new big factory manufacturing all manner of electrical goods, engineering works, a recent extension of the railway system provided temporary employment, and the building sector was enjoying a boom. Although there was still a certain amount of unemployment, it was nothing like it was at the beginning of the 1900s.

Olive at the age of nineteen had married her childhood sweetheart, Jack. Jack was two years older than Olive, and they met when she started attending the local primary school with Jack's younger sister, Eleanor, known as Nelly. Over the years, their friendship had turned to love, and from the age of fourteen, they had become inseparable.

Jack had just qualified as a barber following a two-year apprenticeship when Olive decided to follow in his footsteps. After leaving school, she had commenced a hairdressing apprenticeship that she had only just completed when they married. She became a fully fledged stylist—a title she relished in telling anyone who asked at that time.

Olive used to tease Jack in the early days of his apprenticeship, as she watched him scour fashion magazines and follow the newest trend in hairstyles, especially since Jack himself could take longer to get ready to go on a night out than Olive. She would remind him that the only hairstyles he would be giving his clientele would be a '*short back and sides*'. Of course, he joked that someday she'd be cutting out pictures of the latest hairstyles and colors to put on her wall and reminding her that her future clientele would be local women wanting a style that would be easy to maintain, and not film stars.

Olive would laugh so hard because she knew he was probably right, saying, "The day I tell someone that they should just go for something that was easy to maintain is the day you stop checking your hair in the mirror every half hour, Jack!" He loved her laugh.

Their wedding had been a simple affair at the local registry office. Being immediately after the Great War, money was tight for both families. Both her mother and grandmother had helped her buy a beautiful two-piece suit in dove grey with a matching fascinator hat, which included a veil to one side. Her mother had let her wear the double string of pearls that she had worn at her own wedding. Her bridesmaid was her younger sister, Lillian, who was not too impressed at having to dress up for the occasion. Jack looked dashing in his demob suit along with his mate, Albert, who stood as best man. Together, Jack and Olive looked the perfect couple. The wedding was followed by two nights in a hotel in Blackpool for their honeymoon.

Initially, they lived with Olive's widowed grandmother, Lillian, ten miles south of Preston in a tiny two-up, two-down terraced house until they were able to get their own tiny home on the next street following the birth of Clara, a honeymoon baby. Times were hard, but Olive and Jack were lucky that their tiny home had a toilet in the backyard and that bath night was in front of the fire in an old, tin bath. Clara's sister, named after her grandmother and known as Lilly, was born in 1923.

Olive was able to earn a bit of money to add to Jack's wages by doing the hair of friends and neighbours. This was beneficial for both her and her '*clients*', as a trip to the hairdresser's could be an expense they could ill afford, but she was able to make it more affordable while earning. In 1924, Olive suffered a miscarriage that resulted in irreversible damage to her ovarian tubes, leaving her unable to have any more children. Throughout her pregnancy, many of her clients had showered her with love and good wishes, some even bringing used garments from their own children, who had outgrown them. When she'd lost the child in the seventh month of her pregnancy, they supported her emotionally. For a brief time, she felt like she couldn't go on working and found it difficult facing the same people who had seen her failed pregnancy, fearing their reaction or what they might think. Over time, with the loving understanding of her husband and her many friends, and clients, she grew to accept the fact that she would never give birth again. Olive appreciated the comfort her work and her clients brought her.

In 1925, by pure chance, Jack heard from one of his customers that the Council were redeveloping an area of Preston and were offering a number of shops for sale, for small retail businesses with living accommodation above. Preston Council was attempting to encourage small businesses into this bustling area. What better than a hairdresser? Jack was able to secure a double-fronted shop with three-bedroomed accommodation above where he set up a barbershop and hairdressing salon with the assistance of a mortgage from the Council.

Olive soon made friends with the newsagent next door, Dora Brennan, who had a fourteen-year-old daughter. Dora would look after Clara and Lilly while she worked in the salon. In return, Dora always fell in love with the haircuts Olive tried on her that were on the cutting edge. She loved feeling glamorous, swanky and fashionable.

Money was still tight with very little being left each week after paying the mortgage to the Council, gas electricity and feeding the family, but still the business was their own, and things could only get better. Over the years, she made many friends through the salon, and her daughters' friends' parents, and Preston soon became home. The simple pleasure of bringing a bit of fun into everyone's life made the business side of the salon that much more important to them.

CHAPTER 2

Clara didn't like working in the salon. However, she did like her mother styling her long, blonde hair into the latest fashion. She would spend hours gazing at herself in the mirror, dreaming of looking like Irene Dunn. Unfortunately she couldn't afford the makeup, and her clothes, bought by her mother, were not at all trendy.

This afternoon she and her best friend Mary were going to the Empire to see *Anna Karenina* starring Greta Garbo. Although Mary was her best friend, they were totally different. Mary loved school and wanted to go to college when school finished in the summer and do exams—something Clara would detest. Clara longed to look glamorous, but Mary had no such ambition. She was happy with the way she was and with the clothes her mother bought her.

"Clara," her mother shouted, "will you stop daydreaming and get on with the sweeping up!"

Clara sighed, wishing that time would go quicker and that two o'clock would hurry up. Mary arrived at ten to two, and after getting changed, they made their way to the cinema. On the tram, they chatted about the boys they fancied in school and which shops they would go to after the cinema. After the movie, the girls would giggle and take turns pretending to be Greta Garbo getting ready for the ballroom, feeding their guilty pleasure by picking out the most richly adorned dresses they could find, only to leave empty-handed but full of joy.

Olive's first client of the afternoon was her friend May Matthews for her fortnightly shampoo and set. May told Olive that her sister Doreen Masson would be visiting in three weeks and would like an appointment. Doreen visited May three or four times a year and always came to the salon to have her hair done. Doreen had married a French man shortly after the Great War and moved to Paris. Her husband, Pierre Masson, was a rich businessman working for the French Railways and was often away from home on business. That gave Doreen the opportunity to visit her sister. May was widowed during the war. Her husband left to fight for his country and never came back, leaving her with two young children. She met her second husband when he moved to Preston to work as a foreman in the new paper mill, and her life had turned around. She could now afford her visits to the hairdresser and have a good gossip with Olive.

Jack was busy next door with a queue of men waiting to get their haircut. A few wanted a wet shave; it was a treat when they could afford it.

At the end of the day, Olive went upstairs to prepare Clara's birthday tea. Jack had finished for the day and gone across the road to the Railway Inn for a pint and a game of darts with his mates. Lilly, now almost thirteen, had already peeled and boiled the potatoes and carrots for the cottage pie they would be having for their tea. Olive had made the birthday cake the night before and just needed to add the icing. So, everything was ready when Clara and Mary arrived back from the cinema. They were excitedly telling Olive what a great film it was and so sad they cried.

Mary had bought Clara a small bottle of 'Lilies of the Valley' toilet water, which made Clara feel very grown up. After tea Clara walked Mary part of the way home, making arrangements to meet up the next day to discuss what they could do. That usually meant hanging about in Avenham Park with a group of friends from school.

Clara thought she would stay in bed until late the next day, being a Sunday, but her mother had other ideas. When Clara eventually appeared in the kitchen for breakfast, her mother was making lunch and not happy that Clara had stayed in bed.

"If you think, my girl, that you are going to laze in bed over the Easter holidays, you have another thing coming, and don't think you are going to leave school if you don't have a job."

Clara answered back, saying she was leaving with or without a job, which didn't go down very well with her mother.

"Well, then you will have to work in the salon," said her mother.

"I am not working in the salon. I will find a job," said Clara before slamming out of the house and running to meet up with Mary. They spent the afternoon with their friends, most of the time doing nothing but chatting, as nobody had any money to do anything else.

School finally broke up for Easter, and Clara celebrated with her classmates on her final day at school. She would now seriously have to look for a job. She said goodbye to her teacher Mrs. Harris who wished her good luck. Little did Clara know that her mother had spoken to Mrs. Harris and told her to expect Clara back at school after the holidays, as the prospects of a job at her age were slim.

Once Easter was over, Clara went to every place in town where she would possibly like to work, but there was nothing available. She certainly was not going to work in the mill, she told herself. At the Council offices, they said to leave her name, and they would contact her if anything came up. The local department stores said she was too young and needed to be a year older before they would employ her. She even went to the cotton mill to ask if there were any vacancies in the office, to which they replied, "Can you type?" She couldn't, so they just said no.

Her mother had suggested that she walk up to Fishergate and ask in all the shops there to see if any jobs were available. Perhaps she would do that tomorrow. At this moment in time, she wanted to hang about with her friends while they were still on the school Easter holidays.

In the meantime, Olive was discussing Clara with Jack, "What shall we do with her? She says she is looking for a job, but I have my doubts that she is really trying. She says she won't work in the mill, so what else is there?"

"I am sure something will turn up," said Jack. "Stop worrying."

"It is easy for you to say. She is not under your feet, and she thinks it is beneath her to do a bit around the house. Frankly, I worry that she doesn't care about her future yet."

'*The worst that can possibly happen is that you're right*,' thought Jack, contemplating what Olive said. Except, he was convinced otherwise, seeing their daughter as too afraid to make choices and be disappointed in life outside of the movies. He didn't say anything because he didn't want to worry poor Olive who loved their business and the people who walked in through their door so much that she couldn't imagine what Clara was thinking.

CHAPTER 3

Both Olive's brother, Clifford Rose, and Jack had joined the Preston Territorials in 1914. While Clifford had been sent to France to fight, Jack had stayed in England due to the fact that he was deaf in one ear following a childhood accident. Jack had been part of the Home Defence unit for the entire war, which was a comfort to Olive, as she was able to see him frequently, and he was somewhat out of danger. Clifford was injured in France and before being sent back to fight the enemy, he was nursed back to health, by a French nurse named Jeanne Duval. Clifford fell in love with Jeanne as did the majority of the unmarried injured soldiers in the hospital. They all fell a little bit in love with the nurses caring for them.

However unlike the other soldiers, Clifford had returned to France at the end of the war and married Jeanne. They now lived in a small village in Brittany where they owned and ran a small bar. They had a daughter named Danielle who was a year younger than Clara.

Olive was at work; although being a weekday, it was not very busy. She only had three clients booked for today. Her thoughts were of Clara and what to do with her. During the night, she had had a brainwave, why not send her to Clifford for say three months to give her time to experience another way of life. It might make her see some sense and realise that she needed to go college, so that she would get a good job—one with prospects. This she would need to discuss with Jack at the end of the day.

Jack finished work at six thirty and came upstairs for his tea. Olive had to wait until later to discuss her plans, as both Clara and Lilly were there. After the girls had gone to their rooms, Olive switched off the radio and asked Jack to listen. She explained her plan to write to Clifford and ask him if Clara could go over to France to stay with him and Jeanne for say three months. In exchange Clara would help them in the house or bar and learn some French. Olive anticipated that Clara would soon get bored and want to come home. This would be their leverage to get her to go back to school.

Jack was surprised to say the least. "Have you mentioned this to Clara?" he asked.

"No, I am discussing this with you first."

Jack suggested that she talk to Clara first, but Olive was adamant and said she would write to Clifford the next day and then speak to Clara once she had received a response.

"And," said Jack, "how will she get there? Have you thought this through? It is a long way to go. She is only just fifteen."

"I'll ask Madame Masson. She is always travelling to and from France, and her husband works for the railway in France. I am sure she will know, and she is booked into the salon soon, so I can ask her then," responded Olive.

Olive wrote to Clifford at least twice a year, on his birthday and at Christmas. She knew that a letter took about ten days to reach him. She wrote the letter first thing the next morning before her first client and then quickly popped down the road to the post office to post it at lunchtime. All she had to do now was wait.

Madame Masson came into the salon a few days later dressed in a beautiful fur coat and what appeared to be the latest fashion in haute couture, a classy two-piece suit. She was always very elegant; this was what living in Paris and being married to a rich businessman did for you. She also had no children.

"Good afternoon, Madame," said Olive.

"Call me Doreen. We have known each other long enough to drop the formalities," said Madame Masson. Doreen liked coming into Olive's salon when she was visiting her sister. There was no pretence. Everything was down to earth unlike the salons in Paris. There was the usual small talk while Olive inserted rollers into Doreen's hair. Then she sat under the dryer with a cup of tea and a magazine. Olive was fortunate enough to get unsold out-of-date magazines cheap from Mrs. Brennan, the newsagent next door, for her clients to read in the salon. Occasionally, Mrs. Brennan would exchange magazines for a hairdo.

When Doreen's hair was dry, Olive began to comb it out and style it, and while doing so, she explained her plans for Clara and asked about travel arrangements to France should her brother agree to have Clara. Doreen promised to ask her husband for details on how to get to Brittany plus the cost of the fares. She informed her that she would be speaking to him the next day. Not many people had a telephone at this time, and Doreen explained that she was able to use the public phone at the library and usually phoned her husband a number of times a week.

Olive was losing her patience with Clara. She was always around the house doing nothing but moaning that she was bored. She didn't seem to want to help her mother in either the house or salon and moaned even more when told to do chores like it or not.

CHAPTER 4

It was two weeks later that Olive received a telegram, nervously opening it. The message was simple "CLARA WELCOME STOP LETTER TO FOLLOW STOP CLIFFORD." Olive ran through to Jack and showed him. Now she just needed to tell Clara.

That evening Olive sat Clara down and explained her plan.

Clara was shocked. "I am not going!" she shouted, and she stormed off to her room. Clara sat on her bed and cried, not knowing what to do. She slept very badly that night, her mind in turmoil. The next morning, she got up after her mother had gone down to the salon to give herself some time to think without her mother nagging her. She decided to go and have another look for a job; perhaps she would get a tram and go further out of town. However, it turned into another fruitless day, and it was on her way home that her thoughts went back to her mother's idea and thinking that perhaps it could be an adventure. It was only three months. Then it would be the school summer holidays, so she could spend her days with Mary. '*Yes,*' she thought, '*I will go.*'

Sitting at the dinner table, Clara announced that she had decided that she would go to France and asked when she would be going. Everyone looked at her shocked.

"Okay," said her mother. "I will look into it tomorrow."

Olive had a busy day ahead with four clients' appointments booked, one of which was a perm that took at least two and half hours to complete, and she was just wondering when she would have time to contact Doreen to see if she had managed to get the travel information from her husband when in walked Doreen and May.

"Hello, both of you, I was just thinking of you, Doreen, and was trying to work out how to get hold of you today. I will just finish putting Mrs. Hall's rollers in and put her under the dryer, then I will be with you." Doreen and May took a seat and waited for Olive.

"I am so glad you have come in." She explained that Clara had decided to go to Clifford's and asked whether Doreen managed to get the travel information.

Doreen said yes and that was why she had come into the salon this morning and gave Olive all the details, which she had written down for her. "It is a long journey for someone so young, Olive, and a bit complicated and a lot of hanging around at stations," said Doreen. "In fact, I thought it would be more straightforward than it is."

'*Oh dear*,' thought Olive, thinking that perhaps it wasn't such a good idea after all.

Doreen mentioned that she was returning to France via London, where she would meet up with her husband in two weeks' time and said perhaps Clara could accompany her part of the way.

"That would be tremendous if she could," said Olive.

"Leave it with me. I will get my husband to book the necessary railway and boat tickets. We are speaking later, so all being well, I should come back the day after tomorrow with the details," said Doreen.

"I don't know how to thank you enough. Sorry, I have to get back to work now but will see you soon."

Just as Doreen and May were leaving, Doreen reminded Olive that Clara would need a passport and that she would need to get this attended to as soon as possible.

"Thank you, Doreen, I didn't even think about a passport," said Olive.

Olive told Jack and Clara what Doreen had said while they sat eating their dinner. She told Clara that she would need to go first thing in the morning to the town hall to see about a passport and suggested that she go to Auntie May's house the next day to see Madame Masson.

"She can explain the journey to you. You will also need to go to the bank and order some French francs," said her mother.

Clara was getting quite excited at the prospects of going to France and getting her very own passport; nobody else in the family had a passport. She got up early the next morning and did her chores in the salon before going into town on the tram.

She went to the town hall and got the forms to fill in for her passport. The lady in the office explained that she would need to see her birth certificate and bring the application fee and that it would take at least one week to get the passport. Clara explained that she was going in two weeks and would bring back the form tomorrow. Then she went to the bank and handed the teller a letter from her father giving permission to take money from the bank account and placed an order for some French francs.

"They will be ready to collect in two days," the teller told Clara.

Now that her two jobs were done, she wandered up the main street looking in the shop windows, daydreaming of things to come. All she had to do now was go and see Madame Masson. She caught another tram to Auntie May's house. Auntie May had a very homely, terraced house at the opposite end of town to where Clara lived. It was small but always neat and tidy and smelled of homemade bread. Clara knocked on the door, and Auntie May answered and told her to come in. Clara explained that she had come to see Madame Masson about going to France.

"Yes, yes I guessed that. Come on in. We are just having a cup of tea and a piece of cake."

Clara went into the kitchen. She was a bit nervous, as she had only met Doreen on a couple of occasions.

"Hello, Clara."

"Hello, Madame Masson."

"Don't be silly! You have no need to call me Madame. You must call me Auntie Doreen especially as we are going to be spending a bit of time together."

"Thank you," said Clara.

"Come and sit down next to me and have a cup of tea and some of May's delicious fruit cake. May is the only one I know who makes a fruit cake that is moist and melts in your mouth."

Doreen said her husband had telephoned her that morning with all the details.

"We leave two weeks from today. Firstly, we catch the train to London, where I will meet up with Monsieur Masson, and you must call him Uncle Pierre. We will stay a night or two in London, and then we will get another train to Dover where we will catch the boat to Calais. From there, we will get a train to Paris where I live. I am going to speak to your mother about the possibility of you staying with me in Paris for a week before you then catch a train to visit your uncle. The journey to your uncle's is a bit more complicated, but I will talk you through that nearer the time. Well, what do you think, Clara?" asked Doreen.

Clara was so excited at the prospects of not only going to London but to Paris as well. It would be just a dream come true. She was lost for words.

"Tell your mother I will pop over and see her tomorrow afternoon to discuss the details," said Doreen.

Clara thanked both aunties and virtually danced to get the tram home.

The next two weeks flew by. She had collected her passport and her French francs. Her mother had given her a bit of money to buy a few clothes for the trip. She had borrowed a suitcase from Mrs. Brennan and had packed and repacked her case four times. The difficulty was with what to take and how to get it all in the case. She would be leaving the next morning at eight thirty and her mother was coming to the station. But she would be saying goodbye to her father and Lilly before she left.

She went off to meet Mary from school as she was going to her house for her tea. She was sad to be saying goodbye to Mary, but she promised to write. She told Mary she would be back in about three months, so at least they would have some of the school summer holidays together before Mary went off to college. Clara cried on the way home thinking of how much she would miss Mary.

Clara didn't sleep very well—her mind was all over the place for, although it would be an adventure, she was a bit scared of being on her own, away from her family, in a foreign country and unable to speak much French. She wished now she had taken a bit more notice in French lessons.

The next morning, she was up early and couldn't face having any breakfast. There seemed to be a kaleidoscope of butterflies in her stomach. Daddy's friend, Mr. Byrne, who had a car, had agreed to take them to the station. They arrived with plenty of time to spare, and Auntie Doreen was waiting for them. Her mother was crying as she gave Clara a big hug and kiss and told her that she must write as soon as she arrived in Paris and perhaps send a postcard from London. Clara was crying now as she returned her mother's hug, and then they were on the train and gone.

CHAPTER 5

Clara had only been on a train once before and that was a bank holiday trip to Blackpool with her parents and Lilly. When she boarded the train, she was in an emotional trance. She felt sorrow in the depth of her stomach at leaving her family, and she therefore did not take much notice of her surroundings. She didn't notice the porters fussing around them taking the luggage on board, escorting them to their compartment, and generally making sure they were settled.

It was only later when Auntie Doreen asked if she was hungry and did she want breakfast that Clara realised that there were different sections of the train and that they were in first class. Leaving the compartment, Auntie Doreen instructed her to turn right. When Clara asked what was to the left, Doreen explained that that was where the other sections of the train were, and they were going right to the first-class dining car. Because of Uncle Pierre's position with the French railway, he was able to get preferential treatment on other railway lines, so she always travelled first class. The dining car was nothing like anything Clara had ever seen, the decor was very elaborate, and the staff were very attentive. The breakfast available was vast, leaving Clara at a loss for choice. In the end she chose a bowl of fruit, a bowl of cereal followed by poached eggs on toast with a pot of tea that she shared with her auntie. It was the best breakfast she had ever had.

They returned to their compartment, and her auntie told her that they would arrive late afternoon at the hotel and would have dinner with her uncle Pierre. Then they would be spending two nights in the hotel, giving them a whole day to dedicate to sightseeing in London. The next morning they would catch the train to Dover. There would be a short wait in Dover before they boarded the boat to Calais.

Clara found herself falling asleep and woke up about an hour later. Doreen handed her two books for her to read, the first was *Jane Eyre* by Charlotte Brontë and the second was *David Copperfield* by Charles Dickens.

"I asked your mother if you had read these, and she said no, so I thought you would enjoy them. They will help you pass the travelling time."

Clara thanked her and decided to start with *Jane Eyre*.

The train appeared to go really fast, and the landscapes changed by the minute. Some places were really pretty. Others were just field after field with nothing but bleakness. At lunchtime, Doreen announced that they would go back to the dining car to see what was on the menu. Again, the menu had a variety of meals available, some of which Clara had never heard of. She chose the veal and ham pie with boiled potatoes and vegetables that were so delicious, she cleared her plate. "You must have the pudding," said her auntie.

"But I am stuffed."

"Everyone has room for pudding," said her auntie.

On her recommendation, Clara chose a crème caramel, which she had never had before, and it was just extraordinarily wonderful. Now she really was stuffed.

Before she knew it, they had arrived in London. The scenery started to change and become more built up with houses. Doreen informed her that they were now on the outskirts of London and would be arriving in about twenty minutes. The porters helped them off the train with their luggage. One of the porters took them to the taxi rank to get a taxi to take them to the hotel. Doreen thanked him and handed him a tip.

The drive to the hotel was an eye opener. It was so busy with people and cars. They arrived at a very plush hotel. Again, the porter helped them with their luggage and took the cases to their room. It was a suite of rooms made up of two bedrooms with one bathroom and a sitting area. Her uncle Pierre was waiting for them. He embraced his wife and then came over to Clara and kissed her on both cheeks and said welcome to London. He spoke with a heavy accent that Clara thought sounded very exotic.

"I suggest we order tea and have a rest before dinner and then an early night. You have a full day tomorrow, Clara, with a lot of walking, so you need to be prepared."

The next morning Clara woke up when Doreen knocked on her door and announced that breakfast had arrived. '*Breakfast in the room*,' she thought, '*how exciting was that*.' She went through to the sitting room as the waitress was laying the food out on the table.

"Is all this for us? Surely we will never eat all this!" she exclaimed, pointing towards to table.

"We don't need to eat it all, Clara," said her auntie. "Just fill yourself up, and then we can go out."

They caught a taxi outside the hotel and made their way to Buckingham Palace. It was magnificent. Clara had never seen such a house and was stunned that only one family lived in it. It was so big. Their next destination was the House of Parliament and Big Ben. Her auntie explained that the House of Parliament had been originally called the Palace of Westminster and was where the monarchy lived before Buckingham Palace was built. It was now used by the government.

They went to Harrods for lunch, and her auntie did some shopping while they were there. "We will go to Selfridges later, which will be more to your taste. You will love this store," said her auntie.

They visited St. Paul's Cathedral and Trafalgar Square; they walked for what seemed liked hours, although they had to get a taxi on occasions because of the distance. They arrived at Selfridges at four in the afternoon. The windows were huge and all differently dressed. Auntie took Clara to the teenage dress department and told her to pick a couple of things she would like. She chose a skirt and blouse and a dress with matching cardigan. The dress was in a beautiful baby blue with little pleats at the bottom of the front of the skirt and a little tiny matching cardigan that just covered the top of the arms. Clara couldn't quite believe that she was looking at herself in the mirror.

"You must have some shoes to match, Clara," said her auntie and instructed the assistant to get a selection.

It was a surreal afternoon, and they returned to the hotel laden with parcels. Clara tried all her clothes on again; she couldn't wait to wear them and chose the dress to go to dinner in. Before bed, Clara thanked her auntie for a lovely day out and for the clothes.

Before she knew it, they were on the train to Calais. She had left a postcard at the hotel for them to post to her mother as promised.

The train took a couple of hours and then they had to wait to board the boat. Although Clara had often seen the ships in Preston Docks, she had never been on one, so she was looking forward to her first trip. She felt a bit sick on the trip, but her auntie and uncle tried to take her mind off things by talking about Paris and what they would do while she was there. The trip seemed to take ages, and she couldn't eat anything, as she felt so queasy.

They arrived at a busy Calais, everybody seemed to be trying to get off the boat at once, with porters vying to carry everyone's bags. Her uncle organised a porter and a taxi. They would be stopping overnight in Calais, as it was getting late, and they would take the train to Paris in the morning. They stayed in a lovely hotel again, but this time the food was entirely different and of course everyone spoke French. She couldn't understand a word; they spoke so fast that she didn't recognise any of the words at all.

They arrived at the Gare du Nord in Paris at midday. Clara had thought that London was busy, but Paris was even busier. The cars seemed to be driving all over the road with no rules. A taxi took them to the apartment where her auntie lived. Clara hung onto the door handles of the taxi for dear life. They went so fast, she thought they wouldn't arrive alive.

The apartment was in a fantastic tall, terraced building that stood six stories high with a lift that took them to the fifth floor. The apartment was like nothing Clara had ever seen as a maid greeted them at the door and helped with the cases. Doreen introduced her to Marie the maid and showed Clara her room for the stay that was bigger than her and Lilly's room put together. Marie had lunch ready for them.

"All I seem to do is eat, Auntie," said Clara.

"Well that is what holidays are all about," said her auntie.

After lunch, her auntie went for a lie down, and Marie took Clara on a tour of the apartment. She then went to her room to unpack and wrote a letter to her mother to tell all about the trip and the apartment.

The apartment was on two floors. The top floor where Clara's bedroom was located had dormer windows, and the floor below had huge windows that opened inwards like two big doors. Outside each window were big wooden shutters with a wrought iron Juliette balcony. The apartment had four bedrooms in total. Each had a small bathroom. There was also a sitting room, a dining room, kitchen plus two smaller rooms that were used for what looked like studies.

Clara presumed that her auntie and uncle each had their own study. She described the apartment to her mother in her letter and said she had never seen the likes even in magazines. It was pure luxury. But as Clara thought to herself, she had never really been anywhere before to make a comparison. The apartment was located in Place Dauphine that overlooked a triangular-shaped square with lots of trees and small raised gardens, and as she found out later, there was access to one of Paris's oldest bridges, the 'Pont Neuf'.

That evening Marie served them with a simple dinner consisting of a green salad and lamb chops. Even though it was simple, it was delicious. Clara attempted to help Marie clear the table, but she insisted it was her job and that Clara should sit down. It had been a long day, so Clara decided to go to bed and wished everyone a goodnight. She sank into the feather mattress and immediately fell asleep.

CHAPTER 6

During the following two days, Doreen took Clara sightseeing. They visited the Eiffel Tower, Arc de Triomphe, Montmartre, the Sacre Coeur, and the Notre Dame Cathedral. On one of the days, they took a sightseeing boat trip down the Seine. They ate a sumptuous lunch while floating past all of Paris' magical monuments. Clara had a wonderful time and arrived home each day exhausted.

Her auntie had an appointment on the third day and told Clara that she would need to amuse herself. She decided to visit the Musée du Louvre. With a map in hand, she negotiated her way to the Louvre Palace. She was overawed by the paintings and exhibitions and spent nearly all day looking around, stopping only to eat the lunch provided by Marie.

On the way back to the apartment, she stopped at a small street café for a coffee. There were a number of young people outside drinking coffee and smoking—one of the girls noticing Clara alone. She came over and started speaking to her in French.

Clara responded in her best French, "Je ne parle pas français."

The girl replied, "You are English" in perfect English. "Hello, I am Janet, and I noticed you all alone and was asking you if you wished to join us. My friends are all French, but I will help you speak to them."

"Thank you," responded Clara, "my name is Clara, and yes, I would love to join you."

Janet introduced her new friend, and she explained that she had been in Paris for a year. She was a nanny to three little girls. Today was her day off.

"I have made lots of friends here in Paris, and we meet up for coffee and a chat. I have learned my French here just by chatting to the friends I have made," explained Janet. "What are you doing here, Clara?"

Clara explained that she was in Paris for just a few more days and was then going to the north of France to stay with her uncle. She told Janet that she hoped to learn French and decide what to do with her future.

Clara stayed at the café for about an hour and then went back to the apartment. That night in bed, Clara thought that it could be one of her options to train as a nanny and then return to Paris. She loved the city and was surprised at how friendly everyone was. Even the lady at the bakery where Marie had sent her to get bread took an interest in her. Clara was surprised at how many new words she had learnt in her short time in France.

Soon her visit was over. Her uncle informed her that he had spoken on the telephone to her uncle Clifford and made him aware of the travel plans. He then went through the arrangements for her to get to Plérin, in Brittany, where her uncle Clifford lived.

That night Clara had a restless sleep, worrying about going on her own by train to her uncle Clifford's house even though Pierre had assured her that there would be officials at each station where she would have to change trains. They would be there to help her should she need it.

On her final day in Paris, Doreen took her shopping. They went to Place du Marché. It was a huge open-air market where all sorts of stores displayed their wares. There was a large variety of food stalls to every type of household item imaginable, plus a huge selection of clothing.

"Buy what you want, Clara. Everything is cheap here."

Clara was very apprehensive about buying too much, but every time she showed an interest in an item of clothing, picking it up and examining it, her auntie would say, "If you want this, you must have it." They left the market with bags full of clothes and shoes, plus a new suitcase to accommodate all her new purchases.

Their next stop was Galeries Lafayette, a large department store on Boulevard Haussman only a few blocks from the market where they had lunch. Doreen had ordered some clothing, so after lunch they went to the ladies department where she tried on the clothes. Some minor alterations were needed before they were delivered to the apartment. The clothes were very stylish, more suited to Doreen, unlike the clothes on the market.

Doreen then took Clara to the department that catered to her age and bought her two more beautiful outfits; Clara wondered where she would ever wear such outfits. However, that evening she had her first chance when they took her for a goodbye dinner at a chic restaurant. Clara felt very grown up and had her first glass of champagne.

Then all too soon it was time to say her goodbyes. First, she said goodbye to Marie who said it had been a pleasure to have met her and kissed her on both cheeks. When Clara started to say goodbye to her auntie at the apartment, her auntie hugged her tight. As tears welled up in her eyes, her auntie insisted that Clara must return to Paris and that she had loved having her company and being able to treat her as the daughter she had never had. Crying, Clara left the apartment with her uncle early on a Friday morning. She promised to write and let them know how she was getting on in Brittany.

CHAPTER 7

Pierre had written every detail of the journey down for her, together with the names of the stationmasters at each change should she need it. He made sure she was safely on the train before he hugged and kissed her goodbye and wished her '*Bon Voyage*'.

The train journey was long with the landscape changing from bleak to agricultural, passing through many small pretty villages. Children and farm workers waved at the train as it passed though. There were many stops on the way with passengers getting on and off at the various stations.

Soon, Clara changed trains at Le Mans and Rennes, entering the crowds aware of the feeling of moving with so many strangers on their way somewhere special or usual. She'd never experienced anything like this, and she wondered how many people around her didn't even feel the newness like she did. It seemed so easy to get turned around. At each of these stations, a guard helped her take her luggage on and off the train. They would guide her to the waiting room in readiness for the next train. The longest wait was in Rennes where she had to wait forty-five minutes.

She travelled in first class all the way, and her auntie had given her money to buy food, even though Marie had provided her with a hamper of goodies for the journey. She read her book the majority of the journey and fell asleep for some time. On her arrival in Rennes, she began to get butterflies in her tummy, worried that Uncle Clifford would not be there to meet her. All sorts of scenarios went around in her mind should he not be there.

At Rennes she changed to a smaller train destined for a place called Saint-Brieuc, this town being the nearest to the village where Uncle Clifford lived. She arrived during the early evening with the sun beginning to just go down. A guard helped her with her luggage and took her to the exit.

At first she could see no one waiting to meet anyone. Then she saw a man, come running around the corner towards her, with his arms outstretched. He looked harassed, and he called out, "Clara." With some relief, he hugged Clara, saying hello and kissing her all at the same time.

"I was so worried I was late and that you would be alarmed that no one was here to meet you," he said.

Clara said she had only just arrived and that she was pleased to see him. He thanked the guard and took her luggage over to his parked car. Unlike Auntie Doreen's posh shiny car, Uncle Clifford's was old and a bit battered. He loaded her luggage into the boot and opened the passenger door for her to get in. They drove off on bumpy roads to the home for what she thought would be the next three months.

By the time they arrived, it was dark. Uncle Clifford told her it was a small village with a population of no more than five thousand people. It had an approximate two-mile radius and was three miles from Saint-Brieuc, the main town of the region. He explained that everyone knew everyone else in the immediate area, and families moved not far from where they were originally born with a lot marrying people from the surrounding villages.

Auntie Jeanne, having heard the car, opened the door to welcome them. She kissed her on both cheeks and hugged Clara, waving her into the house where Danielle, her cousin whom she had never previously met, welcomed her. The house was larger than she expected, but it was homey with the bar at the front and the living room and kitchen at the rear. Upstairs were two large bedrooms, a smaller room that was used for storage, and remarkably for rural France, a bathroom. Apparently, the bathroom was Clifford's pride and joy, and he enjoyed showing it off to anyone who was interested. Before joining the army, he had commenced an apprenticeship to be a plumber, so he was able to do all of the work himself. He was one of the first in the village to install an inside bath and toilet and was soon being asked to help others do the same in his spare time.

Downstairs, just behind the bar was a toilet for the customers, again a first for the village, as previously the only toilet was outside. At the rear of the property was a large, overgrown garden with an outhouse, toilet and coal store. At the front of the property, there were a number of bench tables and chairs for the customers.

Jeanne said that Clara would share Danielle's room, and it was all ready for her. Clifford explained that the bar stayed open until 8 p.m. in the winter and 9 p.m. in the summer, however, Jeanne had closed early this evening, as she wanted to be free to welcome Clara. She had prepared a meal, and they all sat down to eat. They asked Clara about her journey and what she had done in Paris. By the time the meal had finished, Clara was ready for bed. She went with Danielle to the room she would share with her for the foreseeable future. Clara tried to chat, but she was so exhausted that she just fell asleep.

The next day Danielle was up early for school. "I have to get a bus to school and it takes about forty-five minutes to get there, so I must go now, otherwise I will be late. See you later," she said, rushing out of the door.

Much to Clara's amazement, Danielle spoke perfect English with a lovely French accent. She was a pretty girl with olive skin, opposite to Clara—whereas Clara's hair was fair, Danielle's was auburn like her mother's—but they were roughly the same height of five feet, four inches.

Clara made her way downstairs to be welcomed by Clifford. Both Jeanne and Clifford had insisted that she drop the uncle and auntie bit from their name. He explained that Jeanne would remain in bed and catch up on a bit of sleep, and as for the next three nights, she would be working nights. Jeanne was a nurse and worked at the hospital in Saint-Brieuc where she was a ward sister. She worked three nights on and three nights off starting 8 p.m. and finishing at 8 a.m. The first of the three nights was always the hardest, as she needed to be rested before the shift started, so she always had a lay-in and then attempted to get a small sleep later in the afternoon.

Clifford showed Clara where everything was in the kitchen and told her to help herself to breakfast. A large black range dominated the kitchen where all the cooking was done. It also heated all the water. It was kept going all day and night and fed with a mixture of coal and logs and anything else that would burn. Above there was a large flue that diverted the smoke out to the back of the building. There was a large dresser, at least eight feet long, against one wall with plates displayed on the shelving and stacks of an assortment of crockery on the top. On the lower shelf, there were hooks from which hung an array of mugs. In the centre of the room was a large wooden table surrounded by ten chairs.

Jeanne came downstairs at 9 a.m. and after her breakfast told Clara that she would be helping with the lunches. They were known as the *'Plat Du Jour'* in French. They prepared them every day, with the exception of Sundays, for the bar.

"Every day we do one dish and a dessert with a basket of bread and a bottle of water for a fixed price. It will be so good to have you here, Clara, to help, as Clifford is always busy preparing and tidying the bar ready for opening at 10:30. We prepare between twenty to twenty-five lunches every day, but we are not always full. It varies from day to day. Twenty-five is the absolute maximum, as you will see the bar is only small. Clifford will show you around shortly."

Jeanne was a handsome woman in her middle thirties with short, dark hair. Clara could see where Danielle got her looks, as she was the image of her mother.

Clara was thrown in at the deep end as soon as all the breakfast dishes were washed and put away then the preparation of the lunches began. Jeanne told Clara that until recently a girl by the name of Marielle came in each day to help her, but that she had left the week before to have a baby, so Clara's arrival was well-timed. On the menu today was coq au vin, which was essentially a chicken stew and would have to be put on to cook quickly as lunch started from 12:30 and finished at 2. The bar then closed for an hour to enable Clifford to have his lunch before reopening.

Clara was given a mound of vegetables to peel, while Jeanne prepared the chicken. All the ingredients were placed in two big pots with wine, stock and herbs, then placed on the cooking range. Together they cleaned the kitchen, ready to serve the lunches. Jeanne did not prepare the desserts herself, she explained. A local lady named Madame Gaudin baked for her and delivered a pie, tart or a gateau every other day, enough to last two days.

Clifford came through to the kitchen and offered Clara a guided tour while Jeanne prepared the coffee for a mid-morning break. The bar was small with eight stools against the bar itself and then eight small tables each with four chairs. There were two windows, a large one to the front of the building overlooking the main village square next to which was the main entrance to the bar. The other smaller window was at the side of the building overlooking the lane. It was a typical French bar with wooden floorboards, a dartboard on one wall and a shelf at one side where there were packs of cards and cribbage boards.

Between the kitchen and the bar was a small corridor in which the toilet was located. Next to this was a door that led to a staircase that took you down to the cellar. The cellar stored all the barrels of beer and other drinks for the bar. Deliveries into the cellar were made from the outside front where a double trap door opened, and the barrels could be rolled directly from the delivery truck into the cellar.

Off the kitchen was a sitting room where there was a settee and two armchairs in front of a blackened fireplace with a wooden surround above which was a shelf full of photos in frames. On the floor was a huge threadbare rug. There was a large window overlooking the back garden dressed with heavy brocade curtains. At the other end of the room were stairs leading to the bedrooms.

After their coffee break the bar was opened and a small number of old gentlemen, the regulars as Clara was informed, arrived for either a coffee or a beer but mostly to chat and play cards. Then lunch commenced; they served mostly men who seemed to appear from nowhere for their lunch; they chatted over a glass of wine or a beer and then disappeared. This was the normal routine, some were the local villagers or local farm workers, others were lorry drivers or delivery men just passing through the village, this being their regular stopping point for lunch. That first day they served nineteen lunches. That meant there was plenty left over for the family's dinner.

Danielle returned from school at 4:30. "At last we can have a chat and get to know each other. Mama said I am to speak to you in French as much as possible so that you can go back home having mastered the language."

Danielle and Clara became firm friends very quickly, and Danielle's friends became Clara's friends.

During that first week Clara learnt a lot about preparing lunches. Jeanne had a diary of what meals would be prepared on certain days. Clara soon mastered what had to be done each day and she attempted to help as much as she could before Jeanne came home from the hospital. She soon became a fixture in the village and was greeted by all she saw when going to the bakers to pick up the bread orders or the butcher for the meat orders.

The village was very small compared to Preston. It was centred around a square, which was dominated by the local Catholic Church, the 'Sacre Coeur'. The square was made up of granite cobblestones with Linden trees planted approximately every six feet. A street encircled the square where the bakers, the butchers and a general store were located. The street had a large deep pavement, and the general store displayed boxes of fruit and vegetables outside.

Within the store, which appeared to sell everything from clothing to foodstuff, was the local post office with a telephone exchange cordoned off to one side. Plérin being the nearest village to the west of Saint-Brieuc was one of the first villages in the area to have a telegraph connection. Not many people could afford to have a telephone installed in their home, instead they relied on the post office for communications. You could go along to the post office and make a telephone call, and the postmaster would take calls and arrange for any message to be delivered to anyone in the immediate vicinity.

All the main businesses had a delivery boy. Each morning and afternoon the boy would collect the orders and load up his bicycle, which had a large basket on the front and back, for the deliveries. He would also collect the future orders from the customers. The boys would often be seen swapping deliveries, if they were going to the same customer in order to save time.

There were four roads leading off the square. On one of the roads, a photographer advertised his services in a small window of his house, offering to take wedding, first communion and family photos to name a few. On another, a lady offered hairdressing from her front room. Directly opposite the church was Clifford's bar.

There was a doctor's surgery attached to which was a pharmacy. Dr. Madec was the only doctor in the area, and his patients came from a number of the surrounding villages. The surgery was open each weekday morning and was managed by his wife with a young girl to assist with menial tasks. The pharmacy was run by M. Hamon, the chemist. He also had a delivery person, but his was a girl, and she had a moped for her deliveries. She was the envy of the boys who wished night and day for a moped like hers.

Clara soon became familiar with the customers consisting mainly of old men that regularly came to the bar. They would sit there most of the day, in their traditional flat caps or berets, playing dominos or cards or just generally sitting outside in the sunshine or inside when it rained. They taught Clara to play poker, cribbage and dominos. She also picked up a lot of the French language from them.

One day one of the men named Claude Guinet wheeled a bicycle around to the bar for her, saying that it was only getting rusty in his shed and thought it might be useful for her. He had oiled it and put new brakes on for her. Clara was delighted and hugged him thank you.

Claude became a firm favourite with Clara. He had been widowed the previous year, and his only son was in the army, so he lived alone. He came to the bar every day for company and to have his lunch which she soon discovered was his only decent meal of the day. When she realised that on a Sunday he was having only bread and cheese, she started making him pies or stews and taking them around to his house on a Sunday morning while the rest of the family were at church. His back garden was an overgrown vegetable garden, and together, over time, they brought it back to life and planted it with cabbages, potatoes, leeks, onions and much more. Clara felt she was helping Claude recover from his wife's death, and thus give him a purpose in life. In turn, Claude helped her clear her uncle's back garden.

Claude suggested that perhaps they could tackle the bar's back garden and grow more vegetables, so with this in mind, Clara asked Clifford's permission, which he gave willingly.

The garden needed a lot of work just to clear it. Luckily at the rear of the garden was a gate that hadn't been used for years given the number of weeds that blocked it from opening. Thus they were able to dispose of all of the rubbish and weeds through the back gate.

The back gate led to a track that was used by the farmers to access their land with their tractors, and the householders whose houses backed onto the track used it to access their backyards or gardens for delivery of coal and other items. The track led from one end of the village to the other with mostly houses on one side and farmer land on the other. Their land was surrounded by five-foot high hedges made up of mostly pussy willow, privet, dogwood and hornbeam bushes plus a lot of weeds and wildflowers such as buttercups and daisies.

Directly opposite Clifford's gate was a section of wasteland that led to a copse of trees that boarded one of the farmer's field; it was here that Claude and Clara deposited all the rubbish ready to burn later.

After two weeks of hard labour, the area was ready. Between them, they decided that a large section would be for potatoes. These could then be stored for future use together with onions and carrots. All these items could not only be stored but used for the bar lunches or, perhaps, suggested Clara, "we could even sell some."

"I think you are getting a bit ahead of yourself, Clara. Nothing has even grown yet," said Claude, attempting to keep Clara's feet on the ground and not let her ideas run away with her.

At the end of the second week, they tackled the large apple tree and two pear trees. Clara picked all the fruit that hadn't been eaten by insects and stored these as Claude instructed her to be used at a later date. Between them, they cut back all the dead branches ready for pruning in the spring. With torn, dirty hands and generally covered in dust and dirt, Clara, totally exhausted but ecstatic with the results, made her way upstairs for a well-deserved, relaxing bath.

Little did Clara and Claude realise but this small venture would be a lifesaver in the years to come.

Claude's next suggestion was to get some chickens. So with her uncle's permission and using the money she had saved from the '*wages*' given to her for working in the kitchen, she bought six chickens. Together, Clara and Claude built a coop, to keep the chickens thus keeping them from digging up the vegetables. They soon started producing more eggs than the family and Claude could enjoy.

CHAPTER 8

The bike given to her by Claude gave Clara the freedom to explore. During the long school summer holidays when all the lunches were finished, she and Danielle peddled to the surrounding areas and on good days went swimming at the beach at Les Rosieres. Clara had learnt to swim at the public baths in Preston and had only been to the seaside once, when her mother and father had taken both her and Lilly to Blackpool. They would be gone all day on a Sunday, meeting up with friends and often cycling all the way to a local fishing port at the entrance of the River Gouët where it flowed into La Manche, and on those days they were exhausted when they came back, as the three-mile cycle ride back was all up hill.

By the time Danielle went back to school, Clara realised that more than three months had passed, and it was time for her to go back home, but she didn't want to go home. She wanted to stay. She loved learning about cooking, and her French had come on so much that she could nearly hold a conversation with the locals. She wanted to be able to harvest the vegetables she and Claude had planted and was worried what would become of her chickens. That evening after the bar had closed, she spoke with Clifford and Jeanne.

Clifford was just about to say how much they would all miss her when Clara said, "Uncle Clifford, do I have to go home? I love it here. I have made so many friends and what about my chickens? How could I leave them?"

Clifford said that she could stay as long as she wanted so long as her mother agreed.

"We don't know how we could manage without you now. You have taken a lot of the work load off Jeanne, and you are like a sister to Danielle."

"Thank you, Uncle. I will write to Mother tomorrow," said Clara.

"However, Clara, you need to slow down a bit. I know you are young and fit, but with the garden and cooking, it is a wonder you are not worn out," said Jeanne.

"I don't see it as work. I love every bit of it, well most of it anyway," said Clara.

The next day Clara wrote to her mother and set out all the reasons why she should stay. She told her all about the vegetable garden and the chickens and also asked her to send a cookery book so she could introduce different dishes to the menus.

Clara had written several letters to her mother since being in France, but they were just short letters, not saying much. This was the longest letter she had every written, and with fingers crossed for a positive reply, she posted it the same day.

Clara was on tenterhooks for the next couple of weeks unable to put her mind to anything while awaiting the reply from her mother. She went through all sorts of scenarios in her mind of how she would make her mother change her mind if she should say no. The letter arrived three weeks later, and her mother approved of her staying, and with the letter, her mother included a Mrs. Beaton cookery book and several magazine cuttings of recipes. Clara was overjoyed and immediately ran into the bar to tell Clifford. '*Now*,' she thought, '*I can plan for the future.*'

That afternoon when the lunches were completed and the dishes washed, dried and put away, she went to Mme Gaudin to put in the order for desserts for the following week.

"Madame, can you teach me to bake?" asked Clara.

"Of course, my dear. As I have told you before, I am finding it difficult to complete all the orders. At my age, I should be resting more; so if you help me, I will in turn teach you how to bake. How about starting now, and then you could come in an afternoon whenever you can?"

Clara was delighted, and her first lesson was Tarte Tatin when she helped Mme Gaudin prepare all the apples and watched while madame prepared the pastry. Over the next month, Clara learned how to cook all sorts of desserts, even bringing with her the cookery book that her mother had sent her to try new ideas. The pastry was a challenge, but in no time at all, she had mastered this and was soon experimenting with recipes on the family. Once the family gave their approval, she then introduced them to the customers. Some were praised, others not, and gradually she built up a portfolio of recipes.

Her experimenting soon extended to the main courses, introducing shepherd's pie, steak and kidney pie, suet pudding amongst others. Again, these were first tried out on the family and then introduced to the customers, with mixed reaction.

At least three times a week, she would help Mme Gaudin, and in return, madame would ask her to bake for her customers. Thus, Clara started to build up her own clientele, and over the next six months, it grew into a small, thriving business.

One of Clara's daily tasks was to collect the baguettes from the boulangerie across the square to go with the lunches. The baker had bought the business six years previously when the then owner died, and his wife wanted to sell the business and move to live with her sister in the next village. The double-fronted shop had been used as a baker's on one side and a pâttisserie on the other, but the new owner, M. LeBrun, was only a baker and therefore only used half of the space in which he sold bread, rolls and buns.

M. LeBrun was always hoping that in the future he would be able to employ a pâtissier and open the other side of his shop, but he barely made enough profit to pay the mortgage plus feed and clothe his wife and three young children, so the chance of employing someone was a faraway dream.

Clara arrived early as usual to pick up the daily order. "Good morning, M. LeBrun," she shouted, as he was not in the shop.

"Good morning, Clara, lovely day. I was just getting your order ready." After a few more pleasantries, Clara asked, "M. LeBrun, would you consider selling a few of my pastries in your shop on a trial basis? I could, say, supply you with six pies, and you could take ten per cent of the sale price in return."

"Mmm ... let me think about it, and I will let you know tomorrow," he said.

The next day the baker said he had considered her proposal and agreed to give it a trial.

"Can you do some items for tomorrow?" he asked. "It's Sunday and being market day, it would be a good day to try this out," he said.

Sunday was always busy in the bar as the market goers from the surrounding area came to the market. The market sold mostly foodstuffs, but there were also a few stalls that sold clothing, hardware, shoes, fabrics and other bric-à-brac. There were also stalls that sold hot food such as whole chickens, crêpes and best of all lovely sausages wrapped in a galette.

Clara was up and baking by 5:30 the next morning. She had decided to bake six Tarte Tatins and twelve éclairs. Everyone had enjoyed her first experiment at choux pastry, therefore, her hope was that these would be a good seller.

Every two weeks or so, Clifford would drive to the Cash & Carry in Rennes. This was the biggest in the area, and Clara had started to accompany him so that she could buy the ingredients for her thriving business at wholesale prices. While in the town, Clifford would visit old friends for a drink in a local bar, leaving Clara free time to roam around the area.

On one of these occasions, she decided to visit local pâttisserie shops to see what they were selling and the prices. She would subtly ask the shop assistant questions regarding the cakes and quite often buy a few of their pastries to examine the contents and structure with a view to copying them. She would always leave the shops with lots of ideas.

Clara delivered her bakes to M. LeBrun in readiness for him opening his shop. She had placed the tarts in boxes that she had bought at the Cash & Carry after seeing them at the pâttisserie and at the time thinking to herself, '*I must get some of those.*' She thought it made them look very professional. She had worked out the price that the baker should sell them for which included the ten per cent to M. LeBrun and a small profit for herself, not the high-end prices she had seen in Rennes but somewhere in between. She left the bakery with her fingers crossed.

At the end of the morning with all the market traders packing up to go home, Clara made her way to the bakers. The shop was just closing.

"Clara, I was going to come and see you after my lunch," said M. LeBrun.

Clara couldn't see any of her baked goods. The shop was completely empty. She was just thinking to herself that perhaps if anything were left she would offer these to the baker's family for their lunch when M. LeBrun handed her some cash.

"I sold everything! I have even been given an order for next week."

Clara was over the moon. Everything sold! And there was an order! This news was more than she had ever hoped for. She left the shop on a high, nearly dancing all the way home.

And so, her small thriving business began to expand. Clara was kept busy giving her little free time.

Jeanne would often complain about the state of the kitchen. "Clara, your pastries are taking over my kitchen. I hardly have any room to make the lunches."

"Sorry, I need to get another table to work on. Perhaps if we moved the dresser into the front room, I could put a table there," said Clara.

"Let's speak to Clifford later to see what we could do," suggested Jeanne.

M. LeBrun had recently opened the other side of his shop to display Clara's wares, his wife had cleaned all the display cabinets, and Clara was absolutely delighted. Although she never filled the cabinets, Clara was happy that at least the customers could see clearly what was for sale.

The same day as Jeanne had moaned at Clara about the state of the kitchen, she was making a delivery to M. LeBrun. She had managed to obtain a small pull-along trolley that had been dumped. Claude had mended the wheel and oiled the others, and Clara had given it a good clean. The trolley was perfect to put her boxes of cakes and pastries in to make her deliveries. Arriving at the bakery, she was telling M. LeBrun about the lack of room in the kitchen at the bar and how she was always in Jeanne's way when she got some great news.

"Yesterday," said M. Le Brun, "a salesman called, and I wanted to try and come and get you, but I was on my own in the shop. Anyway, he was selling electric food mixers." M. LeBrun then went on to say, "You know, I was discussing with my wife only the other day the possibility of you using the bakery kitchen, and then, by pure coincidence, I not only have a salesman visit the shop, but also I hear you say that you are getting in Jeanne's way. So, perhaps you would consider baking from here, Clara. I have the big ovens, and there is a big workbench behind the display cabinets in the other shop for you to work from. Plus, I purchased an electric food mixer, come and have a look," said M. Le Brun, beckoning her next door.

"Wow, how does it work?" exclaimed Clara.

"These are quite a new product. It is called a '*Sunbeam Mixmaster*', and it wasn't expensive. My first thought was of you, so I bought it," said M. Le Brun.

"That is fantastic, and it would make such a difference working from here. I wouldn't have to keep clearing everything away to make room to make the lunches. Imagine the time I would save not having to carry all the items from the bar to the shop," said Clara.

Clara's mind was running on overdrive. She thought, *'I can get up at 5:30 a.m., go to the bakery, do all the baking I need for that day, and then once I have finished, I can go back home, have breakfast and start on the lunches.'* It was a perfect solution. She relayed this plan to M. LeBrun and then ran home to tell Jeanne.

Clara arrived at the bakery the next morning at the crack of dawn with her trolley loaded up with the things she needed to start baking. Mme LeBrun had cleared everything ready for her. At the rear of the pâttisserie-side of the shop was a small work area with a store cupboard, a pantry and a good-sized table with a marble top. In the store cupboard, she found all sorts of paraphernalia—mixing bowls, cake tins, and rolling pins, in fact, everything she needed. There was even a book with a lot of recipes inside. Some she had never heard of, and she couldn't wait to experiment.

CHAPTER 9

The summer school holidays soon arrived, and on the days Jeanne was not working at the hospital, she gave Clara time off to enjoy with Danielle and their friends. This was Danielle's last year at school. In September, she was going to high school or Grandes Écoles to take her entrance exams that would enable her to go to university and study to become a schoolteacher. Her ambition was to teach primary school children, and her hope was that Mlle Ahier, the eldest of the four teachers, would retire from the local school, and she could take over her role. According to Danielle, Mlle Ahier had taught her mother, so she must be ancient.

The local primary school was located behind the church. It was a large granite building and a former convent with the nuns long gone. There was a big courtyard surrounded on three sides by a two-story building. Two priests occupied the far-right hand corner section, and a housekeeper looked them after. The priests took turns to say Mass at the village church and at another church located three miles away in La Ville Fontaine.

The priests could often be seen cycling around their parish, visiting the sick or just generally offering advice. They were well respected in the village. The village doctor's wife, Mme Madec, looked after the church with military precision. She did the organising but not the actual work. This was beneath her, and woe betide anyone who missed their allocated spot on the rota. The rota was made up of local women who would clean and arrange the flowers in the church each week on a voluntary basis.

The school was small—approximately a hundred pupils between the ages of five and eleven years, split between four classes. At the age of eleven, the children would then transfer to secondary school in Saint-Brieuc, a short bus ride away. Every Monday, the children would be given Catholicism lessons by one of the priests in readiness for their first communion. This was a big event in all the regions of France with the girls being dressed up in their white, satin dresses to symbolise purity, wearing veils on their heads kept in place with a wreath of flowers. The dresses were usually passed down within the family. The boys wore long, black trousers, white shirts and ties. Some wore suits or even tuxedos. The children would go in procession through the streets followed by their families all the way to the church to take their first communion and participate in the high Mass. The area bishop would come to the local church to take the Mass, which in itself was an event for the congregation. It was a tradition that a celebration party would follow the First Communion with the entire family gathering to celebrate the event.

Clara and Danielle spent their summer either on the beach, playing boules or hanging around the cafes in Saint Brieuc. They would cycle everywhere. Their group of friends included Léo, a boy slightly older than Danielle, who was in her class at school. He was not exactly good looking, but he had a charm about him that made him endearing to everyone. He stood at approximately five feet, ten inches tall with dark, auburn hair slicked back with hair cream. All the boys seemed to adopt this style.

Clara soon became aware that the friendship between Danielle and Léo was quickly becoming more than just a friendship, and by the end of the summer, Clara was being sidelined on trips to the cinema and nights out by Léo. Not that she minded! She liked Léo, and she could see that he was besotted with Danielle.

At the end of August, Jeanne informed both Clara and Danielle that the next day they would be going blackberry picking. Clara had experienced her first annual picking expedition in her first year in France. She had never tasted a blackberry before and discovered the joys of eating this deliciously juicy fruit straight off the bush. They went off with buckets in hand to a hedgerow about half a mile from the centre of the village. There were about 250 yards of blackberry bushes. They spent about three hours collecting the fruit until their buckets were loaded, and they made their way home full of scratches from the brambles on which the blackberries grew. They would do this trip three times, collecting the fruit at its best before insects invaded the fruits. Jeanne made jam of three varieties, blackberry and apple, just blackberry, and blackberry jelly. All three were delicious. She would make between ninety to a hundred jars. Some she would sell on the market or to the villagers, and the rest would be for family use.

The apples had to be cooking apples, thus, Jeanne couldn't use those from the garden; instead, they were picked from a local farmer's tree. The farmer gave Jeanne the apples for free so long as they either picked up the windfalls or picked them from the tree themselves. In return, Jeanne always gave the farmer some of the jars of the jam she had made. The jam was surprisingly easy to make. The main concern was making sure that it wasn't under or over boiled, but throughout the years that she had made it, Jeanne had become quite the expert. Clara and Danielle would help prepare the fruit, wash the jars to make sure they were absolutely clean, and then cut up grease-proof paper to seal the jars. Later, they would cut circles of gingham fabric to cover the jars secured with a piece of string. Small, sticky labels stating the type of jam in the jar were stuck to each jar. It was great fun. Clara would bake scones that were warm out of the oven and covered with the newly cooked jam. They tasted scrumptious.

Summer ended, high school had ended, and Danielle was now going to University in Rennes. She had passed her higher examinations with distinction. She was now undertaking a two-year teacher training course. Danielle would be staying at the university during the week and came home on the weekends. During this time, Danielle would often be accompanied by Léo. They now appeared to be inseparable. If he didn't come to Plérin, then Danielle would go to stay at his house. Clara began to see less and less of her.

Clara's thoughts often turned to Mary, her best friend from back home. She wondered what she was doing during the summer holidays. Although Clara had written to her on a regular basis, with letters full of news about her new life in France, Mary's letters were short and not very newsy. Clara did wonder if Mary was jealous of her new life and therefore couldn't be bothered to write long letters. This upset her a bit, but she realized she couldn't force a long-distance friendship.

Clara had now been in France just over four years. She had long grown out of all the clothes that she had brought with her and was now at least three inches taller than she was when she left Preston, standing at five feet, five inches or one and half metres. Her hair was slightly darker going from fair blonde to a more honey blonde. She had had it cut periodically, and it now fell in soft waves halfway down her back. It was nearly always tied into a ponytail, as she dreaded anyone finding a hair in the food she cooked.

By the time Clara turned seventeen, Clifford had taught Clara to drive. She would quite often drive to the Cash & Carry to buy the supplies and make deliveries for her flourishing business. She now had customers from various villages within a ten-mile radius of Plérin. She had saved a lot of her money and opened a bank account into which she deposited nearly all her profits.

She was saving up for her own car. A garage had been constructed on the outskirts of the village during the last year. It was a family business run by a father and his son, Henri and Marcel Rouault. There was a large house attached to the back of the garage where both Henri and Marcel and their respective families lived. The garage sold petrol and all sorts of motor parts. There was a workshop at the side of the garage, where repairs were carried out, and on the forecourt, a few cars were displayed for sale.

One was exactly what Clara wanted—a Fiat Topolino Cabriolet in red and black. Clara noticed the car one day when cycling past the garage and stopped and asked M. Rouault how much it would cost. When he told her, she realized disappointingly that she would never be able to afford such a car in the foreseeable future—in fact, perhaps never.

Claude was now seventy-six but still very sprightly, as he still spent nearly every day doing a bit of weeding or harvesting their vegetables, if not in the garden then he could be found in the bar. He had taught Clara to play poker, and she would often sit with him for a game or two. His son had retired from the army and now lived in Switzerland. He had married a Swiss girl some twenty years younger, and they had three children, but Claude very rarely saw them, which caused him some sadness. They wanted him to go and live with them in Switzerland, but he didn't want to leave the village.

"How could I leave my beloved Marie?" Marie was his wife buried in the local cemetery. The churchyard cemetery was behind the school, and Clara would often accompany Claude to visit and tidy up his wife's grave and leave flowers.

The churchyard was a fascinating place with graves going back hundreds of years—some so old, you couldn't read the weathered headstones and others sinking in the soft soil, so they looked like they were about to topple over. There was a small monument at the entrance dedicated to the soldiers of the village who had died in the Great War that listed all the names of the men. Only a small number of the men came home, and of the large number that didn't come home, there were no bodies to bury. So, the villagers with assistance from the church had arranged the erection of a small memorial to give the families somewhere to remember their lost ones and leave flowers.

Each year Clifford would order a sixty-gallon barrel of red wine from a vineyard north of Bordeaux. This was delivered in November to the bar. They would also supply and deliver to a number of hostelries in the Brittany area, and thus the vineyard did not charge for the six-hundred-mile round trip for delivery.

Another of Clara's tasks was to refill the wine bottles in the bar from the barrel of wine stored in the cellar. She did this a couple of times a week. She detested going down to the cellar. Although there was a light, the switch could not be reached until you had gone down two steps by which time she could already feel cobwebs touching her face. She would always take a torch with her, as the single light bulb didn't light up the whole of the cellar. There was a crack of light from the cellar access hatch, and there was also a small window, which was so dirty and covered in cobwebs that almost no light came through. She would fill the bottles as quickly as possible, as she found the cellar very creepy and it smelled of damp and mold. She always imagined that she could hear little scrambling noises that would make her very jittery.

One particular day, she heard a tiny meowing sound. Taking her torch and searching around the cellar, she discovered a black cat snuggled on an old blanket with six tiny kittens.

"How did you get in here?" she said to the cat. It was a bit of a rhetorical question, as the cat could not tell her, obviously. She quickly ran upstairs. "There is a cat with six adorable kittens in the cellar," she announced to Jeanne. She quickly filled a bowl with some water and found a bit of leftover meat. She chopped it up, placed it in a bowl and ran back down the cellar stairs. "Here you are!" she said to the cat who suspiciously smelled the food before gobbling it down and returning to her kittens.

Clara continued filling up the bottles before taking them up to the bar. This was a heavy job, taking the bottles down was okay, but taking them back up, filled, was a bit more of a challenge.

"Who do you think owns the cat and how do you think she got down there?" she asked Jeanne.

"There are a lot of cats in the area, and there is another entrance, although it is difficult to see, and the door doesn't quite fit. So, perhaps she got in that way. Why don't you put a notice in the local shop windows so that someone will come claim her?"

Clara prepared a postcard-size notice and then went around the local shops asking if she could place them in their windows. Sure enough, two days later, Mme Le Pen from just down the road came into the bar.

"You need to speak to my niece, Madame. I will call her for you," said Clifford.

Clara came into the bar, and Mme Le Pen said she had a black cat named Gigi that she hadn't seen for about a week and that she was pregnant. She knew she would be hiding somewhere to give birth. Clara took her down the cellar. *Ma petite beau chat, je me suis demandé étaient vous étiez.* Mme Pen asked Clara if Gigi could stay in the cellar until she could move her and her kittens in about five weeks' time.

"Of course, she can. I will look after her and her kittens, but can I have one of the kittens?" asked Clara.

"Yes, you are welcome to one. It is not easy finding a home for kittens. We usually have them destroyed."

This horrified Clara.

So, after five weeks, Mme Le Pen claimed Gigi and five of the kittens. Clara didn't dare ask about what was going to happen to the other five. She kept a little boy kitten and named him '*Cerfor*'.

"What sort of name is that?" asked Jeanne, after agreeing that Clara could keep one kitten.

"C for Cat, obviously," said Clara, and it sent Clifford into peals of laughter, but the joke was totally lost on Jeanne. Clara loved her little kitten, and soon so did everyone else. He became a fixture in the family and roamed around the house and bar as though he owned the place.

Clara recognized that life for her was changing. Danielle leaving for university, made her think about her future. There was no way she would ever want to return to school. Danielle would make a perfect teacher, but this was not her idea of a career. Clara loved baking and creating new dishes. She often thought of her parents and sister, and yes, she did miss them, and one day she would like to go back to visit them, but her life, at present, was here in France.

Her dreams were to have her own patisserie or teashop in, perhaps, a French city such as Paris. What a joy it would be driving around the city in her little Topolino Cabriolet, with the wind flying through her hair. She couldn't see herself staying in Plérin all her life ending up like Mme Madic, nosing into everybody's affairs and spreading gossip around the village. She liked nothing better than day-dreaming while kneading the dough for the bread, quite often Mme LeBrun would have to bring her back to reality by shouting, "wakey-wakey, Clara, which cloud are you on today?"

CHAPTER 10

Clara realized her responsibilities had grown considerably over the time she had been in France. Both Jeanne and Clifford relied on her to help whenever she could. She would often stand in for Clifford serving in the bar, but on this one particular day, Clifford was in bed with a bad bout of *'man flu'* as Jeanne called it. In reality it was a bad cold. Clara was in the bar washing glasses and generally tidying up when discussions between the regulars became heated. On occasion, she would listen to the regulars chatting usually about politics, which she didn't understand, but she did try and take an interest.

Over the last few years, all the talk had been about the civil war in Spain, and everyone was disgusted at how Franco was treating the Republicans that mostly consisted of the working classes and peasants of the country. There would be heated arguments about what would happen if Spain fell to the Nationalist party, as it would mean that fascists in the form of Germany and Italy would surround France. Some thought that Russia would not let this happen, as they were already supplying the Republicans with weapons and supplies.

However, on this occasion they were talking of the political situation in Eastern Europe and the threat of invasion by Germany. With the mention of the intervention by Britain, her ears pricked-up, and she started to listen to what they were saying. The talk was of Germany wanting to take revenge for their defeat in the Great War and how Hitler had recently invaded Austria.

"Where next?" The men discussed the possibilities and the possible outcome. The conversation became very heated at times. Most of the men in the bar had been too old to fight in the Great War, but many had lost their sons and were frightened for their now grandsons, but some had fought and didn't want to experience the horrors all over again.

Even though the radio was switched on periodically in the bar so everyone could listen to the news, it was not a good reception with a lot of interference and crackling. Clara wished she could read French so that she could read the newspapers, but even though she was now fluent in speaking French, she found it very hard to read. She spoke about the situation with Clifford and Jeanne, and they too were concerned of all the talk.

Over the coming months, Clara with the help of either Clifford or others in the bar would laboriously attempt to read the news in the papers. It was difficult, but Clifford told her the technique he had learned which helped her a great deal. Any spare time she had, she could be found in the bar, listening to the radio and what the customers were saying. She asked questions. She soon learned that Germany had invaded Czechoslovakia. At this point, Clifford started to worry about Clara being in France. He spoke to the local mayor about the best course of action to take.

"She should go home to England, just in case, because if there is another war, then it may be difficult to get her back to England," said the mayor. Clifford even received a long letter from his sister telling him to send Clara home, as they too were worried about the outcome of the situation in Eastern Europe.

"Can't I just become French?" asked Clara.

"I don't think it is that easy," said Clifford.

Clifford paid another visit to the mayor to ask his advice. "My advice to you both is to apply for French identification papers."

"I already have mine," replied Clifford. "I applied for French citizenship after being a resident for ten years, so my papers are all in order."

"If Clara is serious about staying in France, then she needs to go to the embassy in Saint-Brieuc and apply for citizenship. The rule was changed some time ago, and as she is now over eighteen and has been a resident for three years, she should be granted citizenship. I suggest you go with her to vouch for her and take her passport," suggested the mayor.

"Thank you for your help. We will do this," said Clifford.

They went to Saint-Brieuc on Jeanne's next day off after enlisting the help of Marielle, the lady that helped Jeanne in the kitchen before Clara arrived. Marielle would cover the lunches while they were away. They arrived at the embassy and joined the queue and eventually completed the application, which to their surprise was relatively easy. There was an in-depth interview with a government official as to why she wanted to be a French citizen plus a few formalities to be carried out by Clara. She finished these with no difficulties, and her papers arrived three weeks later.

Clara wrote to her mother to try and reassure her that she was just as safe in France as she would be in England; plus, she couldn't just leave, as both the bakery and Jeanne relied on her, but she promised that if the situation became dangerous, then she would not hesitate and come home.

It was a normal Sunday. The market was taking place. The bar was packed with marketgoers when suddenly there was uproar outside with people shouting and crying. Clara and Jeanne ran through from the kitchen where they had been relaxing with a coffee and piece of cake. "What is going on?"

The butcher ran into the bar. "Britain and France have declared war on Germany!" Germany had made an unprovoked attack on Poland, and Hitler had refused to abort his invasion after an ultimatum from Britain. The whole village was in shock.

CHAPTER 11

Danielle came home the following weekend. She ran into the kitchen and fell into her mother's arms, crying uncontrollably and unable to speak.

"Oh, Danielle!" said Jeanne, holding her tightly while she sobbed. "Whatever is the matter?"

Danielle took a few minutes to calm down and then told everyone that Léo had received his conscription papers and had to go straight away.

Every boy aged eighteen and over had to do his national service in the French army for a period of eighteen months. Léo had been given an exemption at eighteen, as he was undertaking a vocational course. However, once the course was finished he would have been expected to do his national service. But with the declaration of war, all the young men had received their call up papers no matter what they were doing, as the French army needed recruits to bolster their regiments in readiness for fighting.

Danielle said that all the boys in her class had gone, and it was rumoured that they had been sent to Belgium to prepare for training to fight the enemy, but that was only a rumour and nobody knew for sure.

"I am so frightened for him. He wouldn't hurt a fly. How is he going to fight and perhaps kill someone?" asked Danielle.

Both her mother and father tried to reassure her, but they both knew all about the monstrosities of war but didn't divulge any of this to her. Danielle went back to the university on the Monday morning with a tiny bit of reassurance from her parents but still extremely upset and worried.

When Clara arrived at the bakery the next morning, she was telling M. LeBrun about Léo. She could see the look of concern on his face but just thought he was worried about the future as was everyone in the village. At the end of the morning, Clara was getting ready to leave when she heard M. LeBrun call her into the family kitchen.

Clara always addressed both M. and Mme LeBrun as such and never used their Christian names. She supposed it was a mark of respect. She knew that M. LeBrun's Christian name was Guilliaume shortened to Gui and that his wife was Simone. They had three children: two boys, Fabien, who was seven years old, and Pierre, who was five, followed by a girl named Cécile, who was three. The boys were at the local school, and Simone would walk them to school every morning with Cécile in the pushchair.

Clara went into the kitchen and asked, "Do you want me?"

"Yes, can you sit down a minute? I just want to talk to you and Simone," said M. LeBrun.

He explained that he had been thinking all morning about Léo, and he realised that at thirty-four he was still eligible to be called up. He had been too young in the Great War to serve in the army, but there was every chance he would have to serve this time.

"So, I need to prepare just in case. After tomorrow, I will teach you both how to bake the bread. Then, you will be able to keep the shop open and make a living if I am not here," he explained.

Simone was beside herself. "No, you can't possibly be called up. Surely you are too old, and you have a family to support."

"I don't think that makes any difference. We have to prepare," he said.

Their lessons started the next day. It was hard work. At the end of the first session, Clara's arms ached from all the kneading, and she only did a small part of the job. What would it be like if she had to do a whole day's batch?

It took them both some time to master the technique, produce a perfect baguette, and going forward, Simone began not only to help her husband but she would also go next door and help Clara. They became firm friends and would chat their way through the morning, with little Cécile attempting to help in the kitchen or play in the garden.

Since the declaration of war in September, everything continued as before. Everybody went about his or her business as though nothing was happening. This period became known as La Drôle de Guerre, or the Phony War. In the spring of 1940, things began to change. Word came through from various sources that The British Expeditionary Forces had arrived on the northwest coast of France. The relief of the British arriving to support the French forces was short-lived with the Germans bombing the North West.

By the end of May 1940, the Germans had invaded Belgium, The Netherlands and Luxembourg. The news was that there were hundreds of refugees making their way through France to escape from their own countries.

This was followed shortly after by The Battle of France fought in Northeastern France. The German forces broke through the ill-prepared French lines, forcing both British and French troops to retreat. It was later described by the British government as a colossal military disaster. It resulted in thousands of troops being evacuated to Britain via the beaches at Dunkirk. With the British, French and Belgium forces retreating, the Germans quickly took over, occupying the whole of northern France. By the end of June 1940, France had officially surrendered to Germany.

The Germans had already taken most of the French army as prisoners of war and deported them to Germany. Some were sent to concentration camps. Others were taken as slave labour to work in German industry or agriculture. The Nazi forces started going from town to town rounding up all men who could be used as free labour. They were sent to work camps in Belgium and Germany. They needed workers in the munitions factories and the farms to keep the German army fed and armed.

Rural guerrilla bands of French Resistance fighters, known as The Maquis, started to become active in northern France. Initially, they were composed of men who had escaped into the mountains to avoid conscription but were soon joined by both men and women wanting to sabotage the German operations wherever they could.

Members of The Maquis forewarned the villagers that Nazi forces were in the area taking prisoners of war. Clifford and many other men of the same age went into hiding. They didn't want to risk being seized even though the Germans were looking for younger men.

While Clifford was absent, Clara took over running the bar. Jeanne told her that on no account should she speak English. One day when a German officer lumbered into the bar demanding to see the proprietor, Clara was struck dumb with fear and quickly ran into the kitchen to get Jeanne.

"I am the proprietor. What do you want?" said Jeanne.

"You have no husband?" asked the officer.

"No, I am a widow," she replied.

"You do not wear widow's weeds. Why is that?" he asked.

"My husband has been dead for a long time. I am too young to continue to mourn, so I no longer wear black," she replied.

"Beer," he demanded, looking at Clara.

With shaking hands, she poured him a small beer that he snatched from her and drank down in one gulp. Also, upon seeing a pile of sausage rolls on the bar counter, he grabbed these and walked out of the bar. They all breathed a sigh of relief. They found out later that his name was Major Lange and the officer in charge in the local area.

Not everyone in the village was so lucky. They heard later that M. LeBrun and Marcel Rouault from the garage had been taken, bungled into a truck containing other prisoners of war. As soon as Clara heard this news, she ran over to the bakery to see Simone.

Simone was inconsolable. Clara took her into her arms and let her cry.

"Thank you, Clara, for coming. I don't know what I will do without Gui, but I know I will have to pull myself together and act normally for the sake of the children. I will see you in the morning as usual," she said, trying to be brave for the children.

Clara didn't want to leave her, but Simone insisted, "I need to pick up the boys from school. It will be difficult telling them that their father has gone," she said.

CHAPTER 12

The villages only saw German troops periodically. At the beginning, it was because they were lost trying to find their way to the West Coast. The Maquis had removed all the road signs to sabotage the manoeuvres of the German troops. They would come into the village to ask the way to their destination, which was a mistake, as the locals never gave the correct directions.

On other occasions, they appeared to enjoy walking through the village to just frighten people, which they achieved. Major Lange more often than not would accompany his troops and when he did, he would always come into the bar. Clara soon learned how to massage his ego, as on his arrival, she would say, "Good morning, Monsieur, how are you today? You look very smart as always in that uniform of yours. I have your beer all ready for you." She would hand him the glass and offer him a delicacy. "I have kept some sausage rolls especially for you in the back."

Clara would go to the kitchen and return with a bag of three or four rolls. "Here you are. I hope you enjoy these," she would say.

"Thank you, mademoiselle, you are very kind."

"My pleasure, sir," she would answer. He would leave with his chest puffed out like a preening peacock.

"How can you do that, Clara, be so nice to that pig of a German?" asked Pierre, one of the bar regulars.

"Easily, he is so arrogant that he thinks I mean every word I say. I am massaging his ego, and I will let you in on a secret. The sausage rolls I give him are destined for the bin. I have either dropped them on the floor, or they are days old. I keep them in a labelled box just in case he comes in. Once I have heated them in the oven, they appear fresh." Everyone in the bar roared with laughter.

"Plus, have you noticed that when he is in the bar, the troops don't come and search the premises, which is good for Clifford?" said Clara.

Food shortages were beginning to hit the villagers. Everyone had received a ration book that entitled them to the basic foodstuffs. They would take the family coupons to the general store, bakery or butcher and get their ration, but the difficulty was that the shops didn't necessarily have the produce to sell.

The villagers were better off than those in the cities, as they were able to grow their own vegetables. A lot of families kept chickens and rabbits that supplemented their rations. Farmers in the area secretly kept pigs and newly born calves, which they would sell on the black market. This was fraught with danger, as if they were caught, there was the possibility they could be arrested and shot.

As part of the rationing system, the bakery was able to purchase bread flour. However, the price was grossly inflated which meant that Simone had to increase the price of the bread. That left everyone unhappy. Some would accuse her of exploiting the shortages even though she tried to explain that her costs had gone up. There were strict regulations in place whereby she could only accept the correct ration coupons in exchange for bread.

Clara continued to help Simone every morning, but the baking of anything other than bread was severely restricted because of the rationing. Quite often Clara would obtain some extra milk from M. Duval, a farmer who had a big dairy herd of cows. She would churn the milk into butter, which, together with the eggs from her chickens, would make a few cakes and pastries. However, she had to be careful where these were sold. Sugar was another scarce item, but Clara soon discovered saccharin as a substitute.

M. Plessis, the arable farmer whose fields bordered the track at the back of the bar, had two young sons, and they would trap wild rabbits. Before the war, they would do this to stop the rabbits eating the crops, but as meat became scarce, they were able to turn this into a small business. They sold the rabbits to the locals.

Clara would often buy a couple of rabbits, as the rationing was also hitting the bar lunches. Clara became adept at serving stews of mostly vegetables with cheap cuts of meat from the butcher or with rabbit.

Coffee was another casualty of war. Old recipes started to emerge using chicory roots or acorns that could be used on their own or mixed with barley. These would be toasted in the oven and then ground down. This was an acquired taste, as it was very bitter.

On one night in early 1941 when Jeanne was on the night shift, Clara was awoken. Clifford was shaking her and whispering, "Wake up, Clara, wake up."

"What is it? What is the matter?"

It was two o'clock in the morning. Cerfar was asleep at her feet and not very happy at being disturbed. Clifford said that he needed her to get up and get dressed quickly. He required her help and told her not to put any lights on. She dressed as fast as she could in her groggy state and made her way downstairs.

"What is it, Clifford?" she asked, feeling quite worried.

"I want your help. Follow me."

He led her out the back door through the garden and out the back gate. Clara recognized Henri Rouault's flat back truck parked in the lane. She followed Clifford to the back of the truck where she could just about make out a man lying there.

"Help me get this man into the house." Clifford held the man by one arm and helped him off the back of the truck. He was moaning in pain.

"Grab his other arm, Clara."

Between them, they managed to get him into the house. The man was unable to put any weight on one foot.

"We need to get him down the cellar," said Clifford.

This they did with great difficulty. The stairs were the biggest problem.

"Clara, ask no questions, just look after him, and try to see to his ankle. I have to go. I will be back later."

Clara laid the cat blanket on the floor and helped the man sit down. She asked him where else he hurt besides his ankle and then realized he was English.

"I think I have only twisted my ankle. I don't think it is broken," said the man.

"You are English?" she asked.

"I am," he replied.

Clara quickly ran upstairs and grabbed the first aid kit that Jeanne had put together and kept in the kitchen in case of emergencies. She helped him remove his boot and tightly bandaged his ankle that was fast becoming swollen. Clara could see he was in a lot of pain, so she gave him an aspirin to ease the discomfort.

"What are you doing here?" asked Clara.

"I think it is best that you don't know too much other than I parachuted in this evening and landed in a tree, then fell to the ground. I will be fine here until Pascal returns," he responded.

Clara went back to bed wondering who Pascal was, but she remembered Clifford saying not to ask any questions. She managed to get a couple more hours of sleep and woke early as usual ready to go to the bakery. Going downstairs, she quickly remembered the airman in the cellar. She looked in on him and found him to be fast asleep. She left him a glass of water and some more aspirin and then made her way to the bakery.

Returning to the bar later, Clifford was waiting for her.

"How is the airman?" Clara asked.

"Comfortable," responded Clifford.

"He will need to stay in the cellar until this evening, and then we will move him out. I have taken some food down to him. Clara, Jeanne will be home soon. You mustn't mention anything to her. The airman knows he must stay completely quiet, and nobody must know he is here. Do you understand? We are in a very dangerous situation," said Clifford very seriously.

"You can trust me, Clifford, I understand," said Clara.

The day progressed as any other day with Jeanne spending the best part of the day asleep, then returning to work in the early evening. Clifford told Clara to go to bed as usual, and he would see her in the morning.

Clara tried to sleep. She tossed and turned in bed, thinking of all the worst scenarios that Clifford could find himself in—from being arrested and shot to being tortured for information regarding the airman. She must have fallen asleep, as the next thing she knew the alarm clock was waking her up.

Everything was quiet downstairs, so she left and made her way to the bakery as normal. The morning dragged by. Clara tried to act normal, but Simone kept asking her if she was all right.

"Clara, you are very distant this morning. Is everything okay? If you are worried about something, please tell me, and I will see if I can help you."

"I am fine, Simone, honestly," said Clara.

On arriving home, Clifford was again waiting for her.

"Is everything okay?" inquired Clara.

"Yes, everything is fine," and that was it. Nothing else was said. This left Clara mystified as to what she should do, but she presumed she was just meant to carry on as though nothing had happened. This is what she decided to do.

Life carried on as normal. There were no visits from the Germans. The only thing to happen out of the ordinary over the following weeks was a directive from the mayor that all radios were being confiscated and had to be deposited at the Mairie. Clara spotted Clifford taking one of his radios to the outhouse and realized he was hiding it.

CHAPTER 13

Almost two weeks later, after finishing at the bakery one Wednesday morning, Clara went to the butcher's as usual to see what was available so she could plan lunch.

"Good morning, M. Gastion. What have you got for me this morning?" asked Clara.

"Only a few scrag ends unfortunately, but before I get these ready for you, can you run a message for me?" asked the butcher.

"A message? What kind of message?" Clara asked.

"Could you just quickly cycle to Claude's and give him these two sausages?" he pleaded.

This baffled Clara. What on earth would Claude want with two sausages? *'He never cooks,'* she thought to herself.

"I will have your order ready for you on your return. Go quickly."

Clara picked up the parcel, jumped on her bike and cycled to Claude's house. She went to his back door as usual and shouted hello as she entered his kitchen. She was surprised to see a tall man standing by the fireplace.

"You must be Clara. I am Michel. Claude has told me all about you." She shook his extended hand. "I am pleased to meet you. I will come straight to the point, Clara," said Michel to a mystified Clara.

Michel explained that he was with British intelligence and that they needed her help. He said he knew she could be discreet following the incident with the airman. But he emphasized that the work of the resistance groups was dangerous, that nobody was to be trusted, and that she should not discuss any task undertaken with anyone—not family or close friends.

"Everyone is out for themselves, Clara. You may think someone is thinking the same as you, but they will do anything to protect themselves," he explained.

"Some people think the Germans will win this war and so France will be under German rule, so they covertly pass information to the Germans in the hopes that they will be looked after by the Germans when the war is won."

Clara listened to all that was said and assured Michel that she would take care and that all her faith was with the British. She promised to do all she could, to help win the war against the Germans and give France back to the French people.

"Thank you, Clara, that is enough said. This is what I would like you to do." Michel explained that she would be known by the code name of Vivienne and that this name would only be known to other resistance workers. He gave her a note and said that she was to deliver it as soon as possible.

"You are to go to La Café Bleu by the Cathedral in Saint-Brieuc, order a coffee and a croissant and sit at a window seat. When the waitress brings your order to the table, you ask her '*is Henri in today?*' and she should respond with '*yes*'. Then you ask to tell him that Vivienne would like to say hello. If by any chance she says '*no*', then drink your coffee and leave quickly. That indicates there is a problem."

Michel informed Clara that Henri would be her cousin and would greet her as such and no doubt exchange small talk about the family.

"You will just need to think on your feet. You must discreetly hand him this message." Michel handed her a folded piece of paper and told her to hide it somewhere safe.

"Henri will then give you a message to give to me. It will either be a note or verbal. If it is verbal, please remember everything he says." Michel suggested that she return home as usual and ask her uncle if she could have the day off.

"I am sure you can make up a story," said Michel.

"Quite easily today, as my aunt is on one of her days off, so it will be no problem," said Clara and off she went.

Clifford didn't question her request and asked her to look out for any supplies while she was in town, reminding her to take the ration books. Clara cycled as quickly as she could, arriving in Saint-Brieuc just before noon. She found the café quite easily and went in and ordered as she had been instructed.

Henri came bounding out of the back, arms open wide. "Vivienne, it has been such a long time! How are your parents?" He kissed her on both cheeks.

"My parents are very well, thank you, and how are yours? Have you seen Grandmamma lately? I saw her two weeks ago, and she was still as grouchy as ever."

Henri laughed and agreed with her.

Clara was surprised by Henri. She was expecting an older man, but he was young, perhaps the same age as her or slightly older, and not quite six foot with jet-black hair slicked back with hair cream. His eyes were an intense dark brown, and his skin was flawless with an olive glow. His fingers were stained with nicotine.

Henri sat down opposite her, and Clara managed to discreetly hand him the message. She drank her coffee and ate her croissant while he read the message. She then realized that the message to go back was going to be verbal. Henri lowered his voice and went on to tell her that there was a bit of a problem in that the informant from the railway had been arrested, and they were urgently trying to get another source to provide the times of the shipment. He was hoping that this would happen in the next couple of days, but in the meantime, there was nothing that could be done.

"I understand," said Clara.

"I must get back to my work. It has been lovely seeing you, Vivienne. Please come and see me again when you are in town." Off he went, waving goodbye.

Clara quickly went to the supplier and managed to get some sugar since that was all that was available, so it wasn't too much of a wasted journey.

She cycled back and went straight to Claude's house. Claude was waiting for her. "Your man will be back in one hour. Do you want to wait and have a cup of coffee with me?"

"Yes, that would be lovely, Claude, but not sure that your home-made coffee has the best taste."

They sat down and gossiped about what was going on in the village and drank their coffee. Michel arrived, and Claude said he was off to the bar and would see her later.

Clara relayed the message, and she could see that Michel was concerned. "I don't know exactly what the message means, but I presume it has to do with the railway. I don't know if it would help, but when I came over to France, I travelled from my home in England, to Paris, with a couple I called aunt and uncle. Although they are not really related, my auntie is a friend of my mother's. Anyway, my uncle was in charge of the railway company in Paris and perhaps could help you," suggested Clara.

"Interesting," replied Michel. "When was the last time you were in touch with them?" he asked.

"I have had no communication since the Germans occupied Paris, as there is no mail, but I do know they remained in Paris," said Clara.

Clara could see that Michel was in deep thought, and she began to think that perhaps she shouldn't have said anything.

Michel then said, "Could you get in touch and sound your uncle out? You would have to be careful, as he may be a German sympathizer," he said.

"The only way I could do this would be to go to Paris. Is this what you want me to do?" asked Clara.

Michel thought for a moment and then agreed that this would be the best course of action—a face-to-face meeting. Michel said he would arrange everything and return in a few days.

"Michel, if something goes wrong, how do I get a message to you? I thought of this while I was cycling to town this morning," said Clara.

"I will give you a contact and code next time I see you," said Michel.

Clara returned to the bar and presented her purchase of sugar to Jeanne.

"Did you have a good day off?" asked Jeanne.

"Yes, I went into Saint-Brieuc and had a coffee with a couple of friends and then got the sugar—that was all they had that we needed—and came back. Made a nice change," she said.

A few days later, she received a message to meet Michel at Claude's. Michel handed her a train ticket and travel papers and told her that she would travel as herself going to visit her aunt and uncle.

"I will leave it to your discretion as to how you ask your uncle to help us." Michel then explained that they required a full itinerary of unusual train movements going from Germany or Belgium to the west coast of France. These trains are destined to ports on the west coast for shipment. They are carrying equipment and munitions to arm the German troops, and we want to try either to intercept or destroy these shipments.

"I will do my best to help you," said Clara.

Michel then went on to give her a contact and code word should she ever need to contact him urgently or if she got herself in any danger.

Clara put arrangements in place to go to Paris so that Simone and Clifford could manage without her for five days.

Clifford dropped her off at the railway station early on the morning of the day she was to travel to Paris and wished her a good trip. The train was later than scheduled, and she found out later was normal. With her small case, she was just about to board the train when a German officer behind her tapped her on the shoulder. She turned around and nearly jumped out of her skin on seeing the officer.

"Let me assist you, mademoiselle," he offered, taking hold of her case before she had a chance to answer. He helped her on board and moved two German soldiers off their seats to make way for her. He stowed her case in the overhead storage area and sat down next to her.

"Let me introduce myself to you, mademoiselle. I am Lieutenant General Hans Klein, at your service."

Besides the major who came into the village, Clara had not had much interaction with the German army and was surprised at how pleasant this officer appeared. He was six-foot-tall, slim with blonde hair, and extremely good-looking. Clara put on her charm and introduced herself and thanked him for obtaining a seat for her. She could see some of the other non-German passengers giving her disapproving looks for fraternizing with the enemy. He asked her where she was going.

"I am going to Paris to visit relatives, my aunt. My mother's sister has been unwell, and my mother doesn't like traveling, so I am going to see her. Then I can report back to my mother," said Clara.

"I am going to Paris also, so I will be able to keep you company," he informed her.

The journey took nearly five hours, longer than it should have taken. There were a lot of unexplained stops. Hans, as he asked her to call him, was thirty-two years old and young to be a lieutenant general. He told her he was married with a little six-year-old girl named Greta. He showed Clara photos of them and appeared to well-up when telling her how much he missed them. In fact, she had his life story in the first hour of meeting.

Clara had brought a flask of coffee and some biscuits with her. She opened her bag and shared them with him.

"What delicious biscuits, did you bake these?"

"Yes," replied Clara.

"I am a cook and a baker, although with all the rationing, it is difficult to bake cakes and biscuits these days." She said this without thinking and then apologized.

"No need to apologize. We are all in the same position. I miss my wife's cooking and have to endure army food or lack of it." He laughed.

Hans asked her about herself, and she tried to keep as near to the truth as possible, leaving out the fact that she was British. Clara found this man very attractive and thought to herself that in another life or another time she could easily fall in love with such a man. But in this present life, and at this time, he was the enemy.

They eventually arrived in Paris, and Hans assisted her off the train and carried her case for her. "How will you get to your uncle's?" Hans asked.

"I will try and get a taxi or a bus," she said.

"It will not be easy getting a taxi. I will help you," he said.

"There is no need. You have already been most helpful," said Clara.

"No, I insist," he said.

They arrived outside the station where a car was waiting for Hans, but before getting into his car, he hailed a taxi for her. On seeing a German officer, a taxi instantly stopped. She thanked Hans for his most enjoyable company on the train and got into the taxi. She gave the taxi driver the address, and she could see the look of disgust on the driver's face. He virtually dumped her at the door without a word or even helping her out of the car, and she was sure he overcharged her as well.

The concierge of the building recognized her from her previous visit and told her to go straight up. He said that he would ring her aunt to inform her that she was on her way up to the apartment.

Her aunt opened the door and took her in her arms. "Speak in French", she whispered to Clara in French quickly, then as she pulled gently away, she said in a normal voice, "My dear, so lovely to see you after all this time. You look so well, and how you have grown." Behind her aunt stood the maid, not Marie but a new one. "This is my new maid, Antoinette."

"Antoinette, this is my niece, Clara," said her aunt.

"Pleased to meet you, Clara."

"Antoinette, please could you make us a cup of tea, and can you stretch dinner to three?" asked her aunt.

"Of course, Madame," said Antoinette.

Her aunt took her through to the living room and closed the door. She lowered her voice and said that she must speak French at all times and that Antoinette was not to be trusted. She told Clara how Marie had just disappeared one day and that the Germans overseeing the railways had recommended Antoinette to her uncle. Both her aunt and uncle felt that Antoinette had been placed with them to keep an eye on them, especially, given her uncle's position with the railway.

Antoinette knocked on the door and carried in their tea.

Her uncle arrived home from work at eight o'clock. He was delighted to see her. Clara was alarmed at how he had changed. He had lost a lot of weight. His hair was now white, and he looked pale and exhausted.

"What brings you to Paris, Clara?" asked her uncle.

"My mother was worried about her sister and sent me to check up on her and report back. You know Mother. She worries that she had heard nothing from you. The mail is non- existent, and she has not been well herself, so she will not travel. I thought I would come and see you for myself to stop her worrying," explained Clara.

Antoinette announced that dinner was ready, and they moved to the dining room.

"Can you get the spare room ready for Clara after your dinner, of course, please, Antoinette?" asked her aunt.

"Of course, Madame, no problem," replied the maid.

By the time they had finished dinner, Clara, excused herself and went to bed. She was so tired she was nearly falling asleep at the table.

The next morning after breakfast, her aunt suggested they go for a walk. While out walking, her aunt told Clara how difficult life was in Paris. Everything is rationed, and even when you go to the shops with your ration coupons, there is nothing there to buy. "That is another reason I am so suspicious of Antoinette. She goes to the shops and brings back foodstuff, which I know is more or less impossible to get. So where does she get it? And she is always lurking about the flat eavesdropping on our conversations."

On their way back to the apartment, they stopped at what used to be her aunt and uncle's favourite restaurant and asked if there was a table available for that evening. They were in luck. So, her aunt booked it for eight o'clock.

Over dinner that evening, her uncle asked for the real reason why Clara had come to see them.

"What makes you think I haven't just come to see you?" asked Clara.

"You lied too easily to us about your mother, so we guessed you had an ulterior motive," replied her aunt.

"How do you feel about the war and the Germans, Uncle? Where do your loyalties lie?" asked Clara.

"What do you think, Clara? I am a Frenchman, and my wife is British. Do you think I would ever take sides with those bastard Germans? They make me work every god sent hour. Sometimes I get paid, and other times I don't. There is always an excuse for non-payment. They are forever checking my work and looking to see what I am doing. They are paranoid, but I am the only one that knows how everything works here in Paris. Most of the other employees have gone, and there are only a few of us doing the work of many. So, I ask again what do you think?" said her uncle.

"Sorry, Uncle, but I had to ask. I am here to ask you if you will help the resistance with information on unusual train shipments coming from Germany or Belgium going to the West Coast," asked Clara.

"Ah! At last I can make a difference, and I know exactly what is wanted. I have noticed certain train journeys are heavily monitored. I would be honoured to help," he said.

Michel had already gone through with Clara how information could be relayed to the resistance through a network of workers. However, she was instructed not to give this information to her uncle in the first instant, but she gave him the telephone number of the post office in the village and told him to phone her when he had information. Thereafter if everything went to plan, and the resistance knew they could trust him, then he would be given a contact in Paris.

Clara spent the next day with her aunt. She discovered that her aunt had had a minor stroke and had been extremely sick. While her aunt took an afternoon nap, she sat reading in the living room. Antoinette offered her tea and then proceeded to virtually interrogate her. Clara, having been forewarned by her aunt, gave Antoinette answers as vague as possible.

Clara's journey home was uneventful. There was no German officer to find her a seat, and she had to squeeze onto a seat with two others—on a seat made for two.

On her return, she met up with Michel and apprised him of how she had got on with her uncle and how he was honoured to help.

It was eight days later when her uncle phoned. The post mistress ran across to the bar and said there was a phone call for her. She quickly went to the phone and made small talk with her uncle. He then proceeded to give her information that she wrote down which included dates, times and places. These meant very little to her. Clara, knowing the information was important, phoned the number Michel had given her and gave the code word to the person who answered the phone and hung up. Not sure what would happen next, Clara went back home.

Clara was on tenterhooks all afternoon. Claude had already been in for his lunch and had gone home for an afternoon siesta, so she did wonder how she would be contacted. But it was not long before Claude was back and asked if she could come and help him with a little job at home. She knew instantly it would be a contact. Michel met her at Claude's house, and she handed over all the information that her uncle had given her.

Michel read it with a big smile on his face. "This is terrific, just what we need. Thank you, Clara."

Clara only received one more call from her uncle and then her role of go-between ceased. Her uncle was given his own code name and direct contact. Thus, the information was passed on quicker.

CHAPTER 14

Danielle had left university in late 1941. The further education system in France had virtually fallen apart. The university in Saint-Brieuc had closed down, as there were insufficient students. All the boys were of the age to either have been taken as prisoners of war or were in hiding. Some had returned to help their families in protected occupations such as farmers. Most of the villagers did not let their children go to secondary school in Saint-Brieuc, preferring to let the children continue at the local primary school. The church had given the school two extra rooms to extend the school, thus enabling them to take the older children.

Danielle was lucky enough to be able to get a position teaching the older children, so she was able to live at home and help out in the bar, taking a bit of the work off Clara and Jeanne. Danielle received mail from Léo intermittently; he was now a prisoner of war in Germany. The letters gave very little information only that he was well.

Jeanne continued to work at the hospital. The hospital was always busy with a lot of injured soldiers being shipped in from other war areas. Jeanne would often have to work long hours, as there was a shortage of trained nurses.

In 1943, Clara turned twenty-three. The men in the bar were always teasing her. Early one afternoon, they were saying to her that by her age she should be married with children.

"How am I supposed to find a boyfriend? There are no eligible men, and then who would look after you lot?" she said. Then by divine intervention, Henri walked into the bar. He came over to Clara and greeted her with kisses on each cheek and ordered a beer.

All the men in the bar started to whistle and cheer, "Clara has found him."

"Stop it, you lot," she said, blushing from head to toe. Henri was a bit perplexed by all of this, but Clara told him to take no notice of the rabble, which only made the men cheer even more.

Clara was unsure what to call Henri. She knew that was his code name but not his real name, however she was saved by Claude.

"And who are you, young man? We didn't know our Clara had a beau."

"My name is Didier, and I am an old friend of Clara's," responded Henri, stretching out his hand to Claude, which Claude took and shook warmly.

"Are you free this afternoon, Clara? Would you like to come out for a drive with me?" asked Didier.

Clifford, who at that minute entered the bar, replied for her saying, "You go, Clara. It will make a nice change for you and give you a bit of a break from us oldies."

"Just give me five minutes, and I will change out of my working clothes," said Clara.

Five minutes later, she was jumping into Didier's car and driving out of the village.

"Where shall we go?" asked Didier. "I am not very familiar with this area, my family lived in the Brest area."

"Let's go down to the beach at Les Rosaires. It is such a nice day. We could walk along the beach." Clara gave him directions, and it took no time at all to get there.

Didier parked the car, and they made their way over the dunes, avoiding the barricade of razor wire, to the beach. Didier took hold of her hand, which made her heart leap. It was such a lovely feeling, one she had never experienced before. She also felt a little embarrassed. After a short time, they stopped and sat down on the sand.

"Tell me about yourself, Clara. Where do you come from and where is your family? I noticed that you called the man in the bar by his Christian name. I thought he was your father at first, but he obviously is not," asked Didier.

Clara's first thoughts were what Michel had said to her to trust no one, but she felt she could trust Didier, especially as it was he who passed messages to her.

She told him all about her family in England and their hairdressing business. She said she was sad that she had not heard from them for such a long time and about her hope that they were safe and well. She told him about her sister who she had not seen for eight years and that she must be all grown up now. She explained that she had taken French citizenship at the beginning of the war so that she wouldn't have to leave the country. She shared all about the cooking and baking that she had learnt since being in France and her love of producing something delicious for others to eat.

"But this is becoming more and more difficult with so much rationing. Perhaps I can cook for you one day," Clara said.

Didier listened intently.

"What about you? Tell me about you."

He told her that he was twenty-seven, was born in France, and that he had one sister by the name of Angela who was a lot older than him, plus a brother who died when he was a toddler. "My father died just after I was born in the Great War. My mother is a bit of a tyrant and lives with my sister in Dinan. My sister is married but had to leave her husband and the place they lived just after the war started."

"How come?" asked Clara.

"It is a long story, which I will tell you sometime."

"How do you make a living?" inquired Clara.

"Wherever I can. Sometimes I get casual work on farms, and I regularly get money from the British in return for helping them. Otherwise, it is difficult. Mostly I live in my car or friends give me a bed for the night. I just wander from one place to another. As a last resort, I go to my mother's, but she is always nagging me about my lifestyle. But there are a lot of men like me trying to help win the war by sabotaging the German's plans. We cannot stay in any one place for long. We just need to keep moving around to avoid being arrested," he explained.

They began to make their way back to the car. "It has been a lovely afternoon, Clara. Thank you for coming out with me. I don't have the opportunity to meet and go out with any girls," he said.

"Neither do I, but in my case boys," responded Clara. "That is why the men in the bar are always teasing me."

"Besides wanting to take you out this afternoon, I had an alternative reason for coming to see you today, Clara. I have a rather dangerous but necessary task to undertake, and I need your help," he asked.

"What is it?" asked Clara.

Didier explained that two young Jewish girls, sisters, had been rescued and needed transporting from a safe house in the Alsace region of France to Nantes where a British plane dropping off a regiment of American soldiers had agreed to make a landing to airlift the girls to Britain.

"The girls arrived at the safe house two days ago, but they cannot stay there long. So we need to move quickly. The plane is scheduled in Nantes in two days' time, and the resistance operating in the Nantes area are preparing a landing strip. Usually the planes don't land, the soldiers are parachuted in and the planes just turn around and go back," he explained. "Are you in?" asked Didier.

"Of course, I am," replied Clara.

"We will leave this evening and travel as far as we can before the curfew. We will find somewhere to park the car unseen and sleep until the morning. It will take us about five hours to drive there," explained Didier.

They made their way back to Clara's house where she explained to her uncle that she had something to do and would be back in three days. Clifford knew not to ask any questions and just told her to travel safely. Clara quickly packed a bag, made a flask of coffee, and filled a tin with the biscuits she had made that morning. On her way out, she remembered that Danielle had some old toys packed in the cupboard under the stairs. She grabbed two soft toys—an old yellow teddy bear and a rabbit with long limbs and floppy ears.

On the journey, Didier said that they would travel under papers in their code names, and he handed Clara both sets so she could memorize the details.

"We will be traveling under the pretence of just having got married. I am taking you to meet my mother in Baccarat, which is about fifty miles from the safe house. We met last year when I moved to near where you live to help my widowed uncle run his farm, and we got married yesterday. Will you remember all of that?" asked Didier.

"Yes, I think it is pretty much straightforward," she replied.

"We are bound to go through a number of checkpoints, so we need to have our story water tight," he said.

"I have papers for the two girls. I am not sure of their nationality or what language they speak, but the family at the safe house will tell us everything we need to know."

The total journey would be about 250 miles, and they stopped before the curfew after travelling about 125 miles without passing any checkpoints. They found a lane off the main road and parked behind a hedge to rest for the night. Clara slept on the back seat, which although uncomfortable, she did manage to get to sleep. At dawn, they drank the coffee and ate a biscuit each before continuing on their journey.

They passed through the first checkpoint with no problem. The soldiers merely looked at their papers and waved them through. They stopped at a village café for breakfast and a toilet break.

Clara was driving as they approached the next checkpoint. "Oh Shit!" she said, waking Didier up.

"What's the matter?" he asked.

"Oh shit! I know that officer." Just as she said this, the officer spotted her. Clara stopped the car and opened the door and got out.

"Hans, how lovely to see you?" said Clara, walking towards him.

"Clara, I cannot believe it. I never thought I would see you again. How are you?" He took both her hands and kissed both cheeks.

"I am well, thank you, and how are you and your family? Are they all well?" she asked.

"Yes, thank you. We are all well, although I have not seen them for some time," he replied.

"What are you doing here?" asked Hans.

"I got married yesterday, and I am on my way to meet my new mother-in-law," she said.

There were two cars in front of Clara—the first one moved off and the second started to move forward. When the second car was cleared, it was Clara's turn to go through the checkpoint.

"I had better move forward, Hans, as the car behind me will start getting impatient," she said.

Clara felt sick with fear, she now had to show her papers at the checkpoint, and they were in a different name.

"Congratulations, my dear," Hans said and walked to the passenger side of the car. Didier wound down the window. Hans extended his hand to Didier.

"Congratulations, young man! You have a beautiful wife. I am extremely envious," said Hans.

Hans walked around the car with Clara. "My very best wishes to you both for the future." He kissed her again and told her to get back in the car, and waving to the checkpoint soldier, he shouted, "You can let these people through. They are friends of mine. Au revoir, Clara, I hope to meet you again one day."

Driving off she waved goodbye to Hans. She drove a further fifteen minutes down the road and pulled over. She was shaking from head to foot and felt physically sick to the point that when she got out of the car, she thought she would vomit. She sat down on the hedgerow with her head in her hands.

"Are you alright? That was certainly a close call. How did you know that officer?" asked Didier.

Clara told him all about her trip to Paris and how she had spent the whole journey with Hans.

Didier took over the driving, and they continued on their journey. All Clara could think of was what if Hans had looked at her papers. How would she have explained the different name? What would have happened to those two little girls?

"I can see you worrying about what happened, Clara, but don't, just be grateful that it turned out okay."

"I know, but I just keep thinking '*what if*'," she said.

They made a second stop in another town and managed to get some bread and cheese to keep them going plus a coffee. After a few wrong turns, they eventually arrived at their destination with Didier reading the map and Clara driving. The safe house was a working farm, and the farmer's wife came out of the house to meet them. Clara stayed in the car while Didier got out. He shook hands with her, but Clara couldn't hear what was being said. The woman was dressed in the typical French apron, and her hair was tied up in a headscarf. She wore clogs on her feet. Clara gave her about fifty years of age if not older, but sometimes with farm workers it was difficult of tell.

Didier waved over to Clara, indicating that she should get out of the car. "This is Mme Solange Kaplan. She has been looking after the girls for the last couple of day." Clara shook her hand.

"I am Vivienne. Pleased to meet you, Mme Kaplan."

"Please call me Solange. Come into the house and have some refreshments and meet the girls. The girls are still a bit traumatized after the long journey from somewhere in the Baltic States. We are not sure exactly, as we have been unable to communicate with them. It has all been hand gestures, so as you can imagine it has been very difficult," said Solange as they made their way to the house.

"We understand that their parents have been killed and therefore are orphans, but we are not sure if they know this or not because of the language problem," she continued.

Solange went into a back room to fetch the girls. They hid behind her as they came into the kitchen obviously very frightened. They were both very slight and appeared small for their age. Solange explained that when they arrived, they both had white blonde hair and that she had dyed it a brownish colour to make them look more French.

Clara went over and knelt down to say hello. "My name is Vivienne, what is yours?"

They didn't answer. Presuming that they didn't understand, Clara pointed to herself and said, "Vivienne." She then realized that perhaps this was the wrong thing to say, as she would have to become '*Mama*' for their journey.

Solange said, "Let's have a coffee and then discuss how we are to proceed."

"Good idea," said Didier.

Solange's husband, Éric, came in from work about an hour later. He introduced himself to Didier and Clara. By this time, Solange was preparing the dinner for them all. Clara offered to help and was given the job of laying the table. They discussed the journey to Nantes over dinner with Didier explaining that he had papers for the girls and that they would sit with the girls after dinner and make them learn their new names and try and make them understand that Didier and Clara would be their parents. Didier told the couple of the problem they had encountered at the checkpoint and said he would take a different route back to avoid this particular checkpoint.

They sat with the girls and although they tried speaking to them in English, Italian, German and French, they didn't understand any of these languages and had to revert to hand gestures. They told the girls their new names. The elder girl was to be Amélie and the younger Estelle. These were the names on the papers. It took some time before Clara was sure that they understood.

Then Clara had to try and tell them that she would be '*Mama*'. The elder girl cried and pushed her away, shaking her head saying, "Nē Nē." Clara took her in her arms and hugged her. She then held her gently by the shoulders and looking into her eyes and pointing to herself, "Mama." It took about half an hour before the little girls called her '*Mama*' and Didier '*Papa*'.

It was getting late, and as they needed to make a very early start, Clara suggested to the girls that they go to bed.

After Solange had taken the girls up to bed, they all discussed at length what would happen the next day. Solange explained that the girls had only one change of clothes, as she had been unable to get any more without drawing attention to herself. "I will give you a blanket, so they can sleep comfortably in the car during the journey." She also said that she would prepare some food and drink for the journey.

They agreed that they would leave at 5:30 a.m.

Solange had made up a room for them for the night. To Clara's astonishment, it was a double bed. Didier laughed when he saw it. "We are not married, Madame!"

"Oh! I am so sorry," she said.

"Don't worry, Madame. I will sleep on the settee downstairs, and Vivienne can have the bed," said Didier.

"Thank you. That's very gracious of you," said Clara, smiling at Didier.

Clara was so tired that she went to sleep as soon as her head hit the pillow. The next thing she knew, Didier was waking her. "Wake up, wake up. It is 5:15. We need to get ready to go."

Clara had a quick wash in cold water and dressed while trying not to shiver too much, then she went downstairs. Didier was loading up the car ready to go. The girls came downstairs, barely awake. Clara kissed both girls and called them by their new names. Solange gave them a piece of bread each with jam on them to eat in the car.

Clara put the girls in the back seat and covered their knees with the blanket. She then gave Amélie the yellow teddy bear and Estelle the rabbit, which they took and cuddled them. Didier thanked Solange and Eric for all their help, and they in turn wished them a safe journey. Didier got into the driver's seat, and they set off. The girls fell asleep after eating their bread and jam, which was relieving for Clara.

It was 9 a.m. before they could see a checkpoint coming up. The girls were still fast asleep, and Clara prayed they would not wake up. Arriving at the checkpoint, Didier handed over all of their papers. The soldier looked in the back at the sleeping girls. Clara asked the soldier to please not wake them up, as they had a long journey and wanted them to sleep as much of the journey as possible.

"Where have you been, and where are you going?" They had already discussed this at length and practiced all sorts of scenarios should they be asked.

"We have just been to see my mother in Baccarat. She had not seen her grandchildren for such a long time, and we are now on our way home to Nantes," responded Didier.

"What do you do in Nantes? Why are you not in service?" asked the soldier sternly.

"I am a farmer, growing crops to feed your troops, sir," replied Didier.

"Ah! Okay, go," said the soldier.

Didier drove off, breathing a sigh of relief. They stopped a few miles down the road and had a cup of coffee and some of the bread that Solange had given them. They swapped places and Clara drove. The girls woke up and Clara turned to them with her finger to her lips, to be quiet as Didier was sleeping.

They were making good time when the next checkpoint came into view. They stopped out of sight and quickly swapped places. Clara spoke to the girls and again indicated to them that they should not speak by placing her finger on her lips. Estelle was cuddling her rabbit and sucking her thumb. Clara also reminded them that she was '*Mama*' and Didier was '*Papa*'.

Didier wound down the window and presented their papers. The soldier looked carefully at the girls. He pointed to Amélie and asked her name. Clara responded for her, and the soldier told her to be quiet. Amélie looked at the soldier with fear in her eyes and said "Amélie." The soldier then looked at Estelle and said, "Then, you must be Estelle." Estelle, with her thumb still in her mouth, nodded in agreement. The soldier returned their papers and waved them through.

"I don't think I can take the stress of another checkpoint," said Clara. "I thought I might pass out with fear when he spoke to Amélie."

"I know. My heart was in my mouth," said Didier.

They stopped in the next village and managed to get some bread and cheese, which they ate, in a lane further down the road. The girls got out of the car, and Clara encouraged them to walk around a bit. She gave them both a hug and sat them on the grass to eat.

They arrived at the designated place in Nantes by seven that evening after stopping several times for something to eat and go to the toilet. The plane was scheduled for midnight, so they had a lot of time to spare. Members of The Maquis soon approached Didier, some of whom he knew. He explained to Clara that there was a big group of them tonight, as they had to prepare an airstrip for the plane to land. The strip had been mostly prepared in advance, but in order to temporarily hide it, they had erected false hedging so that any passing German soldiers wouldn't notice it. They would remove the hedging as soon as they had word that the planes were at the coast.

"Planes?" said Clara.

"Yes, there will be a number of them, but only one will land."

One of the men had a radio and was intently listening with headphones on.

Clara attempted to keep the girls amused. They now seemed to trust her, and she started to teach them a few English words. When they started yawning, she put them in the back of the car to have a sleep. While they were asleep, she wrote a little note.

Dear Amélie,

My name is Clara Pape, and I am the lady who drove you to the plane that took you to England. I am English, and I was born in Preston in the north of England.

I understand that both your parents were killed and that you were rescued by a resistance group in one of the Balkan States and taken to France where I, together with my friend Henri, took you to Nantes to be airlifted to England.

I wish both you and your sister a happy life in England.

Good Luck.

"Vivienne"

    The wireless operator gave the signal that the planes were an hour away. Men appeared from nowhere and soon got into action, removing hedges and laying candle lights for a makeshift landing strip.

    Clara woke the girls and got all their meagre possessions together. She carried Estelle and held Amélie's hand, and they made their way to a position indicated by the men of the resistance. Then she heard the planes and saw parachutes opening above. One plane came into view and gradually landed with a bump on the rough strip. Clara took Amélie's teddy bear, and showing Amélie a piece of folded paper, she tucked it into the teddy's side through a small tear and gave Amélie the teddy back.

    Two men grabbed each girl and ran to the plane, closely followed by Clara. She kissed them both goodbye. The plane virtually without stopping turned around and took off. By the time she and Didier got back to the car, the strip was turned back into fields, and all the men had disappeared.

They drove in the dark to get away from the area before parking in a field for the night. The next morning, they made their way home. The journey was trouble free, passing through only two checkpoints.

"We did well, Clara, don't you think saving those little girls and giving them a new life in England?" said Didier.

"Yes, I am proud of what we did. I just hope they are both alright," replied Clara.

"Can we meet again, Clara? I think we could really get on, and I would love to go out with you," said Didier.

"You mean like girlfriend and boyfriend?" asked Clara.

"Yes, I mean like girlfriend and boyfriend," replied Didier.

"Then, yes, I would really like that too," said Clara.

Didier dropped her off at home, putting one arm around her and kissed her gently on the lips, with the promise that he would see her soon. Clara walked into the house on cloud nine.

Two days later, a sack of flour was left at the back door of the bar. Clara presumed it was a thank you from Michel. Simone was delighted when Clara wheeled it around to the bakery in her cart.

"Let's make a celebration cake. The children could invite a few friends, and we could have a little party," suggested Simone.

"Good idea," said Clara.

CHAPTER 15

It would be two weeks before Clara saw Didier again. He turned up at the bar asking her if she could come out. "Sorry, I can't take you out anywhere fancy, but petrol and money are a bit tight," said Didier.

"I don't need fancy. A walk with you is all that I need," she replied.

They drove down to the coast where the River Gouët met the sea and walked along the seafront as much as they could. There were a lot of German soldiers around, which made them feel uncomfortable. So they went further up the river, had a beer at a bar and chatted. Didier told Clara that the girls had arrived safely in England and had been placed with a childless couple in the country.

"I am not sure exactly where, but they are safe." They returned arm in arm to the car and made their way home.

They met regularly over the next six months. Clara by this time was totally in love with Didier. Her heart skipping a beat each time she saw him.

Although the British and Americans had expelled the Germans from France by the end of 1944 and liberated Paris in August 1944, it was not until May 1945 that the war actually ended with the Germans accepting defeat. This news reached the village very quickly. Everyone made their way to the square shouting, "Viva La France" in celebration. A huge party was organized in the square shortly after with everyone from the surrounding area turning up with food and drink. The celebrations went on long into the next day.

Didier came to see Clara while the celebrations were taking place. He found her with Danielle entertaining the children with games. She turned around and saw him smiling at her. She ran into his arms and kissed him. "It's so lovely to see you come and join the celebrations. I will get you a drink."

"It's good to see you, Clara, but before you run off to get me a drink, there is something I want to ask you," he said seriously.

"And what is that?" she asked.

Going down on one knee and taking her hand, "Clara, will you marry me?" It appeared that everyone stopped what they were doing and looked at the two of them.

Clara, blushing with embarrassment as everyone cheered, said, "Yes, I would love to marry you."

Didier took her in his arms and again everyone cheered.

They married a month later at the local church. Simone made her a beautiful gown out of parachute material, and it was a double wedding. Léo had returned from a prisoner of war camp extremely thin and traumatized, but the first thing he did when arriving home was to contact Danielle and ask her to marry him. She didn't hesitate. She had waited the whole war for him to come home. Now she would nurse him to recovery.

Danielle had a matching dress. They each made themselves a headdress out of wild flowers, and both carried a posy of wild flowers. Simone's daughter acted as flower girl to both brides, and Clifford walked them both down the aisle.

The priest began the service, "At last we have something wonderful to celebrate."

The whole congregation clapped in agreement. It was a heart-warming service with not a dry eye in sight. The only downside was that Clara's mother and father were not there.

Jeanne, Simone and Léo's mother organized the reception. They shared a cake made by Clara and Simone with everyone contributing their rations. The entire village attended together with Léo's family. Everyone provided something, as the country was still on rationing.

Didier's mother, Marie Renaud, and sister, Angela Chevalier, came to the wedding. Angela was very similar in appearance to her brother, slim with black permed hair and olive skin. She was about two inches shorter than Clara and very friendly, welcoming Clara into the family. She explained that she would be leaving France in a few days to be reunited with her husband in Jersey, an Island north of France in the English Channel.

"We were separated when Jersey was occupied at the beginning of the war. Because I was French and not a Jersey person, I had to leave the Island or be interned in a concentration camp, so I obviously chose to return. My mother was also in Jersey at the time, so she could come back to France with me, but Didier had already returned to join the French army," explained Angela.

"I will be glad to get away from my mother. She is very demanding," joked Angela.

The first thing that came into Clara's mind was, '*I hope she doesn't think she is going to move in with us. I want Didier to myself and our cottage is small.*' Clara then was annoyed with herself for having such uncharitable thoughts.

Didier's mother was the same height as her daughter with greying hair and a stout frame. She congratulated Clara after the wedding, kissing her on both cheeks and said, "You will have your work cut out taming my son."

Clara laughed and said that she had no intention of taming him, as he was okay as he was.

"Ah, well time will tell."

Clara took an instant dislike to the woman.

Neither girl had a honeymoon, as the country was still trying to recover from the effects of the war. After the reception, Danielle went home with Léo and his family. They had been given a set of rooms at his parents' house where she would be setting up home and looking after Léo to bring him back to good health. She also hoped to get a teaching job to support them both.

Didier and Clara had found an old cottage on the outskirts of the village to rent and make home. They spent their wedding night in their cottage. Didier was a gentle and considerate lover, and they spent the whole night in each other's arms, exploring each other's bodies.

Over the years, Clara had saved a good amount of money, banking any spare cash she had. She was able to furnish the cottage out of some of her savings, buying anything she could get her hands on to make her home comfortable. Also, lots of her friends in the village gave her all sorts of household items.

She had agreed with Clifford that she would continue to work at the bar as before and would also help out at the bakery.

Her help was required even more at the bakery as Gui had arrived home extremely sick and required nursing by Simone. He could barely walk, and the doctor wanted him to go into the hospital, but Gui refused, saying he wanted to spend time with Simone and the children. He died two months later with the children and Simone at his side.

The funeral took place three days after his death. The church was packed with family, friends and customers of the bakery. The priest gave a moving eulogy, assuring the family that he was now at peace at God's side. Clara felt angry that Gui, after struggling through the atrocities of a war camp and coming safely home to his family, was only able to be with his family a short time before dying.

CHAPTER 16

Didier was helping the French forces to dispose of all of the German artillery, removing the barbed wire from the coastal areas in the north and northwest of France. Help was also sought to rebuild the ports destroyed by the Germans. The government, in an attempt to get the country up and running again, employed locals returning from the war to do reconstruction work. However, France was on its knees financially, and it would take some time to rebuild the country.

He was away from home for weeks at a time as the work took him a long way from home. Thus, life for Clara was very much the same as before they married except that she would go home to her little cottage. Although sometimes, when she worked late in the bar helping Clifford, she would stay in her old room.

With the war ending, Clara was at last able to write to her mother. She sent her photos of the wedding and told her that everyone was safe, but still struggling with rations, explaining that they were luckier than most, as they have gardens to grow things in and that they still had their chickens.

The first letter she received back from her mother was lengthy.
My Dear Clara,

I was so relieved and happy to hear from you. Your father and I were so worried about you especially when news on the wireless and in the newspaper appeared to be all bad.

It has been very difficult for us as well. Rationing was introduced for everything, and it was hard getting anything to make a tasty meal, and you know how I like a cup of tea with sugar. This became a luxury and, in fact, still is, although there are a few more things becoming available in the shops.

The business has also suffered, as you can imagine. All the men were away fighting, so there were fewer haircuts for your father. The women who were left behind had only army pay to support themselves and their children. Therefore, their visit to me was a luxury they could ill afford even though I dropped my prices considerably.

Lilly joined the land army, so at least we didn't have to feed her. She was sent to a farm in Whitby, so only came home now and again. Fortunately though, an American air base was located in Warton Village, and we were asked to take in an airman, so his lodging rent came in handy for the family finances. He is a lovely man and will be leaving us shortly to go back home. I will miss the chocolates and nylon stockings he brings me!

I have some bad news for you. Pierre, the husband of Doreen Masson, has died. You remember them. They are the couple that took you to France with them. Her sister came and told me yesterday. Apparently he had a heart attack. ... Such a shame. Doreen is coming back to live with her sister.

Thank you for the lovely photos of your and Danielle's weddings. I was so sorry to not be there. I liked your description of Didier's mother. I hope she becomes more friendly towards you. It may be that she is protective of her son. Aren't all mothers-in-law the enemy?
Lilly met a lovely, young man while in Whitby. He is a Doctor there. Very young to be a GP, but apparently he took over the practice from his father when he died just before the outbreak of the war. They are engaged and hope to marry before Christmas. She has stayed in Whitby and is helping his mother out at the practice. At least I will be at one of my girls' weddings. I hope you will be able to come over for the wedding. It is such a long time since I have seen you, I hardly recognized you in the photo. You have grown up so much.
I am proud of all you have achieved while you have been in France. Little did I know when I sent you to Clifford that you would still be there after ten years.
Your father sends his love.
Write soon. All my love,
Mum xx
P.S. give my love to Clifford and Jeanne and tell them I will write soon

    Clara read the letter over and over. She couldn't imagine her little sister married and wondered to herself if there was any way she would be able to go to the wedding. She laughed to herself about her mother's idea of mothers-in-law especially as she was to be one herself.

    The news of her uncle's death was not a surprise, as she had received a letter earlier in the week from her aunt.

My Dearest Clara,

I hope this letter finds you and your family well.
Thank you for your letter and the photos of your wedding. Congratulations to you both, and I wish you all the very best for the future.
I write with sad news. Uncle Pierre has died. He came from work a few days ago feeling very tired, so he went to bed. When I went to wake him up for his dinner, he was dead. The doctor said it was a heart attack.
After all the stress of the war, it is not surprising but still a shock for me. He was not old. We still had our retirement to look forward to.
I am going to try and sell the apartment and return to Preston and live with my sister for the time being. I have spoken to an agent who will look after the sale for me. It may not be the right time to sell, so in that case, the agent will try and rent the apartment for me.
I arranged a private funeral that was held this morning. I am feeling very fragile and can't wait to get back to England. Although France holds lots of happy memories for me with Pierre, this has been overshadowed by the last five awful years.
I will write again when I am settled in England. My love and best wishes to you.
Yours, Auntie

Clara had telephoned her aunt as soon as she had read the letter with her condolences; her aunt explained that she was all alone in the apartment. When Paris was liberated, Antoinette disappeared, and she hadn't seen her since, reaffirming her aunt and uncle's suspicions that she was a German spy.

At the end of 1946, Didier arrived home. His work for the government finished. He found it difficult getting a permanent job. He had no professional skills and therefore took casual work wherever he could get it.

It was also at this time that Clara discovered she was pregnant. Although she was delighted and everyone else delighted for her, it couldn't have come at a worse time. She worried how she would manage financially with Didier not having a permanent job.

She saved as much as she could over the next six months. Didier was happy as long as he had money in his pocket to buy himself a beer or two, and he didn't seem to think it was a problem. "You can carry on working after the baby is born. Simone or Jeanne will look after it while you work."

This made Clara worry even more. It was as though the baby was not his responsibility.

Her mother-in-law was delighted with the news and had come on a visit to see Clara and Didier. She asked Clara to call her '*Mère*', but Clara said she would prefer to call her Marie. Marie was not very happy. Angela had given birth to a son exactly nine months after arriving back home in Jersey, and Marie informed Clara that she was lonely living alone and that she missed being with her family. Clara hoped that perhaps she would go to Jersey, but Marie had other ideas.

"You have room here in your cottage, Clara. I could move in with you," she said, looking around their little cottage.

"But when the baby arrives there will be no room, unless you share the bedroom with the baby," said Clara.

Clara knew perfectly well that there was no room for a cot and a bed in this small room.

Clara was relaying this conversation to Jeanne. "Did you know that the priests' housekeeper is retiring? She must be at least seventy and moving to live with her daughter. Perhaps you could mention to Marie that there could be a live-in housekeeping job going," said Jeanne.

"What a good idea! I will do that straight away," said Clara.

Marie went to see the priests, and they were happy to give her the job. "We were just about to start looking for a replacement, so you have come at the right time." Marie moved into the village.

Clara gave birth to her baby girl on August 9th, 1947. She weighed six pounds and seven-ounces. In Clara's eyes, she was beautiful with a head covered in downy, dark hair. Chantal Marie Renard was christened three weeks later. She was the perfect baby, taking to the breast straight away and sleeping peacefully in between. Clara returned to work after four weeks, taking Chantal with her. Her child would sleep soundly in her pram.

Everyone loved Chantal. It was as though she had bought a new future into all their lives. Even Didier cut down on the amount of time he spent in the bar drinking beer. When he wasn't working, he would take the baby for a walk in the pram, most of the time going to visit his mother.

The village was slowly beginning to recover from the after effects of the war, and the bakery got busier as did the bar. Simone's eldest son, Fabien, was now fourteen, had left school, and he now worked in the bakery. Over the years, he had watched Simone and Clara make bread often, helping during the school holidays. He was a natural baker and gradually took over all the baking of the bread. This was a great help to both of them, as now Clara could start work a bit later and concentrate on making the cakes and pastries.

Jeanne's work at the hospital reverted to normal, and she changed her shifts from nights to days. She would work three days on and three days off from 7 a.m. to 4 p.m. Thus, Clara's work on the days that Jeanne worked was full on. She would arrive home completely exhausted, wanting only to put her feet up and rest. Didier demanded his dinner be on the table on time. Quite often, Clara would bring a dish from the bar to save her from cooking.

"I am not eating this shit. Get me a proper meal," he would demand.

"I will have to feed Chantal, bathe her and get her ready for bed first unless you want to do this for me," Clara would say on such occasions.

"No, that's not my job. I will go for a beer while you do all of that." And off he would go, leaving Clara to do everything.

Chantal was eleven months old when Clara found herself pregnant again. She cried when she realized her uncertainty about managing the children. "How will I cope with two babies?" she asked, looking into Chantal's eyes and in return receiving a smile oblivious as to what was being said.

Taking Chantal to work with her was becoming more challenging, as she was now crawling. Clara would place her in a playpen full of toys to amuse her while she worked, but frequently, she would object to being confined to the playpen and start demanding attention. This would make it difficult for Clara to concentrate on her work. Thankfully, Simone's daughter Cécile, who was now eleven, would entertain Chantal, but this was only when she wasn't at school. Clara was becoming more anxious as time went on, especially about what she would do when Chantal started walking.

When Clara expressed her concerns to Jeanne, Jeanne came up with the idea of asking Marielle.

"I will go and speak to her for you," said Jeanne.

"Try not to worry too much. It is not good for that baby inside your belly," said a concerned Jeanne.

"Thank you, Jeanne. You always seem to find a solution to my problems," said Clara, giving her a hug.

Marielle had helped Jeanne and Clifford in the bar before leaving to have her first baby just prior to Clara arriving from England. Marielle's baby was followed by another three years later. Her husband, Pascal, had joined the French Army before the outbreak of war and had continued to fight with the British. When he returned after the war, she had fallen pregnant with her third child, who was now two years old.

Jeanne went to see her and asked her if she could possibly look after Chantal for Clara. "I would love to. It will be company for Annie." They spoke about payment and came to an amicable hourly rate.

"It will only be for a short time, as Clara's second baby is due in March," Jeanne told Marielle. "I doubt she will be able to work with two babies, but you never know."

Jeanne visited Clara on her way back home after seeing Marielle. Jeanne was in the process of telling Clara that Marielle was agreeable to looking after Chantal when Didier arrived home.

"We don't see you here often, Jeanne. To what do we owe the pleasure?" asked Didier.

"I was just telling Clara that my friend Marielle would be willing to look after Chantal while she is at work," said Jeanne, not very happy at having to explain herself to Didier.

Didier was annoyed with this. "Why can't you take Chantal with you? It hasn't been a problem until now."

Clara started to explain but could see that no amount of explanation would satisfy Didier. "We will talk about it later," she said.

Jeanne quickly left, not wanting to get involved. "See you in the morning. Bye-bye."

"I can see my dinner is not ready, again. I am off for a beer," said an angry Didier.

"It is ready!" shouted Clara as he went out the door, slamming it behind him.

Clara gave Chantal her dinner, put her to bed and waited for Didier to return so she could have her dinner with him.

It was two hours before he returned. Clara knew that he had had more than one beer by the way he staggered to the table. "I told you as you were going out that dinner was ready, but you chose to ignore me. Now it is a bit dry." Clara laid out two plates on the table.

He started to eat it, and then he overturned the plate on the table, complaining that the meal was inedible. Clara had started to clear up the mess he had created when he started shouting at her, saying she was useless and couldn't even look after her own child. Again, Clara tried to explain that it was difficult to work and take care of Chantal at the same time.

"Well, give up work, then."

"Yes, that would be helpful, wouldn't it? How would we pay the rent? Certainly not with the wages you give me after you have spent half of it on beer and cigarettes," she shouted back at him.

He grabbed hold of her. "Don't you shout at me," he screamed and slapped her hard across the face.

Clara was stunned. Nobody had ever hit her before, not even her mother or father when she was young and naughty.

Didier stormed off upstairs to bed, leaving Clara in a state of shock, unable to even cry. That night, she slept downstairs. In the morning, when Didier looked at her, he saw a red welt on her cheek. "I am sorry, Clara, my love. Please, forgive me." He tried hugging her, but she was unresponsive. He grabbed a quick cup of coffee and left for work, saying as he went out of the door, "Bye, see you tonight."

Clara dropped Chantal off at Marielle's, saying how grateful she was that she had agreed to look after Chantal and made her way to work. Clara had seen Marielle look at her face with pity in her eyes, but she didn't say anything.

Arriving at the bakery, Clara said very little, getting on with the baking for the day.

It wasn't until Simone brought her a cup of coffee that Simone noticed Clara's face. "What has happened to your face, Clara?" It then dawned on Simone that the mark was that of a hand. "Oh! Clara, my love, why did he do this to you?"

"Don't worry, Simone. It is all sorted out. It was just a mistake," said Clara to an unbelieving Simone.

Jeanne was even more shocked, and Clifford was furious. "I will be having a word with that bastard."

"No, please, Clifford, it will only make matters worse. We have sorted it out. Please don't say anything."

That evening, it was as though nothing had happened. Didier came home and helped Chantal with her dinner and put her to bed while Clara did the dishes and tidied up. He never mentioned again the fact that Marielle was looking after Chantal.

Clara's second daughter was born on March 28th, 1949, weighing seven pounds two ounces and looking exactly like Chantal but with more hair. They christened her Francine Olive Renard. Unlike Chantal, Francine was a difficult baby. She suffered from colic. She would take three times as long to feed than Chantal. At first, Clara didn't know what was wrong with Francine, as no sooner had she fed her and winded her, she would vomit all the milk back up.

Clara soon learned that if she let Francine feed for a short time and then wind her, then she would keep the milk down. The doctor gave her some gripe water to give the baby before a feed, and this helped tremendously. Clara was exhausted during the first two months of Francine's birth. With Chantal, she was able to have a small lie in bed in the morning after her early morning feed, but with Francine she couldn't do this, as she had to attend to Chantal. She barely had time to get out of her nightdress each morning before it was lunchtime. Luckily Chantal still liked a small nap in the afternoon, so Clara could catch up with some sleep then. But trying to muster up enough energy to make Didier's dinner for when he came home from work was difficult. There were still all the other household chores to do, washing, ironing, and cleaning.

Money was extremely tight at this time, as she was not working. She had to rely on Didier to bring home his wages packet intact—it rarely happened. Most of her savings had gone now with only twenty francs in the account that she wanted to keep for a rainy day.

Simone had given her all of Cécile's old clothes, and even Marielle had come around to the cottage with a bag full of clothes that Annie had grown out of. All of these were well received, as Chantal was growing rapidly.

Chantal had started walking at thirteen months, and by the time she was two, she could hold a conversation in both English and French. Often mixing the two languages in one sentence.

Claude would come around with a basket of vegetables and/or eggs for her. He had recruited the help of Simone's middle son, Pierre, to help him with weeding and planting in exchange for some pocket money. That suited both of them. Jeanne offered her money and food. She turned down the offer of money but gratefully took the offer of an occasional ready-made meal.

Clara went back to work when Francine was two months old. Marielle had agreed to take care of Chantal, and Francine would sleep in her pram while Clara worked. The money was a godsend. Although she was still a bit down due to lack of sleep since Francine was still not sleeping through the night, she would wake up in the early hours wanting a feed. Going back to work helped. She could switch off her mind from all the worry about the state of her marriage, and instead of worry about being able to pay the weekly rent on their cottage, she was able to concentrate on baking and the inevitable joy it brought her.

Her mother resumed sending her recipes, and now that she knew about Clara's pastries, she sent a lot of creative pastry and cake recipes.

The bakery was doing well. Simone's boys had repainted the exterior and created a new sign. They had purchased a new blue and white striped awning that improved the appearance. Fabien's new idea was to buy a van and make deliveries to the surrounding areas to increase their sales. Simone embraced Fabien's ideas, as she wanted to keep him in the business even if she didn't agree with some of his suggestions, saying to Clara, "And whom may I ask is going to drive this van? I can't drive, and Fabien will have to wait until he is seventeen."

"If you do get a van, Simone, I will teach you to drive. Imagine what freedom you would have if you could drive and also what it could do for your business," said Clara.

"I will think about it," said Simone.

CHAPTER 17

Clara started experimenting again, initially trying new cakes and pastries out on the customers in the bar and Simone's children before launching them to the paying customers. She wished she could resume selling her wares on the market on Sundays, but she knew she would never have the time. However, she did suggest to Fabien that he try and create new loaves and sell them on the market. Clara's recipes included a seeded loaf, cabbage loaf, plaited loaf and fruit bread. Fabien grasped this idea with both hands, and taking a leaf out of Clara's book, he started experimenting on the family and Clara as his tasters.

His first attempt for a stall on the market was a tremendous success. He set out buttered samples for people to try before buying. He sold out within two hours and his market stall became a permanent fixture.

Simone and Clara were proud of his success. Clara thought to herself, *'Why can't Didier use his initiative and create a job for himself? Fabien is only fifteen and look what he has done.'* She even thought that perhaps he could drive a delivery van for Simone, but when she mentioned it to him, he dismissed the idea as stupid. So, she kept quiet.

Francine was six months old before she slept through the night, much to Clara's relief. She now dreaded her crawling, as she would have to pay Marielle more to look after Francine as well. As it was, Francine showed no interest in crawling. She was happy to sit in the playpen with her toys.

In the six months since Francine had been born, nothing had changed in her marriage. Some weeks she hardly saw Didier, much to her relief, although she did wonder on occasion where he was. But as long as he gave her any wages he received, she didn't complain. Her job and the children kept her busy.

The end of 1949 approached, and Clifford and Jeanne decided to organize a party on New Year's Eve to see in 1950 "a new decade and hopefully improved prosperity," said Clifford. The whole neighbourhood was invited, and tables and chairs were set up outside under a marquee. Clara was quite excited at the prospects of a party and helped Jeanne decorate the bar and marquee.

Danielle, who was five months pregnant with her first child, arrived with Léo the day before with her new record player and a selection of records, with Léo agreeing to keep the music going all night. Between them, they prepared a mass of food.

The party was a massive success. At midnight, everyone cheered the arrival of the New Year. Most of the men were drunk and the women merry. The children were tucked into Jeanne's bed sound asleep. Everyone started to make their way home. Danielle had already gone to bed, and Jeanne suggested that the children stay with her rather than try and wake them up to take them home.

"I will be here first thing in the morning to help you clean up," said Clara, kissing Jeanne goodnight.

She found Didier slumped in a corner and woke him to take him home. On the way home, the cold fresh air aroused him from his stupor. "I suppose you enjoyed yourself. I saw you dancing with all the men, showing me up and making a fool of yourself."

"It wasn't like that at all, I was joining in with everyone else. It was you that was sulking in the corner, getting more and more drunk. Stop trying to spoil things. It was a lovely evening," she said.

She could sense him getting agitated and said no more until she got home.

"Come on, let me help you upstairs to bed," said Clara, taking him by the arm and leading him upstairs.

She was helping him undress when he grabbed hold of her. "Give me a kiss, Clara."

"No," she said in a loud voice, "you are drunk. Just get into bed and sleep it off."

But Didier was not taking no as an answer. He threw her on the bed and lay on top of her, holding her down while she was struggling to free herself from under him, but he was far too heavy.

"Please, Didier, leave me alone," she pleaded.

"You are my wife, and if I want you, I will take you," he shouted.

Despite her protests and her feeble attempts to fight him off, he ripped off her underwear and raped her.

CHAPTER 18

It was a month before Francine's first birthday that Clara suspected that she was pregnant. She went to see the doctor for confirmation.

"Well, Clara, yes, you are definitely expecting another baby."

Clara burst into tears.

"Don't worry. It is natural to be tearful. It is all down to your hormones. Now you look a bit pale, so I will give you a prescription for some iron tablets. These will help you. Come back and see me in a month for a check-up. Now go tell that husband of yours and tell him to let you put your feet up and rest," said the doctor.

"Thank you, Doctor," said a down-hearted Clara.

Clara left the surgery and collected her iron tablets from the pharmacy, feeling nothing—neither joy nor sadness. It was as though her life was worthless, and she couldn't seem to stop crying. She made her way to collect the girls from Jeanne when she arrived. Clara immediately fell into Jeanne's arms, and cried uncontrollably.

"Clara, Clara, whatever is the matter? Did the doctor give you bad news? Please, Clara, try to calm down and tell me," pleaded Jeanne.

"I am pregnant again. What shall I do? I don't want another baby. I can barely manage to feed and clothe these two while I am working. What will I do when I am not working and have another mouth to feed?" said Clara, calming down a bit.

"Oh dear, you know I will help all I can, but Didier needs to get a permanent job. He can't continue drifting from one casual job to another. He has to take responsibility for his family," said Jeanne.

"I know, but you try telling him, because if I say anything, he just hits the roof, and it is me in the firing line. Can't you give me anything to get rid of the baby, Jeanne? As a nurse you must know of something I could do," pleaded Clara.

"No, there is nothing you can take, and abortion is impossible, and don't try a hot bath and gin, that is an old wives' tale. It definitely doesn't work. I am sorry to say this, Clara, but you will have to try and get on with what life throws at you. It will get easier as they grow up. It will be difficult at first, but I am here for you," said Jeanne, trying not to sound too harsh.

The atmosphere was cold and distant between Clara and Didier. When she told him she was expecting another baby, he went berserk. "You stupid woman!" He lifted his hand to hit her, but she quickly moved out of the way, which infuriated him even more. He grabbed hold of her and banged her head against the wall.

"Get rid of it," he said with his face touching hers as he said it. "Anyway, how can this baby be mine? You haven't let me near you for months," he added, virtually spitting out the words in her face.

Clara shouted angrily at him, "After you raped me on New Year's Eve, why would I let you near me after that? That is obviously the night you got me pregnant. I don't know how you have the audacity to say the baby is not yours." She slammed out of the room and told him that from now on he could sleep on the sofa. She was so angry she couldn't even cry. Her head was pounding, and a bump was beginning to come up at the back of her head, and she could feel that it was sticky with blood.

She had been so careful not to get pregnant again taking all the precautions she could, but she could not protect herself from his attack on that night.

It was a week later when Marie came around to visit. Clara guessed that Didier had told her about the forthcoming baby. She told Clara that she had been careless, getting pregnant again. "I suggest you speak to your precious son about that," she said sarcastically.

"Perhaps while you are at it, you could talk to him about getting a proper job. He can't rely on me all of the time. I barely make ends meet now. He never gives me all of his wages. I am lucky if I get half of it. The rest goes on beer and cigarettes."

Clara could see that Marie was not happy about the criticism of her son, but Clara didn't much care. Marie stayed for a cup of tea and a biscuit and played with the girls a bit before leaving. Clara was always resentful of giving Marie a cup of her precious tea. Her mother would always include a packet of tea when she wrote to her. It was something she missed during the war, and it was virtually impossible to get tea in rural France.

Clara tried to take on as much work as she could and would save every spare centime, hiding it, as she knew when Didier was not working. He would try and get beer money from her. She had even caught him searching the cottage for cash.

She had two orders for tiered wedding cakes. Although these were time-consuming, they provided her with a good profit. She would make sugar paste flowers and leaves to decorate the cakes in the evening when the girls were in bed. This was another source of ammunition for Didier to belittle her.

He would arrive home and see her flowers laid out on the table drying and shout, "Get rid of all this shit! I don't want it all over my house," he said nastily.

Clara thought for one minute that he was going to throw all her work on the floor.

"Don't you dare touch it. I have spent hours doing these to earn some money, while all you have done is down pints of beer. Go to bed, and I will tidy away my work," said Clara wearily.

The cakes were beautiful. When they were finished, Clara displayed them in the window of the bakery before delivering them to the wedding reception venues. Everyone that came into the shop admired them. Simone said that if she ever got married again, she would have a cake like that. To Clara's delight, more orders were placed for all sorts of celebration cakes.

As June approached, she had more orders than she could cope with from First Communion to Confirmation cakes. She felt she was letting customers down by saying no to orders. The tradition of the Bishop conducting these two Catholic events once a year resumed in 1946. That year, he was really busy, as none had been conducted during the war years. By 1950, the events were back to a normal number.

Clara, Simone and Fabien worked long hours mixing and baking the cakes, and although Simone could do the icing, she could not grasp the intricacy of making the delicate decorations. This was left to Clara. All the cakes were finished on time and delivered to the customers. All three were jubilant at their success and with the profits that they agreed to share. Clara was building up a nice little nest egg of cash ready for when she had to give up work again.

At seven months pregnant, she felt exhausted all of the time, her ankles were swollen, and the doctor tried to impress on her the necessity to put her feet up to alleviate the swelling. This was easier said than done with two small children and a not very helpful husband.

She was resting one afternoon with her feet up. She had given up work, on the doctor's orders, and there were only five weeks before the baby was due when her mother-in-law arrived unexpectedly. Clara sighed and thought to herself, '*What does she want now?*'

"You look tired, Clara. Shall I make us a cup of tea?" If Clara had not been sitting with her feet up, she would have fallen down with shock.

"Yes, that would be lovely." Then, she started thinking sceptically, *'She is after something. She has never offered to do anything like this for me before.'*

"Where are the girls?" asked Marie.

"Marielle has them for the afternoon so I could have a rest. They should be back soon," replied Clara.

Marie handed Clara her tea, and she had even managed to find the biscuits, which she had placed on a plate for them both.

"Clara ..." Marie began.

'Here it comes,' thought Clara.

"Yes?" responded Clara.

"Well, you know you mentioned about Didier getting a permanent job that pays enough to keep you and the girls and of course the new baby ..." said Marie.

"Yes," said Clara.

"Well, I wrote to Angela, and her husband, Hedley, who has his own farm, and they have agreed to employ Didier full-time. There is accommodation as well," explained a delighted Marie.

"What, in Jersey? You must be joking?" said Clara.

"I will come with you and the family. So don't worry. You won't be on your own," explained Marie.

Clara was speechless. "You expect me and the girls and the baby to leave here and go and live in a place that I have barely heard of, in fact I don't even know where it is, just so Didier has a job? The answer is no. I am not going. He can go if he wants, but I am not moving from here." Clara was angry that all these arrangements had been made behind her back with no consultation. They must have been planning for months.

"Clara, I don't think you realize this, but it is arranged. The plan is to leave as soon as the baby is born," said Marie.

"Well you can un-plan it then. Perhaps you should have thought to consult me before making any plans that involve my life," said Clara, trying not to get too upset.

"Now, don't be like that, Clara. You will have a better life in Jersey. Didier will have a job. You won't have to work. All you will need to do is look after the children," said Marie.

"The answer is still no," said Clara.

"I don't think you quite understand, Clara. The children belong with their father. So if you decide not to go, then Didier and I will take the children with us, and you can stay here," said Marie.

Clara was furious now. "How dare you think you can take my children away from me?"

Marie stood up and said smugly, "I think you will find the law is on our side in that respect," and walked out.

Marielle arrived with the girls and could see straight away that Clara was upset about something. "Go upstairs, girls, and play while I speak to your mamma."

"Whatever is the matter, Clara? Is it the baby?" asked Marielle.

Clara told Marielle everything that Marie had said to her. Marielle was as shocked as Clara. "I don't know anything about the law. You will have to think carefully about what you are going to do." Marielle left, leaving Clara deflated.

Didier and three other men had formed a work gang, going from farm to farm to offer their services as a gang. With the four of them, they were able to quickly plough a field and plant a crop, or whatever was required by the farmer, and then move on to the next job. The money was good when they could get the work, but there were still times of unemployment. Not that Clara benefited from the wage he earned. Most of it was spent on beer before he got home.

Didier was presently away for at least five days, and Marie had obviously timed it just right to impart the news of the proposed move to Clara. She knew this would give Clara a number of days to digest the plan.

Clara went to see Jeanne the next day and told her of the conversation with Marie. She asked her opinion.

"That women is a conniving, old bitch. You need to think carefully about what you want to do, Clara. I am not sure about the law, but why don't you go into Saint-Brieuc now and find a lawyer you can speak to? I will look after the girls," suggested Jeanne.

Clara caught the bus into town and asked at the Mairie if they knew a lawyer who might help her. They gave her a list, and she was able to see someone immediately at the third office she visited.

Advocat Le Fevre was about fifty with receding grey hair. He shook hands with Clara and said she was lucky to see him, as a client he had booked had had to cancel their appointment. He took down a few details from Clara and then said, "Now, what can I do for you, young lady?"

Clara explained the situation and said that she wanted to know if her husband could take her children.

"Well, the law is not clear cut, especially on family matters and the custody of minor children. But what I would say is that if your husband were to go to the courts and request custody of the children, he would have to prove that, firstly he could look after the children, and/or secondly, if it would be in their best interest to be with him, and/or thirdly that you are unfit to look after them," explained the lawyer.

"But surely the children are better off with their mother. I am the one that looks after them now, and I provide everything for them." Clara went on to explain to the lawyer about Didier's lack of employment, saying that when he did work, he failed to hand over all of his wages to help with the family finances. Whereas she worked hard, and all her money went to feeding and clothing the family and paying the rent.

She also told the lawyer of Didier's violence towards her.

"May I ask how you would support the two toddlers you already have and a new baby? How would you be able to work and look after them if you were to decide to stay in France on your own?"

"I have family support and a lady I can pay to look after them while I work. This is what I do at the moment," explained Clara.

"Yes, I understand that, but your husband could say that he will have his mother and sister, neither of whom work, who could dedicate themselves to looking after the children. Also, you said to me that you are originally from England. Therefore, your husband could say that he is concerned that his French children would be taken by you to England, and he would not see them again," said the lawyer.

"Yes, but couldn't I say the same that he wants to take them to Jersey and I wouldn't be able to see them?" she asked.

"I don't think the courts would accept this. They would say that the option has already been put to you to go to Jersey as a family where your husband will have work and accommodation, and you would not have to work and be able to concentrate on looking after the children," he explained.

The lawyer could clearly see that Clara was upset by his remarks and said that he was simply saying it as it was.

"I am not on your husband's side, Madame. I am trying to give you the best advice. In my opinion, I would say that the court would take the side of your husband, but that is just my opinion, I cannot say for certain what decision they would take," he said.

"Thank you," said Clara. "I need to think carefully about my next move. Thank you again for your time."

Despondently, Clara left the lawyer's office, paying the receptionist out of her precious savings.

Clara went home and picked up the girls. She told Jeanne all that the lawyer had said.

"I can't believe that they would take children from their mother! Stay for your dinner, Clara. I don't want you going home on your own while you are so upset."

"Thank you, I will," said Clara.

Clara found it hard to eat anything, she was so stressed by the situation, but made an effort for the sake of the girls who were chatting about what they had done that afternoon. They loved being with Claude, feeding the chickens, collecting the eggs, helping pick peas, and eating more than putting in their baskets. She couldn't imagine life without the two of them.

Didier arrived back home three days later, handed Clara his wages or at least what was left of them. She was too tired to even argue with him about what had happened to the rest of the wage. She could tell that he had already had a few beers. He dumped his dirty washing on the kitchen floor.

Chantal ran over to him, "Papa, Papa! Where have you been? We missed you." Francine followed her on unsteady feet. Didier picked them both up, kissing and hugging them and twirling them around until they were dizzy. They clearly loved their father.

Didier took both girls up to bed after dinner, tucking them in and kissing them goodnight.

Clara had cleared up the dinner things and had just sat down and put her feet up. Didier came downstairs. Seeing her, he sat down. "It's alright for some, sitting down all day resting while I have been working my butt off for you."

"Oh, don't start, Didier. I have only just this minute sat down and anyway the doctor said I must put my feet up to bring down the swelling in my ankles—not that you care," she said.

"You tell me not to '*start*,' but it is you that always '*starts*'. I presume by your attitude that my mother has spoken to you?" he said.

"I don't have an attitude, and yes, your mother has told me of all of YOUR plans. Why did you have to go behind my back and whose plans are they anyway? Not yours—all you think about is your next beer," she said angrily.

"Oh! Here we go again. My only pleasure in life is a beer now and again, and all you do is moan about it. Well, yes, it was kind of my mother's suggestion, but I think it is a good idea, and presumably, you are not in favour of a move," he shouted back at her.

"As I said to your mother, why would I want to go to a place I know nothing about and where I know nobody?" she said defiantly.

"You will have us and my sister," he said.

"I hardly see your mother now. You go away for days at a time, so I don't see how going to Jersey is going to make any difference. Anyway, I don't want to go, so there," she said.

This was like a red rag to a bull. He kicked her chair so hard, it tipped over, and she fell hard onto the floor, hitting her head on the leg of the other chair. He pulled the chair and righted it at the same time he kicked her in the lower back. "Get up you, stupid cow."

Clara couldn't move. Not only was she feeling dizzy, but her bulk was also hindering her from getting into a position to get up.

Didier slammed his way out of the house.

Clara was still on the floor when she was gripped with pain that enveloped her whole body. She tried to restrain herself but was unable to do so and screamed out in pain. This must have woken up Chantal, as the next thing she heard was a little voice saying, "Mamma, Mamma." The pain had been getting worse when Clara suddenly knew that she was in labour.

"Chantal, go get your coat and shoes on and run to Auntie Jeanne's. Tell her to come here. Can you do that? Will you be alright to go on your own?"

"Yes, Mamma, I am a big girl now. I will run all the way," she replied quite excited to be going out on her own but also a bit apprehensive.

It seemed like an age before Jeanne arrived. "I will look after Mamma now, Chantal. You go back to bed." Clara tried to reassure Chantal that she would be okay now that Jeanne was here.

"Clara, what has happened?" Jeanne was very concerned.

Clara attempted to suppress a scream as another wave of pain came over her; Jeanne realized quickly that Clara was in labour.

"Come on. Let's try and get you up off the floor." She grabbed Clara under her arms and between them, they managed to get her standing up. "I need you to get upstairs and on to the bed so I can examine you."

Clara doubled over in pain again. "I don't think I can," she said as her water broke all over the floor. "Jeanne," she screamed. "I want to push. The baby is coming."

Jeanne quickly got her back on the floor and removed her underwear just in time to see the baby's head. A baby girl was born.

Didier walked in amid the chaos. "What is going on? I just walked into the bar, and Clifford told me to get home quickly."

"What do you think is happening? Run and get the doctor—now," demanded Jeanne to a confused Didier.

The doctor quickly arrived. He examined the baby first and announced that she was healthy and a good weight, of four pounds eleven ounces, for a premature baby.

He then examined Clara. Jeanne had already cleaned her and delivered the afterbirth. He soon noticed the cut on her head and cleaned it up and inserted four stitches. "How did this happen?"

"I am not sure. I think I fell against the chair," she said, looking straight at Didier as she said it.

"Let's get you to bed. You need to rest. Here, take this pill. It will help you sleep. I will be back in the morning to check on you and the baby," said the doctor.

Jeanne thanked the doctor and said she would stay the night to keep an eye on Clara and the children and told Didier to go to her house and sleep there.

The girls were up early the next morning, and Jeanne told them they had a baby sister. They were excited to see her and ran downstairs. The baby woke a short time later, and Chantal asked if she could hold her. So Jeanne sat her down on the settee and placed the baby in her arms. Francine came and sat next to her and stroked her head, saying, "Baby." Francine didn't speak a lot, mostly relying on Chantal to speak for her.

"What is her name, Auntie Jeanne?" asked Chantal.

"I don't know yet. We will have to ask Mamma when she wakes up," said Jeanne.

"Shall I go and wake her up?" asked Chantal.

"Yes, I think we will have to, as the baby is hungry, and Mamma will have to feed her," said Jeanne.

Chantal ran upstairs. "Mamma, Mamma, we have a baby sister. Quickly come and see, and Auntie Jeanne says she is hungry and only you can feed her."

Clara had just woken up, still feeling a bit groggy from the sleeping tablet. The doctor had assured her that the tablet would not affect the baby, so she would be able to feed her in the morning. Clara smiled at Chantal's announcement. It was as though Clara didn't know about the baby. She made her way downstairs to the sound of a hungry cry from the baby. Jeanne had a cup of coffee ready for her.

"Here, drink this, and the baby needs feeding, Clara. She is protesting quite vocally," laughed Jeanne.

Clara put the baby to her breast, watched by a fascinated Chantal.

"What is happening, Mamma?" Chantal asked, taking a closer look at the baby suckling.

"The baby is feeding on the milk in my breast," explained Clara.

"Is the baby going to live with us, Mamma, and what is her name?" asked Chantal, still mesmerized by the baby feeding while Clara changed the baby over to the other breast.

"I thought we could call her Liliane, Lilly for short. What do you think? Do you like this name? My sister is called Lillian. Now you have a sister with the same name."

"Yes, I like that, Mamma. ... Lilly." Chantal then looked at Francine and said, "Say Lilly," and Francine repeated "Lilly" much to everyone's amusement.

CHAPTER 19

One month later, in October 1950, they were on the boat to Jersey. Everyone was shocked when Clara announced that she would be moving with Didier and his mother.

There were a lot of tears from Jeanne and Simone. Jeanne hugged the girls. "I will miss these little ones."

Claude held her in a hug. "You have been like a daughter to me. I will miss you more than you realize. Look after yourself and those little girls." With tears in his eyes, he kissed her goodbye.

Clara, with tears falling down her cheeks, promised to keep in touch and to come back and visit.

Clara tried to sound enthusiastic when telling the girls that they would be going on a big boat and travel across the sea to a new house where they would be meeting another auntie named Angela and a cousin named John. But she felt not only apprehensive but also scared for what the future would bring for all of them.

The boat trip was dreadful—two hours of hell in Clara's mind. Both she and Marie were violently sick all the way. The girls appeared to enjoy the rise and fall of the boat. Didier was none too pleased that he was left in sole charge of three little girls.

Didier had been in a slightly better mood since Clara had announced she would move. He kept reassuring her that it would be a new start and that he would cut down on his drinking.

Clara sceptically thought, '*Time will tell!*'

He promised to hand over his unopened wage packet each week—a promise he had kept in the lead up to the move, enabling Clara to save some money, ready for their arrival. He had even helped her pack up their possession.

Hedley picked them up at the harbour, loading their suitcases into the boot of his car. Their larger possessions were being shipped to them and would arrive later. He was a man of few words. He was not a tall man, standing at about five feet, eight inches. His skin was sunburnt, and his hair was grey and slicked-back. He welcomed them all, and they all squeezed into his car—the children sitting on Didier and Marie's knees.

"Look, Mamma, there is the seaside. Will we be able to go to the seaside, and we could go and swim in the sea?"

"Of course, you will, but perhaps we will wait until the summer, as it would be a bit cold now. This is going to be our new home, so we will have plenty of time to explore," said a not-so-convincing Clara.

It was a short drive to Hedley's farm in the Parish of St. Lawrence. Clara thought it looked quite grand with a short, rough drive lined by hedges on either side, leading to a large granite farmhouse with connecting outbuildings on either side of the house. Angela came out to greet them with little John at her side. She hugged and kissed them all.

"It is lovely to see you all. Come in! Come in! I have made us all dinner. I am sure you are hungry after the long journey."

Clara still felt a bit queasy but didn't say anything.

They walked into a large kitchen dominated by a large kitchen table that could easily accommodate ten people. There was a big dresser against one wall, displaying plates of all sizes and designs. On an end wall, in an alcove, was a large AGA with six hot plates for cooking. The mantelpiece above the AGA displayed photos of the whole family, even one of Clara and Didier on their wedding day. To the side of the kitchen was a scullery. The scullery consisted of a big sink with a wooden draining board and a long, but slim, table against the wall where Angela did all the food preparation. At the end of the table was a door leading out to the rear of the property.

"Please, everyone, sit down, and I will serve the food. Clara, there is a highchair for the baby. Mother, get some cushions for the little ones so they can reach the table. Clara, can you help me with the food?" ordered Angela like a sergeant major organizing her troops.

To give Angela her due, she had made a delicious meal. Clara sat Francine in the highchair, as Lilly was too small for it, beside which the baby was happily asleep in the pram donated by Angela.

Between them, they cleared up after dinner with Marie entertaining the children, Hedley and Didier discussing work, and Clara and Angela washed the dishes. While in the kitchen, Angela had confided in Clara that she had no intention of having any more children—one was enough—and had put lots of John's nursery equipment in the cottage for Lilly.

"I have put some essentials in your kitchen to keep you going for the next day or two and made up all the beds for you. You can let me have the bed linen back when yours arrives," said Angela.

Angela then went on to explain where the local shop was and how Clara must come and get milk from her, as well as any vegetables that were grown on the farm. "But I will give these to Didier when they are available to bring home for you."

"Thank you, Angela, you have been so kind and welcoming. I am sure we will all settle down, and it will soon become home," said Clara.

It was dark when Hedley drove them to their cottage, which was a very short journey that they could easily have walked. But with all their luggage, it was easier by car.

Like the farmhouse, the entrance led straight into the kitchen that was furnished with a wooden table surrounded by six chairs. At one end was a large black range that was keeping the room lovely and warm. There was a tiny scullery off of the kitchen.

The first thing that Clara noticed was that there was no sink or running water. "Where is the water supply?" Clara asked Hedley.

"That is outside the back door. You will find a pump just on the right."

Clara was too tired to comment.

The kitchen connected to a small hallway with stairs going up and a door leading to a living area. The living area was quite small but cosy with a fireplace surrounded by a settee and two armchairs. There was a window overlooking the front of the property with a wooden sideboard under the window. The floors were all covered in the same linoleum. A worn rug covered the area between the fireplace and the settee.

Upstairs the landing led to two bedrooms, one to the right and one to the left with a box room in between. The bedroom on the left had a double bed, a wardrobe and a chest of drawers. A rug covered the linoleum at the end of the bed. The bedroom on the right had two single beds and a cot plus a large chest of drawers.

The box room was a bit of a mystery to Clara. She presumed it was a quasi-bathroom. There was a marble washstand with a large bowl. A large water jug stood inside the bowl. Then there was a basket weave, large chair with arms and a high back. On closer examination, Clara discovered it was a commode.

"Where is the toilet?" she asked Hedley.

"Out the back in the outhouse," he answered as though it was a stupid question.

Hedley left then. "See you promptly at six in the morning, Didier – good night," he said as he was leaving.

"Six, that is an early start, lucky I packed the alarm clock in my suitcase," she said, thinking to herself, *'he won't like that'*.

Then, as though he read her thoughts, he looked at her knowing full well his wife knew he wasn't an early riser. He said, "It is a bit early, but the cows have to be milked!"

Clara got the girls ready to go to bed, letting Chantal choose which bed she wanted. She tucked them in with their favourite teddies and kissed them good night.

She quickly fed and changed Lilly's nappy and put her in the cot.

She went downstairs where Didier was just about to take the suitcases upstairs. "What do you think of the place? I am surprised there is no inside toilet or even running water. I wonder where I will do the laundry?"

"I don't know, but I need to get to bed, as I have an early start," said Didier.

"I am coming up as well, I will explore in the morning," said Clara.

It seemed like they had just gone to sleep when the alarm went off. Didier got up and dressed to get ready for work. Luckily, Clara had already unpacked Didier's work clothes in readiness. He had told her the night before that he would not need breakfast before he left or a packed lunch, as Angela would provide breakfast after the milking, and apparently she provided a lunch for all the farm workers.

Clara stayed in bed another hour before Lilly woke up hungry. Lilly had slept through the night at seven weeks old, which was a godsend for Clara.

Clara went downstairs to get some hot water for a wash. She found out that she had to boil a large kettle. It took her some time to find the coal to top up the range that was in an outhouse at the back, next to the toilet. The range was very similar to the one in Jeanne's kitchen, so she was familiar as to how it worked and soon got it up to speed to boil the kettle.

She quickly washed upstairs—it was too cold to linger—and got herself dressed. The girls woke and came downstairs where Clara had cooked them some porridge.

Angela had left a lot of groceries for her, for which Clara was thankful. It would give her time to get her bearings and find out where all the shops were.

"Let's explore, girls."

The pump was just outside the back door as Hedley had said. It was similar to the one she had used in Clifford's back yard to water the plants, so she knew how it worked. There was one big outhouse split into three, one was the toilet, another where the wood and coal was stored, and the other was the washhouse. It had an electric sort of washing machine with a mangle attached and then a large square sink that she presumed was where she would rinse the laundry. There was also a tin bath hanging on the wall.

Attached to the end of the outhouse was a washing line with the other end attached to a pole in the ground.

'At least I have a good place to hang the laundry,' she thought to herself.

At the rear of the cottage was a large field, which looked as though it had recently been ploughed and planted with a crop.

Theirs was the end cottage in a terrace of three similar dwellings, which she presumed was where the other farm workers lived. In the front of the cottages was a grassed area with a small hedge at the end. There was a small path in-between each cottage, leading from the front entrances to a gate that opened onto a lane.

Clara was already planning in her head where she could put her vegetable plot and where she could put some chickens.

Before lunch Clara unpacked while the girls played downstairs. Lilly loved to lie on a blanket on the floor watching Chantal and Francine. After lunch Lilly and Francine went for a nap, and Clara prepared dinner.

'*I will have to go and find the shop tomorrow to get some bread and see what else they sell,*' she thought to herself.

Didier came home exhausted, bringing with him a jug of milk and a cabbage. Clara had put some hot water upstairs for him to have a wash before dinner. They all sat down to dinner. "How did your day go?" asked Clara.

"It is hard work. First we had to get the cows from the field to the milking parlour and then we milked them. And then we had to take them back to the field. The local dairy picks the milk up at 8 a.m., so milking has to be finished by that time. We then had breakfast. Angela cooked us a good breakfast; that is one good thing. Then the rest of the day was spent ploughing a field down the road. There are three of us plus Hedley. Tomorrow we start planting that field with spring cabbages."

"It is a full-on day, then," remarked Clara.

"You are not kidding. We even had our lunch in the field. Angela brought us a basket with French bread and cheese and a flask of soup and left us a flask of tea and some buns for the afternoon break. What did you do today?" he asked.

"Well, I checked out where to do the laundry. There is some kind of boiler that I will have to try and figure out how it works. I still need to unpack and generally look around to see where everything is. Tomorrow, we are going to find the shop."

The next day they set out to find the shop. Clara put Lilly in the pram with Francine perched on the top and Chantal walking holding onto the pram handle. They walked in the direction Angela had told her, along the lane and then onto the main road. After ten minutes of walking, they could see the church. Angela had said that the shop was opposite the church. They passed a small school on the way, and Clara thought to herself that this would be convenient for the girls when they reach school age. She soon spotted the shop that was next door to a public house. She had to leave Lilly outside in her pram, as there was no room in the shop.

She walked in with Chantal and Francine in tow.

Chantal immediately spotted the sweets and in French she said, "Mamma, puis-je avoir quelques bonbons."

Clara longed for the days when customers came to her for sweets. She could barely hide her yearning to ask if any of the local shops needed someone who could bake, but she shoved the feeling aside and looked at the bonbons. She wondered about the quality of chocolate.

There were two customers in the shop, one older woman who was being served and a younger woman waiting. They all looked at her when she entered the shop, and Clara heard the shopkeeper say sarcastically, "Another Frenchy who can't speak English."

On hearing this, Clara in her best English accent said to Chantal, "You must speak in English, lovey," to the astonishment and embarrassment of the shopkeeper. The younger woman couldn't help but suppress a giggle.

Clara looked around the shop, although well-stocked, everything appeared expensive in comparison with French prices. Trying to see something that she could cook for dinner was difficult, and in the end, she decided to buy some sausages, beans and bacon. She picked up some onions and a few basic items and took them to the counter.

"Good morning, Madam," said Clara and gave the shopkeeper her order and then seeing the bread, asked for a loaf.

"Hello, you are new around here," said the shopkeeper as she wrote down the prices of the items.

"Yes, we arrived a few days ago. Are you the only shop in the area?"

"We are. What were you looking for?" she asked.

"I was looking for a butcher," said Clara.

"You would have to go into town for that." She gave Clara her shopping items and gave both Chantal and Francine a sweet each. She wondered where the sweets came from.

"What do you say to the kind lady?"

"Merci, Madame," said Chantal.

"No," said Clara in English. "Thank you, Madame."

"You are welcome. I hope to see you again."

Clara left the shop and found the young woman who had been in the shop talking to Lilly, who was now wide-awake.

The young woman extended her hand. "Hello, I am Audrey."

Clara took her hand. "Hello, pleased to meet you. I am Clara, and this is Lilly, and these two little monkeys are Chantal and Francine. My husband has recently started work at the farm up the road belonging to Hedley Chevalier."

"I know Hedley very well. His father and my father were great friends. I live on the farm on the other side of the main road to Hedley," she said.

They started to walk back home with Audrey chatting away to Clara, telling her all about the area and how the shopkeeper Mrs. Lafolley didn't like the French very much.

"The French men go to the pub next door on pay day and get very drunk and on numerous occasions are sick in front of her shop. As you can imagine she is not happy at having to clean up after them, so that is her reason for not liking them. Unfortunately, she tars them all with the same brush," said Audrey.

Clara asked Audrey about buying supplies. "Come back to my house for a cup of tea, and I will tell you where to go. My mother is there at the moment, looking after my son. He looks about the same age as your Francine, and he will enjoy having some playmates."

Audrey lived in an annex of her parents' farmhouse. The farmhouse looked very similar to Hedley's. She picked up her son, Michael, from her mother's and led Clara and the girls into her kitchen next door.

It was a lovely homely kitchen. Michael took Francine by the hand to show her his toys, and they were soon all sitting on the floor playing.

Clara sat down at the table with Lilly while Audrey made the tea.

"Now tell me what you need to know," said Audrey as she placed a pot of tea and two cups on the table with a plate of biscuits.

"Well, where do you go to do most of your shopping, like the butcher and baker?" asked Clara.

Audrey explained, "Everything is quite easy when you know what's what. The baker will come to you. He makes his round three times a week in his van. He is due tomorrow, so I will ask him to call on you. He usually has a good choice of bread, rolls, doughnuts, all sorts of pastries—if you want something specific, then he will bring it for you. You pay him for what you take.

"The milkman, who you won't need, as I am sure you will get this from Hedley, but if you did, well, he makes his rounds every morning.

"You will have to go to town for the butcher and other things."

"Town! Where is town?"

"Sorry, that is in St. Helier. There is a bus that comes around about every two hours. The bus stop is just past the shop, and you get off at the bus station which is called Snow Hill," explained Audrey.

"The main shopping area starts at the entrance to the bus station. Follow the main street, and everything you need is on this street. It will take you about ten to fifteen minutes to walk to the end. There are three main general stores: Lipton that is about a third of the way down, Le Riches, which is at the bottom of a road that is second on your right as you go down the main street—which by the way is called Queen Street—but I use the Co-op, which is right down the other end, because they deliver your shopping. And when they deliver, you can give them your order for the following week. You should go there first to see what they sell, and you can actually join the co-op, and they give you stamps to collect that give you money back." Audrey was explaining this and drawing Clara a map at the same time.

Pointing to the map she had drawn, Audrey explained where the market was, which housed butchers, fruit and vegetable stalls, bakers and other small shops. Again, Clara couldn't help letting her thoughts wander back to Simone's bakery where she'd developed as a baker. She could only imagine them baking now without her. She wondered whether Simone was still only comfortable making the icing or whether once Clara had left, she had gotten better at the delicate decorations. She couldn't stop herself from getting caught up in the wave of nostalgia and briefly she considered whether she might be able to find work with one of the bakers nearby but immediately pictured Marie's look of disapproval. Any happy feelings she felt from the hopeful possibility immediately faded. She returned to the task at hand and stopped getting distracted by her thoughts, although she could feel a sadness creep over her. She concealed the feeling from Audrey, reassuring herself that although it wouldn't help to tell her about business back at Simone's bakery, where she had thrown herself wholeheartedly into developing her skills at pastries and cakes, the memories would always remind Clara at moments like this.

"I don't suggest you go to town on a Saturday, as it gets very busy, and you spend most of your time trying to get served. Also, I wouldn't take the children. It is impossible to get the pram on the bus." While she poured them another cup of tea and gave the children a biscuit each, Audrey asked, "Did you notice the church hall across from the church?"

"I think so, why?" asked Clara, firmly back in the present moment.

"There is a baby clinic there every other Thursday between ten and twelve. They check the baby over, weigh them and ensure that they have all their vaccinations. They also sell formula milk at a discount. You should take Lilly. They are very good and friendly and give you lots of advice. I think the next one is next week."

"I can't thank you enough, Audrey, for all of this information. I don't know what I would have done without it. Perhaps, you could come around to our house sometime. The children play well together," suggested Clara.

"I would like that," said Audrey.

Clara got ready to go. "It is nearly lunch time. Lilly will be screaming for her bottle of milk very soon." Thanks to Audrey, her nerves were settled, at least for the time being and starting life in their new home.

CHAPTER 20

Clara felt so much happier. She told Didier everything that she had learnt from Audrey and started to make plans to go to town on the following Monday.

The first week went well for Didier. He got paid on the Friday and handed it all to Clara. He reluctantly refused the offer to go to the pub after work with the other men, instead going to see his mother with Clara to ask if she could look after the children while Clara went to town.

Clara caught the bus and enjoyed taking in the sights on the way. The trip was short. They arrived at the bus station within twenty-five minutes. She was a bit baffled at which way to go after leaving the bus but followed other passengers and soon found herself on the main street. She followed her map down to Le Riches Stores that had everything she would need, but since she wanted to see what else was available, she made her way through the market to the co-op.

She went upstairs to the office, and they explained the membership, the placing of orders, and the payment process. She joined up straight away. The lady assistant suggested that she place an order now for basic items for delivery on Friday, as the cut off time was noon that day. The assistant further recommended that Clara go to the store to buy what she needed, and at the same time look to see what other items they sold for future reference.

Clara left the store with a bag full of items. She then returned to the market and purchased the meat and vegetables. She ambled up the main street, looking at all of the shops, enjoying her short period of freedom from the girls. She caught the bus home with plenty of time to spare.

The baker was a jolly man with a white apron. He parked his van in the lane and came to her door with a big basket of his wares. Clara picked out what she wanted, paid him, and asked him if he would like a cup of tea.

"Thank you, my dear, but I have a lot more deliveries to make. I will include you in my round from now on. You don't always need to buy anything. Good-bye." He was gone before she had time to thank him. She wondered about Simone's son, Fabien, and whether he would soon be making the rounds in a van to surrounding areas with their baked goods like they had once talked about. He would be close to driving age by now.

It took two weeks before the delivery van with their possessions arrived from France. The men unloaded them and carried them into the house for her, making her next task the unpacking. She felt proud that in the short time she had been in Jersey, she had sorted out the shops, made a friend, and turned the cottage into a home for them all. She was full of optimism for their new life.

Didier arrived home with his second week's pay packet. They all sat down at the table for dinner, and when they had finished, they sat chatting. Chantal was talking to her father, asking him if she could go and see the cows being milked, when there was a knock on the door. Clara answered it. It was a neighbouring Frenchman.

"Come in!" she said.

He looked straight at Didier, ignoring Clara. "Are you coming to the pub for a pint?"

Didier looked at Clara. "Go," she said discreetly, giving him some beer money.

Didier arrived home shortly after ten, drunk. Clara couldn't quite understand how he managed to get drunk on the money she gave him. He stumbled in, glaring at her. Her blood ran cold as she recognized the look he was giving her.

"You bitch, I suppose you thought it was funny giving me the price for only one pint, humiliating me in front of my friends," he slurred.

"Oh, don't be so stupid. How could I possibly humiliate you? You should have just left after the one pint, saying that you wanted to go home to your family," she said.

He started to come towards her with a look of hate in his eyes.

"Don't you dare touch me," said a fearful Clara, putting up her hands to stop him from coming any nearer to her. But he grabbed her wrists with one hand, pushed her towards the wall with the other hand, and pulled her arms above her head.

"Please, Didier, please let me go," she pleaded.

But he took no notice. He slapped her face over and over. She slowly slid down the wall almost passing out. As she sat on the floor, he kicked her. "Perhaps you will think twice before embarrassing me again," he said.

Leaving her on the floor, he left the room and went upstairs.

Clara managed to crawl to the settee. After the dizziness had passed, she went upstairs and moved Francine into Chantal's bed and then got into Francine's bed.

The week passed as though nothing had happened. There was no apology or a comment. Clara dreaded the next Friday coming around, and she was proven right. He didn't even come home after work. As a consequence, their daily jug of milk didn't arrive. Clara was more concerned now about milk for the girls' breakfast, rather than where Didier was. She knew full well that he would be at the pub.

'*I will go and get some milk before the girls get up,*' she thought to herself.

Didier came home late and very drunk, but Clara had gone to bed, to avoid having to face him. He came into the room, banging into all the furniture. He roughly nudged her.

"Here is my wage packet, bitch."

She half opened her eyes, pretending to have been woken up, as she didn't want a confrontation, while he was in a drunken state. He pulled the bed covers off her.

"Here, take a look," he demanded as he handed her the open pay packet.

She took it and could see straight away that there was hardly anything left. She felt sick at the thought of trying to feed the family on so little money. She knew she shouldn't react but was unable to stop herself.

"You fool. I suppose you like watching your children go hungry. Well it won't only be them, that's for sure," she said, trying to talk quietly so as not to wake the children.

He took hold of her around the neck, started to squeeze and lifted her out of bed at the same time. She attempted to fight back, but he was too strong. She felt herself starting to lose consciousness before he let go. Coughing and gasping for breath, she tried running out of the room, but he caught her with a punch across the back of the head, and as she fell to the floor, he kicked her in the stomach. He then picked her up by the neck and head-butted her unconscious.

When she came around, her whole body was in pain, and her nose was bleeding. She crawled downstairs and washed her face as best she could. She made her way to the settee with a glass of water and some painkillers and lay there for some time before sleep eventually came.

The girls came bounding down the stairs in the morning as usual.

On seeing her mother, Chantal cried, "Mamma, you are hurt," giving her a hug.

Clara tried not to react to the pain from the hug. She had vaguely heard Didier leave for work, so she guessed it must have been about seven thirty. When Lilly began to cry for her morning bottle of milk, Clara knew she would have to go upstairs and get Lilly. She tried to get up from the settee without crying out in pain. She didn't want to frighten the girls.

"Chantal."

"Yes, Mamma."

"Do you remember the way to Auntie Angela's house?"

"Yes, I have been with you lots of times," replied a confident Chantal.

"Do you think you would be able to go on your own?"

"Yes, Mamma. I know my way. It is easy. Just follow the lane to the end."

Clara told her to run upstairs and get dressed. She was so excited at going somewhere on her own that she was back downstairs in a flash. Clara helped her on with her coat and hat and told her to go and ask Granny to come and bring some milk with her. "Now run and watch where you are going."

Clara told Francine to sit at the table and wait there while she fetched Lilly. She managed to get upstairs, but getting down carrying Lilly was a great deal more painful.

It was about half an hour before Marie arrived with Chantal in tow and a jug of milk. She shouted good morning as she entered the kitchen and stopped in her tracks when she saw Clara.

"Oh! My dear girl, what has happened to you?"

Clara wanted to scream at her and say, '*your son did this*', but she knew she couldn't vent her anger at Marie. It wasn't her fault.

"Didier did this, didn't he? I will kill him. How could he? He is a monster. Tell me what happened."

Clara tried to explain as briefly as possible. She didn't want her hating her son.

"I will make sure that Hedley gives me his pay packet in the future, and I will bring it to you. It is only the drink that does this. Now what can I do now to help you?"

To give Marie her due, she stayed all day and helped Clara, even preparing a stew for their dinner. After lunch Marie took the girls for a walk down to the farm, allowing Clara to have a rest. Didier brought them back just before dinnertime.

"I am so sorry, Clara. I didn't mean to hurt you," he said, trying to embrace her.

CHAPTER 21

They had been in Jersey just over two months when Christmas arrived. They were invited to Angela's for Christmas day, and Angela had suggested that they sleep the night thus avoiding having to go home early for the girls' bedtime.

Clara felt embarrassed that she had not had the money to buy any presents. Instead, she made both Marie and Angela some fudge and iced coconut sweets. The girls had helped make the sweets, sitting around the table, helping her decorate the sweets with melted chocolate and sprinkles. They were so proud of themselves. When they had finished, they wiped the mixing bowls with their fingers and licked them clean. Clara revelled in the moment, doing the job she cherished.

Clara found some cardboard and made a box to put the sweets in, which the girls decorated with paint and tied a ribbon around the box. Both Marie and Angela had prized their homemade sweets, not letting anyone else taste them.

Nineteen fifty-one arrived and so did more abuse, although Marie continued to bring Didier's pay packet to Clara on Friday afternoons. This didn't stop him from demanding money from Clara when he got home. He would physically hurt her until she handed over enough for him to go to the pub, then come home drunk and start beating her. She tried shutting herself in with the girls, but this resulted in him banging on the door, so she would have to come out and face him to avoid waking up and frightening the girls.

Life was getting worse for Clara. Some weeks she was so short of money that she would have to send Chantal out to meet the baker to tell him that she didn't need any bread this week or cancel her co-op order.

Clara saw less of Audrey, as she was embarrassed for her to see her cuts and bruises and felt too desperately unhappy to meet up with her.

Clara had attended the baby clinic, as suggested by Audrey, where they had weighed Lilly and checked her over. The last time she went, Lilly had a hearing test. The nurse was concerned and said that she would make an appointment for Lilly to see the specialist at the hospital in town.

The appointment arrived a short time later, and Clara arranged for Marie to look after Chantal and Francine while she took Lilly for her appointment.

Clara took the bus to town, borrowing a pushchair from Angela that could be folded up to go on the bus. Clara had to ask several times for directions to the hospital and eventually found her way. The test was carried out with the specialist saying that Lilly's hearing was fine.

"Perhaps an overzealous nurse," he suggested.

Clara knew she would have a two-hour wait for the bus to take her home, as she wouldn't make it to the bus station before the next bus left. It was now mid-March and still quite cold. She walked with Lilly along the Esplanade, seeing a different part of Saint Helier. There weren't any shops this way. She passed a few hotels and agricultural warehouses. When she came to the end of the road, she saw the booking office for the boat. She stopped to look in the window and noticed various advertisements. On impulse, she went in.

"Can I help you?" said the girl behind the counter.

"Do the boats go to England?" inquired Clara.

"Yes, they go to Weymouth on a regular basis."

"Sorry, but where is Weymouth?" asked Clara.

"It is on the south coast of England," said the girl cheerfully.

"How much is the fare, and do you know how I would get from Weymouth to Lancashire?" asked Clara.

The girl gave her a timetable that included the cost of the fares. She explained that children under two travelled free. She further told Clara about a coach that would take her from Weymouth to anywhere in England, and then she mentioned that alternatively she could get a train to London, and from there, she could get another train to wherever she wanted to go.

Clara also noticed that there was a place that she could change currency. She asked the girl if she could change francs into pounds.

"Yes, bring them in, and we will change them for you."

Clara thanked the girl and left. She made her way up to the bus station with still time to spare. She sat in the bus shelter and read the timetable for the boat.

She still had the francs that she got when she closed her bank account in France. She had kept them for a rainy day, and perhaps now the rainy day had arrived. Clara had had enough of the beatings, the arguments, never having enough money, being so unhappy and living in fear for her life.

And so the seed was sown.

CHAPTER 22

Clara worked out that she had enough money to get the boat and the coach back to Preston, but only for herself!

After another beating, her mind was made up. Leaving the girls with Angela on the pretext of going to town, she caught the bus and went straight to the booking office. After changing her francs, she found she had a bit more than expected, but it was only a small sum that would hopefully cover any food and drink on the journey.

She booked the boat for herself and Lilly, who could travel free, for the following week. She chose one of the only sailing days that left at eleven in the morning, as this would give her plenty of time to get into town and down to the harbour.

She had five days of anguish. 'What sort of mother am I leaving my two little girls?' she thought to herself, but she knew Didier would never lay a hand on them. He loved those little girls. *'When I am sorted out with a job and a home, I will come and get them'*, she would say to herself over and over again. But the anguish continued.

She again asked Angela if she could look after Chantal and Francine, as Lilly had another hospital appointment. Angela didn't ask any questions, just said, "Yes, no problem."

She packed a carpetbag with clothes for herself and Lilly and hid it under the bed. She couldn't take anything bigger, as she would have the pushchair and a small bag with Lilly's nappies and snacks for the journey.

On the morning of her departure, she felt sick with fear. She tried to stop herself from crying as she left Chantal and Francine with Angela, kissing and hugging them good-bye, and telling them that she loved them. She ran back home to quickly collect her bags and made her way to the bus. She kept looking around her, hoping that she wouldn't see anyone that she knew. Making her way down to the harbour, she nearly changed her mind. She couldn't quite believe what she was doing, but then the thought of another beating spurred her on. A member of the crew helped her onto the boat, carrying the pushchair with Lilly in it up the gangplank. She settled them into a seat, and soon, with the sound of the boat's horn, they were off.

The first part of the sailing was rough. Clara felt dreadfully nauseous, but as she hadn't had any breakfast, she wasn't physically sick. Lilly mostly slept. When she did wake up, Clara tried to entertain her with the few toys she had packed. After two hours, they docked in Guernsey and took on more passengers.

The rest of the journey was much calmer. Clara ate one of the sandwiches she had made and drank some of the coffee she had in a flask. They arrived in Weymouth in the late evening. It was already dark and very cold.

Clara asked for directions to the coach station. On arrival at the station, she was told that the next coach was at eight in the morning. This was one thing she hadn't planned for. She asked about nearby accommodations and realized she didn't have enough money to pay for both accommodation and the coach fare. The man in the ticket office said she couldn't stay in the waiting room, as it would be locked for the night and suggested she go to the train station, as the waiting room there wasn't locked at night.

She bought herself a hot drink and a hot pie at the station and found a bench to bed down for the night. It was freezing. She wrapped Lilly up and put the back of the pushchair down so at least one of them would have a goodnight's sleep. Clara had made up several bottles of formula milk, as she could not always supply enough milk herself to satisfy the seven-month-old Lilly. The man at the café had kindly warmed up the bottle for her, so at least she didn't have to worry about Lilly going hungry. Clara didn't sleep at all, anxious that someone would take Lilly or her belongings if she did sleep. It seemed like ages before morning finally came, and Clara could make her way to the coach station.

The driver loaded the pushchair and her carpetbag in the luggage compartment and helped her onto the coach. Clara sat in the back seat in the hope that Lilly would be able to lie down and sleep. The gentle humming of the coach soon sent Clara to sleep with Lilly tucked securely next to her. The journey took seven hours with several stops on the way.

At one stop, the driver gave everyone twenty minutes to get off the coach to go to the toilet and get refreshments. This gave Clara the opportunity to change Lilly's nappy and get a sandwich.

The coach stopped outside of Preston bus station. Clara retrieved her belongings and made her way home. Clara was so tired that she found it difficult to get her bearings. Everything had changed. She recognized a few buildings but couldn't believe how much the main street had altered.

Arriving at the salon, which looked exactly the same, she could see her mother through the window. The bell pinged as she opened the door.

Her mother looked up, taking a double take. "Oh my God! Clara, is that you?" Her mother ran over, taking Clara in her arms. Clara sobbed uncontrollably. "My dear girl, I can't quite grasp that you are here." As soon as she saw Lilly in the pushchair, she said, "Where are the girls and Didier?"

Clara was crying so much that she couldn't speak. Hearing the commotion, her father came through from his shop. It took him some seconds to take the situation in, and on realizing that his daughter had come home, he took over from Olive and held Clara.

Olive went over to the pushchair. "Hello, little one, you must be Liliane. You are a pretty little girl, and you look just like your mummy did when she was a baby with those blond curls and hazel eyes."

Olive lifted Lilly out of the pushchair. "Jack, will you lock up, and I will take Lilly and Clara upstairs?"

Upstairs, Olive put the kettle on. "Now tell me what is going on, Clara, but before you start, Lilly needs a change of nappy. She is soaking wet."

"Sorry, Mum, I thought she would be, but I don't have any nappies left. I only brought a few with me, and I used them all on the journey," said Clara on the verge of tears again. "Sorry, Mum, I can't seem to be able to hold myself back from crying."

"Don't keep saying you're sorry. You look exhausted and very pale. Plus, you are looking very thin, Clara. Try not to worry. I will take care of the two of you. Why don't you run a bath for Lilly? That will give me just enough time to quickly go up to Boots and get some nappies."

"Oh! Mum, please, you have been working all day. I don't want you having to go all the way uptown to the shops. I will go. I can quickly get the bus there before the shops close."

"Clara, we have a little car. I am sure I told you in one of my letters. Anyway, Dad will drive me uptown, and he can wait outside while I run in the shop. Stop worrying. You need to think of yourself and Lilly."

Clara ran a bath for Lilly while her mother and father went to the shops. Lilly loved her bath, and she sat in the warm water, splashing her hands in the water and surprising herself when water landed on her face. By the time she had got Lilly out of the bath and wrapped her in a big towel, her mother had arrived back with two large bags.

"Here are the nappies. I also got some baby toiletries, a couple of nighties and some clothing. Look at these, aren't they cute? I couldn't resist them when I saw them. I didn't realize that Boots sold baby clothes. I also got some formula milk. You need to build yourself up, Clara, and feeding Lilly yourself will not help you or her," said her concerned mother.

"Now, you give Lilly to me, and you go and run yourself a bath and have a good soak. I will bring you that cup of tea that I promised before I left for the shops."

"Clara was almost asleep in the bath when her mother brought a cup of tea to her. Your dad will look after Lilly while I make some dinner. Once we have had dinner, then you need to have an early night. I will pop a hot water bottle in the bed so it is nice and cosy for you. Lilly will have to sleep in the other bed. I will put some chairs in front of it so she doesn't fall out, and we can look for a cot tomorrow."

Clara finished her bath and dressed in her nightclothes. Dinner was ready, waiting for her in the kitchen. She was starving and tried not to wolf it down.

"Mum, do you mind if I go to bed, and we have a good chat in the morning? I am so tired."

"Of course, I don't mind. I said earlier that you needed an early night. I will see to Lilly." Her mother hugged and kissed her goodnight.

Clara slept like a log. She didn't even hear her mother put Lilly to bed or get her up in the morning. When she looked at the clock, it was 11 a.m. She couldn't believe she had slept so long. She quickly got up and got dressed, concerned about how her mother was able to look after Lilly and work in the salon. But she needn't have worried. Lilly was sitting happily on one of her mother's client's knee while her mother was doing her hair.

"Mum, I am so sorry. I have only just woken up," said Clara.

"Don't worry. You obviously needed the rest, and I must say you do look much better than you did yesterday. Now you go and get yourself some breakfast. We will take care of Lilly," said her mother before she called out, "Jean, come here. Let me introduce you to Lilly's mother, my daughter Clara."

Jean Adams came through from the back of the salon. She was a young girl of about eighteen with long dark hair, tied back in a ponytail, dressed in overalls that were identical to Olive's, which had the name of the salon embossed on it.

"Clara, this is Jean, my apprentice. She has been here eighteen months now. I think I told you in one of my letters that I was getting help."

"Hello," said Clara.

"Hello, pleased to meet you. I have heard all about you, and Lilly is just adorable. I want to take her home," enthused Jean.

"She is a monkey. That is for sure," said Clara before going upstairs for breakfast.

It was an early closing day for the salon. After her breakfast, Clara looked around the kitchen to see what she could prepare her parents for their lunch. '*It is the least I can do*,' she thought to herself. There were a lot of vegetables in the pantry, so she quickly set to work to make a vegetable soup. She lightly soaked some bread slices in oil and placed them in the oven with grated cheese on top to accompany the soup.

Clara's parents were delighted with the lunch.

"Thank you. That was delicious and such a treat for me not to have to cook."

"It's the least I can do. Now sit down and have a cup of tea while I clear up and do the dishes."

Lilly was given a bit of the bread soaked in the soup before her bottle. Her face showed that she was not sure what was being given to her, but she opened her mouth for more, which amused everyone.

"Why don't I take Lilly for a walk to the park while you two have a chat," suggested her father.

"Good idea," said her mother, getting Lilly ready for her outing.

After her father left with Lilly, her mother said, "Come and sit down, Clara, and tell me what is going on."

They sat down together on the settee, and Clara told her how she had met Didier and how he had proposed and then got married.

"Everything was fine at first. We had our little cottage, and I was working and bringing home a good wage. After the war, Didier got a short-term job with the government, but after that, he found it difficult to get a full-time job and would drift from one casual job to another. After the birth of Chantal and then Francine, money was very tight, as I couldn't work the same as before, and I had to pay for childcare.

"Didier started drinking more and more, and that was the problem. When he drank, he got angry and took his anger out on me. At first, he would just slap me, which was bad enough, but then he started punching and kicking me. Once, he tried to strangle me. I was embarrassed that this was happening and would cover my bruises and tell people that I had fallen over or bumped into something. But, I could see on their faces that they didn't believe me.

"When he sobered up, he was always sorry, so when the suggestion of moving to Jersey came up and he said it would be a new life, I believed him. But it wasn't, and when by chance, I saw a booking office of the boats to England, I took the hardest decision of my life, to leave."

Clara was by now in floods of tears. "Mum, I have left my two little girls behind. What am I going to do? How will I get them back? I know you don't know the answer, but I can't go back to living in such fear and being so unhappy, but my heart is breaking without them."

Olive was broken-hearted for Clara. "Everything will sort itself out. Try not to worry, just take one day at a time. In the meantime, what are your plans for the future?" asked her mother.

"I was thinking while making lunch that I will try and get a job and then, when and if I get one, then I will sort out a child minder. Once that is all settled, I will then look for a place to live. Will I be able to stay here though until such a time?" she asked.

"You don't need to even ask, Clara. Of course you can stay as long as you need to, and I will help you as much as I can. At least, I have Jean in the salon now to help me, and she has recently received her diploma, so she is no longer an apprentice. She told me off earlier when I introduced her as my apprentice, only in jest I might add," said her mother.

"Thank you, Mum. Until I get a job, I will do all the cooking and housework," said Clara.

"Anyway, what sort of job are you thinking of getting?" asked her mother.

"I thought either a pastry chef or baker or even a cook. All of those, I am good at. I will start looking tomorrow," she said.

She scoured the local paper for job vacancies, and the only one of any interest was a new hotel advertising for staff in all areas. She wrote down the details ready for the morning.

Clara got up bright and early the next morning and prepared breakfast. Once everyone had eaten, she tidied up and got Lilly prepared for the job hunt. Her father gave her some money to help her with bus fares and told her to buy herself some clothes, as she had brought very little with her.

"Thank you, Dad. I will pay you back as soon as I am earning," she said.

"I don't want paying back. I just want you to be happy, my love," he replied.

Tucking Lilly into the pushchair, she set off. Her plan was to go to the hotel first and get an application form, and then go to the Labour Exchange to see what was available there. Afterward, she would go to an agency she had seen in the local paper.

After taking the bus to the nearest stop to the hotel, Clara entered a side door that indicated that this was to be used for job applicants. The girl behind a makeshift desk took her name and asked what post she was seeking within the hotel. Clara told her briefly that she could bake both bread and pâttisserie and generally cook. The girl asked her to take a seat. She tried to explain to the girl that she had only come for an application form, but the girl said that the chef wanted to speak to anyone applying for kitchen jobs before being handed an application form. Clara took a seat, and after a few minutes, she was invited into an office. The girl offered to mind Lilly while she went into the office.

"Thank you very much. That would be a great help!" said Clara, getting up from her seat.

There were two men seated behind a table. They introduced themselves as Mr. Lewis the manager and Mr. Lindsay the chef. "I see your name is Clara Renard and that you are interested in a post in the kitchen. Can you tell us a bit about yourself, and what experience you have?"

Clara described the work she had done in both the bakery and bar and how she had taught herself to produce pastries. She told them about how she had produced cakes for weddings and birthdays and the different types of dishes she had produced for the bar lunches.

"Thank you, Clara." The manager explained more about the hotel and how they would be opening in four weeks' time.

The hotel was named the Royal Park Hotel, and Mr. Lewis said that it had the capacity to take one hundred guests. Although the hotel was new, the premises had previously been an old mill that had been completely refurbished.

"We have already recruited sixty per cent of our staff. Now we will give you an application form to complete, but what we would like you to do is prepare something for us, either some pastries or a lunch dish. What we are looking for is proof of what you can do. We are doing this with all applicants for cooking posts. We want to make sure that we get competent people who will be able to provide our hotel with a good standard of food. If we asked you to come back on Monday and cook us something, what would you choose?" asked the chef.

Clara had to think for a minute and then remember her success with Tarte Tatin. "I would bake you a Tarte Tatin," she announced.

"Excellent choice. We look forward to that," said the chef.

"Can you come at say ten on Monday morning?"

"Yes, no problem," replied Clara.

"We look forward to seeing you then. Can you leave a list with the receptionist of the ingredients you require, and we will make sure they are ready and waiting for you? Please bring your completed application form with you."

Clara thanked them and left the room. She thanked the receptionist for looking after Lilly and asked for some paper and a pen and wrote down what she needed.

Clara was nervous and excited at the prospects of working in the hotel but tried not to get too excited, as she hadn't got the job yet.

Leaving the hotel, she made her way to the Labour Exchange. There she spoke to the person behind the counter, and they went through her options and registered her for a National Insurance card. There were very few jobs that interested her. However, there were a few shop assistant jobs and waitressing jobs should she not find exactly what she was looking for. She then made her way to the agency, which proved a waste of time, as it only offered office jobs. She was left feeling a little downhearted, but at the same time she hoped that the hotel would prove successful.

On her way home, she decided to go and see Auntie Doreen and her sister May. Doreen opened the door and was surprised to see Clara. "My dear, what are you doing here? Come in. Come in. Let me help you with the pushchair."

May busied herself, making tea for them, while Doreen cooed over Lilly. Clara briefly told her auntie why she was back home to her mother and father.

"I can't believe that a man could be so cruel to a woman," said a distressed Doreen.

"Oh! I can," said May. I have seen many women in the same circumstances as you, Clara. I worked for a short-time for a charity helping such woman. The men would spend their entire wage on alcohol, then go home and beat their wives. The family would have gone hungry if it had not been for the assistance of the charity. You were right to leave; most women stay and lead miserable lives."

Clara told them about her job-hunting experience and her hopes for the hotel job. "You must leave Lilly with us on Monday. We would love to look after her, wouldn't we, May?" said Doreen.

"Yes, it would be lovely to have a baby in the house."

Clara finished her tea and thanked them both for their support, leaving a bit more upbeat than when she arrived.

The weekend went quickly. Her mother appeared more excited than Clara at the prospect of the job. She had gone shopping for clothes on Saturday and bought herself two outfits and a pair of shoes. She had also bought Lilly a new coat and some toys.

She was so nervous on Monday morning that she could barely eat any breakfast. She dropped Lilly off at Doreen's and May's and made her way to the hotel.

The chef met her at the entrance and took her for a tour of the kitchen. The kitchen was superb, brand new and state of the art, the likes of which Clara had never seen. The chef showed her where all the equipment was stored and how to use the ovens and hobs. He also showed her the store cupboard should she need additional ingredients.

"Here are the ingredients you requested. I will be next door. Let me know when you have finished."

"Thank you," responded Clara.

She set to work making the pastry first, and then while that was resting, set to work peeling the apples and preparing the caramelized topping. She placed the dish in the oven and hoped it would be perfect. Then, she prepared some vanilla cream to accompany the tart.

While waiting for her tart to cook, she looked around the kitchen, opening all the cupboards. She couldn't believe the number of ovens, hobs and hot plates. There were even griddles that she had not seen before. The walk-in larder and meat safe were huge but not yet stocked with supplies, plus there was a massive refrigerator, again something she had not seen before. When her tart was cooked, she flipped it over onto a plate to cool. It was just perfect. Once cooled, she cut a piece and placed it on a smaller plate with a serving of cream and took it to the chef.

The chef was impressed. "It looks delicious. Now let me taste it," he said as he placed some in his mouth. "Mmmmm! That is delicious. Let me call in the manager so he can taste it."

"Beautiful," exclaimed the manager. "When can you start?"

Mr. Lewis then discussed which position would most suit her, and they agreed on pastry chef. He explained that this position would mean an early start, as some of the bread items would require being freshly baked for breakfast for the guests. Clara explained that she had Lilly and that a 4 a.m. start would suit her fine, as her mother could take care of the baby until she got home from her shift.

"Can I ask you, Clara, where your husband is?" asked Mr Lewis.

"He died," replied Clara.

"Oh! I am so sorry," he said.

Clara didn't know what to say and felt terribly guilty after saying Didier was dead, but there was no going back.

Mr. Lewis asked her to start two weeks later and that before the hotel opened she would work closely with the chef, Mr. Lindsay, in preparing menus and stocking the kitchen. He then told her to obtain two sets of work clothing from a local supplier to be paid for by the hotel.

Clara left the hotel ecstatic, not quite believing that she had got a job so quickly and better still a job cooking. She went along to the supplier and collected two sets of chef's whites in her size. Each jacket had the name of the hotel emblazoned on the front right side of the chest. There was also a cap to tuck her hair into.

She had two weeks before starting her new job. During this time, she cooked the evening meal for her parents and generally helped her mother around the house. She visited Doreen and May a couple of times. They loved seeing Lilly and even offered to look after her while she worked.

She had lost contact with all her school friends, so it was difficult to catch up with them, as so much had changed, and they had all moved on with their lives. Her best friend, Mary, was now married and lived in Leicester, so there was no one of her age to meet up with. Clara had corresponded with Mary over the years and they had regularly exchanged letters before the war, however, during the war all correspondence had stopped. After the war their letters had become increasingly infrequent each getting on with their own lives. She hoped that in the future, she would make new friends perhaps with the people she was going to work with.

"You are very quiet today, Clara. Is something bothering you?" asked her mother over lunch on the following Thursday, knowing very well what was troubling her daughter.

"It's Francine's second birthday today, Mum."

"Yes, I know, lovey. I sent her a card last week just from your dad and me. I just sent our love and included a colouring book and some crayons."

"Thank you, Mum. I couldn't send anything. I don't want Didier knowing where I am," she said.

Whenever Clara thought of her little girls, her heart would break and not a day went by when she didn't think of them and what they were doing and whether they were missing her.

The first week in the job was informal, and she was able to take Lilly with her. Together with Mr. Lindsay, the head chef and three other chefs, they formulated menus for breakfast, lunch and dinner. They had all been given different tasks and shifts. Clara's was to bake all the bread and rolls required for the whole day together with a number of desserts for lunch and dinner. One of the other chefs, Gordon Burton, would cover her shift on her day off, and in turn she would cover his shift on his day off. The head chef had already decided that the menu would be rolled over every two weeks with an occasional special dish of the day, so with this in mind, the two of them, who would be responsible for the breads and desserts, sat down together and planned a different menu for a two-week period together with a number of specials.

The day before starting work properly, she went to bed early with her alarm clock set for 3:30 a.m. There were no buses at that time of the morning, so she knew it would take her almost half an hour to walk to the hotel. With her recipe book and new uniform, she set off full of optimism, arriving in good time.

CHAPTER 23

Clara had been working at the hotel for three months and loved every minute. It was not like a job at all. The work was hard and at times stressful. She had learnt so much from the head chef and from Gordon, and they were never too busy to show her the correct way of doing things or introducing her to new methods of cooking. Gordon was fifty-two years of age and had worked as a chef since leaving the catering corps just after the war. They had become best of friends, and she would often meet up with his wife, Rose, for a cup of tea and piece of cake at the hotel café after work. Rose and Gordon had two children, a boy and a girl, both now grown up with families of their own.

After a month in the job, she had purchased a secondhand bicycle, which was a great asset, getting her to and from work in half the time as walking. She had managed to save a lot of her wages, especially as her mother and father refused to take any money from her. She was hoping to start looking for a place of her own before the end of the year. Life was looking rosy. Her constant sorrow was that she missed Chantal and Francine more and more as the weeks and months went by.

Arriving home from a hard day's work after picking up Lilly one Thursday, she was surprised not to see her mother in the salon. She shouted over to Jean, "Where is Mum, not skiving I hope?" she joked.

"No," said Jean, "she has a visitor, so has finished early."

Clara, intrigued as to whom the visitor could be, mounted the stairs with Lily who was now quite heavy to carry. She could hear her mother speaking to someone in the kitchen.

"Hi, Mum, it's only me," announced Clara.

As she walked into the kitchen, a tall good-looking man in what appeared to be an airman's uniform confronted her. "Ah, Clara, this is Carl Kennion."

He extended his hand to Clara. "Pleased to meet you. I have heard all about you," said Carl in an American drawl.

Clara looked at her mother, bewildered.

"I am sure I told you that we had an American airman billeted with us during the latter part of the war. Well, this is him. He lived here for about a year and a half. It was about that, wasn't it, Carl?" questioned her mother.

"Sure was, ma'am, and your mother treated me like a son, I can tell you that. Who is this little adorable girl, must be your grand-daughter, Olive, a looker just like her Granny and her Mammy, of course."

"You are always full of flattery, Carl. Now stop it and sit down and drink your tea. Clara would you like a cup?" asked her mother.

"Yes, please, Mum," said Clara, setting Lilly down on the kitchen floor amongst her toys.

"I do remember you telling me in one of your letters that you had had an American staying with you," she said to her mother. Then turning to Carl, she asked him if he was in England on air force duty, being that he was in his uniform.

Carl explained that he had returned to close down their base, and he was organizing the shipment of all the equipment at the base back to America. "Once we have cleared everything, then we will officially hand the base back to the British government, and I couldn't come all this way and not visit my *'British Mother'*, especially as she looked after me so well. Now I am sorry to say I must get back as I have a meeting at 2 p.m."

"Will you come back and have dinner with us tonight, Carl? We can catch up on what you have been doing," asked her mother.

"I would like that very much," said Carl. "I will be back then at about 6:30 this evening. Now, I must go." Saying goodbye to everyone, he was gone in a flash.

Olive took Lilly for a walk in her pushchair, and Jack went to meet his mates at the club, giving Clara the chance to cook the evening meal for them all. She had already purchased some steak and kidney to make a pie on her way home. She prepared the flaky pastry in readiness to top the pie, then cooked the meat, and made the onion gravy. The pie would be accompanied by a few boiled potatoes and some green beans. She was lucky enough to be able to get fresh vegetables at a wholesale price from the grocer who delivered to the hotel. She contemplated what to make for dessert from what was available in the cupboard that didn't use too much sugar. Sugar was still rationed, and although they received rations for four people, this didn't go very far. They usually restricted themselves to having desserts after their Sunday lunch. But today with a guest, Clara thought it would be appropriate to make something and eventually decided on fruit flan, using the last tin of mandarin oranges in the cupboard.

Carl greeted Jack with a firm handshake when he arrived and hugged Olive. Clara was busy putting Lilly to bed.

"It's like old times, me coming '*home*' for my dinner, except then I would disappear to meet the guys for a drink straight after dinner," he remembered light-heartedly.

"Come and sit down, Carl. Clara will be down in a minute, and she is going to serve the dinner, which I might add she has cooked for us, so you are in for a treat. Clara is a wonderful cook," said Olive proudly.

They all sat around the table, and Clara brought the plates and placed one in front of everyone.

"Wow, this looks and smells delicious," exclaimed Carl, thanking Clara at the same time.

Over dinner, Carl told them all about how he had gone home six months after the war ended and stayed with his parents for a short-time before going back to his squad and how he had taken the decision to sign on for a further five years.

He explained that this was his last assignment and that when he got back to the US, his five-year term would be finished.

"My parents aren't getting any younger, so I need to go back to the farm and help my father. I will turn forty this year, so I need to settle down. I only have one brother, and he has no interest in the farm. He is a big shot accountant in New York, so it is down to me to eventually take over the business."

Carl, Olive and Jack reminisced over the past, while Clara cleared the table and served the dessert.

Carl offered to help Clara with the dishes. "No, you go through to the living room and sit with Mum and Dad. I will do them," insisted Clara.

"It is the least I can do after that tasty dinner," he replied, insisting that Olive and Jack go and sit down. "I'll wash, and you dry," said Carl, "as you know where everything goes after you have dried them."

"What made you come back to England, Clara, and more importantly, where is your husband?" asked Carl.

Clara was quite surprised by the directness of his question and was trying to think of what to say. She didn't realize her mother was approaching the door when she responded.

"My husband died, so I wanted to come home to Mum and Dad. I didn't want to stay in France on my own with Lilly." Hearing her mother behind her, she instantly regretted her response. She turned around and could see the look of horror and shock on her mother's face.

"I will just make a pot of tea and take it to the living room," said her mother. "Can you bring some cups, Clara, when you have finished the dishes?"

Carl and Clara went to the other room with the cups, and all four made small talk before Carl got ready to go.

"Thank you for dinner—the best I have tasted in a long time. Now, Olive, would you mind if I took your daughter out for dinner as a thank you?" Not even waiting for a response, he looked at Clara and said, "What about tomorrow night I will pick you up at seven?"

Clara was taken aback. "Yes, thank you."

Olive gave a weak smile, saying, "Yes, of course you can, Carl. It would do her good to have a night out," with a hint of sarcasm.

When Carl had gone, her mother came into the kitchen where Clara was tidying up. "What are you playing at, saying, 'your husband is dead'?" That was a nasty thing to say. I know Didier was awful to you but to say he is dead, Clara, how could you?"

"Sorry, Mum, he caught me unawares, and I didn't know what to say. Anyway, it is not as though I am going to be seeing him again after he returns to America."

"I suppose not," said her mother, saying goodnight at the same time, but Clara could hear in her mother's voice that she was not happy.

It was work as usual the next day. Clara kept thinking about what she would wear, as she didn't have anything dressy. She could only hope that it would be an informal restaurant. She was rather looking forward to the evening. She couldn't remember the last time she had been taken to dinner. In fact, she thought to herself *'I have never been taken out to dinner'*.

When she got home from work, she made Lilly's lunch and then had a short nap with her. On waking, she ran herself a bath and washed her hair, ready for the evening. She quickly prepared Lilly's tea and got her ready for bed. Her mother had already said that she would make dinner for herself and her father, so she didn't have to worry about cooking them a meal.

It was a warm day, so Clara put on a light summer frock with a matching cardigan over her shoulders. Carl arrived promptly at seven with a box of chocolates for her mother. Carl could wrap her mother around his little finger. All it took was a present and some flattery.

Carl had a taxi waiting outside and told her he booked a table at the Royal Park for dinner.

"Oh!" she said.

"What's the matter? Is it not a good place?" he asked.

"No, it is a great place. It's just that it is where I work. I haven't actually dined in the restaurant, but I know the food is the best, especially when I cook it," she boasted with a laugh.

"Are you sure you are okay going there? We could easily choose somewhere else," he said.

"No, no that is fine. It will be good to be on the other side for a change."

They arrived at the restaurant and were shown to their table. All the staff knew her and greeted her with a look, especially the waitresses, as if to say, *'Who is this Adonis you are with?'*

The Maître D' came over to the table with copies of the menu. The restaurant had a small a la carte menu as well as the dish of the day. "It's lovely to see you in the restaurant, Clara. Makes a change from the kitchen."

"Thank you, Gerard. Yes, lovely to be served for a change. This is my friend, Carl." They shook hands, and Gerard went through the wine list and made some suggestions.

"Do you have any preference, Clara, or do you just want me to choose a wine?" asked Carl.

"Please, you choose. I am no connoisseur," she said.

Having chosen what they wanted to eat, Pat, one of the waitresses, came over to take their order, and Clara introduced her to Carl. She could just imagine the gossip in the kitchen with Pat giving a detailed account of Carl. He was a good-looking man, tall, well over six feet, with light brown hair slicked back with a side parting. In fact, he looked a bit like Cary Grant.

Clara asked Carl where he came from in America, not that she knew anything about America.

He told her he came from a place called Holly Springs in North Carolina on the east coast of America and that his parents owned a tobacco farm.

"What, you mean you grow tobacco, as in cigarettes?" she questioned.

"Yes, it is a plant. It grows about three feet tall and has big green leaves. These are picked and sent for processing. It is dried and then crushed for use in making cigarettes and cigars," explained Carl.

"Well I never," said Clara. "I hadn't really thought about where tobacco came from. I don't smoke, so it didn't enter my head that it would be a plant," said Clara.

"Now tell me about you, Clara."

Clara told him briefly about France and what she had done during the war, leaving out the resistance work, and that she had decided to come home to England when her husband had died.

"Not much to tell really. I lead a very ordinary life. I like working here though."

She explained her role and her early shift and all about the people she worked with. Whenever a member of the staff came into the restaurant, Clara would tell Carl all she knew about them.

They enjoyed a lovely meal. Clara told Carl that she had baked the rolls that were served to them in a basket with the onion soup that they had both chosen for starters and that she had that morning also prepared the soup. When the dessert trolley came around, she told him which ones she had made or that Gordon had made and she had decorated.

"I am impressed. I can see you are passionate about food," he said.

They chatted easily the whole evening. It was like they had known each other their entire lives.

"I will go and pay the bill and order a taxi," said Carl, getting up from his chair and making his way to the payments desk.

Pat rushed over. "He is a bit of all right. Where did you pick him up from?"

"Pat, really, he is a friend of my parents. He lodged with them during the war. He is only here for a few weeks, then he is going back to America," she explained.

"Well, if he needs anyone to keep him company, mention my name," she laughed and went back to clearing the tables.

Carl came back from paying and said that a taxi would be collecting them in about fifteen minutes.

"I have ordered us an aperitif. I hope you like the one I have ordered for you. Now tell me, when is your next day off?" asked Carl.

"It is Sunday and Monday. It moves forward one day each week and the week commences on a Monday, so every seven weeks I get two days off. It's my lucky week, and I am looking forward to not having to get up early for two days on the trot. Why do you ask?"

"I was wondering if I could take you and Lilly out for the day. I can borrow a car so we could go to Blackpool. I am sure Lilly would love the beach. What do you think?" asked Carl with a pleading look in his eyes.

"Don't look at me with those doleful eyes," she said playfully. "We would both be delighted to go to Blackpool. It is years since I have been there. My parents used to take us when we were little, so it would be great to go again," she said.

"That's a date, then. I will pick you up early, say ten," said Carl.

Gerard came over to their table and told them that the taxi had arrived. They got up from the seats, and Carl thanked Gerard for a lovely meal. Taking Clara's hand, he led her out of the restaurant to the taxi. It was a short drive to Clara's. Carl asked the taxi driver to wait and got out of the taxi and opened the door for Clara to get out.

"Thank you for a lovely evening, Carl."

"My pleasure," he said, leaning over and gently kissing her on the lips. "See you Sunday," he said, getting back into the taxi.

Clara's heart was skipping. '*This is stupid,*' she said to herself. I have only known him a day, and he will be gone in another two weeks.

The house was in darkness. Everyone was in bed, so she quietly made her way to her room. After checking that Lilly was asleep before getting into bed and making sure her alarm clock was set ready for the morning, she got into bed and was asleep as soon as her head hit the pillow.

Clara was ready and waiting on Sunday morning when Carl arrived to pick them up. He said a quick hello to her parents and off they went with Carl at the wheel of his borrowed car. Clara had prepared a picnic for them all to have at Blackpool. They chatted easily all the way there with Lilly sitting on Clara's knee looking out of the window. Carl excitedly told her of his plans for the future of the farm and how he was looking forward to going home to see his parents and friends.

Carl had been born on the farm in 1911, and besides his time in the Air Force, he had lived on the farm all of his life. He had left school at fifteen and joined his father working in the fields helping with the planting and harvesting of the tobacco crops. He loved working with his father, Bill, on the farm, and he had never really wanted to do anything else. However when war was declared in Europe in 1939, his father suggested that Carl enrol in the US Air Force, saying that he had a feeling that a second world war was coming. At the age of twenty-eight, he joined the air force as a junior airman. He was the eldest junior in his squad. By the time America joined World War II in 1941, he had reached the rank of senior airman.

It was years later that Carl discovered why his father had wanted him to join the air force; he felt that Carl needed to go and try another job as his brother had. His brother, Gary, on leaving school, had decided he didn't want to work on the farm instead taking an apprenticeship with a firm of accountants. Bill felt that Carl had not had the chance to try something different.

"I have had enough of the Air Force now, and I feel that I have done my stint for my country and am ready to retire and go and help my father. He is not getting any younger, he will be sixty-six on his next birthday, and there is no one else but me to eventually take over. My brother has his life in New York, and he is not interested in farming, so it's down to me and I am looking forward to working with my Pa again."

It took them an hour to reach Blackpool, and after parking the car, they made their way down to the promenade. They walked a bit with Carl carrying Lilly until they found a suitable place to sit. Carl paid for two deckchairs, and he laid a rug down on the sand for Lilly to sit on. But, Lilly had no intention of sitting on the rug. She was off crawling towards another little girl whose father was making her sandcastles from a bucket. This little girl was taking great delight in destroying the sandcastles as soon as her father had upended the bucket. Lilly watched for a few minutes and then joined in.

"I had better go and buy a bucket and spade. That guy will never be able to keep up with the sandcastles with two little girls smashing them before he has a chance to make them," said Carl.

There were a lot of small tourist shops selling buckets and spades. Carl came back laden with things and soon got friendly with the little girl's father who introduced himself as Barry. Between them, they built a huge castle for the girls and a sand boat for them to sit in while Clara sat and relaxed.

Clara began setting out the picnic just as the mother of the little girl arrived with a picnic basket. She shouted hello and came over and introduced herself as Lucy. "I have been for a walk and thought I had better get back and feed those two," she said, pointing to her husband and little girl whose name, Lucy said, was Patricia. "But we call her Patty. Why don't we share the picnic? The girls seem to be playing well together."

Clara agreed, and Lucy fetched her rug and placed it next to Clara's. When everything was ready, they shouted over to the men.

They all tucked into their food, the girls getting more sand than sandwich in their mouths, even though each mother was trying to keep the sand away. They finished their picnic and packed the remainder back into their baskets.

"It has been lovely meeting you," said Lucy, "but unfortunately we have to go."

"It's been a pleasure meeting you as well and so good that Lilly had a little friend to play with," said Clara, waving them goodbye.

Carl and Clara lay facing each other on the sand with Lilly between them, who was soon asleep.

Carl, looking into Clara's eyes, said, "I think I love you, Clara. I have never felt this way about anyone before. I know I have only just met you, but I can't help how I feel, and this little one ..." he said, pointing to Lilly, "I just adore."

Clara was stunned by this declaration. "Carl, you go home in what ten days? I don't think there is any future in our relationship. There is no way you could come and live here, and you have your parents to think of as well as the farm."

"I know all that, and I thought long and hard before telling you how I feel, but you haven't said how you feel about me, is it all one-sided?" said Carl, looking a bit down-hearted.

"I don't know if I love you, Carl, but in saying that, I do have strong feelings for you, which has surprised me, I feel like I have known you for years, not just a few days," said Clara.

"Then marry me, Clara. Come to America with me."

"What? You can't be serious. What would your parents say, and more to the point, what would my parents say?" said Clara, scared now. How could she marry him? She was still married to Didier.

Carl took her in his arms, almost crushing Lilly in between them and kissed her long and deep.

"Will you think about it, Clara? I will come and see you on Tuesday evening, perhaps take you for a drive, and you can give me an answer then. Promise me you will think about it."

"Yes, I will think about it, and I promise I will give you an answer on Tuesday. Remember I have to go to work early on Wednesday morning, so I don't want to be out late."

They packed all their things away and made their way to the car. Carl chatted all the way home about North Carolina and the relaxed way of life, trying not to influence her in any way but at the same time trying to paint a picture of the life she could have in America.

By the time they reached Clara's house, Lilly was getting grouchy, as she was hungry and tired. Clara kissed Carl goodbye and thanked him for a lovely day. "No, don't thank me, thank you for making it a lovely day for me, and I will see you Tuesday," he said.

CHAPTER 24

The next couple of days were dreadful for Clara. One minute she would be thinking the answer would have to be no and the next yes. She tried weighing up the pros and cons. *'If I went,'* she thought, *'I would have a new life and a new beginning. On the other hand, I would never see Chantal and Francine again.'*

'If I stay, then life could be a struggle. I would have to carry on working like I am doing now. Would I ever be able to save enough to get my own home, and then when I do, get my own home? How will I manage with Lilly? I can't take her around to my mother's at four in the morning, and what happens when she goes to school? How would I take her if I have to go to work?'

These things went around and around in her head. What if this happens and what if that happens? She hardly slept, thinking up all sorts of scenarios.

Tuesday came around all too soon. She made her way to work still tired after not sleeping very well. Gordon was concerned. "What's the matter, Clara? You look like you have the weight of the world on your shoulders," he said.

"Sorry, I am just tired. I didn't sleep very well," responded Clara.

"If you want to talk, I am always hear to listen," he said.

"Thank you, Gordon. You are a good friend," she said, getting back to her work.

Pat had just finished the breakfast shift and came through to the kitchen for a coffee. On seeing Clara, she explained, "Clara, you look like shit. Whatever is the matter? Come and have your break now and sit with me and tell me all about it?"

Clara sat down with her.

"Now tell me what is worrying you. I hope that American guy is not messing you about because I can tell you a few stories about the GIs that were here during the war," said Pat and continued to tell her about one of her friends that was left pregnant by one American who turned out to be married. He returned home, and she never heard from him again. She tried every way she could think of to get in touch with him, and in the end, all she got was a message from his regimental officer just stating that he was married and had made a mistake. There was another who promised marriage and that he would send her a ticket to America, but she never heard from him again. There was one happy ending with another friend. The GI did come back and marry her, and they now lived in Chicago.

"Take care, Clara. They make all these promises just to get your knickers down."

"Pat, you shouldn't be so crude. Anyway, it's not quite like that. He hasn't tried anything on with me, but he has asked me to marry him. I don't know what to do. I really like him, but I am not sure if I love him, but it is something pretty close. Can I tell you something in strict confidence?" asked Clara.

"Of course, you can. I know I sometimes appear to be a gossip and girl about town, but in reality, after my fiancé was killed in the war, I have not looked at another man. Anyone I have ever met doesn't come anywhere near as kind and lovely as he was. I would love to meet someone who I could settle down with and have children, but I don't think I ever will, as I have set my sights so high. Anyway, enough about myself! Let me try and help you solve your dilemma," Pat said, reaching out for Clara's hand in reassurance.

"I had a terrible marriage. My husband would drink too much and beat me up, so when I couldn't take anymore, I ran away with Lilly," explained Clara.

"Your husband is still alive?" exclaimed Pat.

"Yes, so now you can see my problem."

"Oh my God! Clara, you can't possibly marry him, not if you're still married. Couldn't you quickly get a divorce?" asked Pat.

"No, I don't think so. The only grounds I have is cruelty, and from what I understand, it is really difficult to prove. You need all sorts of evidence. I only saw a doctor once, and he didn't really make any comments. The only way I could get a divorce would be for him to divorce me on the ground of desertion, but I am not going to ask, as he would then know where I am, and he might try and get Lilly from me," explained Clara.

"I don't know what to say," said Pat.

"I keep thinking that Carl could offer me a better life. I wouldn't have to work so hard, and I could spend time with Lilly. Whereas, if I stay, my life would continue as it is now and only get more difficult as Lilly gets older. I might have to pay for someone to look after her while I work, and then would I ever be able to afford a place of my own, or if I did it, would it be a struggle?" said Clara.

"Why don't you …," said Pat, "say you will go to America with him but say you don't want to get married again just yet? You could even say that you are willing to change your name to his and even change Lilly's to his if he wants. You could also say that you are prepared to tell his parents that you are married, as I am sure they wouldn't approve of you living together. Then if things don't work out, you could just walk away," suggested Pat.

"Actually, that is not a bad idea. I hadn't thought of that, and at least that way I wouldn't be a bigamist," said Clara, trying to sound light-hearted.

"Thank you, Pat, for listening to me. Even talking to you has helped me feel a bit better. Now my break should have finished five minutes ago. I can see the chef look our way," said Clara, getting up from the table.

"When are you giving him your answer?" asked Pat, taking the coffee cups to be washed.

"Tonight," said Clara.

"Tell me tomorrow how you get on. Good luck," said Pat, making her way to the dining room. Returning home, her thoughts were on how to face her mother and avoid her concerns.

Clara had already asked her mother to look after Lilly, as Carl had asked her out.

"I am really worried about you, Clara. You have not been yourself all weekend. Are you sure there is nothing I can help with?"

"No, Mum, honestly I am fine. I will chat with you when I get home. I won't be late. I've got work in the morning. I have had a lot to think about, but hopefully this will all be resolved tonight. I must go. That is Carl now," she said, getting ready to go downstairs.

Carl was just about to ring the doorbell when Clara opened the door. "Hi, honey," he said, giving her a kiss. Clara's heart leapt as she kissed him back.

"Let's go. I thought we could get some fish and chips and then sit in the park and eat them, not very romantic I'm afraid, but I know you need to get to bed early," said Carl as he drove in the direction of the chippy.

They sat on a park bench with their fish and chips. "I love fish and chips from the chippy. There is nothing more comforting, and it's something I really missed when I was in France," said Clara, trying to avoid the inevitable.

"Have you made your decision, Clara, as I go back on Sunday?" asked Carl.

"Sunday!" exclaimed Clara. "I thought you had another ten days here."

"Unfortunately, the handover of the barracks is almost completed. I tried to delay it, but my commander contacted me this morning to say all the handover papers will be signed on Friday and that a cargo plane is coming on Saturday to be loaded with the stuff that is going back to America. I'll have to go back on the plane as well," explained Carl.

"But that only gives us five day!"

"Four, I will be leaving first thing on Sunday. Clara, please what is your answer? We have so little time together?" pleaded Carl.

"I have thought of nothing else since Sunday and my answer is yes and no. I can't marry you, Carl—"

"Clara, please, why not?"

"Carl, please let me finish. I was going to say I can't marry you, but I will come to America and be your wife but in name only. I have my reasons but please don't ask me what they are. Perhaps in the future, I will explain, but for now my answer is yes."

"Oh my God, Clara, I thought you were going to say no. If you have your reasons, then I will respect those. But my parents would never accept us living together. They are strict members of the Anglican Church," said Carl.

"That is why I said I would be your wife in name only. I am willing to change my name and Lilly's to yours, and we can pretend to be married."

"That won't work. Even if I say to my parents that we got married here, they will still want the marriage confirmed in the Anglican Church." Carl was getting agitated while Clara tried to stay calm.

"What would the church confirmation be? Would it be something like a blessing? They can't marry us again if we say we are already married. We could go along with a blessing."

Carl suddenly got up from the bench and turned to Clara. She flinched and automatically put her hands up to her head to protect herself. "Clara, what are you doing? Surely you didn't think I was going to hit you?" said Carl with a horrified look on his face.

"No, no," she said as she started to cry softly. "I am so sorry, Carl, it is just—"

"You need to tell me what is going on, as I don't understand your reaction."

"I didn't want to tell you this, but now I realize I can't start a married life with you based on lies."

Thinking now she had lost him forever, Clara with a heavy heart proceeded to tell him everything that happened to her in her marriage to Didier, the beatings, the verbal abuse and how she had run away and left Chantal and Francine behind.

"I will understand if you don't want anything else to do with me, Carl. When I told you Didier was dead, I didn't think that I would be seeing you again after that first meeting, so to me it didn't matter. But now everything is different. I would never be able to get a divorce from him, so that is why I suggested we pretend to get married. I am so sorry. Perhaps you should take me home now and we just say goodbye for good."

Clara got up, ready to leave, but Carl caught her elbow and turned her to face him.

"I can't say that I am not shocked by what you have told me, but at least you have been honest and told me the truth, and I can understand how you feel. But, Clara, I love you, and as I told you before, I have never felt like this for anyone. So my offer still stands." He then went down on one knee and said, "Will you marry me?"

"Yes," she said. "I will."

They held each other tightly, kissing and crying at the same time.

"I promise I will make both you and Lilly very happy. Now, let's get you home. Otherwise, you will be cranky in the morning," he said playfully.

Clara pretended to hit him on the arm. "Cheek, I am never grouchy."

He drove her home and promised to meet her from work the next day to discuss the arrangements to get her to America.

Her mother was making a cup of tea in the kitchen when Clara arrived home with a big smile on her face. She kissed and hugged her mother.

"Well, it's good to see you happy. You have looked so miserable the last couple of days. Now tell me, why the big smile?"

Clara sat down at the table with her mother and told her everything that happened and how Carl had asked her to marry him and how she had accepted and that her and Lilly were going to America to start a new life with Carl.

"I am pleased you told him the truth about Didier. You can't start married life on lies. They will only surface at some time in the future. Anyway, how can you marry him?" asked her mother.

"We won't marry. We will just pretend to his parents that we are married, and we will arrange to change my surname and Lilly to his. I must go to bed now. Otherwise, I will never get up in the morning." She kissed her mother goodnight and went to bed.

As promised, Carl was waiting outside the hotel when she finished work. She got in the car, and he kissed her on the lips. "Hello, wife-to-be."

"Hello, husband-to-be." They laughed in unison as he drove off.

"I only have an hour, then I need to be back at the barracks."

"I have to pick Lilly up from Doreen, so I don't have much time either. Perhaps, we can just sit in the café by the station and have a sandwich," suggested Clara.

They found a table and placed their order. Carl explained his plan. "I am going to purchase both of you a boat ticket to New York when I get back to America. Then, I am going to purchase a train ticket to get you from New York to North Carolina. It will be quite a long trip for you both, but to put you on a plane would be too expensive. Is that okay?"

"Of course, it is. It will be an adventure. As long as I know that you are waiting at the other end, what does it matter which way we go?"

They chatted a bit more before Carl said he had to get back to the barracks.

"Why don't you come to dinner tomorrow night, and you can tell my parents? I have already told my mum, but I am sure they would like to hear it from you," she suggested.

"Yes, that would be lovely. Then we can go out on our own on Friday and Saturday before I leave on Sunday," he said.

He dropped her off at Doreen's, kissed her goodbye, and said, "See you tomorrow."

The next few days flew past them. Carl went to dinner and spoke to Clara's parents. They were happy for them but at the same time concerned. Olive told Jack later that evening that she hoped he would send tickets and not just go back and leave Clara waiting.

Jack said he felt that Carl was genuine. "After all, he did spend a long time with us, and we had no concerns then. He was always polite and considerate."

Clara was in tears on Saturday night when they said goodbye, clinging onto him before he drove off, promising to write.

The following week dragged by. A postcard arrived ten days after Carl had left. It was a short message, saying that he had arrived back in Boston and would be leaving for North Carolina in the next couple of days, finishing off with, '*I love you, Carl xxx*'.

The only person she had told at work of her move to America was Pat. She didn't want anyone to know for fear that she could lose her job if they thought she was leaving. So any excitement or apprehension, she had to keep to herself.

It was another three weeks before a bigger envelope arrived for her with an American stamp. She grabbed the envelope and quickly tore it open, reading the three-page letter first. It contained so much information she could hardly take it all in. On the last page, Carl had written that his parents were delighted that he had at last met someone to settle down with and couldn't wait to meet her and Lilly. She read and re-read the letter three times before taking in the travel arrangements. She would be leaving in six weeks. Carl said that he had left plenty of time for Clara to give in her notice to the hotel and get her passport.

'But I am sure you already have one. I forgot to ask you about this,' he wrote. The envelope included all the tickets for her and Lilly.

The next day, Clara gave the chef a month's notice. Everyone was sad that she was leaving. Mr. Lewis said that if things didn't work out that she could come back and that she was an asset they were sorry to be losing.

Time went by quickly. It was Lilly's first birthday three weeks before she was to leave. Olive arranged a little party for her the day after her birthday date, as it was a Sunday. She invited Doreen and May, and Clara invited Gordon, Rose and Pat. Clara baked her a cake in the shape of a teddy bear with a number '1' on it. Pat had bought a bottle of sparkling wine, and the adults toasted Lilly and sang happy birthday to her. Lilly ended up with more cake on her face and down the front of her new dress than in her mouth, but she smacked her lips in approval. It was a bittersweet day, as it was almost a goodbye party as well, but everyone had a good time.

CHAPTER 25

For Olive, Clara's departure date arrived much too soon. She hugged Lilly far too tightly for Lilly's liking, as she struggled to free herself. It was not soon enough for Clara. Her father was to drive her to the docks in Liverpool. Clara had already said goodbye to everyone at the hotel who had presented her with a gift of a silver necklace, and she promised to write as soon as she arrived.

Doreen and May wished her good luck. "I hope it turns out well for you, Clara. You deserve to be happy, write, and tell us how you are getting on." They kissed both Clara and Lilly goodbye.

Clara hugged her crying mother and pried Lilly away from her. "I promise I will write Mum as soon as I arrive."

"Good luck, Clara, and look after my little one. I will miss her and, of course, you so much."

Her father handed her luggage over to a porter at the dock and kissed them both goodbye. "Look after yourself, my dear, and take good care of my little princess," said her down-hearted father as he left her and got in his car and drove away.

Clara was excited and apprehensive at the same time. The ship, the MV Georgic, was huge. A porter helped her to the check-in desk and then handed over her luggage to another porter in readiness for boarding. Clara waited patiently in the queue to board. There were hundreds of passengers milling around her. A girl next to her started cooing and making faces at Lilly who was getting a bit unsettled in her pushchair. Clara turned around to face the girl, who she guessed was in her early twenties, slight with short, dark auburn hair and about the same height as Clara.

"Sorry," said the girl in a strong Irish accent. "I was trying to distract your daughter. I could see she was getting restless."

"That's okay," said Clara. "She doesn't like being restrained in her pushchair. She wants to get out. Hopefully, it won't be long before we board. My name is Clara by the way."

"I'm Niamph Flynn. Are you going to New York?"

"Initially, yes, but only for a night, then I am getting a train to North Carolina," replied Clara.

The queue started to move slowly forward. The porter helped Clara with the pushchair up the ramp, and a steward examined her tickets and directed her to her cabin. Niamph was just behind her.

"Where is your cabin?" Clara asked.

"It is in third class. I am sharing with some other people. It was the cheapest I could get," responded Niamph.

Clara felt a bit sorry for her and said, "Why don't you go and find your cabin and drop your luggage and then come and find me? I am in cabin 401B," said Clara, looking at her boarding card. "Then, we could go and explore together."

"That would be grand," said Niamph. "I will see you soon." She went in the direction given to her by the steward.

It took Clara some time to find her cabin after taking a few wrong turns. A steward arrived a short time later with her luggage. It was a compact cabin with two single beds. She was unsure how she was going to keep Lilly in the bed, but they both had a rail presumably to stop anyone from falling out if the weather got too rough, which Clara thought was not very comforting. The voyage was going to take three days to get to New York. She unpacked her cases and stowed them away under the beds.

Niamph knocked on the cabin door, and Clara let her in. "Quick! The ship is about to sail. Let's go up top and watch it leave," announced Niamph.

They quickly found their way to the top, taking it in turns to carry Lilly. They fought their way forward to find a space on the railings. The decks were crowded with people waving goodbye. Clara and Niamph waved as well but not to anyone in particular. They watched the dock slowly disappear and then made their way below deck.

"Let's find the canteen. I am starving," said Niamph.

They walked around and around several of the upper decks. On passing the formal dining room, Niamph stated, "I don't think you will see me in there, not on my budget."

"You're right, and I don't think Lilly will be welcome in there," said Clara.

They soon found the canteen that was self-service. Carl had sent Clara vouchers that could be used in exchange for meals for both her and Lilly. They walked up and down to see what was available. Clara could see that Niamph was looking at the prices with a frown on her face.

"Let's find a table first, and then decide what we will have," suggested Clara.

At the table, Clara questioned Niamph about her finances.

"I don't have much money at all, but I can afford one dish. I will just have to be careful and keep to a budget. I want to keep some of my money for when I arrive in New York," she said.

"Tell you what, I have vouchers for me and Lilly, and Lilly is not going to eat very much. Why don't you take Lilly's voucher, and we will give her something from each of our plates? We will need to choose something that is easy for her to eat," suggested Clara.

"Thank you, Clara, that is really kind of you, but you don't have to do that. After all, you have only just met me," said Niamph.

"Don't be silly, let's find out what the vouchers get us," said Clara.

They went over to the front desk and asked about the vouchers. The lady explained that there was a voucher for each of the three days on board and that entitled them to a breakfast, lunch and dinner at any of the restaurants on board. She said that the voucher would be marked each time it was used.

"Does that mean we can go to the formal dining room if we want?" asked Clara.

"Yes, the voucher entitles you to eat anywhere on this deck, but not the first-class deck," replied the lady.

Niamph then asked the lady about third-class passengers with no vouchers.

"In that case," the lady informed her, "you need to go to the concierge desk and purchase food vouchers of your choice."

"That's settled. Let's go and choose what we are going to eat," said Clara.

Clara asked the waitress for a high chair for Lilly and settled her in the chair with a bread roll to chew on while she and Niamph went to get their food. They went back to the table with their plates of food, a drink and an extra dish for Lilly.

Niamph took great delight in helping feed Lilly and encouraging her to drink from a cup, so much so her own food nearly went cold but for Clara's intervention.

After dinner, they walked back to Clara's cabin. "I need to get Lilly ready for bed. She is getting tired," said Clara.

"I will go back to my cabin and see you in the morning," said Niamph.

"No, don't go yet. Come in and keep me company for a bit. It is still early," said Clara.

The cabin shared a bathroom with two other cabins. As it was early, no one else was using the bathroom, so Clara was able to give Lilly a bath.

"Please, Clara, can I give Lilly her bath?" begged Niamph.

"Yes, if you want to, but you might get as wet as Lilly. She likes to splash a lot."

Niamph gave Lilly her bath and played splashing with her until the water was getting too cold to continue. She wrapped Lilly in a big towel and took her back to the cabin. Clara passed her Lilly's nappy and nightgown, and Niamph kissed the little girl goodnight, wishing that it were Bernadette. Together, they tucked Lilly up tightly in one of the beds.

Lilly was soon sound asleep.

Clara was intrigued by Niamph's interaction with Lilly, which appeared to be more than just a liking for children.

"Do you have any children, Niamph?" asked Clara. "You seemed to enjoy taking care of Lilly." Niamph tried to answer but was too choked up to speak. Tears began welling up in her eyes.

"Sorry, Niamph. I didn't mean to upset you. Are you okay? Come and sit down," said Clara, quite concerned by Niamph's reaction.

Niamph composed herself as she sat down on the bed. Clara put her arm around her shoulders and tried to comfort her. Silent tears slowly fell down Niamph's cheeks.

"Please don't cry."

Niamph started to speak with a bit of a croak at first. She told Clara that she had a little girl almost the same age as Lilly.

"Where is she?" asked Clara.

"She was adopted by an American couple when she was six weeks old. All I have left of my Bernadette is a bonnet and a photo," explained Niamph.

"I don't understand. Why did you let her be adopted? Couldn't your family have helped you?" asked Clara.

"I come from a very strict Catholic family, and having a baby outside of marriage is a mortal sin and a disgrace on the family. I had no option but to let her go," explained Niamph.

"I still don't really understand. Tell me what happened, and why didn't the father marry you?" questioned Clara.

"I will have to start at the beginning for you to understand the end," explained Niamph.

"I am one of seven children brought up on a farm in a small village in County Westmeath in Ireland. I have three older brothers, all married with children of their own. Two of them still work with my father on the farm. The other one now lives in Dublin. I have an older sister, Nula, who is also married and lives with her husband and two children in a town not far from Dublin. Then I have a younger sister who works as a shop assistant in a nearby town and finally a much younger brother who has Downs Syndrome named Seamus.

"We all went to the village school. My brothers missed a lot of school, as they had to help out at the farm, and my elder sister wasn't interested in school and left at fourteen. But I loved school. I liked learning. So when I reached fourteen, the local priest got me a scholarship to go to high school. My parents weren't happy. They hated '*charity*' as they called it.

"The priests in Ireland are like God—what they say goes—so my parents couldn't object to me going to high school.

"My sister Nula resented me because I had a smart uniform and I was excused from chores to do my homework, whereas she had to look after Seamus and work on the farm that she hated. I left school at eighteen, and the priest arranged a post for me at the local primary school as a teaching assistant. I enjoyed nothing more than teaching the little ones to read and write and getting paid for it. I was allowed to keep a small amount of my wages with the rest going to my mother, which I never resented.

"I had been at the school for four years during which time I had been promoted from teaching assistant to a qualified teacher, when a new headmaster was appointed. Liam Ryan was his name, and he was thirty-five years old and married with two children to a snooty woman who thought she was better than anyone else just because her husband was the headmaster.

"Anyway, at first, I took no notice of his comments. ... you know the sort ... *'you look nice today, Miss Flynn'* or *'I like a well-rounded woman, Miss Flynn.'* Then he asked me to stay after school one day to help with some marking. He sat a bit too close to me, especially for a married man. When we had finished the marking, he told me he found me very attractive and said his wife was no longer interested in him as a husband. Like a fool when he tried to kiss me, I let him.

"To begin with, it was just kissing and touching, but after a few months, he convinced me to sleep with him. Of course, the inevitable happened. It was three months before I faced up to the fact that I was pregnant, and it was four months before I told him. The next thing I know I am called before the school governors and sacked. I tried speaking to him, and I even sent a letter, but he just ignored me. I did think of going to see his wife but couldn't bring myself to do it. My mother had guessed that I was pregnant and told my dad. She said I had brought disgrace on the family and threw me out.

"I didn't know what to do. I went to Nula's. She just laughed and said, '*Well, well little miss perfect is up the duff,*' and told me to get lost. Then, I went to the priest, and he arranged for me to enter a convent that looked after unmarried mothers. It was horrible. The sisters ran a laundry service, and all the girls worked for their keep. It was hard, sweaty work, and you had to work until you went into labour. We weren't allowed to talk to each other while working or at meal times. It was only in our dormitory at night that we could talk in whispers.

"When your baby was born, you had three weeks off to care for the baby and recover. Unfortunately or fortunately, depending on how you look at it, I had to have a caesarean section, so I wasn't able to work for almost six weeks. I had all this time with my beautiful Bernadette. I always knew she was going to be adopted. There was no way I could keep her, but nobody prepares you for the overwhelming love you have for your baby when it is born. After looking after her for six weeks, it was like my heart had been ripped out of me when they took her away.

"I thought I would be able to leave straight away but the Mother Superior informed me that I had to pay them for my keep for the six weeks I wasn't able to work. I was kept a virtual prisoner until I had paid them back. But it was a vicious circle. They paid me a small wage, and then I had to pay for my keep and pay them back what I owed them. It took me nine months before I could leave with just enough money to get me to England and rent digs until I got a job. The priest in Ireland gave me a reference and told me to go to a priest in Liverpool who would help me, and he did. I am going to a Catholic convent school in New York to teach there. … and here I am," finished Niamph.

Clara was horrified at the whole story and how people could be treated so badly. She asked Niamph if she would like to share her cabin for the rest of the journey. "I was going to share with Lilly anyway. I am a bit frightened that she will fall out of bed, so this other bed is yours if you want it."

"You don't need to ask me twice," said Niamph and left to retrieve her luggage.

The rest of the voyage passed in a flash. They became firm friends. Each night, they would sit in the cabin and tell each other their life story. Clara was astonished at the poverty in Ireland, and Niamph was speechless at Clara's bravery not only during the war but also at her decision to leave Didier and her two daughters. They discussed the future and how they would both like to get their daughters back. They cried together and laughed together.

All too soon, they arrived in New York. They had packed the night before and were up on the deck to watch the ship sail into the docks. Clara was being met by Carl's younger brother, Gary, who lived in New York. She would stay with him and his wife overnight. Niamph was to make her way to the convent where she was to work.

They exchanged addresses and promised to write to each other. Both crying, they hugged each other goodbye. Niamph hugged and kissed Lilly, even though Lilly vocally objected. Going through immigration, they lost sight of each other amongst the milling crowds.

Clara, struggling with suitcases and the pushchair, made her way to the exit and instantly saw her name written in large letters on a card held by a man who bore a remarkable resemblance to Carl.

"Hello, I'm Clara."

"Hi, I'm Gary. Lovely to meet the gal that has finally hooked my big brother," said Gary, holding her by the shoulders and planting a kiss on each cheek, much to the surprise of Clara, as she thought it was only the French who adopted this custom.

"And this little gal must be Lilly," he said, tickling Lilly under the chin.

"My driver is waiting over there," Gary said, pointing to a row of cars on the road next to the dockside. He took her cases, and she followed him to a posh, black shiny sedan car.

The driver quickly got out, took her cases and the pushchair, and placed them in the boot.

"As you are only in New York for tonight, I thought you might like to take a drive around the city to see some of the sights before we go to the apartment. Would you like that?" asked Gary.

"Yes, I would love that. Thank you and thank you for meeting me and letting me stay with you tonight. I'm looking forward to meeting your wife and children," said Clara.

The driver drove over the Brooklyn Bridge and proceeded down 4th Avenue, passing the Empire State Building and then on to Times Square, which she almost missed, expecting a square like those in France, but it appeared to be merely a junction with a huge billboard above advertising a film called *The Day Earth Stood Still*.

Then, they drove over the Hudson River to see the Statue of Liberty before making their way to Newark where Gary lived. Clara was mesmerized by the New York buildings, the billboards and the number of cars on the road compared to England.

The driver dropped them outside of the apartment block where they were met by a doorman. "Good evening, Mr. Kennion," he said, opening the door for them.

The apartment was on the fifth floor, and Clara couldn't quite believe her eyes as she walked into the hallway, which was the biggest hallway she had ever seen. Gary led her through to the kitchen to meet his wife, Helen. Helen was tall, about five feet, ten inches, but taller in her three-inch high heels, with flowing blonde hair. She was an attractive woman, not beautiful, but extremely attractive with sharp features.

She welcomed Clara, warmly shaking her hand and bending down to kiss her on the cheek. "Welcome to our home and our family. Come and meet the boys. They are watching television in the den."

Clara, still holding Lilly, followed Helen to find the two boys, Henry, aged twelve, and Kevin, aged nine, who were sitting on the floor watching a small black and white television.

"Switch that off, boys, and come and say hello to your Auntie Clara and cousin Lilly from England."

They politely came over and said hello.

"What time is dinner, Mom? I am starving," said Henry.

"Ten minutes. Now go and wash your hands."

"Boys," Helen said to Clara. "They are always hungry."

"To tell you the truth, there are all girls in our family. I have not had much experience with boys," said Clara.

Helen led Clara through to the dining room, another large stunning room with a round dining table surrounded by ten chairs. Above the table was a staggeringly bright crystal chandelier. The meal was served by a lady named Rosa, whom, Helen explained, looked after the apartment and the boys for her with the assistance of a daily help. The boys chatted non-stop about their day throughout the meal, allowing Clara to enjoy the meal and tend to Lilly.

Gary told Clara that Helen worked as a realty lawyer in the city and that he was an accountant for a family business. "So you can see why we need Rosa, and this is the only time of the day we can catch up with the boys. Hence, the reason they don't shut up."

Clara laughed at this and sadly started thinking that she would miss this with her little girls.

Clara deduced that between them they earned a great deal of money. It explained the beautiful apartment and servants and the enormous diamond ring that Helen was wearing.

After dinner, Clara excused herself so that she could put Lilly to bed. Rosa had prepared a room for them that included a cot, which she informed Clara she had rescued from the garage. Once Lilly was asleep, she joined the family in the living area, another stunning room furnished with three large comfortable sofas. It was like something out of a magazine with a big, low coffee table sitting on a large fluffy rug. The room was subtly lit with standard lamps and walls that were covered in various works of art. Rosa served them coffee while Gary took the boys to bed.

"Tell me how you managed to snag that brother-in-law of mine. I thought he was a confirmed bachelor. You can imagine our surprise when he contacted us and asked us to meet you from the ship and look after you and that you had a one-year old daughter," exclaimed Helen.

Clara laughed at this. "Yes, I can imagine how surprised you would be. Carl was billeted with my parents during the war and while he was in England recently, he went to visit them and that is when I met him."

"Oh! So why didn't you meet him during the war?" Helen asked.

"I was in France. I lived with my aunt and uncle before the war, and when war broke out, I wasn't able to get back."

"What happened to Lilly's father? I am sorry, Clara, I shouldn't be asking you all these questions," said Helen just as Gary came into the room.

"Helen is not interrogating you, is she? I know what she is like. She is so nosey and likes to know everything about everyone she meets. Anyway, I think it is about time we all went to bed. You have an early start, Clara. You need to be at the train station well before the train leaves at ten in the morning," said Gary.

Clara was pleased that she was leaving the next morning. She felt uncomfortable in the apartment. She felt it was more of a show house than a home. Even though it was plush, it didn't have a warm feeling to it.

Helen was up and about early the next morning. She knocked on Clara's door to say goodbye. "I have to be at work early. It has been lovely meeting you, and I'll see you at Thanksgiving."

Clara thanked her for letting her stay the night and said she looked forward to seeing her again.

Clara made her way to the kitchen for breakfast. The boys were getting ready for school.

"Hurry up, boys. Jack is waiting for you," said Gary.

Jack was the driver who she had met the day before, and he obviously took the boys to school.

'What a luxury,' thought Clara, thinking of the time when she had to walk to school every day.

"Jack will take the boys to school then come back for us," said Gary. "We have about an hour for breakfast. That should give us plenty of time."

After breakfast, they arrived at Grand Central Station. Jack had dropped them off outside and was helping Gary get their luggage when she noticed the remarkable building. It was a formidable building. Above the entrance was a large clock with statues of what looked like male angels above. Inside, the building was magnificent, dominated with huge windows on all sides and large supporting pillars. Gary went to find out which platform her train was departing from, leaving Clara to admire the interior of the station.

He led her to the platform where the train was waiting to depart. He helped her find her carriage, kissing her goodbye just as the guard blew the whistle. "Have a good trip and see you at Thanksgiving," Gary said, jumping out of the train and slamming the door.

Clara put her head out of the window. "Thank you, Gary, for everything. I will tell your brother how attentive you have been." She waved him goodbye.

The train journey was going to take about ten hours. Lilly was irritable, and Clara suspected that she was teething again. She had a carriage to herself for which she was grateful, as she was able to let Lilly sit on the floor and play, and, at least, she would not disturb any other passengers with her grizzling. Clara had brought a book with her, which she thought she would finish on the ship, but as it was, she didn't read a page, as she had had Niamph to chat to.

The train had passed out of New York with magnificent views of the Hudson River through to Philadelphia and then on to Washington where the train stopped for fifteen minutes. They passed lots of built up areas and then a lot of flat, open spaces where she could see a few houses in the distance. The train stations were both huge and dirty from all the steam or small, deserted stations. After Washington, the landscape became a bit more interesting with views of woodlands and tree-covered hilled areas. There was another fifteen-minute stop in Richmond. The landscapes from the train were nothing like Clara had ever seen before and travelling over the Lee River was breathtaking.

When it began to get dark, she couldn't see anything other than a few lights in the distance. It wasn't until they went through bigger towns that she could see a bit more.

She managed to buy some food and drinks from the refreshment trolley that passed through the train, avoiding the necessity to go in search of the dining carriage. She slept for a short time and tried to keep Lilly amused, which was quite a challenge in a small space. She knew she must be near her destination, as it was nearly eight o'clock.

She heard the guardsman call, "Raleigh, next stop Raleigh."

She asked the porter for assistance with her luggage and the pushchair and somehow managed to get off the train with a struggling Lilly in her arms. She looked up, and there was Carl, impossibly more handsome than she remembered. She could have cried with relief. She wanted to run into his arms, but a protesting Lilly prevented her.

"Clara," he said, looking into her eyes and grabbing her as closely as he could, trying to kiss her while Lilly protested even more with a loud scream.

"Come here, little lady," he said, taking hold of Lilly, "and let me kiss your mommy."

"The car is just over there in the car park. Here, you take Lilly, and I will take the rest of your stuff,' he said, leading her towards the car.

"How was the journey?"

"Long, and Lilly was restless nearly all the time, but we are here now, so this is the best bit."

Carl opened the car door for her, went around the other side, and got in the driver's seat.

"I have missed you," he said, kissing her again.

"And I have missed you," said Clara with a longing deep in her stomach.

"Mother has been on tenterhooks, waiting for you to arrive. She has been fussing about all day, making sure everything is perfect for you. She has a meal waiting for you, and then she was worried about what you would eat being British. I tried to tell her that you will eat whatever she cooked and that you weren't from another planet, but she still fussed like a mother hen."

Clara laughed at this analogy.

"I hope she hasn't gone to too much trouble, but I am starving. I only had snacks on the train because Lilly was in such a fractious mood I didn't want to take her to the dining car. Her gums are obviously hurting her," said Clara.

It was about a thirty-minute drive. Clara couldn't see much, as it was very dark. It was not until he turned off the road onto a rough lane and she could see lights in the distance that she realized that they had arrived.

He pulled up outside a big two-story building with a veranda going along the front of the building. His parent on hearing the car was waiting on the steps leading up to the front door.

His mother ran over to the car and opened the door. "Oh! My dear! I am so pleased you are here safe and sound. Here, give me the baby."

Clara handed Lilly over and got out of the car. Carl's father came over to her and put his arms around her in a bear hug before Carl had time to get out of the car and make the introductions.

"Let's get you both inside where I can see you properly," said his mother.

CHAPTER 26

Carl had spent an anxious few weeks on arriving home after being away for such a long time. Firstly, having to tell his parents that he had married stressed him out, which in itself was a lie and he didn't like not telling his parents the truth but wanted to protect Clara. Then secondly, telling them she had a child unnerved him. However, Carl felt it was the right time to return to the farm. When he started work again on the farm, Carl realized how much he had missed it and how ready he was to eventually take over the running of the farm from his father.

As it turned out, he worried unnecessarily as his parents were delighted for him and eagerly awaited Clara and Lilly's arrival, as much as he did.

"Now, my dear, I am Hannah, and this is William, but we call him Bill. Carl, take this little lady so I can welcome Clara properly," said his mother as she came over to her, taking hold of both her hands and kissing her on the cheek. "I am delighted to meet you and welcome you to our home. I hope you will both be happy here."

"Thank you. It's lovely to meet you both as well. I am sure we will be happy here," responded Clara.

The door had opened into a large family room which looked like it was multi-functional, as it appeared to be the kitchen with a large stove in a chimney breast on one wall, a large double sink with a draining board under a window draped with net curtaining on the same wall as the door, and then a large triple settee on another wall. In the middle of the room was a huge dining table that could seat at least ten people. There were no floor coverings just bare varnished floorboards. Saucepans and utensils of all sizes and descriptions hung all around the walls. In one of the corners stood a desk with papers scattered on it with a phone perched at one end.

The table was set for four, and a high chair had been placed at one end. In the middle of the table there was a big slab of butter next to a large loaf of bread on a breadboard with a knife by the side that had already been used to cut some of the bread.

"Something smells good," said Clara. "I am starving. I was telling Carl that Lilly was a bit out of sorts on the train. I think she is teething. I have some teething medicine which I will give her now so she is settled in time for bed," said Clara.

"Now, my dear, come and sit down, and I will serve dinner. Bill was moaning that he has had to wait until now for his dinner, so he is starving as well. As you can see, he has already started on the bread and butter. You sit next to the high chair so you can keep an eye on Lilly. Carl, you sit next to Clara," said Hannah.

They all sat down, and Hannah took a big pie out of the oven and placed it on the table together with bowls of potatoes and vegetables.

"This looks delicious. I hope you haven't gone to too much trouble for us," said Clara.

Everyone started to help themselves. Clara felt a bit self-conscious helping herself, but she was so hungry she just went with the flow, getting Lilly a bit of everything and mashing it for her in a small bowl. The food was indeed absolutely delicious.

"Let me help you clear the table, Mrs. Kennion," said Clara.

"You must call me Hannah. We are family now, and would it be okay if Lilly calls me Grandma?"

"I would like that, although she doesn't call anyone anything yet. '*No*' is the limit of her vocabulary at the moment. Would you mind if I put her to bed now? She is rubbing her eyes," said Clara.

"Of course not, I will show you your room while the men clear the table. Carl, take Clara's cases upstairs before you help your dad clear the table. I will put the coffee on when I come down," ordered Hannah.

Hannah showed her to a large bedroom at the top of the stairs. Inside was a king-size bed with a cot to one side. Hannah closed the curtains of a double window, which had a chest of drawers underneath it. There was a triple built-in wardrobe that Hannah opened to show Clara where she could store her clothes. On the other side of the room was a thin, long table with a cane backed chair to one side and a large mirror hung above. Next to that was a sink with two taps. The floor in this room was also varnished floorboard with rugs on either side of the bed. The bed was covered in a beautiful patchwork quilt in a kaleidoscope of colours. There was even a smaller version on Lilly's cot.

"What beautiful quilts! Did you make them?" asked Clara.

"Yes, during the long winter nights, I amuse myself making quilts using any fabric I can get my hands on. The bathroom is next door. I will quickly show you so you know where it is," said Hannah.

There was one hallway that had, from what she could see, five doors that she presumed were other bedrooms. The bathroom was basic with a bath, toilet and sink. There was a mirror above the sink and a bathroom cabinet to one side with a freestanding towel rail with towels on it.

"I will leave you to it. Come down when you are ready," said Hannah as she made her way down the stairs.

Clara gave Lilly a quick wash, changed her into her nightdress, and put her into the cot with a teddy bear that, she presumed, Hannah had left for her. Lilly took only a few minutes to fall asleep.

Clara made her way downstairs to the kitchen where the men were chatting and drinking coffee.

"Come and sit down and I will pour us some coffee. I have made a cake to have with it," said Hannah.

"Here is your coffee and cake. Now let me see your ring," said Hannah.

Clara showed her finger with the cheap wedding ring that Carl had bought her. She felt a bit embarrassed, as she could see the look on Hannah's face when she saw the ring.

"Carl, how could you give this lovely girl a ring like that? Was it the cheapest in the shop?" she asked.

"No, Mum it wasn't like that. I didn't have much English currency to get an expensive ring, and I did promise Clara that when she got here I would take her to get a better one, didn't I, Clara?"

"Yes, he did, Mrs. Kennion, sorry, Hannah. He has promised to get me a better one, but I don't mind. I am not bothered with another one. This will be fine for me. I certainly wouldn't want a flashy one," she replied.

"Hold on a minute," said Hannah as she left the room, returning a few minutes later with a small, beige suede drawstring bag.

"These were my mother's, Carl's grandmother. They came to me when she died. Let's see if they fit you." Hannah took three rings from the bag and took hold of Clara's hand.

"Take your ring off and see if these fit." They fitted perfectly as if they had been made for her. One was a simple gold band, one was a diamond solitaire, and the other was a gold band with tiny diamonds and alternate sapphires embedded in the ring.

"These are beautiful rings, but I couldn't possibly take them."

"Don't be silly. I don't have any daughters to pass them on to, so you and Helen are the next best thing, and I am sure Helen wouldn't want them. Have you seen the size of Helen's rings?" asked Hannah.

Clara laughed. "Yes, I did notice them, especially the diamond one. It is the biggest diamond I have ever seen. They were absolutely beautiful."

"And a beautiful price, knowing my brother and his love of expensive jewellery," said Carl.

"Now, now, Carl," said his mother.

"No, Mum, don't get me wrong. He has worked hard to get where he is. I am not jealous, I am just saying. Anyway, that type of thing is not for me. I would hate having to go to work in a suit and sit in a stuffy office all day. I prefer the outdoor life."

"Yes, I know you do, son. I don't want Clara getting the wrong idea. I love Helen as I would my own daughter, and I was only pointing out that Helen has lovely jewellery," said Hannah.

"I understand," said Clara. "Everyone is different."

"Anyway," said Hannah. "I would like you to have these, and when you get your marriage blessed in the chapel, we will get Preacher Cowan to bless the rings as well."

"Mum, let Clara settle in first, and then we will think about a blessing."

"Sorry, son, I get a bit carried away. Tomorrow, Clara, I will take you on a guided tour of the farm. We are coming towards the end of the harvest, so it is one of the busiest times of the year for the men, and they need to be up early. I think we should think about going to bed. Bill, wake up! It's time for bed," shouted Hannah to Bill, who was snoozing peacefully on the settee.

Carl led Clara by the hand upstairs to their room. "I am sorry that you have been put in this position," he said, nodding towards the bed, "but I could hardly say to Mum that we wanted separate rooms. I will understand if you want to take more time for us to get to know each other."

Clara laughed, slightly nervous. "What would we do, put a pillow in between us? I want to be your '*wife*,' Carl, so let's just accept the situation and start our life together starting now," said Clara as she took a step towards him.

Carl stepped towards her at the same time and took her in his arms, gently kissing her. Any tension between them immediately evaporated, and their kisses became more urgent and passionate. As they separated, looking into each other's eyes, they both started giggling, "Shh! We don't want to wake up Lilly."

They collapsed on the bed and started taking each other's clothes off. Carl held her face in his hands. "I love you, Clara Kennion. Now let's get under the covers so I can ravish you."

They tenderly explored each other's bodies. Clara was lost in a maze of emotions as Carl made love to her slowly at first, then more urgently until she was taken to a sexual height that she had never before achieved. Afterwards, they lay fulfilled in each other's arms and fell asleep.

The alarm woke Carl at six thirty in the morning. He quickly switched it off so as not to wake Lilly. Clara stirred and reached out to Carl. "Good morning, you," he said, leaning over to kiss her. "I have to get up, so don't try and stop me," he teased as he took her in his arms. He couldn't resist making love to her once more.

Clara rolled over, sighing contently and went back to sleep. Lilly woke her an hour and half later, standing in her cot crying to be lifted out. "Come here, sweetheart. Let's get you dressed," said Clara, lying Lilly on the bed, tickling her tummy. "Now you stay there while Mummy gets dressed."

She got dressed and made her way downstairs with Lilly. Seeing Hannah in the kitchen, she said, "Good morning, Hannah. How are you this morning?"

"Ah! Good morning, Clara. Did you sleep well?"

"Yes, thank you, and Lilly is ready for breakfast. I have never known a child who needs her breakfast as soon as she wakes up," said Clara without thinking. Luckily, Hannah didn't pick up on what she said.

"There is porridge already made in the pan on the stove. Here give her to me, and I will put her in the high chair while you get the porridge," said Hannah, taking Lilly.

Clara filled two bowls with porridge and sat down at the table. Hannah fed Lilly while Clara had her breakfast.

"I will give you a tour of the farm when you are ready. Is it okay if I put Lilly on the floor to explore? There is nothing she can hurt herself on. Tomorrow we will go to town and get her some toys, and you will need some more suitable clothing to wear around the place. We can get a lot of rain, so it gets really muddy on the paths. You will need some good boots and a raincoat. You can borrow some boots for today. There are loads in the back dirt room. I am sure there is a pair to fit you. Sorry, Clara, I know I chat too much. Just tell me to shut up. Everyone else does," she teased.

"Thank you," said Clara as she cleared the table and took the dishes over to the sink to wash. As she was wiping the dishes, Hannah suddenly exclaimed, "Clara, look quickly. Lilly is walking." Just as Clara turned in her direction, Lilly promptly fell on her bottom.

"Well I never! What a clever little pumpkin you are," said Hannah. Lilly looked up at her and crawled towards a chair and pulled herself onto her feet. Hannah put her hands out and beckoned Lilly to her. Lilly took three steps and again fell down on her bottom. "Wait till we tell Daddy when he comes home what you can do," she said, speaking to Lilly.

"She will be calling Carl '*Daddy*,' won't she, Clara?" questioned Hannah with a concerned look on her face.

"We haven't actually discussed it, but yes, that is what I would like, and I am sure Carl would want that as well," said Clara.

"Right. Let's get our tour started. We have a couple of hours before I need to prepare lunch."

Hannah led her to the back dirt room as she called it to get a pair of boots. Clara had to borrow some socks as well, as she only had stockings with her.

They went out the back door. Clara found it quite warm, but Hannah said she found it a bit chilly.

"You will soon get used to the climate. I find it chilly because it is usually a lot warmer than this, but you can see over there that the sun hasn't broken through the mountain mist yet," said Hannah, pointing to a mountain range in the far distance.

Clara was overwhelmed by the view. From the back of the house, you could see vast fields of green rows of bushes as far as the eye could see, back dropped by mountain ranges partially covered in a foggy mist. To the right and left of the house were tall trees, and directly at the back of the house was an area enclosed by a low white picket fence. There was a path from the door down to a gate and on either side of the path, there were lawns surrounded by various cultivated and wild flowers.

"This is my little indulgence. I love flowers. I keep this area as my special place to relax when I have time," said Hannah.

Hannah led them up the path and out the gate. Clara saw an enclosure to one side where chickens roamed around pecking randomly, and a large vegetable plot beyond the enclosure must have been at least ten times bigger than the one she had had in France. Two yapping Jack Russell dogs came running up to them, dancing around Hannah on their hind legs.

"Hello, boys," she said, taking two doggy bone biscuits out of her apron pocket to give them.

"This is Buster and Scamp. They are brothers. Scamp is the smaller of the two. They are really good with children, so you won't have to worry about them being around Lilly," said Hannah.

"We grow all our own vegetables. The boys help with the heavy work when they can. Otherwise, me and the other wives look after it," explained Hannah.

They walked beyond the vegetable patch to another paddock area that housed a small herd of goats.

"We keep goats for their milk, and they are also handy at keeping the weeds down. But, we have to be careful, as they would eat the crops if you let them. If they are not in the paddock, we keep them on chains so they can only reach the weeds," explained Hannah.

As they walked from the paddock, a row of single-storey stone huts came into view. There were about ten of them each with a front door and a window on either side of each door. In the front, each had a neat, little garden. One had a pram outside and another had two little black boys playing football.

"These are the workers' cottages."

"My ancestors originated from Scotland. Would you believe they came here in the mid-eighteenth century and started this farm? From what I can gather from the old accounting books and diaries they left behind, it took them over a hundred years to get it to this size. They used slave labour in those days, and we still have some of the descendants of those same families working for us. I might add that the living conditions are much better now than they were then. All the cottages have a bathroom of sorts and a kitchen with running water," Hannah was explaining when a large black lady came out of the door where the two boys were playing.

"Morning, Betsy," shouted Hannah as she walked towards the woman with Clara in tow.

"Betsy, this is my daughter-in-law, Clara, and my new granddaughter, Lilly."

Clara extended her hand. "Hello! So pleased to meet you. Are these your sons?"

"You are trying to flatter me, young lady. These are my grandsons, Ethan and Thomas. Boys, come and say hello to the lady."

The boys came over and politely said hello.

"They are my daughter's boys. She is working with her husband." Betsy pointed towards a field in the distance where Clara could see a number of workers. "She only picks during harvest to help out."

"Can Clara look inside your cottage, Betsy? I want her to see all of the farm," asked Hannah.

"You don't have to ask, Hannah, just go in."

Clara followed Betsy into the cottage. She was surprised at how homely and cosy it was. The cottages were deceptive from the outside, as inside was a living area, kitchen and bathroom with a sort of sit-in bath in the shape of an armchair that Clara found quite amusing and two bedrooms. Betsy explained to Clara that she lived next door in a much smaller cottage and that she shared the bathroom with her daughter.

"Thank you, Betsy. Have a lovely day," said Hannah.

"Betsy is retired now but still lives on the farm. Her husband—who worked for us as did his father before him—died two years ago. We adapted the cottage next to her daughter's for her. She now helps out with the workers' children, and she sometimes helps me out in the house," explained Hannah as they made their way towards the front of the house. "I grew up with Betsy. In fact, she is my best friend," said Hannah.

As they approached the front, Clara could see it was a striking white colonial two-story house. Circular pillars supported the front veranda. Above the veranda canopy, she could see five windows with shutters on either side. An assortment of chairs sat on the veranda, including a rocking chair with a cat sleeping contently on a cushion. There was another huge tree to the right of the house of the same variety as she had seen on the other side, which Hannah told her were white oaks. The whole place was a luscious green no matter which way you looked.

"What a beautiful place you have, Hannah."

"Yes, we are lucky, and you are seeing it at its best. Those mountains are the Appalachian Mountains, and we get many hikers passing this way in the summer months. The Bass Lake is not far from here, and the boys used to cycle down to swim there when they were young. It is a lovely safe place for children to grow up in. Now let's get inside and prepare lunch for the workers.

"There are six of us for lunch today including you and me," explained Hannah.

"I hope you will let me help you, Hannah. I don't want to sit around doing nothing," offered Clara.

"Carl has already told me that you are an accomplished cook, and an extra pair of hands is always welcome. I have panned fried chicken with roasties and green beans. I made an apple pie yesterday that we will have for dessert with custard," she said.

You prepare the beans, and I will do the potatoes. Will Lilly be okay playing on the floor? I found some building blocks in the loft for her to play with until we get her something better tomorrow," said Hannah.

They set to work preparing the lunch while Lilly played happily on the floor. The men arrived for their lunch at twelve thirty. While Bill and the other two workers sat down at the table, Carl came over to Clara.

"How was your morning?"

"Good, your mother showed me around, and I am impressed by everything I have seen so far. I think there is still quite a bit more for me to see. It is a fantastic place, and the views are unbelievably stunning. I can see why you wanted to come back home," exclaimed Clara.

"I am pleased you like the place. I will take you down the valley after work. I want to show you something," he said, pecking her on her cheek before sitting down for lunch.

The men discussed the crops over lunch and the jobs planned for the afternoon before they left to continue their work.

"Hannah, you go and sit out front with Lilly and have a rest while I do the dishes and tidy up. I will bring you a glass of lemonade when I am finished," suggested Clara.

Hannah didn't have to be asked twice. She picked Lilly up and went and made herself comfortable on the rocking chair on the veranda, moving the disgruntled cat from its sleeping place. When Clara went out with the lemonade after clearing up, she found both Hannah and Lilly fast asleep. Clara sat down and drank the lemonade herself, thinking that she must get the recipe to add to her collection—it was delicious.

She had limited the amount of personal items she had brought with her besides all of her clothes, but she did bring her collection of recipes. The scrapbook was now bulging with her collection containing not only the ones she had written in the book but also the cuttings her mother had sent that she had glued into the book. She had also brought the box she had started to accumulate with items for Chantal and Francine. She wanted them to know that she had never forgotten them if and when they should meet in the future.

Lilly woke up first, and she woke Hannah.

"I can't believe I fell asleep," announced Hannah as Clara took hold of Lilly and put her down on the veranda.

"I will go and get you a drink. I did bring one out to you, but as you looked so peaceful, I didn't want to disturb you, so I drank it." Clara went and got her a drink and came back with one for Lilly as well.

"If you are willing to look after Lilly, I will do the jobs you had planned today. It will give you a bit of a break, but, saying that, Lilly might be more work."

"Thank you, Clara. That would be a great help, and as far as I am concerned, Lilly is a joy to look after, not a chore. There is nothing to do upstairs. I always make the bed when I get up unless I am changing the bedding, and I do this every Monday. Usually I clean the bathrooms and sweep upstairs every other day, that is if it's needed, so let's leave it for now. But I do sweep downstairs every day and try and keep the kitchen as clean as I can. I do the washing whenever I have enough to fill the machine, but I do this in the morning so that I can hang it out to dry. But I need to prepare dinner. I thought I would do a chicken and vegetable soup, using up the remainder of the chicken from lunch," said Hannah.

"Okay," said Clara. "I have already tidied the kitchen, so I will start on the soup. Where will I find the vegetables?"

Hannah showed her the larder where she kept the entire foodstuff. The larder was well stocked with everything you could possibly need. Hannah pointed out sacks of potatoes, onions and various root vegetables and told her that any other vegetable would have to be picked from the vegetable garden. Next to the larder was a small scullery where there were oversized saucepans and baking trays of all descriptions and sizes all set out neatly on shelves that covered each wall. Behind the scullery door hung a selection of aprons.

Clara picked an apron that fit her and set to work on the soup. After picking the meat from the carcass of the chicken, she set the bones to boil while she went out to the garden to select some vegetables. '*I love this garden*,' she thought to herself as she picked the vegetables and herbs for the soup.

Going back in the kitchen, she suddenly remembered that she had forgotten to ask Hannah about bread to go with the soup. She searched the kitchen and larder, panicking that she would have to bake a loaf when she spied a large tin with '*BREAD*' written on it. She lifted the lid and she breathed a sigh of relief. There sat two loaves. She shredded the chicken, prepared the vegetables and added herbs to her soup and put them on the stove to simmer.

She sat outside for a short time with Hannah, and they planned the next day's shopping. "When do you bake bread?" Clara asked.

"I try and do it every other day or at least every two days, and I make enough to last at least two days. Can you make bread?" asked Hannah.

"Yes, in fact bread and pastry are my specialties," said Clara.

"Oh, Clara, you are a godsend. I am sixty-four now, and I have been finding the housework much harder to do these last few years. Betsy comes and helps me now and again, but she is not much younger than me, and she helps her daughter. In fact, only a couple of months ago, I said to Bill that I was thinking of employing someone to help me, but I hadn't actually got around to doing it. Then when Carl announced he was leaving the army and coming home, Bill was relieved, as he is not getting any younger either, and although he has a good workforce, he needs someone to eventually take over from him. ... And then when Carl announced he had gotten married and was bringing an English wife with him, I was concerned that she/you would be a city type, but how wrong was I? Now thankfully I have you to help me," said Hannah.

"I know how you feel. It worried me that I was arriving at your home with a baby in tow, and I wondered how you would react to me. But Hannah, I am not the type to sit around and do nothing all day. I have worked since I was fifteen and don't intend to stop now, so rest assured that I will do anything and everything to make your life easier," said Clara.

Carl arrived back from work early. "Mum, I am going to take Clara from you, is that okay, and will you watch Lilly while we are gone?" he asked.

"Of course, son, she is in the kitchen. You have found yourself a good one there, son," said Hannah as she shouted for Clara.

Carl put his hand out for her to take. "Come on, let's go and see the valley I mentioned at lunch time."

"Can you watch the soup for me, Hannah, while I go with Carl?" asked Clara, grabbing hold of his hand ready to be led away.

"Your mum didn't take me this way. What is all this land yours as well?" she asked as they walked in the opposite direction of the workers' cottages.

"Yes, all ours up to those line of trees." He pointed to the trees in the distance. "Now this is what I want you to see," he said as they approached a neglected house. "This used to be the house of the slave master and then head foreman of our workers, but hasn't been lived in for at least fifty years," explained Carl.

"What a shame to let such a lovely building be left and not lived in," said Clara.

Carl explained that at the end of the abolishment of slavery the slave master had fled the farm in fear of his life when there had been a concern that the slaves might rise against him. His four-times-great-grandfather had then appointed a head foreman to run the farm. That role had continued until it was taken on by his grandfather who lived in the main house then, which meant that this house was left unoccupied.

"Anyway, the reason I have brought you here is that I intend to renovate the house for us. What do you think?"

"I think that would be wonderful! Can we look inside?" said an emotional Clara.

Carl unlocked the front door, and they went inside. Dust and cobwebs were everywhere. A mouse scurried past her. She instantly screamed and jumped backwards.

"You wimp," said Carl.

She playfully punched him on his arm. "I am not scared of a little mouse. It just gave me a fright, that's all!"

Clara looked into all the rooms. Going upstairs, there were five bedrooms. "We can turn this room into a bathroom, and this room can be Lilly's, and this one can be ours and—"

"Not so quick. Let's get a builder in, and he will tell us the best room for the bathroom. This will be your project," he said.

"Really, I can't wait. When can the builder come?" asked an excited Clara.

Going back downstairs, Clara mentally turned all the rooms into what she wanted. She then went out the back and could see where she would plant vegetables and have an herb garden. She was so excited. She could hardly contain herself.

"Come on, let's make our way back. I might just be able to get in touch with a builder Dad uses."

On the walk back, Carl told her to get some more appropriate clothing on their shopping trip planned for the next day. "You need to get yourself some denims and sturdy boots. You can't be going around the farm in ballot pumps and pretty dresses. I will give you some money to spend."

"I can't take your money, Carl. I have some I can use," said Clara.

"Don't be silly. You are my wife, and I want to take care of you and Lilly," he said, planting a kiss on her cheek.

The next morning, Clara was up with Carl. She left the bedroom door open so that she would be able to hear Lilly when she woke up. She had made breakfast and was in the throes of making bread when Hannah appeared.

"Good morning, and why are you up so early, Clara?"

"Good morning, I am starting as I mean to go on. From tomorrow, you can have a little lay in and I will do breakfast. Now sit down, and I will serve you," instructed Clara.

Hannah sat down, and Clara served her with porridge and a cup of coffee followed by two slices of toast.

"This is a treat," said Hannah just as Lilly gave out a scream announcing that she was awake. "I will go and get her," said Hannah.

"Will you wash and dress her? The clean clothes are on the chair," asked Clara.

"My pleasure, better than having to make bread," said a delighted Hannah.

By mid-morning, with the bread baked and Betsy in charge of lunch, they made their way to Raleigh. Hannah drove the Chevrolet pick-up truck. She pointed out various places as they made their way to Raleigh. She drove around the town and showed Clara where the best places were and what to buy at those particular stores before pulling up outside of Hamrick's, a vast department store that appeared to sell everything.

They collected a trolley and entered the store. Clara couldn't believe her eyes. There were shelves stocked to the ceiling with goods. They made their way to the clothing section. She immediately saw the denims that Carl referred to. Unsure of the size she would take, she asked an assistant if there was a place where she could try on the clothing. The assistant directed her to the fitting cubicle, taking two different sizes that she thought might fit her. She had never worn trousers, and all she could think when looking at herself in the mirror dressed in the denims was WOW. She purchased three pairs, several t-shirts with both short sleeves and long sleeves, a waterproof coat with a removable lining, a pair of plimsolls and a pair of sturdy boots plus socks.

They then went to the children's section where they got a few items for Lilly plus her first shoes. Finally, they went to the toy section.

Hannah was in heaven. "A little girl to buy for at last," she said and piled a separate trolley with a doll pram, dolls, and a small trike. After more than an hour in the store, they left and made their way home. Hannah had also purchased some balls of wool.

"I can't wait to knit some clothes for Lilly's dolls," said an excited Hannah.

Clara modelled her new denim jeans to Carl in the privacy of their bedroom.

"Well how sexy do you look in jeans," he said, grabbing hold of her, and throwing her on the bed. He smothered her in kisses. "Now take them off," said Carl playfully, "or I will rip them off you."

CHAPTER 27

Over the following three months, they all settled into a routine. Clara looked after the house and did the cooking with Hannah. Hannah took great pleasure in looking after Lilly. Lilly's vocabulary was increasing day-by-day. Grandma became gamy, mummy became mama, daddy became dada, and grandpa became dapa.

In turn, Lilly was always asking for Gamy and not Mama, not that Clara minded. She loved to see the two of them together.

The builder came to look at Valley House, so named by Clara because of its location. Clara told him what she wanted, and he told her what she could have, leaving the two of them to meet somewhere in the middle. The work, he told her, would take approximately six months to complete, and she couldn't wait. Carl tried to rein her back and bring her back to reality, reminding her of the costs involved in not only the renovations but to furnish it afterwards.

Thanksgiving came and went. Gary, Helen and the boys arrived the day before, greeted at the door by the yapping of Buster and Scamp, and stayed for five days in total. It was lovely for Hannah to have the entire family together. The boys loved the farm, spending their days outdoors getting covered in mud. Gary went through the farm accounts and discussed with Bill and Carl how they could improve the profits. Helen relaxed on the veranda with Hannah and Clara.

Thanksgiving lunch was an extravaganza of food, mostly prepared by Clara. A large plump turkey with all the trimmings was presented for Carl to carve followed by a traditional pumpkin pie and cream. Clara had made a thanksgiving cake that looked too good to eat decorated in sugar paste flowers and berries.

Clara was sorry to see them go, as she had struck up a firm friendship with Helen. They talked effortlessly about anything and everything, both having the same sense of humour. Helen helped her do the washing up and preparing meals.

During her time in America, Clara had written regularly to her mother and Niamph and once to Jeanne. Jeanne had written back surprised to hear that she had moved to America and with the sad news that Claude had died. Clara was shocked and upset by the news. This was the first person close to her that had died. The letters from Niamph were mixed. She found the job fulfilling, but she still desperately mourned the loss of her baby. She was always asking after Lilly, wanting to know if she was walking and words she was learning. Clara supposed that she could then relate Lilly's progress to that of Bernadette.

On her thirty-second birthday, Clara suspected she was pregnant. She discreetly asked Hannah for the name of a doctor she could go and see. With a knowing smile, Hannah gave her the name of their doctor, and the next day he confirmed her pregnancy. She felt guilty telling the doctor that this was her second pregnancy as opposed to her fourth, but being that he was the family doctor, she felt it was safer to keep her secret to herself and Carl.

That night in the privacy of their bedroom, Clara said to Carl, "I have two surprises for you," taking off her dressing gown and revealing herself dressed in a black, lacy baby doll pyjama set.

"WooHoo," he said. "I can't wait for the second surprise," grabbing hold of her and kissing her neck.

"Stop it," she said, giggling.

"Come on, what is the second surprise?" demanded Carl impatiently.

"I'm pregnant."

Clara couldn't quite make out whether the look on Carl's face was surprise or shock or perhaps both.

"Wow," he cried, "wow, I'm going to be a daddy," lifting her off her feet and swinging her round. "I can't believe it. Are you sure?"

"Yes, I went to the doctor this morning. He thinks I must be eight weeks, so it will be due in about September or October." Before Clara could finish the sentence, Carl was out of the door and running down the hallway to his parents' room.

Knocking on their door, he shouted, "Mum, Dad, we are having a baby!"

His mum opened the door with a big grin on her face. "Congratulations, son. I am thrilled for you both."

His father was not quite so thrilled, as Carl had woken him up. "Yeah, yeah, son, see you in the morning."

Clara shouted to him, "Come on and leave your mum and dad to go back to bed."

He was so excited, bounding back to their room, picking up Clara and hugging and kissing her. She eventually managed to get him to go to bed.

"I want a boy," he said. "What shall we call him?"

"I think we will just have to take what we are given. It could be a girl, especially given my track record," she whispered.

Cuddling close to her, he whispered, "I don't mind what we have. I just can't believe I am going to be a daddy."

The next six months flew past. Everyone tried to get Clara to slow down and rest, but she felt full of energy and was enjoying every minute, even though she had a huge belly, much bigger than her previous pregnancies. She felt she must be having a boy, as this pregnancy was so different from her others.

Valley House was now finished and just needed furnishing. Carl insisted that they wait until after the birth of the baby to move, as he didn't want Clara doing too much heavy work and he knew that she would insist on moving furniture around if they moved in.

But then tragedy struck.

Bill came back from work late afternoon as usual with Carl following him shortly after.

"I think I will just go upstairs and lie down for a bit, love. Give me a shout when dinner is ready," he said to Hannah.

"Are you okay?" asked Hannah.

"Yes, fine just a bit tired, that's all," Bill replied as he went upstairs.

Hannah shouted to him several times that dinner was ready, but she received no response.

"Carl," she asked. "Can you pop upstairs and wake your dad and tell him that dinner is ready?"

Carl ran up the stairs two at a time to get his father. He shouted his name as he opened the door. His father appeared to be fast asleep, but when Carl went to shake him awake, he discovered that his father was dead.

The whole house was in shock. An ambulance and the doctor were called, but he was pronounced dead. The doctor suggested that he must have had a heart attack, but a post mortem would have to be held to ascertain the cause of death.

The shock left Hannah speechless. They had been childhood sweethearts and married for forty-six years. During that time, they had never spent a night apart. She didn't even seem able to cry. The doctor told Carl that he would give her a sedative and come back in the morning to see how she was. Clara sat with her until she fell asleep.

On seeing the ambulance, the workers who lived on the farm came over to see what was happening. On hearing the news, they and their families gathered around to show their respects, all as shocked as the family.

Carl phoned his brother, who said he would be with them as soon as he could get a flight. He hoped it would get him there in the morning.

Nobody could face eating. Carl and Clara went to bed but couldn't sleep. They clung to each other all night. Carl was deeply concerned for his mother and the future of the farm.

Hannah refused another sedative in the morning. She sat at the kitchen table, holding Clara's hand. "What will I do without him, Clara? He has been my life. I can't imagine never seeing him walking through that door ever again." Eventually, Hannah sobbed uncontrollably. Carl came into the kitchen at that point, took hold of his mother in his arms, and they both cried together.

The funeral was held five days later. The post mortem had revealed a massive heart attack. Helen arrived on the morning of the funeral, leaving the boys with her parents. She helped Clara and Betsy prepare the food for the wake. The chapel was packed to overflowing with mourners from all over the area, and Bill was buried in the cemetery close by.

Although a solemn affair, everyone had a happy story to tell about Bill. They all shook hands with the family, expressing their condolences as they left the wake. Hannah put on a brave face and thanked everyone for coming.

Helen left for New York the next morning, telling Clara to call her if she needed any help with anything. Gary stayed another week to help Carl sort out Bill's affairs. The lawyer arrived the day after the funeral and read the will to the family. Bill had left the farm to Gary and Carl equally with a proviso that Hannah be looked after for the rest of her life. The lawyer advised them to have the farm and the land valued for probate purposes and that he would draw up the necessary paperwork transferring the ownership.

Before Gary left for New York, the lawyer had drawn up an agreement whereby it was agreed that Carl would continue to run the farm, take a wage and look after their mother. They agreed to give their mother an allowance and that the remaining profits would either be invested to improve the farm or split equally between them.

The day after Gary left, Clara went into labour. This was the turning point for Hannah, having no time to dwell on her grief, as she had to suddenly take on the responsibility of looking after the family.

On the fourth of September 1952, Jeffrey William Kennion came into the world. Carl was over the moon. "A boy. I told you it would be a boy—a son—wow!" Kissing Clara on the forehead, he took hold of his baby son. Hannah and Lilly came upstairs to welcome the new arrival.

Lilly jumped on the bed to give her mother a kiss. "Mama's got a baby," she announced to everyone's amusement.

"Yes, Mummy's got a baby. This is your brother, Jeffrey," said Clara, looking at Hannah and added, "Jeffrey William, in fact, we named him after Bill."

"Thank you, Clara," she said, tears welling up in her eyes while she took the baby from Carl. "He is beautiful."

Carl had already re-arranged the rooms, giving Lilly her own room directly opposite Hannah's. They told her she was a big girl now and would have a big girl's bed. The room had recently been redecorated in readiness for the arrival of the baby for Lilly with pink flowery wallpaper and matching curtains. Lilly was delighted with her new big bed, jumping up and down on it.

They explained to her that the baby would now have the baby bed and sleep in Mummy and Daddy's room until he was a big boy. Lilly didn't seem to be concerned, but as the months went by, she would often sneak into Hannah's bed during the night.

After Bill's death, there was no way that Clara and Carl could move out of the farmhouse, so their plans to move into Valley House were put on hold.

Although all of their lives had changed with Carl taking over the role of running the farm and having to do all of the paperwork, Hannah taking on the responsibility of the children, and Clara taking care of the house, they remained tight knit, supporting each other at every turn.

Clara and Carl's second son, Timothy Carl, was born on the eleventh of December, 1955 just after Lilly had started at the local primary school.

The house felt a little empty without Bill and Lilly. Clara sensed that Hannah often appeared to be lonely, and she tried her utmost to keep Hannah involved in the busy life of the farm. At least with the growing family, it seemed to Clara that the house and this family could keep the business from suffering, something that always weighed heavily on her given what her mother and father went through during the war and how it impacted their lives and their family finances. Maybe life would stop bringing surprises.

CHAPTER 28

One Sunday morning, when Lilly was five and about a month after Timothy's birth, just as Hannah and Betsy were about to leave the house for the chapel service, Lilly came into the kitchen dressed in her best outfit.

"Mummy," she said, standing in front of Clara with her hands on her hips. Clara could barely keep herself from giggling, as this was the stance that Hannah took when she was about to make an announcement.

"Yes, sweetheart," exclaimed Clara.

"Mummy, I need to go to chapel with Gamy and Auntie Betsy," announced Lilly.

"And why is that?"

"Because I want to learn to sing, and Auntie Betsy says she learnt to sing at chapel."

Everybody in the kitchen was by now in fits of laughter, except Lilly who took exception to being laughed at.

"Of course, you can go to chapel, sweetheart, if Gamy and Auntie will let you go with them," said Clara.

"Can I, Gamy? Please, please, can I come with you?" pleaded Lilly.

"Hurry up then and go get your hat, as we are going now, and we don't want to be late," said Hannah.

So started Lilly's weekly attendance to chapel.

"I don't go to all of the service, Mummy. I go to Sunday school first, and then all the children go to the last part of the service. I am learning all the words to the songs. Miss Matthews says I am really good at singing."

"That's good, sweetheart, but I think the songs are called hymns."

"Yes, I just forgot the word. Miss Matthews says that all children should be baptised because if they aren't, they won't go to heaven. Have I been baptised, Mummy, because Miss Matthews says that my name is not in the book?"

"And what book is that, sweetheart?" asked Clara, thinking to herself that Miss Matthews needs to be shot.

"I don't know, but she has got a book with all of the children in it. She said that Jeffrey and Timothy are not in it either. I need to be baptised, Mummy, because I don't want to go to that other place. I want to go to heaven."

Carl came into the room and caught the tail end of the conversation.

"Daddy, I need to be baptised because Miss Matthews says—"

"Yes, yes, I heard what you said to Mummy. Let me talk to Mummy about it. Now go and find Gamy. I think she is feeding the chickens with Jeffrey."

When Lilly had left the room, Carl looked at Clara, and they both chuckled.

"I am sure Miss Matthews means well, but I could kill her. Fancy telling the kids that they won't go to heaven if they are not baptised! It's enough to give them nightmares. But on a serious note, Lilly was christened in a Catholic Church in France when she was about two weeks old, so what do I do now?" asked Clara.

"I am not sure. I can't imagine Pastor Cowan being happy that Lilly is Catholic. Perhaps just let her be baptised again. I don't see it would matter that much," replied Carl.

Clara mentioned the conversation she had had with Lilly to Hannah. "I didn't like to say anything to you about the children being baptised, as I know both you and Carl are not interested in going to chapel. If it was up to me, I would get them done, but it's your decision."

Lilly didn't mention the conversation again, but the next Sunday, Pastor Cowan invited himself to lunch. Clara presumed that either Hannah or Lilly had mentioned the prospect of being baptised to him.

"Thank you for having me to lunch, Clara," he said, extending his hand out to Carl and shaking it brusquely. They all sat down to lunch, with the Pastor giving a disapproving look at Buster and Scamp sitting under the table waiting to be fed scraps of food. Luckily, Lilly chatted non-stop throughout the meal, which covered up the stilted conversation of the adults. At the end of the meal, Betsy took Lilly and the boys to play with her grandsons.

"I presume you have come to ask about the children being baptised, Pastor," said a straight-talking Clara, "as it's not often we see you."

"Well, yes," said the surprised pastor. "Lilly told Miss Matthews that she wants to be baptised, so I thought I would come and talk to you about it. I know she wasn't born here, so I wasn't sure if she had already been baptised, and I know that the boys haven't because I would have done it."

"Carl and I discussed the possibility when Lilly mentioned it and have no objection, especially as Lilly is quite concerned by Miss Matthews' remarks about her not going to heaven," said Clara, slightly sarcastically, hoping that the Pastor picked up on this, but it went right over his head.

"Excellent, excellent," he said quite animatedly. "I think we could arrange it for the end of the month. I will confirm it tomorrow. I just need to double check my diary."

'*Oh yes,*' thought Clara to herself, '*I bet he has already checked his diary.*'

Lilly was ecstatic when they told her. "Can I have a new dress, Mummy, because Miss Matthews said that I would have to have a proper dress so that everyone knew it was me being baptised? Will Jeffrey and Timothy be dressed up too? I can't wait to tell my friends at school tomorrow. A lot of my friends go to my chapel as well, Mummy, so they will see me," said Lilly, barely coming up for air.

Clara said to Carl later, "That child can talk the hind legs off a donkey."

Carl laughed. "I have never heard that expression before, but I get the gist. At least when she is around, you don't have to say anything just sit back and listen."

Hannah offered to take Lilly to get her new dress and had already rescued Carl and Gary's christening gown from the attic. "Little Timothy can wear this. I just need to wash it, as it has been in a chest in the attic for almost forty years."

Clara had to admit that it was a lovely gown, but she still had a feeling that Hannah was behind this entire baptism affair, and it was not just Miss Matthews putting it into Lilly's head. But she felt she would go along with it. She didn't want her children being different from the others, as she knew that Hannah would want to take Jeffrey to chapel as soon as he was old enough.

As Clara had expected, the date was confirmed for the thirtieth of January. The family arrived at the chapel all dressed up. Lilly in a beautiful lacy white dress and matching hair band to keep her blond curls out of her face, Jeffrey in a white roper suit with matching jacket and white bow tie, and Timothy in the christening gown and wrapped in a shawl, as it was a chilly day. Carl was in his best and only suit, and Clara had bought herself a navy blue, fitted woollen dress with a matching bolero jacket and hat.

"Wow," commented Carl on seeing Clara in the clingy dress, patting her bottom playfully. "You should get dressed up more often."

"Cheek! I thought you liked me in denims?"

The pastor welcomed them and told them that he had reserved the front row for them. The normal Sunday service was held first, with Lilly staying with them, as she didn't want to go to Sunday school because she didn't want to get her dress dirty. At the end of the service, the pastor announced that the baptisms would be taking place and welcomed the congregation to stay and witness the event. Most of them did to Clara's astonishment.

Timothy had slept the entire service but woke up when the pastor took him, held his head over the font and poured water over his head at which point Timothy let out an almighty scream. Nobody could hear a word of what the pastor was saying after that, and as soon as she was able, Clara took Timothy from him and tried to calm him down. The procedure for Jeffrey and Lilly was slightly different, as the pastor could hardly pick them up and pour water over their heads. He just anointed them. At the end, the pastor welcomed the children into the family of the chapel.

"Now, before everyone leaves, I have one last duty," the pastor announced to the congregation. "You all know Carl Kennion, the father of the children that have just been baptised, but not many you know his wife, Clara. Will both of you kindly come and join me?" Clara handed Timothy to Hannah, and she and Carl made their way to the front.

"What is this about?" Carl whispered to Clara.

"I don't know. Sounds a bit fishy to me."

"Carl and Clara, on this auspicious day, I would like to bless your marriage so that it is recognised in the eyes of God and welcome you, Clara, into our community."

To both Carl and Clara's absolute astonishment, the pastor proceeded to go through the marriage ceremony. They both felt obliged to follow the pastor's instructions rather than make a scene in front of the whole congregation. He finished by saying, "And I now pronounce you man and wife." Everyone stood up and clapped.

Carl took Clara in his arms and kissed her, then whispered, "Did he just marry us?"

"Not sure, but it sounded like it."

As they walked out of the chapel, everyone they met congratulated them, which was met with a false smile and a '*thank you*'.

The drive home was tense. Carl was furious at his mother, as he was sure that she had instigated the so-called blessing. Luckily, Lilly chatted in her usual manner all the way home.

After lunch, when the two little ones were having their nap and Lilly had gone out to play, Carl tackled his mother. "How could you do that to us? We had already said that we didn't want a blessing as neither of us attend church?" said Carl angrily.

"I am sorry, son. I didn't know he was going to do that there and then. He mentioned to me the possibility of a blessing and that perhaps he could do it after the baptisms, and I did say it was a good idea, but nothing more than that. I was as surprised as you. But it was a lovely service, don't you think? It's nice to know that you are now properly married in the church and not merely in a registry office," replied Hannah. "I am going to see Betsy," she said and quick as a flash left the house.

Carl took Clara in his arms. "I am so sorry."

"You have nothing to be sorry about. I don't think he could have married us because surely we would have had to sign the register or at least be given a marriage certificate. Anyway, let's not dwell on it. I'm sure your mother wouldn't have purposely deceived us. To me, it's the pastor that is devious. I don't really like him very much. Let's hope that Lilly gets fed up of Sunday school and that this is just a phase she is going through," said Clara.

Shortly before Timothy's first birthday, the family celebrated Thanksgiving with Helen, Gary and the boys arriving for the annual holiday. Gary would always go through the farm's accounts, but on this occasion, he asked for a family meeting to discuss accounts.

"There is nothing wrong, is there?" Carl asked Gary.

"No, you are doing a fantastic job, and the profits are up on last year. Helen and I have discussed our share, and we want to suggest that you should try and buy us out. You do all the work, and I just sit in New York and take the profit. It's about time you took over the sole ownership," said Gary.

"Oh, yes, and how am I supposed to raise enough money to buy you out? Let's get real. I may have a bit put by, but not enough," said Carl.

"Don't worry about that. I could arrange to get you a very good rate on a mortgage through one of my contacts. What do you think?" asked Gary.

"Well in principal, yes, but it would have to be a good deal," said Carl sceptically.

"If you think about it, Carl. It would be no different from paying me my share of the profit. It would just mean that you would be paying the mortgage, plus interest of course. Anyway, leave it to me, and I will speak to a couple of my contacts and put a package together for you to consider," said Gary.

It took a month for Gary to come back to the farm accompanied by a mortgage broker. They sat down with Carl and Clara and went over the accounts and the mortgage details. While Gary and the mortgage broker had lunch with Hannah, Carl and Clara left the room to discuss the offer.

"It's a good offer," said Clara. "It means that we will be paying less on the mortgage repayments than we are now paying Gary. I know it will take us twenty years to repay the mortgage, but at the end, the farm will be ours or at least yours, and we can do what we want without having to ask Gary every time we want to buy something. What do you think?" asked Clara.

"It's a big debt, what happens if the crop fails or—"

"Or what, Carl? We have to take a risk," said Clara.

"Okay, let's give Gary our decision before I change my mind or find another IF!" said Carl.

The farm was theirs and so was the mortgage, but Clara had plans—big plans.

CHAPTER 29

Over the time Clara had been in North Carolina, she had noticed that coaches of tourist and hikers would pass the farm. On several occasions, they had stopped and driven up to the house asking questions about the crops and usually asking if they could use the bathroom. This annoyed Hannah intensely, making them use the outside lavatory.

"Cheek of people, thinking they can just turn up here to use our facilities on the pretence of wanting to look around the farm and admire the view."

Clara had once suggested that the tourists did appear to be interested in the area and what crops they grew only to be put down by Hannah.

Clara invited the builder who had renovated Valley House to come and see her.

"What are you up to, Clara?" asked Hannah.

"Wait and see," said Clara, wanting to keep her idea to herself for now. The builder met her at Valley House, and she explained her plan to him.

"That's a brilliant idea." He went on to explain what could be done to change the layout of the house and the costs involved. All she had to do now was convince Carl and Hannah.

The next day Clara went to the tourist office in Raleigh and got details of the tour companies that provided tours of the area and asked about advertising in the next tourist brochure. She then went to Hamrick's to price out various items, asking the manager about a bulk buyer discount, which she managed to negotiate to a high rate.

That evening, with all the children in bed, she sat down with Carl and Hannah to put forward her idea.

"What have you been up to today, Clara? You are being very secretive," said Hannah.

"Sorry, but I wanted to collect all the information I needed before I put my plans to you both," said Clara.

She gave them her list of costs, estimations and budget forecasts, which she had meticulously worked on all afternoon, and then went on to explain her idea.

"I want to open up a tearoom in Valley House," she announced.

"A tearoom?" questioned Carl.

"Yes, just hear me out please," she pleaded.

"Downstairs would be where we would serve the customers and have a small kitchen, upstairs would be the bathroom facilities, and the three bedrooms that could be used for passing hikers if they wanted a stop-over or to say stay a few nights. I have put it all there," she said, pointing to the estimate given to her by the builder.

She continued as she looked at the estimate with them, "Here are the cost of converting the downstairs, to make one large tearoom that would double as a dining room for any visitors staying over, and the cost of installing two bathrooms with wash basins upstairs. The bedrooms and bathrooms would remain as they are and so would the kitchen."

Carl was speechless. "You have done all this on your own?"

"Yes! And if you look at the builder's estimate, it includes changing the driveway so coaches or visitors arriving by car can park outside Valley House. And ... I spoke with the manager at Hamrick's today about supplying all the equipment, and he offered me a very favourable discount if I buy everything from him. He even said that if he didn't have what I wanted, he would get it for me. Well, what do you think? A good idea or not?" asked Clara, feeling very pleased with herself.

"And this is the profit we, well you, could make?" questioned Carl, looking at her workings.

"Yes, but I would need capital to start. I know we have a rainy-day fund in the bank, so I either could use this or I could ask the bank for a loan."

"If I could butt in here," said Hannah. "How on earth could we possibly do this? We are pushed enough now, Clara. What with looking after the house, the garden and three children. It would be too much. I am not getting any younger, Clara. Even now, I have to have a rest every afternoon."

"I have thought of that," she said.

Clara had continued to write to Niamph, and the past two years had been happy for Niamph. She had met '*the man of her dreams*' as she described him, and plans were in place for them to be married. But in her latest letter, Niamph had written that the relationship had ended:

'*I foolishly thought it was better to tell Patrick everything about me before we married, not wanting to hide anything from him, but I was wrong. When I told him about Bernadette, he walked out on me. I tried to reason with him, but obviously, he didn't love me enough. I am heartbroken, Clara. I thought the hurt I felt at losing my baby was bad enough, but I have now lost the only man I have ever loved. I feel sometimes that I don't want to go on with my life. It's as if the whole world is against me.*'

Clara had written back straight away, trying to console her friend, which was difficult in a letter, and had invited her to come and stay with her for a while.

Clara went on to tell Carl and Hannah about Niamph's letter and how she had written and asked her to come and stay with them. She hoped that perhaps they would agree to have Niamph stay and work with them.

"But if she says no, then we would see about employing some full-time help, and I have budgeted for some help in my figures. Of course, Hannah, I do realise we can't do it on our own," said Clara.

"Can I sleep on it, Clara?" asked Hannah.

"I agree, Mum. I want to think about it as well," said Carl. "Let me go through the farm accounts and your figures, and we will discuss it again tomorrow night."

Clara was a bit deflated, as she had been so excited about the whole project that she thought everyone else would be as well, but she realised that it was a big commitment that could not only be a success but also a failure.

Lilly was now six and had been at school for a year. Every day Hannah or Betsy would walk her down the drive to the road where the school bus would pick her up and drop her back at the end of the day. The day after their discussion, she could see Hannah walking back from taking Lilly to the bus through the kitchen window. Then, she saw Carl intercept her as she neared the house.

From what she could see, they were having a heated discussion. *'No doubt about my proposal,'* thought Clara.

Hannah appeared to storm off in the direction of the house with Buster and Scamp at her heels. Clara pretended to be busy, giving the boys their breakfast when Hannah came in banging the door behind her.

"Men," she said as Carl came marching in behind her.

"Look you two, I don't want you falling out over my plans. Let's just forget I ever said anything. It was only an idea after all. And ... you are right, Hannah, how could we take on another job? We have enough as it is," said Clara.

"No, you have got us wrong. We are not falling out over your plans. We both think it is a fantastic idea, and in fact I have even got another idea to enhance yours."

"Well, what are you arguing about then?" asked Clara.

"I want to give you the money to get you going, but Carl doesn't want me to give it to you, but as I have tried to explain to him, I have money sitting in the bank that I don't need. You two provide me with everything I need except for my clothes, and I don't buy many of those. It seems to me that I could invest in your project and you could repay me in the future with interest," explained Hannah.

Clara was so surprised she had to sit down. She was so happy she could have cried. "I thought you hated the idea when I saw you arguing. Thank you for your offer, Hannah," she said, turning to Carl. "I think we should take your mum's offer. If we put in fifty per cent and your mum puts in fifty per cent, we could be partners in this new business and split the profits. That way your mum is not putting in all her savings," suggested Clara.

"Okay, then. You two have worn me down," sighed Carl, "but I want a proper agreement put in place. I don't want Gary saying that we have fleeced Mum of her money."

"Agreed," said Hannah. "Now let's have a cup of coffee and some of that banana cake you made yesterday, and you can tell us what your idea is before you go back to work."

Carl explained that his idea was to turn one of the barns into a kind of museum of old farming equipment.

"When you said, Clara, that some of the tourists were interested in the farm, you were right. I remember one man asking me all sorts of questions about the rusty old things that are lying around the place. I thought we could get all those old things and put them in the big barn. There is nothing much else in there. Then we can label them saying what they are and their purpose. We could also perhaps put old pictures of the farm around the walls, even old newspaper cuttings."

"And," said Clara, "we could make a charge for them to go in or ask for a small donation."

"Or," said Hannah, "we could give them free entry if they buy something in the tearoom."

"That's a brilliant idea. Now I must get back to work or the men will be sending out a search party for me," said Carl.

As Clara and Hannah got stuck into the morning's work, they discussed excitedly what they would sell in the tearoom and how much they would charge, each coming up with new and different ideas. In the end, Clara suggested that they needed to sit down with a notebook and write down everything.

"Let's go down to Valley House after lunch with the boys, and tomorrow, I'll ask Betsy to look after the boys, and we can go to town and see the bank manager," said Hannah, who was now more excited than Clara.

It took three months to get everything ready. They were so proud of the results. Ten tables covered with red and white gingham tablecloths, each ready to accommodate four people, occupied two of the ground floor rooms that had been knocked into one. They had hung pretty net curtains at the windows, all made by Hannah. The kitchen and scullery had been knocked into one and now had a new double stove with two ovens and worktops on either side. On the adjacent wall, a worktop ran along the entire wall that held a big electric urn for making teas. There was shelving above the worktop filled with matching floral cups, saucers and plates of different sizes. The cupboards below the worktops held matching teapots, milk jugs and sugar basins. On the opposite wall stood their pride and joy, a freestanding double refrigerator with an icebox. In fact they were both so taken with the refrigerator, they made Carl buy one for the farmhouse. The only thing they hadn't finished were the bedrooms. The driveway had cost much more than anticipated, so Clara and Hannah decided to leave the furnishing of the bedrooms to avoid going over their budget.

All they had to do now was wait for the tourists. Advertisements had been put in the tourism brochure for the area and in the tourism offices in both Raleigh and Charlotte. They had offered a tour company an incentive if they brought their coaches to the tearoom, and there was a signpost at the end of the drive.

Niamph had arrived the month before the work had finished. She had grabbed the opportunity to leave New York and make a fresh start. Clara was concerned at first that Niamph would miss teaching and find the work at the farm a bit mundane. But those fears soon faded. Niamph enjoyed family life, and she relished looking after the children. Clara loved having her around. She was someone of her own age, and they would talk about anything and everything, confiding in each other like only two women could.

Valley Tearooms opened for business on the first of May 1956.

The tour company that Clara had originally contacted sent a representative to visit the tearoom. He looked very official when he arrived with a clipboard in one hand. He extended his other hand to shake hands with Clara and then shook Hannah's. He introduced himself, "Mike Loftis. Pleased to make your acquaintance, ladies."

"Thank you for coming, Mr. Loftis. I am Clara Kennion, and this is my mother-in-law, Hannah Kennion. We are partners in this new venture," said Clara.

"Please, call me Mike."

As they walked from the farmhouse to the tearoom, Mike took copious notes. They showed him around the bathroom facilities upstairs first and then all around the downstairs area.

"I am impressed. It all looks very *'quaint,'* if that is the right word, just what our clientele are looking for. They don't want to stop at a diner. They much prefer a small family place like this. Is it possible to see your menu?" asked Mike.

Clara handed him a copy, explaining that they would make sandwiches to order so as each one would be fresh, that there would be a homemade soup of the day that would come with freshly made crusty bread, and that cakes would all be homemade. "Our intention is to provide a light lunch and afternoon tea, opening the tearoom from say noon to four in the afternoon. Obviously, if we are a success, then we could open either earlier or later, but we need to see how things pan out," explained Clara.

"That sounds perfect, and I can happily say that we will make you one of our stops. Now you spoke of incentives. ..." said Mike.

"Yes, my idea was to either give the driver or your firm a percentage of what their tour group spent or even a one-off payment so long as you could guarantee us so many coaches a week," said Clara.

"Mmm ... I wouldn't want the driver to have anything, as he usually gets tips at the end of each tour, and depending on the nationality of the group, they can be quite substantial. So I would prefer to negotiate a one-off payment. If I could, say, guarantee five coaches a week for lunch and five for afternoon tea, what sort of figure would you have in mind?"

"Oh! I didn't think there would be that many, so I will need to discuss it with Hannah. Are there really that many tourists a week?" asked Clara.

"Here is our brochure." He handed both Clara and Hannah a copy. "If you look at the various itineraries we do, you'll notice the coaches that come from the south. It is those that you would provide with afternoon tea, as we stop in Charlotte for lunch before travelling north for an overnight stop and then come across from Charleston or down from Richmond. That group would require a light lunch. Perhaps I could look around the museum you mentioned while you discuss a figure," suggested Mike.

Although Carl and the men had cleared the barn and placed all the old equipment they could find in the barn, they hadn't yet completed the project. They had done this between seasons, and the planting took priority over the museum. She walked Mike to the barn and explained that there was still work to be done, but hopefully he would get the gist of how it would look when finished. She explained the intention of putting labels on the old equipment and machinery, detailing the purpose and what was now used in its place and also the photos and cuttings to be placed on the walls.

Mike did a small tour of the barn and spoke to Carl while Clara and Hannah discussed the figure they should offer Mike.

"I think we should offer him a lower figure than we want to pay and see what he says, then, at least, we have some power to negotiate to the higher amount," said Clara. Hannah agreed.

Clara was quietly excited about this new venture, and the possibility of guaranteed customers gave her plans an extra boost. Her dream was suddenly about to become reality.

Clara invited Mike for some refreshments so they could negotiate the amount to be paid.

Mike left pleased that he had negotiated a reasonable sum, and Clara was very pleased that they had negotiated somewhere towards the lower sum.

CHAPTER 30

Niamph, having arrived in an emotional state, was now in a better place thanks to the loving environment that she found at the farm. Not that everything was perfect, but the arguments that did arise were soon settled, and no ill feeling lingered. She felt she had found the perfect job looking after Clara's children, especially Lilly. Whenever Lilly passed another hurdle in her growing-up stage, Niamph would imagine Bernadette doing the same.

The front parlour of the farmhouse was rarely used. Everyone preferred the comfort of the kitchen. Niamph noticed that there was an upright piano in the parlour the very first time she went into the parlour to clean. When she polished it, she noted that it was made of a beautiful ebony wood with a walnut inlay. She lifted the lid, and on playing a few notes, she could hear that it had not been used for some time, as it was way out of tune. She asked Clara if anyone played the piano.

"Not since I have been here. It just sits in the corner doing nothing. You will have to ask Hannah. Why do you ask?" responded Clara.

"It just seems such a shame for such a lovely instrument not to be played," replied Niamph.

Niamph asked Hannah about the piano that evening at dinner.

"My mother used to play it. She was a lovely pianist, and she tried to teach me, but unfortunately, I am tone deaf and the boys thought only sissies played. My father bought it for her as a wedding present, and nobody has played it since she died. Do you play?" asked Hannah.

"Yes, my grandmother taught me. We had a piano at home but not one nearly as good as yours. When I was young, I would play and everyone would sing. It was a grand time. I haven't played for such a long time. I just hope I haven't forgotten how. Would you mind if I got it tuned, and, perhaps, I could teach the children to play? Have you heard Jeffrey play his little xylophone? He definitely has an ear for a tune," said Niamph.

"It would be wonderful to hear it played again. I will ask the man who tunes the organ at the chapel if he will do it for us."

As it turned out, Lilly had no aptitude to play. Niamph would sit with her trying to teach her the scales, but she couldn't even grasp these. She did love to sing as Niamph played. Unfortunately, her singing was very off key, but she enjoyed it "and that is the main thing," said Niamph to the family as they endured another rendition of '*We're off to see the Wizard*' from the Wizard of Oz that her class was going to be performing at the end of the term.

Lilly would become very indignant when Buster and Scamp howled as soon as she started to sing, much to the amusement of the rest of the family.

Niamph would sit Jeffrey on her knee so he could reach the keys. At the tender age of four, he could play a simple tune. Niamph would play first, and he would copy.

"That boy definitely has potential to make a good piano player. He can play by ear," Niamph told Clara. "When he is a bit older, you should think about getting someone to teach him how to read music."

"I'm not sure what use that will be to him when he starts work on the farm," responded Clara. "But, perhaps, when he starts school, he might be able to learn."

Niamph felt that Clara was being dismissive of Jeffrey's potential talent but vowed to herself that she would teach him what she could even if she herself couldn't read music.

Although Niamph's main job at the farm was to help with the children, she would muck in and help wherever she was needed. When the family was discussing what was to be done to bring the museum up and ready for the tourists, she offered to help.

"I know my way around a library, so I could go into town and do some research and see if I can get copies of old photos and perhaps newspaper cuttings," suggested Niamph.

"That would be great, and your writing is so neat. You could write out the description of the machinery to put next to each item," said Clara.

"I have some old photos in the attic that I will get out for you as well. You can sort through them to see if any would be of use," said Hannah.

With Hannah agreeing to look after Jeffrey and Timothy, Niamph cadged a lift on the school bus to town. Carl had promised to teach her to drive but hadn't got around to it, and the buses to town that passed the farm were very infrequent.

The bus driver gave her directions as to where to find the library. It was a good size, as you would expect from a town the size of Raleigh, and located on the ground floor of a large old building in the centre of the town. Niamph explained to the librarian what she was looking for, and the women directed her to the archives. After spending about an hour researching, she found quite a large amount of items that would be of interest. She wrote down the details in her notebook. When she was about to leave, the librarian suggested that she visit the local newspaper office, giving her instructions as to how to get there.

"They should have lots of old newspapers for you to look through, and the editor there, James Hartley, is a helpful man. Good luck," said the librarian as she left.

Niamph found the newspaper office of the *'The Raleigh Post'* without any problem. She passed a stationery store on the way and went in and purchased some stiff cards, coloured paper, glue and other items she thought might be useful to assist in displaying the information she had gleaned at the library.

The newspaper office was a double front shop on one of the side streets off the main street. As she opened the door, a bell rang. There was a long counter behind which stood all sorts of printing presses. A tall, good-looking man with unruly, wavy brown hair came to the counter. "And how can I help you today? It's not often we have such pretty ladies coming in here," he said, pushing his fingers through his hair.

"Are you Mr. Hartley?" asked Niamph.

"I am, and whom may I ask wants to know?" he said.

Niamph told him who she was and what she was doing and asked if he had any old newspapers that she could perhaps look through.

"We have thousands of newspapers in the basement, going back over fifty years and, yes, you are welcome to go through as many as you like. I must warn you first that it is a very dirty job as you can see," he said as he showed her his black, print-stained hands. "But I may be able to save you some time," he added as he lifted part of the counter and beckoned her through.

"Some years ago, I did an article on farming in the area and how it had progressed. You are more than welcome to a copy of this. Now follow me and be careful how you go. These presses have some sharp edges." He led her to a back room with floor-to-ceiling shelving filled to capacity with large books. Each one was labelled with its contents and the date.

"These books cover the last four to five years. The older ones are downstairs," he explained.

He went along one of the shelves until he found the book he was looking for. He stood on a stool to reach down and placed it on a long table in the middle of the room.

"Here, this is the one," he said as he opened it for her and flipped through the pages to find the article.

"Sit here and read it. See if this is the sort of thing you are looking for," he instructed.

He left her to sit and read the article, which took her about thirty minutes, as she had to re-read some parts. When she had finished, she went to find him in the front of the shop.

"Well, what do you think? Is it what you were looking for?" he asked.

"And more," responded Niamph. "Can I copy it? How much will you charge me to copy it?" she asked.

"There is no charge. If you had read the article in the paper when it was printed, it would only have cost you the price of the paper, and I can copy it for you," he said, walking over to a smaller machine. "This is the latest invention for copying it called a Xerox machine. You put the piece of paper that you want to copy in there and out comes a copy under here. You wait for it to dry and hey! Presto, you have a copy. We are up to date here with our technology," he said proudly.

He unscrewed the pages from the book and copied them for Niamph.

"Now, while these are drying, let's go have lunch," he suggested.

"I didn't realise it was that time already. Yes, now that you mention lunch, I am hungry," replied Niamph.

They went to a diner just across the road. James ordered a burger and a coke, and Niamph ordered a sandwich and a coffee. "Please let me pay. It is the least I can do after all your help," said Niamph.

"Only on condition that I pay for dinner," replied James.

Niamph was a bit taken back. "Are you asking me to dinner?"

"I surely am," he said.

"Then, I accept," she replied.

Over lunch, Niamph asked him seriously about payment, and he asked that the articles displayed be attributed to him and his paper. "It will be a bit of free advertising for me, and speaking of advertising, I hope you will consider advertising your museum and tearoom with my paper. We need all the revenue we can get," said James.

"I don't see why not, especially given all your help," said Niamph.

After lunch, they made their way back to the newspaper office. James placed the copied articles into a file for her to carry home.

"Would you like to look at some old photos of the area? I have heaps of those," he said as he led her to the back room. "Wait here, and I will go downstairs and get you some."

James returned a few minutes later with a document box of envelopes each holding a large amount of photos with the negatives attached. She spent the next hour looking through them and chose about twenty photos that she thought would be appropriate.

"I will have to charge you for these, as the photographic paper is too expensive for me to give away," explained James.

"Of course, I must pay. There are a lot of photos here," said Niamph.

"I will have them ready for you the day after tomorrow. Perhaps, I could deliver them to you, and then we could go to dinner?" suggested James.

Niamph thanked him and told him that would be perfect and that she looked forward to it.

She left the shop feeling quite elated. Not only had she gotten all the information for the museum, but she also had a date. '*Wait until I tell Clara*,' she thought.

James turned up to pick Niamph up for dinner as he had promised with all the photos she had chosen. He had even enlarged some of them for her. Niamph invited him into the kitchen to meet Clara.

"Clara, this is James."

They shook hands. Clara said she was pleased to meet him as Carl came into the room.

"James, what are you doing here? Bud, I haven't seen you in ages. How are you?" exclaimed Carl, taking hold of James's hand and shaking it firmly. Then he looked at Niamph and the penny dropped. "Oh! You're Niamph's date. Clara just told me that Niamph had a date, but she didn't say who with." He laughed.

"Good to see you too, Bud. I am fine. I can see you are well, and quite a family you have now."

"Yeah, three kids now—quite a house full. So you are off to dinner? Now no sweeping our best helper off her feet. We need her here," teased Carl.

James laughed as he took Niamph's hand and led her to his car.

He drove to a little restaurant on the outskirts of Raleigh. He was the perfect gentleman, holding the chair for her to sit down and ordering her cocktail while she chose what she wanted to eat.

"Tell me about yourself, Niamph," he asked.

"Well, I am thirty-one. I come from a small village in Ireland," she explained.

"I wondered what your accent was. So you're Irish, right?" asked James.

"Yes, that's right. I met Clara on the ship on our way to America when she was coming to be with Carl and I was going to New York. I stayed in New York teaching at a Catholic school until two months ago when I came here," she said.

"Why did you leave Ireland? Seems a long way from New York," he asked.

"To be totally honest, to escape from the heartache of having my baby taken away from me. Now tell me about yourself," said Niamph.

"Oh! I don't know how to follow that. I want to ask more. Are you married?" he asked.

"No, I am not. Are you?" she said defensively.

"Sorry, let's start again, and no, I am not married. Let's order first. Do you know what you want?"

They gave their order to the waiter, and James ordered a bottle of white wine to accompany the meal.

"You are unusually forthright, Niamph, for a first date, not that I mind," said James.

"I'm sorry too. It was rude of me. Please tell me about you," she said.

"I am forty-five, same as Carl. We were in school together. When I left school, I joined my father at the newspaper. He died five years ago, and I took it over, so I have lived here all my life. As you were so honest, I will tell you that I was engaged to a girl named Louise for three years. We had been together for five years and were going to be married when she drowned in a boating accident on the lake not far from here," he said.

"Oh my god! I am so sorry. How did it happen?" asked Niamph.

"We were in a small rowing boat on the lake, and we were mucking around when she dropped her oar in the water. I jumped in to retrieve it, and as I tried to get back in the boat, it tipped over, and she got trapped underneath. I tried to dive under to get to her, but every time I tried to get hold of her, she slipped from my grip. Other people on the lake tried to help me, but by the time I got her to the lakeside, it was too late," he said with tears welling up in his eyes.

"That is terrible," said Niamph, taking hold of his hand to comfort him.

The food arrived. As they ate, James told her all about the newspaper business and how he had increased the circulation since taking over from his father and his plans for expansion in the future.

Niamph told him all about Ireland and growing up with her brothers and sisters and how she had met Clara on the ship.

They finished their meal and walked to the car. As James drove her home, he asked if he could see her again. "Yes, I would like that," she replied.

It was five dates later that Niamph told him the story of Bernadette and explained why she had told him on the first date of her existence. "I didn't want to get emotionally attached to you, then for you to finish with me when you found out that I had had a baby. I couldn't go through another heartache. I have had enough already in my life."

"I understand, and thank you for telling me. You are the first person that I have dated who I have told about Louise. It still hurts to talk about her, but as time goes by, it gets better."

Their relationship steadily grew and soon became a permanent fixture and James a regular visitor to the farm.

CHAPTER 31

The opening of the tearoom was planned to coincide with the first coach load of tourists. Clara, Hannah and Niamph had sat down and discussed at length the allocation of jobs and soon realised that they couldn't do everything between just the three of them. They agreed to initially employ a waitress and a person to wash the dishes. They were surprised at the number of applicants they received from the advertisement placed in James's newspaper, mostly from students from the university in Charlotte.

They chose two young girls, Nancy and Barbara, both nineteen, students and friends.

"Would it be possible for us to share the roles? Say I do the tables one day and Barbara does them the next? That way one of us is not washing dishes all of the time," asked Nancy.

"If you are happy to do this, then yes that would not be a problem. Do you have any other questions?" replied Clara.

"Yes, can we keep any tips that we receive?" asked Nancy.

"Oh! I hadn't thought about tips. I don't see why not. Perhaps, we could put a container by the till so if anyone wants to leave anything, they could use this. Would you like to find a container and perhaps put a label on it so people know what it is for? Then, I suggest you share it between yourselves at the end of the day since you are sharing the job," replied Clara.

The girls turned out to be the perfect fit. Each had a sunny personality and interacted with the customers effortlessly.

Hannah and Clara had agreed that they would run the kitchen. It was a steep learning curve during that first week for them, as they soon realised that sandwiches had to be pre-made and bread had to be cut and buttered in advance. The very first coach arrived with thirty tourists aboard. Trying to take orders and getting all that food served in good time was a mammoth task.

At the end of the first day, they all sat down in the tearoom kitchen exhausted, realising that they hadn't quite got the demographics right. Nancy suggested that both she and Barbara should take the orders when the customers arrived, and then one of them could make the drinks while the other served them.

"This would then give Hannah and me time to prepare the food, and then you could both serve it. That's a brilliant idea, Nancy," said Clara. "You should go into business management when you leave the university."

Following that first week, the running of the tearoom settled into a routine. The girls would recommend the sandwiches that were pre-made and the cakes that hadn't sold from the previous day. After the coach parties left, they would wash the dishes and tidy the tearoom in preparation for the next day.

As the first month progressed, Hannah soon realised that she couldn't cope with the work involved in the tearoom. Each morning, Clara would do all the baking, leaving Hannah to prepare the soup, but there was still the house to clean, the washing to be done, the vegetable plot to be attended to, plus the many other jobs required to run the house.

"I am almost seventy, Clara. I just get too tired," Hannah explained.

"I should have realised, Hannah. I am so sorry. I was so wrapped up in making a success of the tearoom that I forgot to take into consideration what was happening around me. Let me think of a solution. In the meantime, you stay home."

That evening, feeling tired, Hannah had gone to bed early, as had been her habit since the beginning of the year. Niamph had gone out with James, leaving Clara to freely discuss with Carl what they should do.

"I thought I would ask Nancy and Barbara if they had a friend who may be interested in a job and that would help with the tearoom and then perhaps we could look to employ someone to help in the house. What do you think?" asked Clara.

"The tearoom is doing well, so we can well afford to pay another wage without the profits being effected too much. The farm is faring even better, especially with the price of tobacco up this year compared with the same time last year. Thinking about it, you know, I took on that chap last week, the one that has moved into old Joe's place," said Carl.

Old Joe was a retired worker who had stayed on rent-free at the cottage after working for Carl and his father for over forty years and had sadly died the previous month. Clara had to think for a minute, then remembered that Hannah had mentioned that she and Betsy had had to clear the cottage of old Joe's possessions and clean up the place.

"Yes, I do remember. I should have gone around and introduced myself to him and his wife, but it completely slipped my mind. I hope they don't think me rude. I will pop around in the morning," said Clara.

"What I was going to say is that ... and by the way, would you believe it, but his name is Joe as well? ... anyway, he asked me if there was a job going for his wife. I did say she could do some picking when the season starts, but to be honest, she didn't look the picking type. He introduced me to her, but I can't remember her name. Why don't you ask her if she wants to take over the housework? That would be the perfect solution, and we could easily afford to pay her to work full-time," suggested Carl.

The next morning, after making the bread dough and leaving it to prove, Clara made her way over to old Joe's cottage. She knocked, and a lady, who Clara guessed was in her early thirties, answered it. She was about five feet, four inches tall with her dark hair tied back in a ponytail.

"Hello, I am Clara Kennion, and I should have come earlier to welcome you," said Clara, extending her hand to shake hands with the woman.

"Hiya, so pleased to meet you. I am Sally. Come in."

Clara was pleasantly surprised when she went into the cottage kitchen. Sally had decorated it with a pretty, light lilac paint, and the table was covered in a floral tablecloth with a vase of wildflowers in the middle. There were new rugs on the floor, and the chairs each had floral seat covers on them.

"I can't believe what you have done in such a short space of time. It looks lovely and homely," said Clara.

"I haven't got anything else to do while Joe is at work. I got the paint cheap in town, and the man in the shop told me what to do. It is the first time I have done any painting, so I am really pleased with myself. Although, I did get more paint on me than I did on the walls at one point. Would you like a cup of coffee? There is a pot on the stove," asked Sally.

"I'm sorry. I just don't have time, I need to put my bread in the oven to bake ready for lunch but perhaps another time. My husband said that Joe had mentioned that you were looking for a job, is that right?" asked Clara.

"Yes, it is. I got the newspaper last week, but there was nothing suitable in it, and we don't have a car yet. It would be difficult to get anywhere from here. The buses don't seem to be very regular. Why do you ask?" she said.

"You're right about the buses, although there are plans to increase the number of buses since they have built the new road by New Hill, but it may be some time. Anyway, I am looking for someone to help me at the farmhouse. It would be housework, I'm afraid. Nothing exciting. Cleaning, washing and a bit of cooking. Do you think you would be interested?" asked Clara.

"When can I start? I am going crazy here. There is only so much cleaning you can do in a place this size," said Sally.

"Now!" said a relieved Clara.

"Let me leave a note for Joe," said Sally. "Will I be able to come back at lunchtime to feed Joe?"

"If you don't mind helping with the lunch for Carl, the foreman and one of the other men, then you can tell Joe he can have his lunch at the farmhouse with them," said Clara.

As they walked over to the farmhouse, Clara explained what she wanted Sally to do and said that Hannah would show her where everything was.

Sally arrived in the farmhouse kitchen to what seemed to be organised chaos. Hannah was sitting, having her breakfast. Timothy was in his high chair, screaming at Niamph because he wanted to feed himself, two dogs sat at each side of the high chair waiting to see what came their way. Jeffrey was demanding strawberry jam on his toast instead of black currant, and Lilly was practicing her song for the Wizard of Oz.

"Shh! Everyone, this is Sally, and she is going to be helping us," shouted Clara.

"Hannah, Sally is here to help you with everything, and I mean everything. You are from today going to take a well-earned rest, and I don't want to see you in the tearoom either, although can you still do the soup for me?" She laughed.

"Of course, I can. Pleased to meet you, Sally. Welcome to our mad house. Lilly, hurry up, or you will be late for the bus," said Hannah.

All Clara had to do now was arrange for extra help in the tearoom, which proved almost as simple, as Nancy had a friend, Lottie, who agreed to start the next day.

The tearoom was proving to be a great success, as not only the tourists but also locals started coming for afternoon tea or lunch. Clara had to increase the lunch menu and introduced homemade Quiche Lorraine with salad, scrambled eggs with toast and a variety of salads. Lottie volunteered to help Clara with the cooking which was a great help, as it was becoming impossible for her to do it on her own.

The baking of the bread for sandwiches gradually became unworkable, not only the baking but also the cutting since they couldn't provide uniform slices for sandwiches. When a baker turned up one day touting for business, Clara felt he was heaven-sent. After tasting his pre-sliced bread and being impressed at the quality and taste, she placed a daily order. She now had more time to concentrate on the cakes and lunches.

The day of Lilly's school production of the Wizard of Oz arrived. The entire family including Niamph and Sally sat in the front row of the school hall. Lilly was one of two narrators and knew her lines by heart and in fact Niamph said to Clara, "So do I."

Lilly was so excited that she could barely contain herself, talking non-stop in the car on the way to school. She had a new dress, a pretty blue floral one with a belted waist with a full skirt and a little white collar.

She informed Clara, "Mummy, I have to have a new dress, as Miss Adams says we have to look our best because all of the audience will be looking at us."

Clara felt sure that the audience would all be looking at their own children and not Lilly.

James had also come along in a professional capacity, as he would be writing a review for his paper, which he told Lilly would include a photo. "I will try and get you in the photo so you can be in my paper."

Lilly felt very important at the thought of having her picture in the newspaper.

The production was hilariously brilliant given the ages of the cast. One little girl wet herself on stage and had to be quickly removed by Miss Adams. Another little boy was so nervous, he couldn't get his lines out. The younger ones, all dressed as munchkins, sat in the front surreptitiously waving to their parents, and the singing was more shouting than singing at one point. But they got a standing ovation at the end.

The production coincided with the last day of the term and Lilly's first year at school. Clara and Carl had gone along to the school to parents' evening a few days earlier to receive Lilly's end of year report. They were pleasantly surprised that Miss Adams gave Lilly a glowing report, saying that her reading was that of a child two years her senior, and her writing was coming along nicely.

"She has a passion to please and an enquiring mind which will take her a long way in life," said Miss Adams. "I chose her as a narrator for our end-of-term production because she speaks beautifully—clear and precise for her age. However, I must add that once she gets chatting, it is very hard to stop her."

Clara and Carl laughed at this statement, as they were well aware of Lilly's chatting ability.

When Clara relayed Miss Adams's comments to Niamph the next day, Niamph said, "She has an enquiring mind, alright. Some days I think to myself if she asks me one more time, '*but what if this or what if that*' and '*did you know Auntie Niamph*,' I will scream. But she does love to read, and I always get a load of books from the library for her and Jeffrey."

Niamph looked after the children during the long summer holidays with some help from Gamy. Lilly would help her show the visitors around the museum and soon knew as much as Niamph about the machinery on show.

Niamph relished the museum, always adding new interesting facts, usually supplied by James or from books she found in the library. Her enthusiasm overflowed onto all the visitors to the museum, and as a consequence, the visitors would nearly always leave a contribution in the box provided.

The summer soon ended, and Lilly went back to school for her second year, and a month later the tearoom closed for the season.

The takings and profit exceeded all expectation, and Clara thanked the girls for all the efforts with an end-of-season bonus. Nancy and Lottie promised they would be back the following year, whereas it was Barbara's final year at university. As she explained to Clara, she would be entering the world of full-time employment, all being well.

Clara felt a sense of achievement as she cleaned and shut up the tearoom for the winter months. She was looking forward to a long-earned rest, but at the same time, she was looking forward to opening up the tearoom again the following year.

.

CHAPTER 32

Time flew past, and before they knew it, the time came for Jeffrey to start school. He could already read the basic starter books, count to one hundred, recite the alphabet and write out his name and simple words. But it was his musical ability that astounded everyone that heard him play the piano. Clara had already spoken to Miss Adams before he started and asked about music lessons and was disappointed to find out that the school did not have a music teacher.

It became apparent after his first year at school that his learning ability and progress far outweighed his classmates. Miss Adams suggested that he apply for a scholarship to a private independent school in Raleigh that had a large music department.

Clara took him for the interview that included a small test. He passed with flying colours and impressed the interview panel with his eloquent replies to their questions. Clara explained that Jeffrey's teacher had recommended their school because of its musical department and that Jeffrey could already play a number of tunes on the piano.

"We can definitely offer Jeffrey a place at our school, Mrs. Kennion. However, it will not be a full scholarship, but we will offer you a fifty per cent reduction in fees for the first year. We will then review this arrangement this time next year with a view to a full scholarship thereafter. I will put this in writing to you, and, perhaps, you could confirm your agreement by signing the letter and returning it to us," explained the headmaster. He shook hands with both Jeffrey and Clara. "It's been a pleasure meeting you, young man, and I hope we will see you in September," he said.

Jeffrey was quiet all the way home, and it was only when they got home and Niamph asked him how he got on, that he expressed his concerns at going to this new school.

"It is so big, Auntie Niamph." Then turning to his mother, he said, "What happens if I get lost and can't find my classroom, and I am late for lessons?"

"Oh, sweetheart, is that your only worry?" said Clara. "I thought you were quiet on the way home because you didn't like it."

"No, I thought it was great. Did you see the science room and the music room had loads of instruments?" said Jeffrey.

"Of course, I saw them. I was with you, silly," said Clara.

When the letter arrived a few days later, Clara and Carl discussed it at length.

"Do you think it is fair on Lilly and Timothy that Jeffrey is treated differently by going to this school?" Clara asked.

"Let's ask Lilly what she thinks," suggested Carl—so they did.

"Well, I think that Jeffrey is very clever, Mummy. I wouldn't want to go to another school because all my friends are at my school. I think Jeffrey should go to this special school so he can learn more music because, you know, Mummy, he loves music. ... and I won't have to look after him on the bus," said Lilly.

Clara looked at Carl, stifling a laugh. "Well is that any clearer?" she said.

In the end, they agreed that he should go, and it turned out to be one of their best decisions, as Jeffrey flourished, moving from elementary to intermediary music in the first two years. He excelled in all subjects, but music was his passion.

Carl knew, and so did Clara, that Jeffrey would never take over the farm when the time came. That role would be taken by their rough and tumble son, Timothy. Timmy liked nothing better than play fighting with Carl on the floor, which Jeffrey hated. Whenever Carl tried to get Jeffrey to join in, he would back away, saying, "No, Daddy, I don't want to play fighting," leaving Timmy and Carl to it.

Hannah's beloved Jack Russells, Buster and Scamp, were now eighteen years of age, a good age for a small dog. It was Buster who, after months of doing nothing but either sleeping in his basket cuddled up to Scamp or lay on Hannah's knee, started to show signs of distress. When he cried all night and seemed unable to settle, Hannah called the vet. The vet, after examining him, said he appeared to have a neurological disorder and suggested it would be best for Buster to be put to sleep. The entire family was distraught; nobody wanted to make a decision. However, after a second distressful night, they agreed it would be kinder to put him out of his misery.

They all missed him, but Scamp missed him the most. Within two weeks, Hannah discovered him in his basket one morning. He had died in his sleep.

Shortly after, James turned up at the farm with a present for the children. Knowing how upset they had been at the death of Buster and Scamp, he thought this was a perfect present.

"Guess what I have for you?" he asked, holding his coat closed.

"Tell us, Uncle James, please, please," begged Lilly.

"Is it some sweets? I like sweets," said Timmy just as a little sound came from James's coat.

"I hope that is not what I think it is," said Clara.

James looked a bit sheepish as he opened his coat. There sat an adorable yellow Labrador puppy.

"Can I take him?" said Jeffrey, putting out his hands and gently taking the puppy from James.

James explained that he had reported on an abandoned Labrador Bitch that had been found on the roadside with her puppy at her side. The mother had died a short time later, and he said that when he went to take a photo of the puppy at the animal shelter, he couldn't resist but to take the puppy home. "I thought of your children as soon as I saw him all on his own in a cage at the shelter, so I asked if I could take him," he said.

"We can keep him, can't we, Mummy?" said Lilly.

"Please, Mummy! Look! He likes me," said Jeffrey as the puppy was licking his face.

"I suppose, but we have to ask Daddy," said Clara.

The children instantly ran to find their father who was upstairs. "Daddy, Daddy," they all shouted, running up the stairs.

"Where is the fire?" asked Carl.

"Daddy, James has bought us a puppy. Come and see him. Can we keep him, Daddy, please, please?" urged Lilly.

"Let me get down the stairs first," said Carl.

Carl was deluged with pleas from the children as he walked into the kitchen. He shook hands with James. "How are you, Bud? What chaos are you causing today?" Carl asked jokingly.

Clara handed him the puppy. "This is the chaos. Isn't he adorable?"

The children all appeared to respond at once, "Can we keep him, Daddy, please, please, Daddy, can we keep him?"

"I don't see why not, but you three will have to look after him. Me, Mummy and Gamy have enough to do, and until he is grown up, you will have to make sure he doesn't wander off," said Carl.

"Oh, thank you, Daddy, thank you," they all said at once.

"He can sleep on my bed," said Jeffrey.

"No, I want him to sleep on my bed," said Lilly.

"He is not going to sleep on anyone's bed. He will have his own bed in the back room. In fact, I don't want him upstairs at all, especially as he will need to be toilet trained," said Clara sternly.

"What shall we call him?" asked Lilly.

All three debated on a name. Lilly wanted to call him Fudge because he was the same colour as fudge. Jeffrey wanted to call him Barney because he looked like Barney the Bear, and Timmy was not quite sure. Looking around the room for inspiration, he finally said Biscuit.

"Daddy, you choose," said Lilly.

"I will put all three names on a piece of paper, and Mummy can close her eyes and choose," said Carl.

Clara wrote down each name on individual scraps of paper and folded them. Carl held them while Clara closed her eyes and chose the name.

"And the winner is," Clara said as she unwrapped the paper, "Biscuit."

Everyone cheered, and so Biscuit became a member of the family, causing absolute chaos at first by chewing anything and everything until he had his own things to chew on. He was a quick learner and in no time at all was house-trained. Although Clara had banned him from going upstairs, she would often find him asleep on Jeffrey's bed in the morning. He grew to be a lovely well-behaved dog.

While the children were at school, he would wander around the farm, knowing who would give him the best treats. He uncannily knew what time the school bus arrived back at the end of the school day and could be found sitting near the bus stop waiting for the children.

Clara sat at the desk on the morning of the ninth of August, 1960, writing a card to Chantal. Her baby became a teenager today. She sat wondering what her baby looked like now that she was a young lady. How tall was she? Did she remember her mamma? The tears tumbled down her cheeks, her heart breaking as she remembered that last day.

Carl came quietly behind her, putting his arms around her shoulders and resting his chin on her head.

As they stood there together, Lilly suddenly came into the room. "What's the matter, Mummy, why are you crying?"

"Nothing, sweetheart, just Mummy being silly," she reassured as she quickly dried her tears. "Now I must get back to the tearoom or else there will be nothing to eat. Would you like to come with me?" she asked Lilly.

Carl gently kissed her and left to go back to the fields as she and Lilly made their way down the valley to the tearoom.

CHAPTER 33

Niamph and James had now been an item for three years. They were content in their relationship. On the anniversary of Louise's death, they sat on the bank of the lake—James remembering that awful day, and Niamph lying down on the grass sunning herself. In his own way, James loved Niamph. He hadn't actually told her, as he would often wonder to himself what exactly love was. Whereas, Niamph knew that James loved her. He didn't have to say the word. It was the way he stroked her arm or her back or her neck or her hair when they were together, or the way he looked deeply into her eyes before he kissed her.

They were the best of friends. They discussed anything and everything. Nothing was out of bounds. Niamph often talked about Bernadette and James about Louise. She wasn't jealous of Louise, as she understood the feeling of losing someone close to you and how you need to talk about them from time to time.

On this particular day at the lake, James lay on his stomach next to Niamph, tickling her nose with a piece of grass until she opened her eyes. He smiled down at her and said, "Why don't we get married?"

She replied, "Yes, why don't we."

He still didn't tell her he loved her, but he didn't have to. They both knew.

Niamph and James made the announcement to the family that evening. Everyone was delighted.

"About time," said Carl to James, shaking his hand in congratulations.

"Can I be bridesmaid, Auntie Niamph? Please, please, I so want to be a bridesmaid. Bella was a bridesmaid last year, and can I have a pink dress? I don't want a blue dress because Bella had a blue dress. Please, please?" pleaded Lilly.

"Hold on, Lilly. We haven't even discussed the wedding yet," said Niamph.

James butted in, "Of course, you will be Niamph's bridesmaid. You would be our first and only choice," he said to an excited Lilly.

Lilly had been best friends with Bella since they had met at school on that first day and had been joined at the hip ever since. Lilly would often stay over at Bella's house, and Bella would often stay over at the farm. If anyone thought that Lilly could chat, then they hadn't met Bella who could out-talk anyone. They were a perfect match. On the nights that Bella stayed over, no one got any sleep, as the girls appeared to chat at the top of their voices all night. Clara would have to keep going into the bedroom to tell them to keep the noise down.

Niamph and James went to the church to see the new priest, as Niamph called him, not sure what they were called in a Protestant Church. Pastor Cowan had now retired, and the Reverend Kisro had taken over the role as minister. He was much more approachable and understood exactly what they wanted when they explained that they wanted a simple service, as neither of them were regular churchgoers. The wedding was planned for a Saturday at the beginning of September.

Clara planned the reception. "I will close the tearoom on that day, and we will do a glorious buffet. The girls can serve the drinks. ..." She listed all the things she was going to do. Clara was more excited than Niamph, who was extremely nervous.

Niamph had chosen a pale, pink silk, calf-length fitted dress with laced, three-quarter length sleeves. The lace also covered the bodice of the dress to just below the waist. Her hair had been put up in a bun and real flowers arranged on a clip that went around the bun to which was fixed a pink veil that just touched her shoulders. She looked stunning.

Lilly was dressed in an identical-coloured sleeveless, taffeta dress that was fitted at the waist. The knee-length skirt was fitted with a stiff petticoat that made it flare out. There was a big pink silk belt around the waist that was tied at the back into a bow.

Niamph carried three white lilies tied together with leaves and a pink ribbon. Lilly carried a little posy of different coloured flowers.

The moment Niamph walked into the chapel on Carl's arm followed by Lilly, everyone turned around. When James eventually turned and saw her, he cried. Silent tears fell down his cheeks. As Niamph reached his side, he lifted her veil and drew it back, only to see that she had tears welling up in her eyes as well.

"You look beautiful," he whispered, taking her hand and kissing her fingers.

She whispered back, "You don't look too bad yourself."

Rev. Kisro conducted the service. The words of the service were slightly adapted, as they had requested. When he said, "I now pronounce you man and wife. You may now kiss the bride," everyone stood up and applauded.

After signing the register, they walked out of the church and were rained with rice and confetti. The photographer that worked at the newspaper took the photos and then they all departed for the reception. Before getting in the car, Niamph walked slowly and purposely through to the cemetery, and holding James' hand, she placed her bouquet on Louise's grave. They stood for a moment hand-in-hand before James led her away.

The reception was informal and simple just as Niamph had wanted. Everyone helped themselves to food, and the girls from the tearoom went around refilling empty glasses. Clara had hired some additional tables and chairs and put them outside together with an array of picnic blankets on the grass, allowing everyone to relax. Carl delivered a short speech followed by a toast with champagne to the happy couple. Everyone stood up with a deafening shout of "to the Bride and Groom." Clara had made them a beautiful two-tier cake with pink, sugar paste flowers and topped with a model of a bride and groom. They cut the cake together, and pieces were handed out to all the guests.

Lilly had the best time of her life, as she informed everyone afterwards and placed a photo of herself and Niamph in pride of place on her bedroom wall. She kept a copy of the newspaper article of her performance in the Wizard of Oz on her dresser, feeling as courageous now as the Cowardly Lion finally became to be himself. She was becoming herself.

Niamph and James left for a short honeymoon on Lake Michigan in Chicago.

James' mother, Martha, and sister, Faye, had attended the wedding. His mother had left Raleigh shortly after his father had died and moved to Maine to live with his sister and her family. At the time, she felt that there were too many memories in Raleigh, so James had taken over both the business and living accommodation above and paid his mother rent. The day before the wedding, Martha had handed James the deeds to the property as a wedding present from both her and Faye.

"Mother, you can't do this. It is not fair on Faye. She would inherit half in due course," he said.

"I have discussed this with Faye, and when I die, she will inherit the cash I have sitting in the bank. I still have the life insurance money from when your dad died. I honestly don't need much to live on. I don't pay rent on my granny flat, and I have most of my meals with Faye, so I hardly spend anything. I want you and Niamph to have it so you can make it your own," said Martha. "She is a lovely girl, James. You make sure you look after her, and I wish you both all the happiness in the world. And ... I look forward to more grandchildren." She laughed, hugging her son.

Niamph and James took a train to Charlotte where they were spending the night before taking an airplane to Chicago the next day. James told Niamph about the wedding present from his mother. Niamph was overwhelmed.

"That is so generous of her. I will write and thank her when we get back home. I can't wait to decorate your '*bachelor*' apartment," she said.

"You can make all the changes you want. It hasn't been decorated in years, but not too floral, please," he teased.

Unbeknown to Niamph, James had booked the bridle suite. The porter carried their suitcases to the room. As he opened the door for them, James whisked her off her feet and carried her into the room. He gently tossed her onto the bed. The porter discreetly left, closing the door behind him. James jumped on the bed next to her.

"Hello, Mrs. Hartley, at last I have you all to myself," he wrapped his arms around her and gently kissed her.

"Sounds like mister newspaper editor isn't running any local news this week, except announcing that you got married and hopefully … nothing about this!" She drew closer to him with a sly smile.

"Well, it's the best front-page news the town is going to see! Minus, of course …"

He kissed her more passionately. She returned his kisses with her arms around his neck. They undressed each other slowly, James running his hands over every part of her body, gently removing her underwear. Niamph felt a bit embarrassed laying on the bed with no clothes on, but when James removed his underwear and danced around the room stark naked, she started to laugh, which took all the embarrassment away. James made love to her like she was the most precious thing in the world, kissing her ears and neck, sending a delightful sensation down the whole of her body. She arched her body to meet his and reached an orgasm like she had never ever experienced in her life. Afterwards, they lay on the bed with a contented smile on their faces and drank champagne provided by the hotel.

Niamph told Clara when she arrived home that she hardly saw anything of Chicago.

"How come?" asked Clara.

"We spent most of the time in bed making love," she said giggling.

While Niamph and James were on their honeymoon, North and South Carolina were hit by Hurricane Donna. It was the strongest hurricane that anyone had ever experienced. It had started as a category 4 but fortunately dropped to a category 2 by the time it hit the Eastern sector of North Carolina. They were fortunate enough to be protected to a certain degree by the Appalachian Mountains, but it still brought winds gusting up to 100 mph.

One field of tobacco was completely destroyed, while the other three were saved from the worst of the winds and suffered only minor damage. The old barn had its roof blown away with the debris scattered all over the surrounding area. Some of the trees lost branches, but the huge 300-year-old oak in the valley was completely blown over.

The children lay in bed petrified as the winds howled around the farmhouse. Lilly jumped into bed with Hannah and hid under the covers, while the boys got into bed with Clara and Carl. Biscuit hid under the bed. Carl wanted to go out and see the damage being caused, but Clara stopped him, saying it was too dangerous. They stayed awake all night, listening to things banging and crashing around them.

It took the whole workforce a few weeks to clear the debris and remove the damaged crops. They had to plough the field totally ready for replanting.

The insurance assessor arrived with his clipboard, making notes of the damage and taking photos. He assured Carl that the claim wouldn't take too long to settle. "You have fared better than most. Those in Wilmington were badly hit."

They were both sad at the loss of the oak tree in the valley. Carl had remembered helping his grandfather build the wooden bench that sat around the tree and reminisced about the many family picnics that they had had under the tree. Clara remembered how in the early days of her arrival in Holly Springs they sought privacy during the evenings, sitting under the tree discussing the future and even laying on the grass and making love under the moonlight.

"Once we have cleared the tree away, we will plant another one," promised Carl. "One good thing is that we will have enough logs to last us for years."

It was around this time that Carl was approached by a television broadcasting company. They were looking for a suitable site to erect a television mast to cover the area. The representative, who had introduced himself as Ron Larkin, walked around the farm with Carl and suggested a suitable spot for the mast that would not interfere with the workings of the farm. Carl invited him into the kitchen to discuss the logistics of erecting the mast.

"It will be in the region of 60/70 feet high," explained Ron, showing Carl a diagram of how it would look and explained how it would be erected.

"We will be able to drive our construction equipment along the path at the edge of your fields without causing any damage," he explained.

"I am not sure," said Carl. "That field suffered a lot of damage in the storm, and it has just been planted with next year's crop, so the last thing we want is for this new crop to be damaged in anyway."

"You will be well compensated by my company, Mr. Kennion, and every care will be taken not to do any damage," he said.

"In what way will I be compensated? Please call me Carl."

"Well there will be an initial payment and thereafter an annual rental fee. I might add that other landowners have opted for the installation of a television set in their home instead of the initial fee, perhaps you may wish to consider this," said Ron.

"Let me just go and call my wife and see what she thinks," Carl went to the back door and shouted to Clara to come in.

Carl introduced Clara to Ron and asked him to explain to Clara what he had already told him.

"Wow, a television. The kids will love that. I think we should definitely accept the offer," said an excited Clara.

That evening when everyone was sat at the table for dinner, Carl said to the children, "Guess what we are getting?"

"Not another baby," suggested Lilly.

"No," said Clara, "not another baby."

"We are getting a television," said Clara excitedly, but no one seemed to respond or be excited.

"What's a television?" asked Timmy.

It was at this point that she realised that the children hadn't seen a television, and no one in their area had one, hence the need for the mast. When she explained what it was, they then took an interest.

"So it's like a cinema in your house but smaller?" asked Lilly.

"Exactly," replied Clara.

Timmy had never been to the cinema, so he was totally bemused. Lilly spent the whole evening telling everyone in the greatest details what a television was, even though she had only seen one once at Gary's and she had only been a baby at that time, therefore, there was no way she would remember. This amused the adults to no end.

The television arrived at the beginning of 1961. The whole family was intrigued by it. Timmy wanted to know how the pictures got into the box. So did Clara and Carl, but they didn't dare say they didn't know, just said that it came through the aerial on the chimney. When he persisted with "but how?", Lilly answered, "It's like magic, be quiet so we can listen."

Although it was a novelty at first, with the children running home from school so they could switch it on to watch the children's programmes, when summer came around again, they preferred to be outside.

CHAPTER 34

Within six months of her marriage, Niamph announced that she was pregnant. James was over the moon, phoning his mother first to tell her and then telling everyone he came into contact with.

Niamph told Clara, "He would put an announcement in the paper if I let him."

Clara laughed. "Well, with all the reconstruction he's been printing about ever since the hurricane, I bet many of his readers wouldn't mind a good news, feel-good story!"

At first Niamph combined her time between organising the redecoration of their home and visiting the farm to help Hannah and look after Timmy, but when Timmy started school the term after his fifth birthday, she came less frequently. As her pregnancy progressed, her visits were for pleasure not work. James tried to cosset her, telling her to take it easy, but she told him that she would go crazy doing nothing all day.

When the tearoom opened again for the season, she would come every day for a few hours to show the visitors around the museum, which now had a new roof. Luckily the contents of the museum had suffered only minor damage during the hurricane that Niamph with Carl's help had quickly fixed.

At seven months pregnant and according to Clara "looking like a house," Niamph started to become tired and her ankles and legs would become swollen if she stood for any length of time. Consequently, when she went to the doctor for her regular monthly check up, he referred her to the antenatal clinic at the local hospital. The midwife took her into a cubicle and checked her over and looked over her notes that her doctor had provided. She told her to lie on the bed so that she could feel her tummy.

"Everything seems absolutely fine, Mrs. Hartley. Now I will just listen to the baby's heartbeat."

Niamph was intrigued at this. No one had done that when she was expecting Bernadette. The midwife put the heart monitor earphone to her tummy and moved it around a bit, listening intensely.

"I will just call the doctor," she said.

"Is everything okay?" said a worried Niamph, now wishing she had let James come with her.

"Yes, nothing to worry about. I just want the doctor to listen to the baby," said the midwife.

The doctor entered the cubicle. He was younger than Niamph expected. He took the listening device from the midwife and placed it on Niamph's tummy. As he moved it around her vast tummy, he kept saying, "Ah."

"Well, Mrs. Hartley. I have some good news for you. Well, I hope it's good news." He grinned. "You are having twins."

"Twins, no, are you sure?" said a surprised Niamph.

"Yes, I can hear two heartbeats. Otherwise, the midwife tells me you are fine, but you will have to put your feet up a bit more. We don't want those ankles swelling up too much. An extra baby means extra weight to carry around, so remember put your feet up or at least don't stand up for any length of time. Now we would like you to come back every two weeks until two weeks before your due date, so we can keep an eye on you," he said, then he left.

The midwife helped her off the bed. "See you in two weeks, Mrs. Hartley."

Niamph went home in a daze. When she arrived, James was working in the office. On seeing her face, he said, "What's the matter? Are you okay? You look—"

Before he could finish the sentence, she said, "We are having twins!"

"Twins! No, twins? Are you sure?"

"That's what the doctor told me. I can hardly believe it," she said.

Niamph couldn't wait to tell Clara, and she went to the farm the next day to impart her news.

"Twins? Wow that is fantastic! No wonder you are so big," declared Clara.

"That means I will have to knit another set of clothes, but I am delighted for you. Imagine all of your family in one go. Well done, my girl," said Hannah.

The babies were due in late September, but by the end of August, the doctor was concerned about her high blood pressure and that she was slightly anaemic. At first she was ordered to go to bed and stay there and rest, but it soon became apparent that this was not working. The doctor recommended that the babies be delivered as soon as possible.

"I am sorry, Mrs. Hartley, but I want to do a caesarean section, and I would like to do this tomorrow. I will arrange for you to go to the hospital this afternoon, and we will keep an eye on you overnight and prepare you for the morning," said the doctor.

"My wife is not in any danger, is she?" asked a worried James.

"Not at the moment, but I think it would be prudent to deliver these babies now to avoid any problems that could occur if we leave her to go full-term. My main concern is her blood pressure," the doctor informed James.

James spent the night with Niamph in the hospital, sleeping on the armchair in her room, not wanting to leave her on her own. He telephoned Clara to tell her what was happening.

"Telephone if there are any changes, and I will come to the hospital straight away. Otherwise, I will be there in the morning to hold your hand," she teased. "Give Niamph my love and tell her I am thinking of her. See you in the morning and try to get some sleep," she said.

Clara spent a restless night worrying about Niamph and went to the hospital as soon as the children had gone off to school.

James met her in the reception. "How is she?"

"Good. She slept better than me but was very nervous this morning. They took her to the operating theatre about fifteen minutes ago. The doctor said it wouldn't take very long, so let's get up to the ward quickly," he suggested.

As they arrived in the waiting room outside the maternity ward, Niamph's midwife came to see James.

"Congratulations, Mr Hartley! You have two beautiful baby boys."

"My wife, is she okay?" asked an anxious James.

"Yes, she is absolutely fine. The doctor is just stitching her up now, and you will be able to see her in about half an hour. Now would you like to see your sons?" asked the midwife.

"Oh Yes, yes please. Can our friend come as well?" asked James.

"Yes, of course, she can. Follow me."

They were able to view the babies through a window. The two little tiny boys with nappies that appeared bigger than them lay in individual cribs.

"Aren't they beautiful? They look so perfect and so tiny," said James with tears running down his cheeks.

"In fact for twins born three weeks early, they were a good weight. Baby one was exactly five pounds, and baby two was five pounds three ounces," said the midwife.

"No wonder poor Niamph was so big! Imagine if she had gone full term!" exclaimed Clara.

"I will take you to her room. She should be back by now. Usually it is husbands only at this time, but as you have a private room, your friend can come with you. She will be a bit groggy until the anaesthetic wears off," said the midwife.

Niamph was fast asleep, so James and Clara went to the cafeteria to have some lunch before returning to Niamph's room just in time to see her wake up. The midwife made them wait outside while she checked Niamph over.

"You can go in now. I will go and get the babies so she can see them. I won't be long," said the midwife.

Niamph sat up in bed. James went straight to her. "Honey, how are you?" he asked, kissing her and then attempted to hug her.

"Be careful, I am a bit sore," said Niamph.

"Sorry, honey. Are you okay?" he said, sitting down next to the bed and holding her hand.

"Yes, I am fine. Have you seen our babies? What are they like?" she asked.

"They are absolutely beautiful and so tiny, but the midwife said they were a good weight. I can't remember what she said they weighted now. She has just gone to get them," he said.

Clara came over and gave her friend a kiss. "Well done. I have seen them through the window as well. ... Ah! Here they are now." Clara held the door open as two midwives wheeled two little cribs into the room.

One of the midwives helped Niamph sit up, placing pillows behind her to make her comfortable while the other handed her the first baby. "Here is baby one, and he weighs five pounds. I will give baby two to Daddy, and he weighs just three ounces more. Now, I don't want you overtiring yourself, so I will be back in twenty minutes to take the babies back to the nursery. Then, you can have a good rest before feed time," said the midwife.

"I will go now, Niamph, and let you two get acquainted with these little ones. I will be back tomorrow," said Clara, kissing her goodbye.

"Oh, James, he is so perfect. Can we swap? I want to say hello to '*baby 2*'. What shall we call them? I was so convinced I was having a girl that I didn't think of any boys' names," she said as they swapped babies.

"Hello, precious," she said, stroking the baby's soft cheek.

Both babies had a covering of downy, dark hair and little heart shape lips, and Niamph thought they were the most beautiful things in the world.

"What about Scott and Stephen?" suggested James.

"I like Scott but not Stephen. It would mean they would have the same initial and that could be confusing. What about ... Bradley?" said Niamph.

"Scott and Bradley. Yes, and perhaps one could have my dad's name as their second name and your dad's for the other one."

"No, I don't want my dad's name, not after the way he treated me, but could I have Bernard, would you mind?" asked Niamph.

"Of course, I don't, so it's Scott Charles and Bradley Bernard—perhaps not. No, the other way sounds better, Scott Bernard and Bradley Charles," said James.

The midwife arrived to take the babies to the nursery, and James left to let Niamph have a rest.

"I will be back this evening," he said, kissing all three of them.

Clara arrived exactly as the visitors' bell rang. Niamph looked the picture of health.

"I can see you are much better today than yesterday. I have brought you some flowers from the kids. They picked them this morning. ... and some chocolates so you can indulge yourself while you can. How are these little ones?" she said, going over to the cribs. "Oh, they are asleep. I wanted to hold them, but I suppose I will have to wait," said Clara.

"Thank you. I will enjoy eating those, and thank the kids for me for the flowers. Yes, I am feeling a lot better today but still very sore, which is to be expected. I remember it took a few weeks with Bernadette. The boys only wake up to be fed, which the midwife said is normal at this stage. Come and sit down," said Niamph.

"Have you decided on names yet?" asked Clara.

"Yes, this little one is, Bradley Charles, Charles after James's dad, and this little one is Scott Bernard," said Niamph, pointing to the individual cribs.

"Bernard for Bernadette, I presume," questioned Clara.

"Yes, what do you think?"

"I think that it is lovely, Niamph," said Clara.

"I am so glad I had boys, Clara. If I had had girls, I would have felt like they were replacing Bernadette, and I wouldn't want that. How would I be able to face Bernadette in the future with a girl? How would she take it? At least with boys, my hope is that she will accept them as brothers,' said Niamph.

"Oh, Niamph," said Clara, taking her hand. "I just hope that one day your dream of seeing her will come to fruition. Lilly is dying to see the boys, but she is not allowed to visit. I asked the midwife, and she said she has to be sixteen, so she will have to wait until you get home," said Clara.

"The doctor has said that I must stay in for at least another six days," said Niamph.

"Well, make the most of it because it is bad enough doing the night feeds with one baby, never mind two. I will come and help you every day. I have already told the girls at the tearoom. At least, it is coming towards the end of the season, so hopefully may not be so busy. Hannah said she would help the girls as much as she can," said Clara.

"You are a good friend to me. Thank you. I am sure James will help as much as he can, but you know men. They have good intentions but are mostly useless," laughed Niamph.

"Ah, I think I heard a murmur," said Clara, going over to one of the cots as Scott opened his eyes and yawned. "Hello, sweetheart. Would you like Auntie Clara to pick you up? Can I?" Clara asked Niamph.

"I don't think I will be able to stop you!"

Clara came to the hospital every day until Niamph was discharged. Then, for the next few months, she helped Niamph at home. Lilly adored the boys at first sight, wanting to help Niamph as much as she could, or, at least, as much as Niamph would let her.

CHAPTER 35

By 1964, Lilly had been at junior high school for three years and was about to enter senior high in the tenth grade. She would start studying for a high school diploma at the end of twelfth grade. A great debate took place as to what subjects she would study. Besides the core subjects, she chose ancient history and domestic science, which amused Clara to no end because Lilly took no interest in cooking at all. But she did take an interest in everything old. Her history teacher had studied archaeology and history at university and would often take his class to visit museums or any exhibitions that involved anything remotely to do with archaeology. They had even been on a few archaeological digs. His enthusiasm had rubbed off on Lilly, and you would often find her reading books on the subject, even asking Carl if he had ever dug anything up in the fields when ploughing.

"We're in North Carolina, Lilly, not Rome. I am hardly going to be digging up an ancient pot or whatever it is they find in these places."

"I know that, Daddy, but I thought you might find something."

"Sorry to disappoint you, honey, but the only things we dig up are stones and more stones."

"When I grow up, I want to be an archaeologist," she announced, having a bit of a problem pronouncing the word.

At eighteen, Lilly, having achieved scores of fours and fives in her advanced placement exams, gained a place at the University of North Carolina (UNC) almost three hundred miles away to study archaeology.

The summer before university, Lilly worked helping Clara either in the tearoom or showing the visitors around the museum. She loved the museum and was always reading books to find ways to improve and enhance it.

One hot day in August, Hannah was sitting on her rocking chair in her usual place on the veranda with Biscuit at her feet when Lilly came home. Biscuit was now becoming very slow in his old age, preferring to spend his days sleeping than anything else. Not wanting to wake her Gamy straight away, Lilly thought, '*I will go and get her a glass of cold lemonade.*' As she was about to wake her, she realised something was wrong. "Gamy, Gamy!" she said, gently touching her on the arm, but there was no response. Dropping the lemonade, she quickly ran to the tearoom, shouting for her mother.

"Mum, Mum, come quickly. Something is wrong with Gamy," shouted Lilly with tears streaming down her face.

"Calm down, Lilly. What do you mean '*something is wrong*?'" said Clara, running after Lilly, who was now on her way back to the farmhouse.

"Mum ... I think she is dead."

"Don't be silly. She can't be. I only spoke to her about an hour ago," said a concerned Clara.

Clara walked onto the veranda, and on touching Hannah, she realised that Lilly was right. "Run and get your dad!"

Clara went inside and phoned for the doctor.

Carl came running with Lilly not far behind. He quietly approached Hannah, gently taking her hand.

"Mum! Oh, Mum," he said with tears in his eyes.

The funeral was held five days later. As with Bill, the church was packed to overflowing.

Carl and Gary slowly followed the coffin down the aisle followed by Helen and Clara and all the grandchildren. They were all still in shock at Hannah's sudden death. The service was conducted by Reverend Kisro, and she was buried next to her beloved Bill.

The lawyer read the will to the family the next day, and Carl and Gary were surprised at how much money she had, which she had bequeathed to the five grandchildren in equal proportions. The lawyer explained that she had decided that Carl and Gary had already inherited the farm from their father and thus her decision to leave everything to the grandchildren.

Hannah was sorely missed. The farmhouse was so quiet without her even Biscuit appeared to miss her. He would roam from room to room as though looking for her.

At the end of September, Lilly left for the university. She had bought herself a car out of her inheritance, loaded it up with her possessions, and drove off with a promise to phone as soon as she arrived.

"See you all at Christmas."

It was a sad moment for Clara—her baby leaving home.

Jeffrey was in his last year at the music academy that he had joined at fourteen. He was now sixteen. He had bought himself a guitar with part of his inheritance and was in the process of teaching himself to play it. At the end of the last semester, his teacher had told Carl and Clara that besides being a gifted musician, he was also a talented poet. Clara already knew that her sensitive eldest son was a talented musician, but the poetry bit came as a complete surprise. She was more surprised to hear that he had won a variety of competitions.

On the way home from the parents' evening, Clara said, "Why didn't you tell us about the poetry competitions you have won?"

"I was a bit embarrassed. It's bad enough the guys at school teasing me never mind Lilly and Timmy," said Jeffrey.

"I am sure they wouldn't tease you," said Clara.

"They would, Mum. They tease me about playing the piano, calling me Liberace and asking me where my candelabra is," he said.

"Well you should take no notice. They are only jealous that they can't play. I am proud of you, son, and that is all that matters," said Clara.

"Thank you, Mum."

During the Easter holidays of 1969, Jeffrey asked Carl if he could turn part of one of the barns into a practice area for his band.

"What band?" asked Carl.

"Me, Johnny, Gerry and Joel have decided to form a band, but we need somewhere to practice," said Jeffrey.

"You could use the back room of the new barn, but you will have to clear all the stuff out of it first," said Carl.

"Gee thanks, Dad."

The next day the boys spent the whole day clearing the area and turning it into a studio, as the boys referred to it. Gerry was a bit older than the others and had recently passed his driving test. He had borrowed his dad's pick-up truck, and they had loaded it up with second-hand equipment that the boys had clubbed together to purchase. The '*gear*,' as the boys referred to it, was quickly installed in the '*studio*'.

"Mum."

"Yes, Jeffrey," said Clara, busily trying to bake a batch of cakes for the tearoom.

"Do you think I can move the piano to our studio?" asked Jeffrey.

"I don't see why not, but you better ask your dad, as it was Gamy's piano," suggested Clara.

That evening, Clara noticed that the piano was missing. "So you let him move the piano, then?" she asked Carl.

"Yes, I thought that perhaps we could redecorate the parlour, make it a bit more comfortable. It hasn't been decorated for years," said Carl.

"Good idea, we could do it during the winter when I am not so busy," suggested Clara.

The boys started practicing their music.

"Thank goodness we don't live near anyone else. Have you heard the noise coming from the barn?" said Carl.

"It's the '*studio*,' and it's called '*music*,'" replied Clara.

"Music, well I have never heard '*music*' like that. It's just a noise. In fact, if you stand outside, all you can hear is boom, boom, boom," said Carl.

"As long as they are enjoying themselves, that's the main thing, at least it keeps them out of trouble," said Clara.

When it came to the summer school holidays, Clara told Jeffrey, or Jeff as he liked to be called, which Clara found really difficult, that he would have to help out either around the farm or in the tearoom. "You are not going to spend all summer bumming around doing nothing, or in your studio playing all day. You will have to do some work like your brother and sister," demanded Clara.

"Okay, Mum, but I would prefer to help you. I don't really want to get my hands dirty helping Dad," he said cheekily.

He joined the girls in the tearoom sharing their duties. Her now five-foot-seven handsome son with his deep brown eyes and brown, floppy hair, so long that Clara made him tie it back when he was working, was a hit with both staff and customers. He would teasingly flatter the older ladies and flirt with the younger ones. The tips that season doubled over previous years much to the delight of the girls.

When a customer was indecisive about which cake they wanted, he encouraged them to buy two and take one home. Clara purchased takeaway boxes, which proved highly successful. Soon everyone was taking out, either buying a whole cake or taking a piece of cake away with them.

Jeffrey was due to go to the University of Carolina Music Academy in October. However at the beginning of September, he announced that he had a recording contract and the band was leaving for Los Angeles in the following week.

To say that Clara and Carl were shocked was an understatement. "What do you mean you've got a recording contract?" said Carl angrily.

"Calm down, Dad!" said Jeffrey.

"Don't you tell me to calm down!" said Carl.

Clara stepped in at this point, telling Carl to sit down and listen and asking Jeffrey to explain to them what exactly was going on.

Jeffrey sat down and calmly explained that during the summer the band had sent off recordings of the band playing a number of songs that he had written to various record labels, and to their surprise, they had received an offer from not only one but two companies.

"And you are telling me that people will buy records of that noise that we hear coming from your '*studio*'?" asked Carl.

"Oh, Dad! That noise as you describe it is garage rock, and, yes, people do buy the records. We may fail miserably, but unless we try, we won't know, Dad. I hope that you and Mum will wish us good luck," explained Jeffrey.

"Sorry, son. I shouldn't have sounded off, but this is all alien to me and Mum. But as you say, if you don't try, then you won't know. So good luck, son," said Carl.

"Has this band of yours got a name?" asked Clara.

"Yeah, we have called ourselves, *'The JayJays'*. We wanted to call ourselves *'The Hollies'* as in Holly Springs, but there is already a British band called that. So as all our names begin with *'J'*, except for Gerry but his sounds like it begins with *'J'*, we opted for *'The JayJays'*. What do you think?" asked Jeffrey.

"Well, I don't know, but I am sure it will be fine," said Clara unconvincingly.

When Jeffrey told Lilly and Timmy about his recording contract, they were really excited for him. "Imagine! We might have a famous brother," said Lilly.

"What like Liberace?" said Timmy jesting.

In the second week of September 1969, shortly after his seventeenth birthday, Jeffrey departed for Los Angeles and fame.

Their first record was released in November 1969 called *'Your Love is My Love'*. Jeffrey sent a copy of the record to Clara a week before its official release. Clara rushed into town to buy a record player. She had never felt a need to buy one before, especially as Lilly had bought herself one two years previously. However she had taken it to university with her. Clara phoned Niamph, asking her to come to the farm that afternoon if she had time.

"I have got a surprise," she said, which intrigued Niamph.

With the record player all set up and ready to play, Clara put the record on the turntable, and the needle lowered itself automatically. They both stood there looking at it turn around when the musical introduction started. They sat down to listen. When it had finished, they turned to each other and started laughing.

"What did you make of that?" asked Clara.

"I don't know, but it wasn't Perry Como!" exclaimed Niamph.

"I'll phone him tonight and tell him we like it. What do you think?" said Clara.

"I agree and tell him I will go and buy a copy, so at least he will have one sale," teased Niamph.

After they had had a cup of tea and the boys had exhausted themselves running around outside, Niamph went home to tell James all about it.

Carl listened to it that evening before Clara phoned Jeffrey.

"I think it is growing on me," said Clara. "What do you make of it?"

"Well, I thought it was an indefinable noise coming from the barn, sorry '*studio*,' when they were practicing. Now I know it definitely was an indefinable noise," said Carl.

"I will tell Jeffrey that you like it then!" Clara laughed.

She spoke to Jeffrey later that evening and told him that they had all listened to his record, and they all thought it was great. Timmy grabbed the phone from her. "Hiya, Bud, groovy record. Don't listen to Mum. She knows nothing about rock music. It will be number one next week."

Timmy ended the call and went to his room, commandeering the record player. Clara and Carl just looked at each other trying not to laugh.

The record didn't make number one. In the first week, it went to number ten in the charts and stayed in that position for several weeks before it gradually dropped out of the top fifty. Their next record proved more successful going to number four, but their third record did go to number one. The whole family was ecstatic, and Clara threw a party to celebrate.

CHAPTER 36

The farm over the years had expanded considerably and was now almost fifty per cent bigger than when Carl took it over from his father. They recently purchased two large fields to the north of the property. With more land, came the need for more workers and extra equipment.

When Carl's father ran the farm, he and a number of tobacco farmers in North Carolina had formed a co-operative to ensure that each farmer received the same price for their tobacco from the big processing companies. The bigger farmers felt it was unfair that the smaller farmers could not get the same price for their crops, just because the bigger farmers had more bargaining power. The co-operative met approximately once a month to discuss new methods, new machinery and generally socialising. On occasions, they would have a guest speaker or a presentation by manufacturers. The venue was alternated so that the travelling distance was not always in one grower's favour.

James was visiting Carl on one occasion when a neighbouring farmer, named Ernest Watkins, dropped in to see Carl. "I just dropped by to see if there was anything interesting at this month's co-op meeting. My daughter had a baby that day so I daren't come. My wife would not have been very happy," he jokingly said.

"Not a lot. Mike Oldham is having problems with his men. I've got a leaflet on some new irrigation system but nothing of great interest. Oh, and a chap brought along a brochure on work wear, you know overalls, hats, gloves, that sort of thing," said Carl.

James listened to the two men and said, "Don't you produce a newsletter of the meeting for those who can't attend?"

"No, I don't think there is a need. We just tell each other the news," said Carl.

"How many members are there?" asked James.

"I think we are up to just short of seventy-five," replied Carl.

"And how many of those come to the meeting?" asked James.

"I suppose about forty maybe fifty. Why do you ask?"

"Well I was just thinking that perhaps I could produce a newsletter for you," suggested James.

"I don't think we could afford that, Bud. We pay an annual subscription, but that covers the cost of booking a venue and paying any speaker that wants paying. I can't imagine the members wanting to pay for a newsletter," said Carl.

"They wouldn't have to pay, not if I received income from advertising. Tell you what. Perhaps, I could come to your next meeting and then produce something, send it to all your members and take it from there," suggested James.

"Well we haven't got anything to lose, so yes, come along. You could give us a talk on how you think a newsletter would help us," said Carl.

James thought this was a perfect opportunity to expand and diversify his business.

Over the years, the circulation of his newspaper *'The Raleigh Post'* had increased vastly due to the increase in the population of Raleigh and the surrounding area. The weekly newspaper became untenable due to the amount of news being received together with the requests for advertising space and gazette notices.

When James took the decision to change the weekly paper to a daily paper, he looked for alternative premises to house the new and much larger printing presses that he would need to produce a daily paper. Fortunately, an advertiser answered his problem when he requested an advert to be placed in the paper, advertising units for rental on a new industrial estate on the outskirts of town. James immediately asked to view them and found the perfect unit to fit his needs.

He raised a loan using the house as collateral. He purchased two new printing presses, employed two further reporters and moved all his archives into the new premises. Niamph had conversion plans before even James had moved everything out, but James said they needed to maintain a presence in the town. Niamph agreed to take over the running of a small office-cum-shop and turn the remainder of the ground floor into a family kitchen/dining room.

Niamph loved her little shop. The front was half the size from when James had it. She added all sorts of items of stationery for sale. Her idea of introducing a new format to the family notices proved popular and lucrative. She would suggest to the customer that the announcement be placed in a bordered box headed by a logo such as a stork for a birth, two entwined rings for an engagement, or a pair of bells of a marriage, showing them pictures of formats they could choose from. She would advise other advertisers how best to display their advert and the best day to do it. The paper now included a daily crossword—one easy and one hard. She was in talks with a local artist to create a cartoon strip with a view to introducing a weekly children's page.

James and Niamph discussed at length his idea for a newsletter for the co-operative, and she agreed to phone around to farming suppliers to see if they would be interested in advertising in this proposed new venture. Instantly, she had a vision for the *'Farmers Monthly'* and after speaking to numerous businesses, she received a lot of positive responses from potential advertisers.

James attended the co-operative's next meeting and took with him a mock-up of the proposed paper. This was met with enthusiasm and after a unanimous vote of the members, the '*Farmers Monthly*' was born. Initially, he sent each member a free paper and placed copies of the paper at various businesses around Raleigh for anyone wishing to pick up one free of charge. After six months, the popularity of the paper was so successful he took the decision to launch the paper to the paying public and increased the number printed. However, he continued to provide free copies to all members of the co-operative.

CHAPTER 37

With Lilly at university and Jeffrey in Los Angeles, there was only Timmy left at home. When he reached the age of fifteen, he wanted to leave school and work full-time with Carl on the farm, saying to his father that school could teach him nothing that would be of use to growing tobacco.

"I know, son, but the law says you have to stay at school until you are sixteen. There is nothing I can do about it. If you don't go to school, then it's not only you that will be in trouble but us as well," said Carl.

Timmy wasn't happy and stormed off to bed.

When Carl discussed the situation with Clara, she said that she would try and get an appointment with Timmy's headmaster to seek clarification.

She met with the headmaster, Mr. A'Court, a few days later and explained that Timothy wanted to leave and work on the farmer.

"Our other son is not interested in farming, but Timothy is, and when my husband retires, it will be Timothy who takes over. Surely, it is best that he starts learning now, especially as he doesn't want to continue at school," said Clara.

"I am sorry, Mrs. Kennion, but this is not my decision. Personally I agree with you, but leave it with me, and I will make a few enquiries. I will come back to you."

And true to his word, Mr. A'Court contacted them and requested that both Clara and Carl come and see him.

"I have spoken to the head of education for the state, and he has suggested an alternative for Timothy. I am not sure if he will want this, but it is a part solution, and in my opinion a very good alternative. There is a department linked to the University of North Carolina that offers an eighteen-month '*Agricultural and Horticultural*' course. It is an actual working farm and offers all aspects of husbandry together with farm management and accounting. If it is the intention that Timothy will eventually take over the farm, then this course would be invaluable," explained Mr. A'Court.

"And this would be acceptable as part of his education instead of going to school?" asked Clara.

"Yes, the head of education said they would accept this. Now the only downside, if you can call it that, is that firstly you would have to pay for the course, and secondly Timothy would have to live on the farm for the whole length of the course. Here is a brochure, and you will see it is a non-profit making farm. All the students work it seven days a week," he said.

"Well I think this would be perfect. Let's hope that Timothy does as well. We will speak to him tonight and let you know, thank you," said Carl.

"Yes, thank you, Mr. A'Court," said Clara.

That evening, Clara called Timmy down from room. "Timmy, Timmy, come down here. We want to talk to you."

"Mum, can you stop calling me Timmy. I am not ten years old. Everyone else calls me Tim."

"Sorry, '*Tim*,' now sit down. Your dad and I want to talk to you," said Clara.

Carl explained their conversation with the headmaster and told him all about the course. Finally, he handed Tim the brochure to read, saying that if he agreed, they would inquire about enrolling him in the course as soon as possible.

"I think it would help with the running of the farm in the future. It would give you all the up-to-date methods, and also, the management and accounting would be invaluable. I suggest you read the brochure and think about it and give us your answer tomorrow," said Carl.

"Okay, Dad, I must admit it sounds interesting. Let me sleep on it," said Tim.

Tim needed no more convincing. Having read the brochure, he thought it was a fantastic idea, and two months later, he joined the next intake of students.

He would come home for a weekend every three months or so and be full of suggestions of how the farm could improve productivity or changes that should be implemented, much to the annoyance of Carl.

Carl told Clara, "I can't wait for him to go back to college. He is driving me mad."

Tim enthusiastically told Clara how they worked seven days a week, starting at six every morning to milk the cows. "Well, we take it in turns," he explained. Then, he shared how every weekend, they attended a farmers' market to sell the produce, again taking it in turns, and how he had been to several agricultural trade fairs and was amazed at the machinery that was available. He even bought Clara a present.

"I got this at the exhibition I went to last weekend," he said.

"What is it?"

"An electric adding machine," he said, showing her how it worked.

"Imagine how much time it will save you when you are doing the books," he said enthusiastically.

"Gee thanks, son, just what I have always wanted," she said teasingly.

On one of his next visits, he bought her an accounting contraption. "Look, instead of a book for your accounts, you have this." He showed her how you could add and remove pages of ledger sheets by undoing screw type clips at the rear of the folder.

"This way, you don't have to get a new accounting book each year. You just take out the old sheets and add the new ones, and on ones that you don't use much, you can just draw a line and start a fresh," he explained.

"Oh," said Clara, not quite understanding how it would work. "Thank you. Perhaps when you take over the books you can use this, but at the moment I like the books I use, and that's because I understand them," said Clara.

"Oh, Mum, you have to move with the times," he said.

"Yes, son, and I will—one day."

Tim finished his course, graduating with distinction certificate. Clara and Carl stood proud at the graduation ceremony.

Tim already knew he would work with his father, because that was always what he had wanted to do since a young age. Working on the land was, to him, extremely satisfying, watching the crops he had planted grow and harvested. He had lots of ideas to bring the farm into the twentieth century with the latest equipment and farming methods. It would take time, but he knew one day, with a little bit of persuasion, his father would come around to his way of thinking. He just had to bide his time.

Clara and Carl had redecorated the parlour with a stripy wallpaper of pale beige and cream. A carpet in light brown with a pattern of orange and cream swirls had been laid, and they had chosen a sandy-coloured, three-piece settee suite. A new sideboard in light oak with two-sided cupboards and four drawers in the middle standing on four spindle legs now stood against the wall where the piano had been. A matching coffee table sat in front of the settee. They had even bought a larger television set that stood on its own stand facing the settee.

They spent quiet evenings together, snuggled up on their squishy settee, watching television or listening to the radio with Biscuit at their feet. They enjoyed this quiet time with no children around to worry about. Some evenings, they even managed to go to the cinema to see the latest film or have dinner with James and Niamph if they could get a babysitter.

Their peace was soon broken. Jeffrey came home for a quick visit. He arrived early one Friday evening to his parents' surprise. He walked into the kitchen just as Clara was getting ready to serve up dinner.

"Hiya, Mum," he said, nearly making Clara drop the pan she was holding.

"Oh, Jeffrey, you gave me a fright! How lovely to see you," she said, going over to him and giving him a hug.

Her shy, sensitive baby boy was now a strapping, six-foot-tall man. In the nine months since she had seen him, he appeared to have not only grown but also matured. His luscious locks still too long for Clara's liking but envied by many girls.

"Why didn't you tell us you were coming home? I would have come and picked you up," said Clara.

"I wanted to surprise you, and I knew if I told you, you would be rushing around making sure everything was clean and tidy, which it is anyway. I have hired a car to make it easy for me to get around while I am here. And, Mum, call me Jeff. Everyone else does," replied Jeffrey.

"How long are you here for, '*Jeff*'? It's hard, you know, calling you Jeff after all these years. You will always be Jeffrey to me, but I will try," she said.

"I have only just arrived, and you are asking how long I am here for," joked Jeff. "Unfortunately, only for four days, just long enough for me to say hello to everyone."

"Such a short time! Never mind. It is lovely to see you. It is so quiet here for your dad and me without all you kids around," said Clara.

"One of the reasons I am here, Mum, is to get my birth certificate. We are off to England at the end of July for three months, and I need to get a passport," announced Jeff.

"Wow! You will love England. Will you be able to go and see your grandma and grandpa? They would just adore seeing you," asked Clara.

"Yes, that is another reason for coming so I could get their address. We are playing in Manchester first, and I remember you saying that they didn't live far from there, so I plan to go and see them for a few days. But don't tell them. I want it to be a surprise. We are only a support band, but our last gig is at a new festival called '*The Glastonbury Fair*' in Somerset, which I think they said is in the south of England. A lot of famous acts are going to be there. Have you heard of David Bowie or Joan Baez or Traffic?" asked Jeff.

"I have heard of Joan Baez and David Bowie but not Traffic, although I might have heard them play if they have been on our radio without knowing who they are," said Clara.

Carl was thrilled to see Jeff, bombarding him with questions of what he had been doing and how much money he was making.

"You know, Dad, we were lucky that Gerry's dad is a lawyer. He went over our management contract and negotiated lots of the finer details that we wouldn't have known about or what certain things meant. We have spoken to lots of other new bands, and their contracts are just diabolical. They are barely making enough money to live on, whereas ours is all in our favour. We haven't made a fortune yet, but we have rented a great apartment in LA, and I have bought myself a Chevy Corvette in black. You should see it, Dad. It makes a great noise," said Jeff, full of enthusiasm.

During the four days Jeff was home, he went to see some of his buddies and also popped in to see Niamph and James.

He thanked James for the two-page spread on the band that he had put in the newspaper. "I am sure it helped with sales," he told James. "I am glad you put in the bit about Niamph getting me into music, because I wouldn't be here today without her," he said, hugging Niamph.

All too soon the visit was over.

"Don't forget to give your grandma a hug and kiss from me," said Clara, crying as he left.

True to his word, Jeff went to see his grandparents following their event in Manchester. Arriving at the hairdressing salon, he opened the door to the ladies' salon, and he immediately saw his grandmother, recognizing her from photos. She sat behind a small desk and looked up as soon as she heard the bell over the door ring.

"The gents' hairdresser is next door, lad," said his grandmother.

Jeff couldn't help but laugh. She obviously thought he needed a haircut.

"Hello, Gran," he announced.

Olive looked bemused at this young man. "Jeffrey?"

"Yes, Gran," he said, walking over to her and putting his arms around her and kissing her cheek. He couldn't believe how short she was, barely five feet, one inch.

"Ah! Jeffrey, it is so good to see you! I can't believe how grown up you are. Your mother hasn't sent me any photos of you since you were about fifteen."

"Jean, Bev," called Olive to her assistants, "come and meet my grandson."

Bev was in awe. She recognized Jeff from her teen magazine. She could hardly speak. She couldn't entirely take it in—she was face to face with a pop star.

Jean shook his hand and said hello. Olive looked at Bev and said, "What is the matter with you? Come and say hello."

"Wow, Olive, it's Jeff from the JayJays," speaking to Olive as though Jeff wasn't in the room.

"Well, I don't know about that, but he is Jeffrey, come and say hello," said Olive.

"I can't believe it ... hello, my friends will be so envious. I have never met anyone famous before. Can I have your autograph?" said Bev, spluttering over her words.

Jeff laughed. "I don't know about famous but pleased to meet you both, and yes, I will give you an autograph."

"Come on, Jeffrey, come and see your grandfather, and then we will go upstairs for a nice cup of tea," said Olive.

Jack was delighted to meet his grandson, shaking his hand and then hugging this tall, strapping lad. "You need a haircut, lad. I could fit you in for a short back and sides," he joked.

"Thank you, Granddad, but I will give your offer a miss," Jeff said.

Jeff told his grandparents all about the events he had played at in Manchester and then the group's upcoming appearance at Glastonbury. He offered them some tickets to come and see him at Glastonbury.

"I think we are a bit old for that lad, but thank you anyway. How long are you stopping?" asked his grandmother.

"Sorry, Gran, only a couple of hours. We have a busy schedule, and I have to get back to Manchester this evening," replied Jeff.

Olive loved hearing all the news from Clara and the family. Jeff's visit was over all too quickly, and he promised to return when he was next in England.

CHAPTER 38

Clara's next visitor was Lilly. At almost twenty-one, she had just completed her final examination at her university and was awaiting her results.

"Mum ..."

"Yes, sweetheart," said Clara, waiting for the question.

"Professor Hatcher, you know my archaeology tutor, has been invited to a '*dig*' by one of his friends who is an archaeology tutor in Boston, and he can take four students with him. And he has asked me. What do you think?" asked Lilly.

"That's great! I am sure you would love it," replied Clara.

"It's during the summer holidays, so I won't be able to help you with the tearoom. Is that okay? It's an opportunity I might never get again," said Lilly with a plea in her voice.

"Well, it will have to be, won't it? It hasn't given me much time to get a replacement, but I will contact the university tomorrow or one of the girls that is already coming to see if they know anyone who would fill in for you. Where is this '*dig*'?" asked Clara.

"Italy."

"Italy! How wonderful, but how much is that going to cost?"

"Don't worry, Mum. I will use Gamy's money, and I have savings from when I have worked and from the good allowance you give me, Mum. So, money is no problem," she declared.

"It's not the money, Lilly. I was just surprised, that's all. Italy is a long way away. How long will you be gone?"

"We go the second week of July for two months. I will be back again in plenty of time to start my teacher training course."

Lilly had decided at the beginning of the year that she would continue at the university and take a course that would convert her degree into a teaching degree. Her plans would be to try and teach archaeology at a university. She had been accepted on a course starting in the second week of October and was looking forward to it.

When Carl came in from work, Lilly excitedly told him all about the '*dig*' and how they would be sleeping in tents and cooking all their own meals over a fire. "I don't need to take much with me, just a sleeping bag and my clothes, as everything else is already there," she explained.

"Well, it sounds like just your sort of thing. When do you go?" asked Carl.

"Second week of July. Oh, Mum, I need my birth certificate to get my passport. The Prof is getting all the application forms, and he will organise the passports and all the flights for us. I will just give him a cheque for the total. The Prof said that we shouldn't take too much cash with us but take traveler's checks instead, so I will go to the bank tomorrow and get some," explained Lilly.

Clara's heart sunk. '*Her birth certificate,*' she thought.

That night in the privacy of their bedroom, they discussed what they should say to Lilly. "As soon as she sees her birth certificate, she will know," said Clara with tears slowly falling down her face.

"We should have told her before now," said Carl regretfully.

"I know, I am just trying to think how I will tell her now after all this time, because I will have to tell her tomorrow. She leaves in two days." Clara sobbed.

Clara didn't sleep all night, trying to think of how she would tell Lilly, but there was no easy way.

"Do you want me to be there when you tell her? It might be better coming from both of us," said Carl.

"No, I think this is something I have to do on my own. At least this way, I can be the enemy, and she has you to come to after," Clara said, exhausted from having no sleep.

Lilly went to the bank before Clara had time to speak to her. "You have to order the traveler's checks, so I will have to come back to collect them before I go, or the manager says you could collect them for me and give them to me at my graduation. You are coming to my graduation aren't you, Mum, and Dad?" said Lilly without taking a breath. Ever since she was able to speak, Lilly would always tell you everything in one breath.

"I went to see Auntie Niamph and the boys. I can't believe how much they have grown since I saw them last," said an excited Lilly.

"Let me get a word in. Yes, of course, we are coming to your graduation, and yes, I will pick up the traveler's checks from the bank. Now, on a more serious note, I need to speak to you, Lilly," said Clara, already beginning to feel tears well up.

"Mum, what's the matter?" said a concerned Lilly.

"Sit down, sweetheart. There is something I need to tell you," said Clara.

She handed Lilly her birth certificate.

"Before you look at this—"

It was too late. Lilly immediately opened up the certificate and started to read it.

"Mum, I don't understand. This is all in French," she said while continuing to read it.

"Mum … who is Didier Jean Renard?"

"Your father, Lilly," said Clara in a whisper.

"But I don't understand. Are you telling me that Dad is not my father and that this Didier is?" said a confused Lilly.

"Let me explain," said Clara.

"No! Mum, what is there to explain? Just tell me who is my father?" shouted an angry Lilly.

"Please, Lilly, let me explain," said Clara, trying to stay calm.

"No! Mum, I don't want an explanation. I just want to know who my father is?" shouted Lilly again.

"Please, Lilly, your father was my first husband, a French man named Didier Renard. It is a long story—" started Clara.

"Just cut to the chase, Mum. I don't want a long story," shouted Lilly.

"I ran away from him, Lilly, with you, and that is the last time I saw him when you were almost seven months old. I then met Carl, and I came to America to be with him. But, Lilly, Carl is your father for all intents and purposes," said Clara, trying to explain.

"I can't believe that you haven't told me before. Why wait until now for me to find out? Were you ever going to tell me, Mum?" sobbed Lilly, getting up and running out the front door.

Clara sat in shock. Crying, she held her head in her hands.

Lilly ran down to the fields in search of her father. "Daddy, Daddy," she shouted, falling into his arms. "Please tell me it's not true, please, Daddy," she said, sobbing in his arms.

Carl tried to calm her down by holding her tight and stroking her hair. "I am so sorry. We should have told you before, but the opportunity never seemed to arise. Let me tell you from the minute I met your mum, I loved her and I loved you. You are my daughter, Lilly, even though my blood doesn't run in your veins, you are my daughter," he said soothingly.

Lilly left the next day to go back to university; she refused dinner and was gone before Clara got up without saying a word.

They received their invitation to Lilly's graduation and sat with all the other proud parents watching all the students receive their graduation certificates. After the ceremony, Lilly was very cool with them. Clara handed her the traveler's checks that she had collected from the bank and gave her some lira as a present. Clara tried to hug her daughter to wish her luck on the trip, but Lilly just stood there coldly, although she did return her father's hug. Professor Hatcher took Clara to one side and told her not to worry that he would look after her.

"She will be a different person when she comes back, and hopefully, she will be able to put all of this upset behind her," said the professor, obviously aware of the story of Lilly's father. "I will make sure she writes to you, but, in any case, I have your address, so I will keep you posted on our progress."

"Thank you, Professor, that is very kind of you."

When Clara got home, there was a letter waiting for her from England. She didn't recognise the writing straightaway. It was only when she opened it that she realised it was from her father. This was most unusual, as it was always her mother that wrote to her. Her immediate thought was that something had happened to her mother, and she started to read the letter anxiously.

My Dearest Clara,
I am writing to you instead of your mother, as today you had a visitor, and after hearing her story, I felt I had to write.

I was in the salon when I saw this young lady looking in the window. She appeared to hesitate, walking past and then coming back. I went to the door and asked if I could help her, thinking that perhaps she was lost.

Anyway, she asked if Clara Pape lived here, and I explained that I was your dad and that you lived in America. I could see she was quite distressed, so I invited her upstairs for a cup of tea. She told me she had come quite a long way in search of you and that she was disappointed not to see you.

I didn't quite understand who she was, so I obviously asked the question as to who she was and how she knew you.

Her name is Olga, but she said you might remember her as Amélie, and she told me the story of how you and, I presume, Didier had rescued her and her sister during the war and took them to safety. She explained that she and her sister had been adopted by a British couple, and she now lived in London.

Her story brought me to tears, Clara, and I just had to write and say how proud of you I am that you were able to carry out such a selfless act when you were so young.

I hope you don't mind, but I gave her your address, and she will be writing to you.

Your mother is well. We are contemplating selling the business and retiring. Neither of us does much in the salon now, as the youngsters tend to run it for us. So, next time your mother writes, we may be relaxing in a retirement bungalow somewhere by the sea.

My love as always,
Dad xx

Clara read the letter twice, remembering that day they drove to Nantes. Her own daughter wasn't willing to understand that decisions were made during the war that were not easy to make, and yet, this letter momentarily filled the emptiness in her heart. As she held the letter, she hoped with all of her heart that Lilly would find it in her heart on her trip to show some empathy towards her some day and at the very least gain what she could from the dig in Italy but come to terms with their past. All Clara could do was wait, unbearably.

CHAPTER 39

Lilly left for Italy with the professor and three other students, Jenny, Peter and Ross. Each had their rucksacks and sleeping bags. It was the first time any of them had been on an aeroplane, and they were all apprehensive, especially when they saw how big the plane was. Lilly sat next to Jenny, and they chatted about university and about what they were going to do next in between sleeping and reading their books. Jeffrey had sent her a Pentax camera as a graduation present, so she read the instruction leaflet from cover to cover. She had already taken some experimental photos of the family, and she intended to improve her photography technique so she could take photos of any finds she might make at the dig.

They were going to a site in Lombardy called Bagnolo Stele located in Northern Italy. The flight took over thirteen hours, as they stopped over in London to refuel. At first, it was a novelty being on the plane, but after landing in London, they dreaded getting on the plane again. They were all tired and bored.

After arriving in Milan, they were driven for nearly two hours to the site—all of them slept on the mini bus. The professor woke them, "Right, you guys, let's get out and collect all your gear from the back." They were all a bit groggy. "Let me introduce you to my friend from Boston, Professor Alan Wilson. Now, guys, we are no longer at university, so you are to call me Steve and Alan, Alan," said the professor.

Four students stood behind Alan.

"Perhaps we can introduce ourselves," said Alan. "Starting with you, Millie, just say a bit about yourselves."

Each took turns introducing themselves to the group.

"Hiya, my name is Millie. I am from Boston, and I am studying the history of art and archaeology."

"Hi, my name is Gill, and I am also from Boston, and I am studying geography and archaeology."

"Hi, my name is Joe, and I am from Rhode Island, and I am studying archaeology."

"And, ok, I'm last. I am Harry, and I am from New York, and I am studying archaeology."

"Now, my bunch, starting with you, Lilly," said the professor.

"Hiya, I am Lilly. I am from North Carolina, and I am studying history and archaeology."

"Hi, I am Jenny. I am from South Carolina, and I am studying geography and archaeology."

"Hi, guys. I am Peter. I am from West Virginia, and I am studying history and geography."

"And looks like I'm the last one. I'm Ross. I am from Ohio, and I am studying archaeology and English literature."

Alan showed them around and finally showed them where the campsite was. Lilly had agreed to share a tent with Jenny. It was a fairly small ridge tent in a line with another, at least, thirty tents. The professor was lucky he was sharing a caravan with Alan. There was a building behind the tents where there was a shower block, a common room and a large kitchen.

"I thought the Professor said we would be cooking on a camp stove, but there is a range in the kitchen," said Lilly.

"Perhaps he didn't know there was a kitchen, or perhaps he was just teasing us," said Jenny.

They put all their stuff in the tent.

"How are we supposed to get dressed in here?" asked Jenny.

"I think I will just take my shorts and t-shirt and change in the shower block," said Lilly.

"Good idea, I will come with you," said Jenny.

In addition to Lilly's group of four, there were already twenty people working on the site. Alan showed them where they would work and told them what to wear. He showed them what had been unearthed that day. There were two girls behind two large tables, taking the finds and labelling them and marking on a map where that particular piece had been found.

"You will each have a turn of recording the finds. This makes it fairer, as I know everyone wants to be at the site trying to uncover a Roman urn," he jested.

They were handed their equipment: a small paintbrush, one medium-size trowel and a tiny one. Lilly looked at Jenny and then looked at their '*equipment*' and laughed. "I was perhaps expecting a bit more than this," said Lilly.

"Yes, I was as well," said Jenny.

The time flew by. They worked all day, enjoying every minute. Whenever one of them found anything, they would show their neighbour, and then take it over to the table. Lilly would take a picture of hers with her camera, which was always close by.

The archaeological site was a settlement dating back to prehistoric times; they had unearthed a number of stone carvings, numerous pieces of pottery and cooking implements. All these indicated that the area had been some type of commune or village.

The most significant find was an elaborate mosaic floor, covered in years of dirt and mud. It was explained to the team, that this indicated the centre of the village. Given its extravagance, it would have been the dwelling of the village elder.

Lilly had found the whole experience fascinating and wished she could have stayed longer.

Each evening, they would shower, take turns cooking for their group, then sit outside around a campfire and sing or tell each other stories. There was great camaraderie between them.

On Saturday nights, they would walk down to the local village and take over the bar, the old Italian men looking at them in wonder. They would drink the local beer and sing all the way back to the site.

Towards the end of their time, they went down to the bar, as usual stopping off for a pizza on the way. Lilly found herself sitting next to Millie. She wasn't too sure about Millie who was obviously from a very posh family from the way she talked and the way she expected other people to do things for her. Nobody did; they just showed her how to do it.

"It amazes me," said Lilly to Jenny, "that she doesn't even know how to wash her clothes. I wonder how she managed at university."

"She would have just gone out and bought some new ones," joked Jenny.

Millie got very drunk that evening and told Lilly how she hated her parents and that she didn't want to go home.

"My whole life has been a lie, and THEY have been lying to me all this time. I hate them. It will serve them right if I never go back," she said, slurring her words.

Lilly tried to humour her and said that everyone hated their parents at one time or another, thinking how at this present time she hated her mother.

"Yes, but for me to find out I am adopted at the age of twenty-one and by accident is just not on. I bet if I hadn't come here and needed a passport, I would never have known, and they don't care how I feel," said a sobbing Millie, who then stormed off back to the site.

Lilly could empathize with Millie. She was still angry with her mother but was trying not to think too much about her situation. She wanted to enjoy her time in Italy, knowing full well that she would have to face the facts of her birth when she returned home.

In the morning, Millie carried on as though nothing had happened.

"Do you think Millie remembers her outburst last night?" said Jenny to Lilly.

"I am not sure. Perhaps she was so drunk she has forgotten," replied Lilly.

"Or, she is so embarrassed she has chosen to forget," suggested Jenny.

Peter, Ross and Joe were discussing going to Paris. They had all agreed that it was a bit silly coming all the way to Italy and not going to see a bit more of Europe, before going home.

This seemed to be a good idea to Lilly. She didn't want to go home just yet, although she had written to both her mother and father and told them how she was getting on. She was still trying to come to terms with Carl not being her father. She asked Peter if she could tag along.

"Of course, you can. We are going to catch a train down to Rome and then on to Paris and then to London before going home."

"Well, I am going to Ireland," announced Millie.

They all looked at her, surprised at her announcement.

"Why Ireland?" asked Joe.

"To find my real mum," she said, turning her back on the group and flouncing off.

The professor gave those not going home with him their travel documents, telling Lilly to take care and advising her to contact a travel agent, as she would need to change her airline ticket to return home. "Make sure you write home and tell them where you are. Otherwise, they will worry. Promise me you will do this," he said.

"Yes, I promise," said Lilly reluctantly.

Unbeknown to Lilly the professor had written to Clara and Carl, giving them a short progress report, telling them that Lilly appeared happy and was enjoying her time in Italy and not to worry too much. He felt sure that the family's problems would soon be resolved.

Alan and Steve treated them all to dinner on their last night and thanked them for all their help. "We have made a few good significant finds, so thank you for all your efforts. I hope you have enjoyed yourselves? Now raise your glasses *'to us all'*." He stood up and raised his glass of wine.

Everyone joined in, "To Us."

Lilly said goodbye to Jenny and promised to keep in touch as the four of them made their way to Rome.

Rome was magnificent. They went from museum to museum. They saw the Colosseum and the Pantheon, and they spent half a day examining the Roman Forum and drank beer and coffee near the Trevi Fountain. Four days later, they caught a train to Paris.

After wandering the streets, they soon found the rooms in a hostel that the tourist information desk at the Gare du Nord had suggested. They were to stay in Paris for four days before going on to London. They took a sightseeing bus around the city and had dinner at the foot of the Eiffel Tower.

Lilly wished she had taken more notice of the French her mother had tried to teach her when she was younger, and she now realised why her mother was fluent in French.

The next day, they went from the Notre Dame to the Arc de Triomphe and spent the late evening eating at a restaurant in the Latin Quarter. The boys wanted to go and see the Catacombs the next day, but Lilly said she would give this a miss and go window-shopping along the Champs-Élyseés instead. She stopped for coffee and a pastry at one of the many cafes along the street next to a tourism information centre. There was a map of France on the wall that caught her eye. When she had finished her coffee, she went into the centre.

"Bonjour, mademoiselle, puis-je vous aider?"

"Sorry, I don't speak French. Do you speak English?" asked Lilly.

"Yes, I do, mademoiselle. How can I help you?" said the assistant in perfect English.

"I was wondering if you could show me on the map where a place called Plérin is?" asked Lilly.

"Well I have not actually heard of it, but I have a detailed book of maps here. Let me see if it is in the index." The assistant opened a large book and turned to the back page.

"Yes, here it is." She turned to another page and showed Lilly one of the pages.

"Where exactly is that on the big map?" asked Lilly.

The assistant went to the map on the wall and showed Lilly where it was, and then pointed to Paris so she could see how far away it was.

"How could I get there? Is there a train, do you know?" asked Lilly.

"I am sure there is a train, but you will need to go to the train station to find out," the assistant suggested.

Thanking the assistant for her help, she made her way to the train station. Here she was able to establish that she could get a train quite easily. The man at the station pointed to the platform she would need and gave her a timetable that detailed the stops to a place called Saint-Brieuc, being the nearest town to Plérin.

Lilly wasn't too sure if she wanted to go, but she had a natural urge to see the place she was born. *'And why not while I am so close? Surely it wouldn't hurt just to see, then I could go to London after and meet up with the boys'*, she said to herself. By the time she met up with the boys for dinner, she had changed her mind several times.

Early the next day, she found herself sitting on the train. She was full of apprehension and wished she had asked her mother more about her time in France, but it was too late now. She knew her real father was no longer in Plérin, as her mother had said she didn't know where he was when Lilly had demanded, "And where exactly is this father of mine now?"

All her mother had said was, "I am sorry, Lilly, but I don't know."

While on the train, Lilly was playing out all sorts of scenarios in her head, all of which she would tell herself were stupid even to think of. '*I am just going to look and then go to London.*' Although she hadn't thought about how she would get to London from there. '*I should have thought of that,*' she thought to herself. '*Perhaps I will have to go back to Paris.*' It was while sitting watching the scenery pass by that Millie suddenly jumped into her head. Millie had reminded her of someone, but she couldn't think whom. When she had been in Italy, she had gone through all her friends at school, then all her friends at university but just couldn't think who she reminded her of. Then she realised it was Auntie Niamph. '*Of course,*' she said to herself, '*she has her mannerisms. ... the way she moves her hands and tilts her head when she talks ... and her hair is exactly like Niamph's, and on reflection there was a slight resemblance.*' Pleased with herself for solving her dilemma, she thought no more of it.

She arrived at the station. It appeared to be deserted, although a couple of other passengers had got off with her. She followed them to what she presumed would be the exit, hoping to find a taxi, but there were none in sight. She began to make her way back into the station to see if there was anyone to ask about a taxi when she heard a man shout, "Taxi, madam?"

She turned around, and there was a battered black Citroen with a '*Taxi*' sticker on the side. "Yes, please," she said, getting into the back with her rucksack.

"Où voudrais-tu aller, madam?"

Lilly guessed he was asking her where she wanted to go and replied, "Plérin."

The journey took no more than twenty minutes, and she was pleased that she had cashed sufficient traveler's checks to buy some francs, as she wasn't sure how long the journey would be and how much the taxi would cost. Luckily, she knew the French word for church and asked him, "L'eglise, s'il vous plait," as she felt sure every village in France had a church. When he didn't answer and just carried on driving, she knew she was right.

The taxi driver dropped her off in a square just by the church as she had asked. She looked around not really knowing what to do now that she was here. The church door was open, so she decided to start there. The priest was walking up the aisle as she entered.

"Hello," she said. "Do you speak English?"

The priest looked up and smiled, "Bonjour, mademoiselle, no English."

'*Oh! What shall I do now*?' she thought to herself, but the priest walked past her and beckoned her outside. He then pointed to a bar across the square.

"English, English," he said, pointing again.

She made her way to the bar. There were a couple of men sitting outside drinking beer. She went inside where there were more men who all appeared to stop speaking as she entered and turned to look at her. She felt embarrassed with everyone looking at her.

There was an old man behind the bar, staring at her. He instantly called out, "Jeanne, Jeanne."

An old lady came out from the back. She followed the man's stare. "Oh my God, Clara."

"No, no, I am Lilly," she said.

"I can't believe my eyes, Liliane. You are just like your mother," said the lady coming over to her, kissing her numerous times on each cheek and hugging her.

"Come into the back! I am your great-auntie Jeanne, and this is your great-uncle Clifford."

Lilly went to put out her hand to shake his, but he took her by the shoulders and kissed her again numerous times on each cheek.

"Come and sit down. Get her a drink, Clifford. Now tell me why you have come. Your mother never said you were coming. Oh, I am so pleased to see you again. I never thought this day would come," said Jeanne not letting Lilly get a word in. "How is your mother? She writes but not often enough," asked Jeanne.

"She is fine, and to answer your question, she doesn't know I am here. I am sorry to say that I didn't know you two existed. ... Well that's not quite true. I have heard your names, but I didn't know who you were or that you lived here," answered Lilly.

Clifford gave her a glass of lemonade and explained that he was her grandmother's brother. "Your mother lived here with us for fifteen years. She was like a daughter to me. She was fifteen when she arrived, and we still miss her. Now how long are you staying because you must stay with us," said Clifford.

Lilly was a bit distracted by the photos on the mantelpiece, some which appeared to be of her mother.

"I only came on an impulse. I was in Paris with some friends, and I had an urge to see where I was born and here I am. I will only stay a few days," explained Lilly.

"Well, you must stay here with us," said Jeanne. "You can stay in your mother's old room."

"Sorry, Lilly, but I must get back to the bar, or my customers will be helping themselves to drinks," Clifford said, leaving the room.

Lilly got up to have a closer look at the photos. She recognised a young version of her mother that she presumed was taken on her wedding day.

Jeanne stood up. "That is your mother and my daughter, Danielle. They had a double wedding, and they looked lovely in their parachute dresses."

"What are parachute dresses?" asked Lilly.

"They got married just after the war had finished, and there were no fabrics available then. We still had rationing, so your mother's friend, Simone, made the dresses out of parachute material. You must go and say hello to Simone. She would be delighted to meet you," explained Jeanne.

"Where is your daughter and are those her children?" asked Lilly, pointing to the photo of two little girls clinging onto a tiny baby in a christening robe.

"My daughter lives in Bordeaux now, and she has two boys," said Jeanne, looking at Lilly questioningly. "Don't you recognise that little one?" she said, pointing to the baby.

"No, should I?" asked Lilly.

"That is you with your sisters," exclaimed Jeanne.

Lilly felt faint. "My sisters! I don't have any sister. I have two younger brothers," said Lilly.

Jeanne looked at her with the realisation that Clara hadn't told her about her sisters.

"Oh, my dear. I am so sorry. Sit down! You look very pale," said Jeanne.

With tears falling down her cheeks, Lilly murmured, "I didn't know I had two sisters. Why didn't my mother tell me? I have only just found out that my dad is not my father. Now I discover I have two sisters. I just can't believe my mother would do this to me."

"I am sure she had her reasons. This photo was taken just before she left France, and she was desperately unhappy. She didn't want to go, but your father insisted," said Jeanne.

"I don't understand. Why was she unhappy and where did they go? I thought she was in England before she went to America," said Lilly.

"Lilly, it is difficult for me to explain, especially as Didier is your father, but he wasn't very nice to your mother and made her very scared and unhappy. They went to Jersey to start a new life, as your father put it, but it was no different from her life here. And from what I gather, he beat her once too often, and she ran away. She wrote to me at the time to tell me she was with her mother, your grandmother, in England but not to tell Didier if he ever asked, describing how she could only take you with her. She was distraught at leaving your sisters but hoped that one day she would be able to get them back. But she knew Didier would never let her take the girls away from him," explained Jeanne.

"I still don't quite understand. Why did he beat her and where is Jersey?" asked Lilly.

"Unfortunately, he drank too much and when he got drunk, he got violent, and he blamed your mother for anything and everything. ... Jersey is a small island between France and England. As far as I am aware, your father and sisters are still there. I thought at one point she would come back here, but then I think she was frightened of losing you, so she stayed in England," explained Jeanne.

"I have so many questions I hardly know where to start. When was the last time you saw my sisters and what are their names?" asked Lilly.

"I haven't seen them since the day they left with you. They are Chantal and Francine. Chantal was such a brave little girl. It was she that came running to me for help on the night you were born. She was only three, and she ran from where you lived about a quarter of a mile away from here. I missed you all so much," said Jeanne with tears welling up in her eyes, remembering that night.

Lilly wanted to ask about her father but felt that Jeanne didn't like him very much, and she didn't want to hear anything negative that Jeanne might say about him.

Jeanne showed her where she would sleep, and Lilly insisted on making up the bed, as Lilly didn't want to give the old woman any extra work.

Over dinner that evening, Lilly told them all about the farm and her brothers and how her mother had opened the tearooms. In bed that night, she realised how proud of her family she was and how much she missed them all. After a restless night, she made the decision to travel to Jersey to find her father and her sisters.

In the morning after breakfast, a couple arrived, Marie and Jean. Jeanne explained, that the couple had been helping her and Clifford, for over a year but were now going to take over the bar. "Your uncle and I are getting old, and we find the work too tiring, so we have decided to retire. Danielle has invited us to live with them. We are looking forward to moving," she said.

"Auntie, I have decided to go to Jersey. Do you know how I can get there?" asked Lilly.

"Let's go and get the bread for lunch, and then we will get the bus into town and go to a travel agent and find out. Your mother went by boat, but we do have an airport now, so perhaps you may be able to fly there. We will find out," said Jeanne.

They walked down to the bakery. Simone was behind the counter, and Lilly could see her take a second look at her and then at Jeanne. Simone spoke to Jeanne in French, and Lilly heard her mother's name being used. Then Jeanne introduced her to Simone. Simone hugged and kissed her just twice, once on each cheek, held her face, and looked into her eyes, saying something to her in French.

"She is saying how much you look like your mother and how pretty you are just like your mother."

"Merci," said Lilly.

Jeanne and Simone spoke for some time, giving Lilly time to take photos of the shop. A man came through from the back. "This is Simone's son, Fabien. He now runs the business for her."

Lilly shook his hand and asked if she could take a photo of them both to show her mother.

As they made their way back to the bar, Jeanne told her about the village and how her mother had worked at the bakery for some years, helping Simone during the war after her husband was taken by the Germans. "She was a good girl and worked so hard. Everyone loved her. Now I must quickly drop off the bread for Marie," said Jeanne.

They caught the bus to town, and Jeanne explained her surroundings and how the village had expanded. "Your mother would hardly recognise it now." The bus stopped by the train station, which she remembered from the day before, and they made their way to a travel agent. The lady in the agency explained that she could either take a plane—and there was one the following day—or go to Saint-Malo and get the boat. She further explained that the plane would be quicker and more convenient but more expensive, whereas the boat was much cheaper but took longer, and she would have to travel to the port. Lilly chose the plane and quickly went across the road to the bank to get some more francs while the travel agent made the booking.

Jeanne showed her around Saint-Brieuc, and they stopped at a small café for lunch before making their way home again. Lilly took lots of photos, using up an entire roll of film, feeling sure her mother would like to see the places as they were today.

Her flight was at one o'clock the next day, and Jeanne arranged a taxi to take her to the airport. "Your visit has been so short. Next time, you must come to see us in Bordeaux and meet my daughter. They have a campsite, so there will be plenty of space for you to stay."

"I will, Auntie, and thank you for everything." Lilly felt very sad to be leaving but at the same time apprehensive as to what was to come next.

The airport was tiny and the plane even tinier. There were only seven passengers and the pilot, leaving three empty seats. They all squeezed in after climbing into the plane via the wing.

"This is amazing," she said to the lady sitting next to her who was unfortunately French, so didn't understand her.

The trip took no more than twenty minutes, and Lilly quickly took out her camera when she saw land approaching, taking photos from the air. It was a bit of a bumpy landing, and Lilly grabbed the seat in front of her, feeling sure they were about to crash. Soon, the plane came to a stop and then taxied to the terminal. It was a bit more difficult getting out of the plane than it was getting in, but she made it.

After collecting her rucksack, she was making her way through to the exit when she spotted a tourism information desk.

"Hello, can I help you?" asked the lady.

"I was going to ask you if you speak English, but you have answered my question." Lilly laughed nervously.

"Yes, we speak English here. I often get asked that question, so you are not the first. Now how can I help you?" she asked.

"I think I will only be here a few days, so I need a hotel," requested Lilly.

"Yes, no problem a good hotel would be the *Pomme D'Or*. It is in the centre of town and a bit more expensive than a guest house. Or would you prefer something cheaper?" she asked.

"No, that hotel will be fine."

"Okay, I will just phone them to see if they have any vacancies," she said, picking up the phone.

"You are in luck. They have one single room left. Shall I book it for you?" she said, holding her hand over the speaker of the phone.

"Yes, please," replied Lilly.

The lady gave her a map of the island and directed her towards the taxi rank.

"Thank you very much for your help. ...Oh, what money do you use here? I only have francs," asked Lilly.

"We use sterling. If you go over there to the Bureau de Change, they will change your francs for you," said the lady, pointing to her left.

Lilly thanked the lady again and went and changed her francs.

A row of taxis was outside, and she got into the first one and gave the driver the name of the hotel.

"Your first visit to the island, miss?" he asked as he began their journey to the hotel.

"Yes, I am just here for a few days," she replied.

"Are you American?"

"Yes, how did you guess?" she asked jokingly.

He laughed and then proceeded to tell her all the places she should try and see while on the island. He pointed out a few of the sights as they drove along the coast, then sooner than she expected, he drew up in front of the hotel.

"I want to go to this address this evening at about five thirty. How long would it take from here?" she asked the taxi driver.

"Only about twenty minutes, miss, maybe a bit longer if there is a lot of traffic but not much more. Would you like me to take you, miss?" he asked.

"I don't know," she said hesitantly, thinking about what she was going to do for the next three hours.

"Tell you what, miss. If you want me to pick you up at say three thirty, I could take you for a trip around the island, show you a few of the sights before dropping you off at that address. I wouldn't charge you the full fare," he said.

"That would be great. Thank you. Shall I wait here at three thirty?" she asked as she paid him.

"Yes, miss, see you later," he said as he drove off.

She went into the hotel, checked in and took her rucksack up to her room. She had quite a bit of time before the taxi came back for her, so she went downstairs and asked the receptionist the way into the town.

Walking up to the main street, she spotted a bank and went in to change some of her traveler's checks. She asked the bank clerk the rate between dollars and pounds, as she was getting a bit confused about how much one pound was worth. The clerk explained.

"Now, I understand. Thank you," said Lilly.

She walked down the main street and went into a café. She had a bit of lunch.

Before going back to the hotel, she went into the post office that she had noticed earlier. Asking the counter clerk if she could send a telegram to America, she found out she could, and she sat down and drafted a short telegram to her mother.

'SEEN AUNTIE JEANNE. NOW IN JERSEY. GOING TO FIND MY SISTERS. LOVE YOU.'

After giving the counter attendant the wording for the telegram and paying him, she made her way back to the hotel to wait for her taxi.

The taxi driver, who introduced himself as Mike, drove her all around the island telling her where they were. "This is the east side of the island, and that big castle there is Mont Orgueil Castle."

The trip continued with him pointing out the sights and giving her a bit of the history attached to the sight. They stopped every so often so Lilly could take some photos. They finally stopped on the north coast, and he pointed out where puffins could be seen nesting at certain times of the year.

"We are very close to the address you gave me, miss, so are you ready to go now?" he asked.

"Yes, I think so. Can I pay you now? Thank you so much for taking me around. It has been very interesting, and I have lots of photos," she said nervously.

"Are you okay, miss? You look a bit pale," he asked.

"Yes, I am fine, just very nervous. I am meeting some family for the first time, or, at least, I hope I am," she said.

"Well, good luck, miss," he said, driving towards their destination.

"Here we are, miss. It is that house just down that track. I can't go down, as there is a tractor in the way," he said, pointing across the narrow road.

As they came to a stop, from the front passenger seat of the taxi, Lilly saw two girls not much older than her walking down the opposite side of the road, arm in arm, chatting away. She suddenly saw them wave to someone. At first, she thought it was her, but when she got out of the taxi, she saw a man standing at the end of the track and realised they were waving at him. As Lilly closed the taxi door and the taxi drove off, the man looked in her direction.

He stood in the road at the entrance to Rotherwood Farm. She knew instantly it was her papa. How, she didn't know. Perhaps it was just instinct. Auntie Jeanne had given her the last address she had for her father. He was staring her way. She wasn't sure if she was imagining it or was engaged in wishful thinking, but she was certain he mouthed her name.

She crossed the road, thinking to herself that she would merely ask this man if he knew the family she was looking for, but she didn't need to say anything. He continued to mouth her name repeatedly. He put his arms out and held her shoulders and looking directly at her.

Time appeared to stand still as he looked at her, staring in what appeared to be disbelief.

"Liliane," he finally said.

"Papa," she replied.

"My Liliane, my baby, is it really you?" he asked pleadingly, as though he couldn't quite believe his eyes.

"Yes, Papa," she cried, tears running down her cheeks. They hugged, and Didier held her away from him so he could take a good look at his youngest daughter.

One of the two girls gasped, 'Mamma,' as the other girl's gaze followed her sister Chantal's eyes to see where she was looking. Within seconds, Chantal was almost running towards her father and Lilly.

As the three of them hugged and cried, Lilly felt overjoyed. Slowly, Francine crossed the road as she watched the three of them embrace. Lilly was finally meeting her two sisters and being held by her father. Lilly felt like she couldn't have asked for more. Her trip to Europe had been everything she hoped. Her mother briefly crossed her mind as she wished she could see all of them together, meeting for the first time.

As the three of them pulled apart, she hugged Chantal again and then immediately embraced Francine. She took a moment to look at her two sisters. Their appearance was so different from her own. They were dark like their father, whereas she was blonde like their mother. She felt an instant warmth from Chantal but not from Francine.

Lilly looked a bit confused, but the feeling passed when she was overcome by her papa's overwhelming fervor that swept her and Chantal away from the middle of the road.

"Let's go home," said her papa.

Her papa's warm hand on her back guided her along with Chantal inside to share their first meal together. Lilly was ready for this wonderful chance to rest and get to know the sisters and father she had never known. Francine lagged at a distance behind them as Lilly and Chantal walked arm in arm, chatting away, and their papa brought them into their warm home.

THE END

Printed in Great Britain
by Amazon